THE MAMMOTH BOOK OF

SCIENCE
FICTION

THE MAMMOTH BOOK OF

SCIENCE FICTION

Edited by Mike Ashley

ROBINSON
London

Constable & Robinson Ltd
3 The Lanchesters
162 Fulham Palace Road
London W6 9ER
www.constablerobinson.com

First published in the UK by Robinson,
an imprint of Constable & Robinson Ltd 2002

Collection and editorial material copyright © Mike Ashley 2002

A copy of the British Library Cataloguing in
Publication Data is available from the British Library.

ISBN 1-84119-375-5

Printed and bound in the EU

10 9 8 7 6 5 4 3 2

Contents

Copyright and Acknowledgments

First published in *Astounding SF*, September 1957. Reprinted by permission of the Laurence Pollinger Literary Agency on behalf of the author's estate.

"A Ticket to Tranai" © 1955 by Robert Sheckley. First published in *Galaxy*, October 1955. Reprinted by permission of the author.

"A Death in the House" © 1959 by Clifford D. Simak. First published in *Galaxy*, October 1959. Reprinted by permission of David W. Wixon on behalf of the author's estate.

"The Very Pulse of The Machine" © 1998 by Michael Swanwick. First published in *Asimov's Science Fiction*, February 1998. Reprinted by permission of the author.

"The Last Days of Earth" © 1901 by George C. Wallis. First published in *The Harmsworth Magazine*, July 1901. No surviving estate.

"Firewatch" © 1982 by Connie Willis. First published in *Asimov's Science Fiction*, February 1982. Reprinted by permission of the author.

Introduction: The Next Step

Mike Ashley

Science fiction has been called the literature of ideas, and it is certainly that. But it's also something else. It's about change – the changes arising from those ideas.

What fascinates me about science fiction (or "sf" as I tend to abbreviate it), and what draws me back to it time and again, is to see the wonder of human imagination about ourselves and the universe and to discover how each individual writer has used their skill, knowledge and, above all, imagination to develop an idea and see what it does. It's the old question that provoked the study of science in the first place: "What if?" And the answer to that always results in change. It may be for good – one step onward; it may be for bad. A lot of sf serves as a warning to humanity about the perils of change.

You'll find both kinds of stories here: those that take us one step forward – sometimes a whole load of steps forward – and those where we step backward. And there's even a few where we step sideways.

There are stories set on other worlds, stories where beings from other worlds come to us; stories of robots and time travel and genetic engineering, and utopias, dystopias, impossible problems, catastrophes and ultimate apocalypses. All the stuff of science fiction. But above all they're about people and how they have reacted to these discoveries, ideas and changes.

When I started to compile this anthology I wanted to select a wide range of the most intriguing and challenging science fiction published over the last forty or fifty years. Because science fiction deals with change and technology it is easy for some sf to date rapidly. Even the best written story, which was highly regarded fifty years ago, may not hold up well today because of the considerable changes that have affected science and society in the last twenty years. Science fiction may try and make predictions, but it's seldom very good at it. Very few stories hit the mark as regards the Internet, for instance, or the rapid growth in mobile phones, in computers, in the fall of the communist Eastern bloc in Europe, the rise in the drug problem. So even when I revisited many of my favourite stories from years ago, they did not all stand up well today.

But I still achieved my aim. This anthology contains twenty-two stories. Two of them – by Stephen Baxter and Eric Brown – are brand new, written specially for this book. Another two – by Frank Lillie Pollock and George C. Wallis – are real "golden oldies" from a hundred years ago. The other eighteen stories are pretty much evenly selected from the 1950s and the 1990s with a smattering in between. The result is the best of the old and the best of the new, each one posing challenging and different ideas.

Suppose, for instance, we find a drug that allows you to access your other selves in other realities. How would you police that? That's what Greg Egan tackles in "The Infinite Assassin". What is reality and what is dream? Both Robert Reed and Kim Stanley Robinson approach that in very different ways. Are aliens already here and we just don't realize it? See how H. Chandler Elliott and Mark Clifton deal with that. Can you really have an impenetrable object? That's what Colin Kapp poses in "The Pen and the Dark". Brian W. Aldiss and John Morressy, on the other hand, look at the effects and outcomes of genetic engineering, while Connie Willis considers just what else might have been helping us during the Second World War. And what would really happen if you entered a black hole? Geoffrey Landis takes us to the ultimate in "Approaching Perimelasma".

There's plenty more. If you want aliens, try the stories by Eric Brown, Peter Hamilton, Michael Swanwick and Clifford Simak. If you want a sardonic view of other societies, try Robert Sheckley and Philip K. Dick. And if you want the end of the world, try the two apocalyptic classics.

There should be something for everyone. Everything you could ever imagine is all just a step away. Have fun.

Mike Ashley

Ulla, Ulla

Eric Brown

When Eric sent me this story I was delighted, because it was the ideal way to start this anthology – combining the old with the new. Eric Brown (b. 1960) emerged on the sf scene in 1987 with a series of inventive stories in Inter-zone *that led to his first published collection* The Time-Lapsed Man *(1990). Other stories will be found in* Blue Shifting *(1995) whilst his novels include* Meridian Days *(1992),* Engineman *(1994), and the excellent* Penumbra *(1999).* New York Nights *(2000) marked the start of his* Virex *trilogy, SF thrillers set in 2040 featuring private eyes and virtual reality. The other titles are* New York Blues *and* New York Dreams. *You can find out more on his website* < *www.ericbrown.co.uk* > .

After the debriefing, which lasted three days, Enright left the Kennedy Space Center and headed for home. He drove south to the Keys in his '08 Chevrolet convertible, taking his time now that he was alone for the first time in three years. For that long he had been cooped up in the *Fortitude* on its voyage to Mars and back. Even on the surface of the planet, beneath the immensity of the pink sky, he had never felt truly alone. Always there were the voices of McCarthy, Jeffries and Spirek on his com, and the prospect of the cramped living quarters on his return to the lander.

Ten kilometers south of Kennedy, on the coast road, he pulled into a parking lot overlooking the sea, climbed out and stared into the evening sky.

There was Mars, riding high overhead.

He considered the mission, but he had no original take on what they had discovered beneath the surface of the red planet. He was as baffled as everyone else. One thing he knew for certain, though: everything was different now. At some point, inevitably, the news would break, and things would change for ever.

He had been allowed a couple of hours with Delia after quarantine, before being whisked off to the intensive de-briefing. Of course, he had not been cleared to discuss their findings with her, the one person in his life with whom he had shared everything. She had sensed something, though, detected in his manner that all was not right. She had been at mission control when the first broadcast came through from Mars, but Director Roberts had cut the transmission before anything major had leaked.

He shivered. The wind was turning cold.

He climbed back into his Chevrolet, reversed from the lot, and drove home.

He left the car in the drive and walked around the house.

The child's swing, in situ when they had bought the place four years ago, had still not been removed. Delia had promised him that she would see to it while he was away.

She was sitting in the lighted conservatory, reading. She looked up as he pushed through the door, but made no move to rise and greet him.

"You weren't due back until tomorrow," she said, making it sound like an accusation.

"Let us off a day early. Thought I'd surprise you." He was aware of the distance between them, after so long apart.

Over dinner, they chatted. Small talk, the inconsequential tone of which indicated that they both knew they were avoiding deeper issues. She was back teaching, three days a week at the local elementary school. Ted, her nephew, had been accepted at Florida State.

He wanted to tell her. He wanted to tell her everything that had happened on Mars. He had always shared everything with her in the past. So why not now?

Mission confidentiality? The papers he had signed seven years back on being accepted by NASA?

Or was it because what they had discovered might have been some kind of collective hallucination? And Delia might think that he was losing it, if he came out and told her?

A combination of all the above, he realised.

That night they made love, hesitantly, and later lay in a parallelogram of moonlight that cut across the bed.

"What happened, Ed?" she asked.

"Mmm?" He tried to feign semi-wakefulness.

"We were there, in mission control. You were out with Spirek. Something happened. There was a loud . . . I don't know, it sounded like a landslide. You said, 'Oh my God . . .'. Roberts cut the link and ushered us out. It was an hour before they got back to us. An hour. Can you imagine that? I was worried sick."

He reached out and stroked away her tears.

"Roberts gave us some story about subsidence," she said. "Then I heard you again, reassuring us that everything was okay."

They had staged that, concocted a few lines between them, directed by Roberts, to reassure their families back home.

He shrugged. "That's it. That's what happened. I was caught in a landslide, lost my footing." Even to his own ears, he sounded unconvincing.

Delia went on, "And then three days ago, I could tell something wasn't right. And now . . . You're hiding something."

He let the silence stretch. "I'm hiding nothing. It's hard to readjust. Imagine being stuck in a tin can for three years with cretins like Jeffries and McCarthy."

"You're too sensitive, Ed. You're a geologist, not an astronaut. You should have stayed at the university."

He embraced her. "Shh," he said, and fell silent.

He dreamed that night. He was back on Mars. He could feel the regolith slide away beneath his boots. The sensation of inevitable descent and imminent impact turned his stomach as it had done all those months ago. He fell, tumbling, and landed in a sitting position. In the dream he opened his eyes – and awoke suddenly.

He gasped aloud and reached out, grabbed the head-board. Then it came to him that he was no longer weight-less, floating in his sleeping bag. He was on Earth. He was home. He reached out for Delia and held her.

In the morning, while Delia was at school, Enright took a walk. The open space, after so long cramped in the *Fortitude*, held an irresistible allure. He found himself on the golf course, strolling along the margin of the second fairway in the shade of maple trees.

He came to a bunker and stopped, staring at the clean, scooped perfection of the feature. He closed his eyes, and jumped. The sensation was pretty accurate. He had stepped out onto Mars again. He felt the granular regolith give beneath his boots.

When he opened his eyes he saw a young girl, perhaps twelve years old and painfully pretty. She was standing on the lip of the bunker, staring down at him.

She was clutching a pen and a scrap of paper.

Beyond her, on the green, two men looked on.

"Mr Enright, sir?" the kid asked. "Can I have your autograph?"

He reached up, took the pen and paper, and scrawled his name.

The girl stared at the autograph, as if the addition of his signature upon the paper had invested it with magical properties. One of the watching men smiled and waved a hand.

Delia was still at school when he got back. The first thing he did on returning was to phone a scrap merchant to take away the swing in the back yard. Then he retired to his study and stared at the pile of unanswered correspondence on his desk.

He leafed through the mail.

One was from Joshua Connaught, in England. Enright had corresponded with the eccentric for a number of years before the mission. The man had said he was writing a book on the history of spaceflight, and wanted Enright's opinion on certain matters.

They had exchanged letters every couple of months, moving away from the original subject and discussing everything under the sun. Connaught had been married, once, and he too was childless.

Enright set the envelope aside, unopened.

He sat back in his armchair and closed his eyes.

He was back on Mars again, falling . . .

It had been a perfect touchdown.

The first manned craft to land on another planet had done so at precisely 3.33 a.m., Houston time, 2 September, 2020.

Enright recalled little of the actual landing, other than his fear. He had never been a good flyer – plane journeys had given him the shakes: he feared the take-off and landings, while the bit in between he could tolerate. The same was true of spaceflight. The take-off at Kennedy had been delayed by a day, and then put on hold for another five hours, and by the time the *Fortitude* did blast off from pad 39A, Enright had been reduced to a nervous wreck. Fortunately, his presence at this stage of the journey had been token. It was the others who did the work – just as when they came in to land, over eighteen months later, on the broad, rouge expanse of the Amazonis Planitia.

Enright recalled gripping the arms of his seat to halt the shakes that had taken him, and staring through the viewscreen at the rocky surface of Mars which was rushing up to meet them faster than seemed safe.

Jeffries had seen him and laughed, nudging McCarthy to take a look. Fortunately, the air force man had been otherwise occupied. Only Spirek sympathized with a smile; Enright received the impression that she too was not enjoying the descent.

The retros cut in, slamming the seat into Enright's back and knocked the wind from him. The descent of the lander slowed appreciably. The boulder strewn terrain seemed to be floating up to meet them, now.

Touchdown, when it came, was almost delicate.

McCarthy and Jeffries were NASA men through and through, veterans of a dozen space station missions and the famous return to the moon in '15. They were good astronauts, lousy travelling companions. They were career as-

tronauts who were less interested in the pursuit of knowledge, of exploration for its own sake, than in the political
end-results of what they were doing – both for themselves
personally, and for the country. Enright envisaged
McCarthy running for president in the not too distant
future, Jeffries ending up as some big-wig in the Pentagon.

They tended to look upon Enright, with his PhD in
geology and a career at Miami university, as something
of a make-weight on the trip.

Spirek . . . Enright could not quite make her out. Like the
others, she was a career astronaut, but she had none of the
brash bravado and right-wing rhetoric of her male counter-
parts. She had been a pilot in the air force, and was along as
team medic and multi-disciplinary scientist: her brief, to
assess the planet for possible future colonization.

McCarthy was slated to step out first, followed by Enright. Fancy that, he'd thought on being informed at the
briefing, Iowa farm-boy made good, only the second human being ever to set foot on Mars . . .

After the landing, Jeffries had made some quip about
Enright still being shit scared and not up to taking a stroll.
He'd even made to suit up ahead of Enright.

"I'm fine," Enright said.

Spirek had backed him up. "Ed's AOK for go, Jeffries.
You don't want Roberts finding out you pulled a stunt,
huh?"

Jeffries had muttered something under his breath. It had
sounded like "Bitch," to Enright.

So he'd followed McCarthy out onto the sun-bright plain
of the Amazonis Planitia, his pulse loud in his ears, his legs
trembling as he climbed the ladder and stepped onto the
surface of the alien world.

There was a lot to do for the two hours he was out of the
lander, and he had only the occasional opportunity to
consider the enormity of the situation.

He took rock samples, drilled through the regolith to the
bedrock. He filmed what he was doing for the benefit of the
geologists back at NASA who would take up the work when
he returned.

He recalled straightening up on one occasion and staring,

amazed, at the western horizon. He wondered how he had failed to notice it before. The mountain stood behind the lander, an immense pyramidal shape that rose abruptly from the surrounding volcanic plain to a height, he judged, of a kilometre. He had to tilt his head back to take in its summit.

Later, Spirek and Jeffries took their turn outside, while Enright began a preliminary analysis of the rock samples and McCarthy reported back to mission control.

Day one went like a dream, everything AOK.

The following day, as the sun rose through the cerise sky, Enright and Spirek took the Mars-mobile out for its test drive. They ranged a kilometre from the lander, keeping it in sight at all times.

Spirek, driving, halted the vehicle at one point and stared into the sky. She touched Enright's padded elbow, and he heard her voice in his ear-piece. "Look, Ed." And she pointed.

He followed her finger, and saw a tiny, shimmering star high in the heavens.

"Earth," she whispered, and, despite himself, Enright felt some strange emotion constrict his throat at the sight of the planet, so reduced.

But for Spirek's sighting of Earth at that moment, and her decision to halt, Enright might never have made the discovery that was to prove so fateful.

Spirek was about to start up, when he glanced to his left and saw the depression in the regolith, ten metres from the Mars-mobile.

"Hey! Stop, Sally!"

"What is it?"

He pointed. "Don't know. Looks like subsidence. I want to take a look."

Sal glanced at her chronometer. "You got ten minutes, okay?"

He climbed from the mobile and strode towards the rectangular impression in the red dust. He paused at its edge, knelt and ran his hand through the fine regolith. The first human being, he told himself, ever to do so here at this precise location . . .

He stood and took a step forward.

And the ground gave way beneath his feet, and he was falling. "Oh, my God!"

He landed in a sitting position in semi-darkness, battered and dazed but uninjured. He checked his life-support apparatus. His suit was okay, his air supply functioning.

Only then did he look around him. He was in a vast chamber, a cavern that extended for as far as the eye could see.

As the dust settled, he made out the objects ranged along the length of the chamber.

"Oh, Christ," he cried. "Spirek . . . *Spirek!*"

He stood in the doorway of the conservatory and watched the workmen dismantle the swing and load it onto the back of the pick-up.

He'd been home four days now, and he was falling back into the routine of things. Breakfast with Delia, then a round of golf, solo, on the mornings she worked. They met for lunch in town, and then spent the afternoons at home, Delia in the garden, Enright reading magazines and journals in the conservatory.

He was due to start back at the university in a week, begin work on the samples he'd brought back from Mars. He was not relishing the prospect, and not just because it would mean spending time away from Delia: the business of geology, and what might be learned from the study of the Martian rocks, palled beside what he'd discovered on the red planet.

Roberts had phoned him a couple of days ago. Already NASA was putting together plans for a follow-up mission. He recalled what McCarthy and Jeffries had said about their discovery, that it constituted a security risk. Enright had forced himself not to laugh out loud, at the time. And yet, amazingly, when he returned to Earth and heard the talk of the back-room boys up at Kennedy, that had been the tenor of their concern. Now Roberts confirmed it by telling him, off the record, that the government was bank-rolling the next Mars mission. There would be a big military presence aboard. He wondered if McCarthy and Jeffries were happy now.

The workmen finished loading the frame of the swing and drove off. Delia was kneeling in the border, weeding. He watched her for a while, then went into the house.

He fetched the papers from the sitting room where he'd discovered them yesterday, slipped under the cushion of the settee.

"Delia?"

She turned, smiling.

She saw the papers and her smile faltered. Her eyes became hard. "I was just looking them over. I wasn't thinking of . . ."

"We talked about this, Delia."

"What, five years ago, more? Things are different now. You're back at university. I can quit work. Ed," she said, something like a plea in her tone, "we'd be perfect. They're looking for people like us."

He sat down on the grass, laid the brochure down between himself and his wife. The wind caught the cover, riffled pages. He saw a gallery of beseeching faces staring out at him, soft focus shots manufactured to pluck at the heart-strings of childless couples like themselves.

He reached out and stopped the pages. He stared at the picture of a small blonde-haired girl. She reminded him of the kid who'd asked for his signature at the golf course the other day.

And, despite himself, he felt a longing somewhere deep within him like an ache.

"Why are you so against the idea, Ed?"

They had planned to start a family in the early years. Then Delia discovered that she was unable to bear children. He had grown used to the idea that their marriage would be childless, though it was harder for Delia to accept. Over the years he had devoted himself to his wife, and when five years ago she had first mentioned the possibility of adoption, he had told her he loved her so much that he would be unable to share that love with a child. He was bullshitting, of course. The fact was that he did not want Delia's love for him diluted by another.

And now? Now, he felt the occasional craving to lavish love and affection on a child, and he could not explain his uneasiness at the prospect of acceding to his wife's desires.

He shook his head, wordlessly, and a long minute later he stood and returned to the house.

The following day Delia sought him out in his study. He'd retreated there shortly after breakfast, and for the past hour had been staring at his replica sixteenth-century globe of the world. He considered crude, formless shapes that over the years had been redefined as countries and continents.

Terra incognita . . .

A sound interrupted his reverie. Delia paused by the door, one hand touching the jamb. She was carrying a newspaper.

She entered the room and sat down on the very edge of the armchair beside the bookcase. He managed a smile.

"You haven't been yourself since you got back."

"I'm sorry. It must be the strain. I'm tired."

She nodded, let the silence develop. "Did you know, there were stories at the time? The Net was buzzing with rumours, speculation."

He smiled at that. "I should hope so. Humankind's first landing on Mars . . ."

"Besides that, Ed. When you fell, and the broadcast was suddenly cut."

"What we're they saying? That we'd been captured by little green men?"

"Not in so many words. But they were speculating . . . said you might have stumbled across some sign of life up there." She stopped, then said, "Well?"

"Well, what?"

"What happened?"

He sighed. "So you'd rather believe some crazy press report –?"

She stopped him by holding out the morning paper. The headline of the Miami Tribune ran: LIFE ON MARS?

He took the paper and read the report.

Speculation was growing today surrounding man's first landing on the red planet. Leaks from NASA suggest that astronauts McCarthy, Jeffries, Enright and Spirek discovered ancient ruins on their second exploratory tour of the red planet. Unconfirmed reports suggest that . . .

Enright stopped reading and passed the paper back to his wife.

"Unconfirmed reports, rumours. Typical press speculation."

"So nothing happened?"

"What do you want me to say? I fell down a hole – but I didn't find Wonderland down there."

Later, when she left without another word, he chastised himself for such a cheap parting shot.

He hadn't found Wonderland down there, but something far stranger instead.

So the leaks had begun. Maybe he should tell Delia, before she found out from the paper.

For the rest of the morning, he went through the pile of letters that had accumulated during his absence. He replied to a few and discarded others. Just as he was about to break for lunch, he came upon the letter from Connaught in England, with its distinctive King's head stamp.

He wondered what strange theory his eccentric pen-pal might have come up with this time.

He opened the letter and unfolded a single sheet of high quality note paper. Usually there were dozens of pages in his tiny, meticulous handwriting.

Enright read the letter, no more than three short paragraphs. Then he read it again, his mouth suddenly dry. He lay the sheet on his knee, as his hands were trembling.

Dear Ed, he read,

I have been following your exploits on the red planet with interest and concern. By now you will have returned, and I hope you will read this letter at the earliest opportunity. I was watching the broadcast from the Amazonis Planitia, which was suddenly terminated in strange circumstances . . . I wondered if humankind had at last found that life once existed on

Mars. Ed, my friend, if you did indeed discover something beneath the sands of Mars, I think I can furnish
an explanation.

If you would care to visit me at the Manor at the
earliest opportunity, I have a rather interesting story
to tell.

If you need further convincing that your trip might
prove worthwhile, I can but write the words: *Ulla,
ulla* . . .

>   Your very good friend, Joshua Connaught.

Enright read the letter perhaps a dozen times, before
folding it away and staring at the far wall for long minutes.

If the original discovery had struck him as an irresolvable
enigma, then this only compounded the sense of mystery.

He reached for the phone and made immediate plans to
fly to England.

Later, over lunch, he told Delia that NASA had
recalled him. He'd be up at the Space Center for just
under a week.

"Is it about . . . about what happened on Mars?"

How much to tell her? "Delia, when I get back . . . I
think I'll be able to tell you something, okay?"

And the words Connaught had scrawled at the end of his
letter came back to him.

Ulla, ulla.

He had fetched up on his butt at the bottom of the landslide
and stared about him in wonder. The dust had settled, and
bright sunlight penetrated the chamber for the first time in
who knew how long?

Through the dust and the glare he made out an array of
towering shapes ranged along the walls of the chamber. He
had fallen perhaps fifty feet, and the shapes – the machines
– were almost that tall.

"Oh, Christ," he cried. "Spirek . . . *Spirek!*"

In his ear he heard, "You okay, Ed? You hear me? Are
you okay?"

"Sal! You gotta see this."

"Ed, where are you?"

He looked up. Sal was a tiny, silver-suited figure bobbing about on the lip of the drop, trying to see him.

He waved. "Get yourself down here, Sal. You've gotta see this!"

In his head-set he heard McCarthy shouting, "What's going on out there, Enright? Spirek?"

"You getting the pics, McCarthy?" Enright asked.

"Is the camera working? The picture went haywire when you fell."

He checked the camera. It had ceased filming at some point during his descent. He activated it again and swept the head-mounted lens around the chamber. He could see now that a section of the ceiling had sunk over the years, and the pressure of his weight upon it had brought the slab crashing down, and tons of sand with it.

McCarthy: "It's all hazy, Enright. Can't see much."

Enright stood, tested his limbs. He was fine. No breaks. He stepped forward, out of the direct sunlight, and stared at the ranked machinery that disappeared into the perspective.

"Hell fire in heaven!" Jeffries murmured.

Spirek was still peering down at him, unsure whether to negotiate the landslide.

"Ed, are you gonna tell me?"

He peered up at her. "Get yourself down here, Sal."

She hesitated, then stepped forward and rode the sliding sand down to him like a kid on a dune.

She lost her footing and sprawled on her back. Enright helped her up. He was still holding her hand, staring past her face plate to watch her expression, as she turned and looked down the length of the chamber.

She said nothing, but silver tears welled in her eyes.

Then, without a word, spontaneously, they embraced.

Hand in hand, like frightened kids, they walked down the chamber.

They approached the machinery, the *craft*, rather. There were dozens of them, each one tall and columnar and bulky. They were dark shapes, seemingly oiled, silent and static and yet, every one upright and aimed, seemingly poised with intent.

Then they came to a smaller piece of machinery, perhaps half the height of the columns. Enright stopped, and stared.

He could not help himself: he began weeping.

"Ed?" Sal said, gripping his hand in sudden fear.

He indicated the looming, legged, vehicle.

She shook her head. "So what? I don't see . . . ?"

In his head-set, Enright heard McCarthy, "Hey, you two oughtta be heading back now. Sal, how much air you got there?"

Sal swore. "Dammit, Ed. We gotta be getting back."

He was staring at the vehicle, mesmerised. "Ed!" Sal called again.

Reluctantly, Enright turned and followed Sal back up the landslide to the Marsmobile.

England, in contrast to sun-soaked Florida, was caught in the grip of its fiercest winter for years. From the window seat of the plane as it came in to land, Enright stared down at a landscape sealed in an otherworldly radiance of snow. This was the first time he had seen snow for almost twenty years, and he thought the effect cleansing: it gave mundane terrain a transformed appearance, bright and pristine: it looked like a land where miracles might easily occur.

He caught a Southern Line train from Heathrow to the village of Barton Humble in Dorset, and from there a taxi to Brimscombe Manor.

For the duration of the ten mile drive, Enright stared out at a landscape every bit as alien and fascinating as the terrain of Mars. He seemed to be travelling deep into the heart of ancient countryside: everything about England, he noted, possessed a quality of age, of history and permanence, entirely lacking in the American environment to which he was accustomed. The lanes were deep and rutted, with high hedges, more suited to bullock-carts than automobiles. They passed an ancient forest of oak, the dark, winter-stark trees bearing ghostly doppelgangers of themselves in the burden of snow that limned every branch.

Brimscombe Manor, when it finally appeared, standing between the forest and a shallow rise of hills, was vast and sprawling, possessed of a tumbledown gentility that put

Enright in mind of fading country houses in the quaint black and white British films he'd watched as a child.

The driver took one look at the foot-thick mantle of snow that covered the drive of the Manor, and shook his head. "Okay if I drop you here?"

Enright paid him off with unfamiliar European currency, retrieved his bag from the back seat, and stood staring at the imposing façade of the Manor as the taxi drove away.

He felt suddenly alone in the alien environment. He knew the sensation well. The last time he had experienced this gut-wrenching sense of dislocation, he had been on Mars.

What the hell, he wondered, am I doing here? He had the sudden vision of himself, a US astronaut, standing forlornly in the depths of the English countryside on a freezing December afternoon, and smiled to himself.

"*Ulla, ulla*," he said, and his breath plumed in the icy air before him, the effect at once novel and disconcerting. "I'm going mad."

He set off through the snow. His boots compacted ice crystals in a series of tight, musical squeaks.

A light burned, orange and inviting, behind a mullioned window in the west wing of the Manor. He climbed a sweep of steps and found a bell-push beside the vast timber door.

Thirty seconds later the door swung open, and heat and light flooded out to greet him.

"Mr Enright, Ed, you can't imagine how delighted I am . . ."

Within seconds of setting eyes upon his long-term correspondent, Enright felt at ease. Connaught had the kind of open, amicable face that Enright associated with English character actors of the old school: he guessed Connaught was in his early sixties, medium height, a full head of grey hair, wide smiling mouth and blue eyes.

He wore tweeds, and a waistcoat with a fob watch on a silver chain.

"You must be exhausted after the journey. It's appalling out there." He escorted Enright across the hall. "Ten below all week. Record, so I'm told. Coldest cold snap for sixty years. You'll want a drink, and then dinner. I'll show you to your room. As soon as you've refreshed yourself, join me in the library."

He indicated a room to the right, through an open door. Enright glimpsed a roaring open fire and rank upon rank of books. "This is the library, and right next door is your room. I hope you don't mind sleeping on the ground floor. I live here alone now, and since Liz passed away I don't bother with the upstairs rooms. Cheaper just to live down here. Here we are."

He showed Enright into a room with a double bed and an *en suite* bathroom, then excused himself and left.

Enright sat on the bed, staring through the window at the snow-covered lawn and the drive. The only blemish in the snow was his footprints, which a fresh fall was already filling in.

He showered, changed, and ventured next door to the library.

Connaught stood beside a trolley of drinks. "Scotch, Brandy?"

He accepted a brandy and sat on a leather settee before the open fire. Connaught sat to the right of the fire in a big, high-backed leather armchair.

He surprised himself by falling into a polite exchange of smalltalk. His curiosity was such that all he wanted from Connaught was an explanation of the letter which he carried, folded, in his hip pocket.

Ulla, ulla . . .

He fitted sound-bites and observations around Connaught's questions and comments.

"The flight was fine – a tailwind pushed us all the way, cutting an hour and a half off the expected time . . .

"England surprises me . . . Everything seems so old, and *small . . .*

"I'm impressed by the Manor . . . We don't have anything quite like this back home."

And then they were discussing the history of manned space exploration. Connaught was extremely knowledgeable, indeed more so than Enright, in his grasp of the political cut and thrust of the space race.

An hour had elapsed in pleasant conversation, and still he had not broached the reason for his visit.

Connaught glanced at the carriage clock on the mantel-shelf. "Eight already! Let's continue the conversation over dinner, shall we?"

He ushered Enright along the hall and into a comfortable lounge with a table, laid for two, in a recessed area by the window.

A steaming casserole dish, a bowl of vegetables, and a bottle of opened wine, stood on the table.

Connaught gestured to a seat. "I hire a woman from the village," he explained. "Heavenly cook. Comes in for a couple of hours a day and does for me."

They ate. Steak and kidney casserole, roast potatoes, carrots and asparagus. They finished off the first bottle and started into a second.

The night progressed. Enright relaxed, drank more wine.

The amicable tenor of their correspondence was maintained, he was delighted to find, in their conversation. He contrasted the humane Connaught with the bullish egomania of McCarthy.

Ulla, ulla . . .

Suddenly, the conversation switched – and it was Connaught who instigated the change.

"Of course, I watched every second of the Mars coverage. I was glued to the Net. I hoped and prayed that your team might discover something there, though of course I was prepared for disappointment . . . I'll tell you something, Ed. I harboured the desire to be an astronaut myself, when I was young. Just a dream, of course. Never did anything about it. I fantasised about discovering new worlds, alien civilizations."

Enright smiled. "I never had that kind of ambition. I slipped into the space program almost by accident. They wanted a geologist on the mission, and I volunteered." He hesitated. "So when I stepped out onto Mars, of course the last thing on my mind was the discovery of an alien civilization."

"I was watching the cast when you fell. The moment you said those words, I knew. Your tone of disbelieving wonder told me. I just knew you'd found something."

Connaught refilled the glasses. "What happened, Ed? Tell me in your own words how you came to . . ."

So he recounted the landing, his first walk on the surface of Mars, and then his second. He worked up to his fall, and the discovery, like an expert storyteller. He found he was enjoying his role of raconteur . . .

They arrived back at the lander, after the discovery, with just four minutes' air supply remaining.

McCarthy and Jeffries were standing in the living quarters when they cycled through the hatch and discarded their suits. They were white-faced and silent.

Enright looked around the group, shaking his head. Words, at this moment, seemed beyond him.

McCarthy said, "Mission control went ballistic. You should hear Roberts. Wait till this breaks!"

Sal Spirek slumped into a seat. "We're famous, gentlemen. I think that this just might be the most momentous occasion in the history of humankind, or am I exaggerating?"

They stared around at each other, trying to work out if indeed she was exaggerating.

Enright was shaking his head.

"What is it?" Sal asked.

He could not find the words to articulate what even he found hard to believe. "You don't understand," he began.

Sal said, "What's wrong?"

"Those things back there," Enright said, "the cylindrical rockets and three-legged machines." He stared around at their uncomprehending faces. "Have none of you ever read *The War of the Worlds*?"

Six hours later, with the go ahead of Roberts at mission control, all four astronauts suited up and rode the Marsmobile to the subterranean chamber.

As he negotiated the sloping drift of red sand, Enright half-expected to find the cavern empty, the cylinders and striding machines revealed to be nothing other than a figment of his imagination.

He paused at the foot of the drift, Sal by his side, McCarthy and Jeffries bringing up the rear and gasping as they stared at the alien machinery diminishing in perspective.

He and Sal walked side by side down the length of the chamber, passing from bright sunlight into shadow. He switched on his shoulder-mounted flashlight and stared at the vast, cylindrical rockets arrayed along the chamber. They were mounted on a complex series of frames, and canted at an angle of a few degrees from the perpendicular.

They paused before a smaller machine, consisting of a cowled dome atop three long, multi-jointed legs.

McCarthy and Jeffries joined them.

"Fighting Machines," Enright said.

McCarthy looked at him. "Say again?"

"Wells called them Fighting Machines," he said. "In his book –"

He stopped, then, as the implications of what he was saying slowly dawned on him.

He walked on, down the aisle between the examples of an alien culture's redundant hardware. The atmosphere within the chamber was that of a museum, or a mausoleum.

McCarthy was by his side. "You really expect us to believe . . . ?" he began.

Spirek said, "I've read *The War of the Worlds*, McCarthy. Christ, but Wells got it right. The cylinders, the Fighting Machines . . ."

"That's impossible!"

Enright said, "It's all here, McCarthy. Just as Wells described it."

McCarthy looked at him, his expression lost in the shadow behind his faceplate. "How do you explain it, Enright?"

He shrugged. "I don't. I can't. God knows."

"Here!" Spirek had moved off, and was kneeling beside something in the shadow of a tripod.

"The hardware wasn't all Wells got right." She gestured. "Look . . ."

Mummified in the airless vault for who knew how long, the Martian was much as the Victorian writer had described them in his novel of alien invasion, one hundred and twenty years before.

It was all head, with two vast, dull eyes the size of saucers, and a beak, with tentacles below that – tentacles that Wells had speculated the aliens had walked upon. It was, Enright thought, more hideous than anything he had ever seen before.

Enright walked on, and found more and more of the dead aliens scattered about the chamber.

Jeffries said, "I'll get all this back to Roberts. We need to work out strategy."

Enright looked at him. "Strategy?"

Jeffries gestured around him. "This is a security risk, Enright. I'm talking an A1 security risk, here. How do we know these monsters aren't planning an invasion right now? Isn't that what the book was about?"

Enright and Spirek exchanged a glance.

"The Martians are dead, Jeffries. Their planet was dying. They lived underground, but air and food was running out. They died out before they could get away."

"You don't know that, Enright. You're speculating."

Enright strode off. He needed isolation in which to consider his discovery.

He found other chambers through giant archways, and a series of ramps that gave access to even lower levels. He imagined an entire city down there, a vast underground civilization, long dead.

Sal Spirek joined him. "How did Wells know?" she asked. "How could he possibly have known?"

Enright recalled the last time he had read the novel, in his teens. He had been haunted by the description of a ravaged, desolate London in the aftermath of the alien invasion. He recalled the cry of the Martians as they succumbed to a deadly Terran virus, the mournful lament that had echoed eerily across an otherwise deathly silent London. "Ulla, ulla, ulla, ulla . . ."

"What was it like when I looked upon those ranked machines?" Enright shook his head. "I felt more than I thought, Joshua. I was overwhelmed with disbelief, and then elation, and then later, back at the ship, when I thought about it, a little fear. But at the time, when I first saw the machines . . . it came as one hell of a shock when I realized why they were so familiar."

Connaught was nodding. "Wells," he said.

Enright let the silence stretch. "How did you know?" He leaned forward. "How did Wells know?"

Connaught stood. "How about a whiskey? I have some fine Irish here."

He moved across the room to a mahogany cabinet and poured two generous measures of Bushmills.

He returned to the table. Enright sipped his drink, feeling the mellow burn slide down his throat like hot velvet.

"My great-grandfather, James," Connaught said, "inherited the Manor from his father, who built the Manor in 1870 from profits made in the wine trade. James was a writer – unsuccessful and unpublished. He wrote what was known then as scientific romances. He self-published a couple of short books, to no great notice. To be honest, his imagination was his strong point – his literary ability was almost negligible. To cut a long story short, he was friendly with a young and aspiring writer at the time – this was around the 1890s. Chappie by the name of Wells. They spent many a weekend down here and swapped stories, ideas, plots, etc . . . One story James told him was about the invasion of Earth by creatures from Mars. They came in vast cylinders, and stalked the earth aboard great marching war machines. Apparently, my great-grandfather had tried to write it up himself, but didn't get very far. Wells took the idea, and the rest is history. *The War of the Worlds*. A classic."

Connaught paused, staring into his glass.

Enright nodded, his mind full of H.G. Wells and James Connaught discussing story ideas in this very building, all those years ago.

"How," he asked at last, "how did your great-grandfather know about the Martians?"

He realized that he was drunk, his speech slurred. The sense of anticipation he felt swelling within him was almost unbearable.

"One night way back in 1880," Connaught said, "James was out walking the grounds. This was late, around midnight. He often took a turn around the garden at this time, looking for inspiration. Anyway, he saw something in the sky, something huge and fiery, coming in from the direction of the coast. It landed with a loud explosion in the spinney to the rear of the Manor."

Enright leaned forward, reached for the whiskey bottle, and helped himself.

"James ran into the spinney," Connaught continued, "after the fallen object, and found there . . . He found a huge pit gouged into the ground, and in that pit a great cylindrical object, glowing red and steaming in the cold night."

Enright sat back in his chair and shook his head.

Joshua Connaught smiled. "You don't believe me?"

"No, it's just . . . I do believe you. It's just that it's so fantastic . . ."

Connaught said, "My great-grandfather excavated the pit and built an enclosure around it, and it exists to this day. I've shown no one since Elizabeth."

Enright experienced a sudden dizziness. He made a feeble gesture.

Connaught smiled. "It's still there, Ed."

Enright shook his head. "*It*, you mean . . . ?"

"The Martian cylinder, and other things."

Enright downed the last of his whiskey, felt it burning his throat.

Connaught stood. "Shall we go?"

Enright stood also, unsteadily. "Please, after you." Swaying, he followed Connaught from the room.

He expected to be taken outside, but instead Connaught led him through a narrow door and down a flight of even narrower steps. A succession of bare, low-watt bulbs illuminated a series of vaulted cellars, the first chambers stocked with wine, the later ones empty and musty.

They walked along a narrow red brick corridor.

"We're now passing from the Manor and walking beneath the kitchen garden towards the spinney," Connaught reported over his shoulder.

Enright nodded, aware that he was sobering rapidly with the effects of the cold and the notion of what might imminently be revealed.

The corridor extended for five hundred yards, and terminated abruptly at a small wooden door.

Connaught drew a key from the pocket of his waistcoat and opened the door. He stood aside, gesturing for Enright to enter.

Cautiously, he stepped over the threshold.

He faced an abyss of darkness, until Connaught reached past him and threw a switch.

A dozen bare bulbs illuminated a vast rectangular red-brick room. The walls were concave, bowed like the hull of a galleon. A series of rough wooden steps led down to the floor, again of red brick.

The cylinder lay in the centre of the room, a long, gun-metal grey column identical to those he had seen in the chamber on Mars. At the facing end of the cylinder was a circular opening. Beside the cylinder, laid out lengthways, was one of the Fighting Machines.

Enright climbed down the steps, aware that his mouth was hanging open. He walked around the cylinder, its dimensions dwarfing him and Connaught. He reached out and touched the icy cold surface of the cylinder, something he had been unable to do on Mars. He inspected the tripod, marvelling at the intricacy of the metalwork – crafted far away on Mars by a race of beings long dead and gone.

"According to the story," Connaught said, "that night James crouched on the edge of the pit and watched fearfully as the great threaded stopper slowly unscrewed and fell out. He waited, but hours elapsed and nothing emerged other than a strange, other-worldly cry, 'Ulla, ulla, ulla, ulla.' It was daybreak before he plucked up the courage to scramble down into the pit and approach the cylinder. There were three beings in the craft, he could see by the light of dawn, but they were dead. Fortunately, the spinney was on his land, and anyway the trees concealed the pit from view. Over the course of the following year, working alone, he built this construction around the craft, and then devoted the rest of his life to the study of its contents. He and his son, my grandfather, reconstructed the tripod you see there. They even attempted to preserve the dead aliens, but they rotted almost to nothing with the passage of years."

Enright looked up. "Almost nothing?"

Connaught walked over to a raised wooden platform. Upon this was a big desk, and piles of papers and manuals, illuminated by a reading lamp. He gestured to a bulbous preserving jar, floating in which was a grey-brown scrap of what looked like hide.

"This is all that remains of the first alien beings to arrive on planet Earth," Connaught said.

"Did James show Wells all this?" Enright asked.

Connaught shook his head. "It was a strict secret, at the time known only to James and his son. As I said, he gave Wells the idea as a fiction, but supplied him with detailed drawings of the cylinder and the other machinery, and even of the aliens themselves, and their death cry."

"And you've never shown anyone outside the family, until now?"

Connaught smiled. "By the time my father found out, the truth of what had happened was lost in time. My grandfather was old when he showed my father the cylinder – his memory was not what it was. My father took the story with a pinch of salt. He rationalized that James had manufactured the cylinder himself, and the tripod. My father sealed the chamber, and only showed it to me when I was down here exploring, and asked about the mysterious bricked-up door."

"And yet you believed James's story?" Enright said.

Connaught hesitated. "I was at Oxford in the seventies," he said, "studying ancient literature. Later I found myself working for the government, decrypting codes . . . When I inherited the Manor, I inspected this chamber and everything it contained."

He moved to the desk and unlocked a drawer. From it he produced a thick, silver object that looked something like a book.

He laid it upon the desk and opened the cover. The pages were also silver, manufactured of some thin metal-like material, and upon each leaf of the book Enright made out, in vertical columns, what might have been lines of script. But it was a script unlike any he had ever seen before.

"James discovered this in the cylinder. For years and years he worked at decoding the book from the stars, as he called it. He failed. When I came across it, I began where my great-grandfather had left off."

Enright stared at him. "And you succeeded?"

Connaught bent and unlocked another drawer. From this he lifted a more conventional manuscript, a ream of A4 paper in a clip folder.

"I succeeded. Last year I finished translating the book. Much of it is an encyclopaedia of their world, a history of their race. Mars was dying, Ed. Millennia ago, the beings that had dwelled on the surface of the planet were forced to move underground, out of the inhospitable cold. Their numbers dwindled, until only tens of thousands survived. They realised that they had to leave their planet."

"And invade Earth," Enright finished.

But Connaught was smiling and shaking his head. "They were a peaceful people. Only in Wells' fiction were they belligerent."

He reached out and opened the cover of his translation. "Please," he said.

Enright stepped forward, his pulse pounding, and read the first paragraph.

We of the fourth planet of the solar system, the planet we call Vularia, come to the third planet on a mission of peace. Although our kind has known enmity, and fought debilitating wars, we have outgrown this stage of our evolution. We come with the hope that our two races might join as one and explore the universe together . . .

Enright stopped reading, aware of the constriction in his throat. He leafed through over five hundred pages of closely printed text.

He thought of McCarthy, and Jeffries, and the military operation underway right at this minute. He smiled to himself.

"Over half a million words," Connaught said. "You can hardly begin to conceive what a treasure it is."

Enright turned and walked away from the desk. He stared at the cylinder, and the so-called Fighting Machine.

Behind him, Connaught was saying, "My great-grand-father guessed that they were dying before they arrived on Earth – that it was not an earthly virus that ended their existence, but one of their own. How wonderful it might have been, had they survived."

Enright turned. "Why, Joshua? Why have you shown me all this? Your translation?"

"Why else? This has been a secret long enough. Now, my life's work is finished, the translation done – I would like to receive acknowledgement, in due course. I summoned you here so that you might take this copy of the translation back to America, to answer the mystery of what you discovered beneath the sands of Mars."

He gestured towards the door. "Come, it's cold in here. Shall we retire to the library for a nightcap?"

With one last glance at the Martian machines, he turned and followed Connaught from the chamber.

On the flight back to America, Enright dreamed. He was in London, but a London laid waste by some apocalyptic war. He strode through the ruins, listening. He was not alone. Beside him was a child, a small girl, and when he looked upon her he was filled with a strange sense of hope for the future, a hope like elation. The girl slipped a hand in to his, and at that moment Enright heard it. Faint at first, and then stronger. It was the saddest, most haunting sound he had ever heard in his life.

"Ulla, ulla, ulla, ulla . . ."

He awoke with a start. The sensation of the small, warm hand in his was so real that he glanced at the seat beside him, but it was empty.

The plane was banking. They were coming in to land at Orlando.

Enright checked beneath his seat to ensure that he still had the briefcase containing the Martian translation.

We of the fourth planet of the solar system, the planet we call Vularia, come to the third planet on a mission of peace . . .

He smiled to himself, closed his eyes, and thought of Delia, and home, and the future.

Deathday

Peter F. Hamilton

Peter Hamilton started writing at about the same time as Eric Brown, though his emphasis was less on short fiction than on increasingly breeze-block size novels which pumped life back into the grand space opera of old. His Night's Dawn trilogy – The Reality Dysfunction (1996), The Neutronium Alchemist (1997) and The Naked God (1999) took the struggle of life and death to the ultimate. The following story, one of his earliest, is another struggle for life or death, but on a rather smaller scale.

Today Miran would kill the xenoc. His confidence had soared to a dizzying height, driven by some subconscious premonition. He knew it was today.

Even though he was awake he could hear the ethereal wind-howl of the ghosts, spewing out their lament, their hatred of him. It seemed the whole world shared in the knowledge of impending death.

He had been hunting the xenoc for two months now. An intricate, deadly game of pursuit, flight, and camouflage, played out all over the valley. He had come to learn the xenoc's movements, how it reacted to situations, the paths it would take, its various hiding places in rocky crevices, its aversion to the steep shingle falls. He was its soul-twin now. It belonged to him.

What Miran would have liked to do was get close enough so he might embrace its neck with his own hands; to feel the life slipping from his tormentor's grotesque body. But above all he was a practical man, he told himself he wasn't going to be asinine-sentimental about it, if he could pick it off with the laser rifle he would do so. No hesitation, no remorse.

He checked the laser rifle's power charge and stepped out of the homestead. Home – the word mocked him. It wasn't a home, not any more. A simple three-room prefab shipped in by the Jubarra Development Corporation, designed for two-person assembly. Candice and himself. Her laugh, her smile, the rooms had echoed with them; filling even the glummest day with life and joy. Now it was a convenient shelter, a dry place from which to plot his campaign and strategies.

Physically, the day was no different to any other on Jubarra. Gloomy leaden-grey clouds hung low in the sky, marching east to west. Cold mist swirled about his ankles, coating grass and rocks alike in glistening dewdrops. There would be rain later, there always was.

He stood before her grave, a shallow pit piled high with big crumbling lumps of local sandstone. Her name was carved in crude letters on the largest. There was no cross. No true God would have let her die, not like that.

"This time," he whispered. "I promise. Then it will be over."

He saw her again. Her pale sweat-soaked face propped up on the pillow. The sad pain in her eyes from the knowledge there was little time left. "Leave this world," she'd said, and her burning fingers closed around his hand for emphasis. "Please, for me. We have made this world a lifeless place; it belongs to the dead now. There is nothing here for the living any more, no hope, no purpose. Don't waste yourself, don't mourn for the past. Promise me that."

So he had held back the tears and sworn he would leave to find another life on another world; because it was what she wanted to hear, and he had never denied her anything. But they were empty words; there was nowhere for him to go, not without her.

After that he had sat helplessly as the fever consumed her, watching her breathing slow and the harsh stress lines on her face smooth out. Death made her beauty fragile. Smothering her in wet earth was an unholy sacrilege.

After he finished her grave he lay on the bed, thinking only of joining her. It was deepest night when he heard the noise. A muffled knock of rock against rock. With a great effort he got to his feet. The cabin walls spun alarmingly. He had no idea how long he had lain there – maybe hours, maybe days. Looking out of the door he could see nothing at first. Then his eyes acclimatized to the pale streaks of phosphorescence shivering across the flaccid underbelly of the clouds. A dark concentration of shadows hovered over the grave, scrabbling softly at the stones.

"Candice?" he shouted, drunk with horror. Dark suppressed imaginings swelled out of his subconscious – demons, zombies, ghouls, and trolls, chilling his bones to brittle sticks of ice.

The shadow twisted at his cry, edges blurring, becoming eerily insubstantial.

Miran screamed wordlessly, charging out of the homestead, his muscles powered by outrage and vengeance-lust. When he reached the grave the xenoc had gone, leaving no trace. For a moment Miran thought he might have hallucinated the whole event, but then he saw how the limestone had been moved, the rucked mud where non-human feet had stood. He fell to his knees, panting, stroking the limestone. Nauseating fantasy images of what the xenoc would have done with Candice had it uncovered her threatened to extinguish the little flicker of sanity he had remaining. His future ceased to be a nebulous uncertainty. He had a purpose now: he would remain in this valley until he had ensured Candice was granted the dignity of eternal rest. And there was also the question of vengeance against the monster desecrator.

Miran left the grave and walked past the neglected vegetable garden, down towards the valley floor. The hills of the valley were high prison walls, steep slopes and cliffs smeared with loose stone and tough reedy grass. They reared up to create a claustrophobic universe, for ever preventing him from seeing out. Not that he had any desire to, the memory of all things good dwelt between the hills.

The river ran a crooked course ahead of him, wandering back and forth across the valley floor in great loops, fed by countless silver trickles which seeped out of secret fissures high in the forbidding massifs. Long stretches of the low meadowland below the homestead were flooded again. Skeletal branches and dead rodent-analogue creatures bobbed lazily on the slow flow of muddy water. Further down the valley, where the river's banks were more pronounced, straggly trees had established a hold, trailing weeping boughs into the turbulent water.

This was his land, the vista he and Candice had been greeted with when they struggled through the saddle in the hills at the head of the valley. They had stood together lost in delight, knowing this was right, that their gamble had paid off. They would make their life here, and grow crops for the ecological assessment team's outpost in return for a land grant of twenty thousand acres. Then when the colonists started to arrive their vast holding would make them rich, their children would be Jubarra's first merchant princes.

Miran surveyed the valley and all its wrecked phantoms of ambition, planning carefully. He had abandoned yesterday's chase at the foot of a sheer gorge on the other side of the river. Experience and instinct merged in his mind. The xenoc had been skulking along the base of the valley's northern wall for the last two days. There were caves riddling the rock of the foothills in that area, and a scattering of aboriginal fruit bushes. Shelter and food; it was a good location. Even the xenoc occasionally sought refuge from Jubarra's miserable weather.

He stared ahead. Seeing nothing. Feeling around the recesses of his mind for their perverse bond.

How it had come about he never knew. Perhaps they had shared so much suffering they had developed a mental kinship, something related to Edenist affinity. Or perhaps the xenoc possessed some strange telepathy of its own, which would account for why the ecological investigators had never caught one. Whatever the reason, Miran could sense it. Ever since that night at the grave he had known of the other's presence; moving around the valley, sneaking close, stopping to rest. Weird thoughts and confused images oozed constantly into his mind.

Sure enough, the xenoc was out there to the north, on the hummocks above the flood water, picking its way slowly down the valley.

Miran struck out across the old fields. The first crops he'd planted were potatoes and maize, both geneered to withstand Jubarra's shabby temperate climate. The night they had finished planting he carried Candice out to the fields and laid her lean body down on the new furrows of rich dark humus. She laughed delightedly at the foolishness that had come over him. But the ancient pagan fertility rite was theirs to celebrate that night, as the spring winds blew and the warm drizzle sprinkled their skin. He entered her with a fierce triumph, a primeval man appeasing the gods for the bounty of life they had granted, and she cried out in wonder.

The crops had indeed flourished. But now they were choked with aboriginal weeds. He had dug up a few of the potatoes since, eating them with fish or one of the chickens that had run wild. A monotonous diet; but food wasn't an interest, just an energy source.

The first of the morning drizzles arrived before he was halfway to his goal. Cold and insistent, it penetrated his jacket collar and crept down his spine. The stones and mud underfoot became treacherously slippery.

Cursing under his breath, he slowed his pace. Presumably the xenoc was equally aware of him. It would soon be moving on, building valuable distance between them. Miran could move faster, but unless he got within a kilometre he could never hope to catch it in a day. Yet he didn't dare take any risks, a fall and a broken bone would be the end of it.

The xenoc was moving again. Throughout the intermittent lulls in the drizzle Miran tried to match what he was sensing in his mind with what he could see.

One of the buttress-like foothills radiating out from the base of the mountain ahead of him had created a large promontory, extending for over half a kilometre out into the flood water. It was a grassy slope studded with cracked boulders, the detritus of past avalanches. The oldest stones were coated with the emerald fur of a spongy aboriginal lichen.

The xenoc was making for the promontory's tip. Trapped! If Miran could reach the top of the promontory it could never hope to get clear. He could advance towards it down a narrowing strip of solid ground, forcing it to retreat right to the water's edge. Miran had never known it to swim.

Gritting his teeth against the marrow-numbing cold, he waded through a fast icy stream which had cut itself a steep gully through the folds of peat skirting the mountain. It was after that, hurrying towards the promontory through slackening drizzle, that he came across the Bulldemon skeleton.

He paused to run his hands reverently over some of the huge ivory ribs curving above him. The Bulldemons were lumbering quadruped brutes, carnivores with a small brain and a filthy temper. Their meat was mildly poisonous to humans, and they would have played havoc amongst pioneer farming villages. A laser hunting rifle couldn't bring one down, and there was no way the Development Company would issue colonists with heavy-calibre weapons. Instead the Company had cleared them out with a geneered virus. As the Bulldemons shared a common biochemistry with the rest of the planet's aboriginal mammalian species it was tacitly assumed in the boardroom to be a multiple xenocide. Billions of fuseodollars had already been invested in exploring and investigating Jubarra, the board couldn't afford to have potential colonists scared off by xenoc dinosaur-analogues. Too many other colony worlds were in the market for Earth's surplus population.

The virus had been ninety-nine per cent successful.

Many of Miran's dreams were of the fifty million xenoc ghosts. If he had known of the crime beforehand, he would never have taken up the Development Company's generous advance colonizer offer. Throughout history there had never been a planet so sinned against as Jubarra. The ghosts outnumbered the ecological assessment team twenty thousand to one, engulfing them in tidal waves of hatred.

Maybe it was the ghosts who had disturbed Jubarra's

star. The astronomers claimed they'd never seen an instability cycle like it before. Three months after he and Candice arrived in the valley the solar observatory confirmed the abnormality; flare and spot activity was decreasing rapidly. Jubarra was heading straight for an ice age. Geologists confirmed the meagre five thousand year intervals between glacial epochs – they too had seen nothing like it. Botanists, with the wonder of hindsight, said it explained why there were so few aboriginal plant species.

The planet was abruptly declared unsuitable for colonization. The Jubarra Development Company went bankrupt immediately. All assets were frozen. The Confederation Assembly's Xenological Custodian Committee filed charges of xenocide against the board members.

Now the army of civil engineering teams designated to build a shiny new spaceport city would never arrive. No one would come to buy their crops. The ecological assessment team was winding up their research. Even the excited astronomers were preparing to fly back to their universities, leaving automatic monitoring satellites to collect data on the rogue star.

The shutdown had killed Candice. It broke her spirit. With her enhanced immunology system she should never have succumbed to the fever. But if it hadn't been the germs it would have been something else. All they had laboured over, all they had built, all their shared dreams had crumbled to dust. She died of a broken heart.

The xenoc was coming back down the promontory; moving as fast as it had ever done. It had realized its mistake. But not swiftly enough. Events were tilting in his favour. Soon now, so very soon.

Miran had reached the foot of the promontory. Now he scrambled over the deep drift of flinty stones that'd cascaded down its side from an eroded cliff higher up the mountain, hurrying for the high ground of the summit. From there he could cover both sides with the laser rifle. Small stones crunched loudly underfoot, betraying the urgency of his pounding feet.

The drizzle had stopped and the weak grey clouds were lifting, letting the sunlight through. Candice had loved the valley at moments like this. Her sweet nature prevented her from seeing it as anything other than an enclave of rugged beauty. Every time the sunbeams burst past the turbid curtains of cloud she would stop whatever task she was doing and drink in the sight. With its eternal coat of droplets the land gleamed as new.

Waiting for us to bring it to life, she said. To fill it with people and joy. A paradise valley.

He listened to her innocent sincerity, and believed as he had never believed in his life before. Never in all the months they spent alone together had they quarrelled; not even a harsh word had passed between them. There couldn't be a greater omen of a glorious future.

They worked side by side in the fields by day, using every hour of light to plant the crops. Then at night they made love for hours with a ferocity so intense it almost frightened him. Lying together in the warm darkness afterwards they shared their innermost thoughts, murmuring wondrously of the life their loving would bring to her womb.

Miran wondered about those easy days now. Had the xenoc watched them? Did it spy on their frantic rutting? Listen to their quiet simple secrets? Walk unseen through the new terrestrial plants they had infiltrated across land won in blood from its kind? Look up to see the strange lights in the sky bringing more usurpers? What were its thoughts all that time while its world was ravaged and conquered? And how would it feel if it knew all its race had suffered had turned out to be for nothing?

Miran sensed the xenoc's alarm as he reached the promontory's spine. It had stopped moving as he jogged up the last few metres of coarse, tufty grass. Now he was astride the spine, looking down the tapering spit of land.

The tip sank below the sluggish ripples of brown water six hundred metres ahead of him. There were several clumps of large boulders, and a few deep folds in the ground. But nothing which could offer secure cover.

The xenoc was retreating, slinking back to the tip. Miran couldn't see any scrap of motion; but he'd known all along it wasn't going to be easy. He didn't want it to be easy. Infrared sensor goggles, or even dogs, would have enabled him to finish it within days. He wanted the xenoc to know it had been hunted. Wanted it to feel the nightmare heat of the chase, to know it was being played with, to endure the prolonged anguish and gut-wearying exhaustion of every creature that was ever cornered. Suffering as Candice had suffered. Tormented as the ghosts tormented him.

Miran began to walk forward with slow deliberate steps, cradling the laser rifle. He kept an eager watch for any sort of furtive movement – shadows flittering among the boulders, a swell of ripples gliding along the boggy shore. Perhaps a faint puff of misty breath; that was something the xenoc could never disguise. Whatever illusion it wore was of no consequence now. He had it. He would draw it into his embrace and slay it with loving tenderness. The final act of this supreme tragedy. A benevolent release for the xenoc, for the ghosts, for Candice, and for himself. The xenoc was the last thread binding them in misery. Its death would be a transcendent kindness.

With four hundred metres left to the promontory's stubby tip he began to detect the first flutterings of panic in the xenoc's thoughts. It must be aware of him, of the deadly, remorseless intent he harboured. Cool humour swept into his mind. *You will burn,* he thought at it, *your body devoured in flames and pain. This is what I bring.*

Drowning in wretchedness and loathing, that was how he wanted it to spend its last moments of life. No dignity. No hope. The same awful dread Candice had passed away with, her small golden world shattered.

He looked down into one of the narrow crinkled folds in the ground. Stagnant water was standing in the bottom. Tall reeds with magenta candyfloss seed clusters poked up through a frothy blue-green scum of algae, their lower stems swollen and splitting. Glutinous honey-yellow sap dribbled down from the wounds.

Miran tried to spot some anomaly – a bulge in the grass like a giant molehill, a blot of algae harder than the rest.

The wind set the reeds waving to and fro. A rank acidic smell of rotting vegetation rolled around him. The xenoc wasn't down there.

He walked confidently down the promontory.

Every step brought a finer clarity to the xenoc's thoughts. It was being laid bare to him. Fear had arisen in its mind, to the exclusion of almost every other thought. A chimerical sensation of wrinkling stroked his skin; the xenoc was contracting, drawing in on itself. A protective reflex, seeking to shrink into nothingness so the terrible foe would pass by unknowing. It was rooting itself into the welcoming land, becoming one with its environment.

And it was close, very close now. Bitter experience gave Miran the ability to judge.

As the day belonged to him, so the night belonged to the xenoc. It had returned to the homestead time and again. Creeping up through the dark like a malevolent wraith. Its obscene presence had corrupted the sanctuary of Miran's dreams.

Often after sleep claimed him he would find himself running down the length of the valley with Candice; the two of them laughing, shrieking and dancing through the sunlit trees. It was the valley as he had never known it – brilliant, warm, a rainbow multitude of flowers in full blossom, the trees heavy with succulent fruit. A dream of Candice's dream.

They would dive cleanly into the blue sparkling water, squealing at the cold, splashing and sporting like young naiads. Each time he would draw her to him. Her eyes closed and her neck tilted back, mouth parting in an expectant gasp. Then, as always, her skin grew coarse, darkening, bloating in his grip. He was holding the xenoc.

The first time he had woken shaking in savage frenzy, arms thrashing against the mattress in uncontrollable spasms. That was when their minds had merged, thoughts twining sinuously. His fire-rage became the ice of deadly purpose. He snatched up the laser rifle and ran naked into the night.

The xenoc was there; outside the paddock fence, a nebulous blot of darkness which defied resolution. Its presence triggered a deluge of consternation to buffet his already frail mind, although he never was quite sure whether the tumult's origin lay in himself or the monster. Miran heard the sound of undergrowth being beaten down by a heavy body as the xenoc fled. He fired after it, the needle-slim beam of infra-red energy ripping the night apart with red strobe flares, illuminating the surrounding countryside in silent eldritch splendour. Puffballs of dense orange flame bloomed in front of him. Some of the drier scrub began to smoulder.

Miran had sat in the open doorway for the rest of the night, guarding the grave. A thick blanket tucked round his shoulders, taking an occasional nip from a bottle of brandy, the laser rifle lying across his lap. When dawn broke, he had set off down to the river on the trail of the xenoc.

Those first few weeks it couldn't seem to keep away. Miran almost became afraid to dream. Dreams were when the xenoc ghosts came to haunt him, slipping tortuously through his drowsy thoughts with insidious reminders of the vast atrocity humans had wrought on Jubarra. And when Candice rose to comfort him the xenoc would steal her from him, leaving him to wake up weeping from the loss.

Miran reached the downward slope at the end of the promontory. The nail of the finger, a curving expanse of gently undulating peat, wizened dwarf bushes, and a scattering of boulders. Thick brown water lapped the shore a hundred metres ahead.

The xenoc's presence in his mind was a constant babble. Strong enough now for him to see the world through its weird senses. A murky shimmer of fog with a cyclonic knot approaching gradually. Himself.

"Come out," he said.

The xenoc hardened itself, becoming one with the land.

"No?" Miran taunted, heady with the prospect of victory. "Well, we'll see about that."

There were five boulders directly in front of him. Big ochre stones which had fallen from the mountain's flanks far above. Splodges of green lichen mottled their rumpled surfaces. A sprinkling of slate-like flakes lay on the grass all around, chiselled off by a thousand winter frosts.

He lined the laser rifle up on the nearest boulder, and fired. The ruby-red beam lashed out, vividly bright even by day. A small wisp of blue smoke spurted from the stone where it struck, blackened splinters fell to the grass, singeing the blades. The thermal stress of the energy impact produced a shrill slapping sound.

Miran shifted his aim to the second boulder, and fired again.

The third boulder unfolded.

In the camp which housed the ecological assessment team they called them slitherskins, a grudging tribute to the xenocs' ability to blend flawlessly into the background. Rumours of their existence had circulated ever since the primary landing, but it wasn't until the virus was released that a specimen body had been obtained. Some of the xenobiology staff maintained their ability to avoid capture confirmed their sentience; it was an argument the Custodian Committee would rule on when the hearings began.

The few autopsies performed on decomposing corpses found that they had gristle instead of bone, facilitating a certain degree of shapeshifting. Subdermal pigment glands could secrete any colour, camouflaging them with an accuracy terrestrial chameleons could never achieve.

Miran had learnt that those in the camp, too, feared the night. During the day the xenocs could be spotted; their skin texture was too rough even if they adopted human colouring, and their legs were too spindly to pass inspection. They were nature's creatures, suited to wild woods and sweeping grasslands where they mimicked inert objects as soon as they sensed danger approaching in the form of the Bulldemons, their natural predators. But at night, walking down lightless muddy tracks between the camp's prefabs, one uncertain human silhouette was indistinguishable from another.

The camp's dwindling population kept their doors securely locked after nightfall.

When it stood up, the xenoc was half a metre taller than Miran. As its knobbly skin shed the boulder's ochre, it reverted to a neutral damp-looking, bluish-grey. The body abandoned its boulder guise, sagging into a pear shape standing on two thin legs with saucer feet; its arms were long with finger-pincer hands. Two violet eyes gazed down at Miran.

Resignation had come to the xenoc's mind, along with a core-flame of anger. The emotions sprayed around the inside of Miran's skull, chilling his brain.

"I hate you," Miran told it. Two months of grief and venom bled into his voice, contorting it to little more than a feral snarl.

In one respect the xenoc was no different to any other cornered animal. It charged.

Miran let off three fast shots. Two aimed at the top of the body, one dead centre. The beam blasted fist-size holes into the reptilian skin, boring through the subcutaneous musculature to rupture the vitals.

A vertical lipless gash parted between the xenoc's eyes to let out a soprano warbling. It twirled with slim arms extended, thin yellow blood surging from the gaping wounds. With a last keening gasp, the xenoc crumpled to the ground.

Miran sent another two laser pulses into what passed for its head. The brain wouldn't be far from the eyes, he reasoned. Its pincer hands clutched once and went flaccid. It didn't move again.

Distant thunder rumbled down the valley, a sonorous grumble reverberating from one side to the other, announcing the impending arrival of more rain. It reached Miran's ears just as he arrived back at the homestead. There was no elation, no sense of achievement to grip him on the long walk back. He hadn't expected there would be. Fulfilment was the reward gained by overcoming the difficulties which lay in the path of accomplishment.

But Jubarra offered him no goals to strive for. Killing the xenoc wasn't some golden endeavour, a monument to human success. It was a personal absolution, nothing more. Ridding himself of the past so he could find some kind of future.

He stopped by the grave with its high temple of stones to prevent the xenoc from burrowing to its heart. Unbuckling his belt, he laid the laser rifle and its spare power magazines on the stones, an offering to Candice. Proof that he was done here in the valley, that he was free to leave as she'd wished.

With his head bowed he told her, "It's finished. Forgive me for staying so long. I had to do it." Then he wondered if it really was over for her. Would her ghost be lonely? A single human forced to wander amongst those her race had slaughtered indiscriminately.

"It wasn't her fault," he cried out to the xenoc ghosts. "We didn't know. We didn't ask for any of this. Forgive her." But deep down he burned from bright flames of shared guilt. It had all been done in his name.

Miran went into the homestead. The door had been left open, there was a rainwater puddle on the composite squares of the floor, and a chill dankness in the air. He splashed through the water and slipped past the curtain into the hygiene alcove.

The face which looked back from the mirror above the washbasin had changed over the last two months. It was thin, pinched with long lines running down the cheeks. Several days' worth of stubble made the jutting chin scratchy. The skin around the eyes had darkened, making them look sunken. A sorry sight. He sighed at himself, at what he had allowed himself to become. Candice would hate to see him so. He would wash, he decided, shave, find some clean clothes. Then tomorrow he would hike back to the ecological team's camp. In another six weeks there would be a starship to take them off the planet. Jubarra's brief, sorry chapter of human intervention would cease then. And not before time.

Miran dabbed warm water on his face, making inroads on the accumulated grime. He was so involved with the task his mind dismissed the scratching sounds outside, a part of the homestead's normal background noises: the wind rustling the bushes and vegetables, the door swinging on its hinges, distant gurgling river water.

The clatter which came from the main room was so sudden it made his muscles lock rigid in fright. In the mirror his face was white with shock.

It must be another xenoc. But he had felt nothing approach, none of the jumble of foreign thoughts leaching into his brain.

His hands gripped the basin in an effort to still their

trembling. A xenoc couldn't do him any real harm, he told himself, those pincer fingers could leave some nasty gouges, but nothing fatal. And he could run faster. He could reach the laser rifle on the grave before the xenoc got out of the door.

He shoved the curtain aside with a sudden thrust. The main room was empty. Instead of bolting, he stepped gingerly out of the alcove. Had it gone into the bedroom? The door was slightly ajar. He thought he could hear something rustling in there. Then he saw what had made the clattering noise.

One of the composite floor tiles had been forced up, flipping over like a lid. There was a dark cavity below it. Which was terribly terribly wrong. The homestead had been assembled on a level bed of earth.

Miran bent down beside it. The tile was a metre square, and someone had scooped out all the hard-packed earth it had rested on, creating a snug cavity. The bottom was covered in pieces of what looked like broken crockery.

The xenoc. Miran knew instinctively it had dug this. He picked up one of the off-white fragments. One side was dry, smooth; the other was slimed with a clear tacky mucus. It was curved. An egg.

Rage boiled through him. The xenoc had laid an egg in his homestead. Outsmarting him, choosing the one place Miran would never look, never suspect treachery. Its bastard had hatched in the place intended for his own children.

He pushed the bedroom door fully open. Candice was waiting for him on the bed, naked and smiling. Miran's world reeled violently. He grabbed at the doorframe for support before his faltering legs collapsed.

She was very far away from him.

"Candice," his voice cracked. Somehow the room wasn't making sense. It had distorted, magnifying to giant proportions. Candice, beloved Candice, was too small. His vision swam drunkenly, then resolved. Candice was less than a metre tall.

"Love me," she said. Her voice was high pitched, a mousy squeak.

Yet it was her. He gazed lovingly at each part of the

perfectly detailed figure which he remembered so well – her long legs, firm flat belly, high conical breasts, the broad shoulders, over-developed from months spent toiling in the fields.

"Love me."

Her face. Candice was never beautiful, but he worshipped her anyway. Prominent cheekbones, rounded chin, narrow eyes. All there, as delicate as china. Her soft smile, directed straight at him, unforgettable.

"Love me."

Xenoc. The foetus gestating under his floor. Violating his dreams, feeding on them. Discovering his all-enveloping love.

"Love me."

The first post-human-encounter xenoc; instinctively moulding itself into the form which would bring it the highest chance of survival in the new world order.

Its slender arms reached out for him. A flawless human ribcage was outlined by supple creamy-white skin as it stretched.

Miran wailed in torment.

"Love me."

He could. That was the truth, and it was a tearing agony. He could love it. Even a pale monstrous echo was better than a lifetime without Candice. It would grow. And in the dark crushingly lonely hours it would be there for him to turn to.

"Love me."

He wasn't strong enough to resist. If it grew he would take it in his arms and become its lover. Her lover, again. If it grew.

He put his hands under the bed and tugged upwards with manic strength. Bed, mattress, and sheets cartwheeled. The xenoc squealed as it tumbled onto the floor.

"Love me!" The cry was frantic. It was squirming across the floor towards him. Feet tangled in the blankets, face entreating.

Miran shoved at the big dresser, tilting it off its rear legs. He had spent many evening hours making it from aboriginal timber. It was crude and solid, heavy.

"Love me!" The cry had become a desperate pining whimper.

The dresser teetered on its front legs. With a savage sob, Miran gave it one last push. It crashed to the floor with a hideous liquid squelch as it landed on the xenoc's upper torso.

Miran vomited, running wildly from the bedroom, blind, doubled up in convulsions. His mad flight took him outside where he tripped and sprawled on the soggy ground, weeping and pawing at the soil, more animal than human.

A strained creaking sound made him look up. Despite eyes smeared with gritty tears, he saw the rock at the top of the grave cracking open. A tiny arm punched out into the air. Thin flakes went spinning. The hand and arm worked at enlarging the fissure. Eventually a naked homunculus emerged in jerky movements, scattering fragments of shell in all directions. Even the xenoc eggs had the ability to conform to their surroundings.

Miran watched numbly as the homunculus crawled down the pile of sandstone lumps to join the other two humanoid figures waiting at the base.

In the homestead the safest identity to adopt was a love object, cherished and protected. But outside in the valley survival meant becoming the most ruthless predator of all.

Between them, the three miniature humans lifted up the laser rifle. "Hate you," one spat venomously. Then its fist smacked into the trigger.

Miran couldn't believe his own face was capable of expressing so much anger.

The Infinite Assassin

Greg Egan

Though younger than either Eric Brown or Peter Hamilton, even if only by a matter of months, Greg Egan (b. 1961), had already been selling fantasy and science fiction in his native Australia for four years before their debut. Since then he has established a reputation as "one of the genre's great ideas men" as The Times *declared. Egan, like Hamilton, always goes for broke – nothing's too big for his imagination. His novel* Quarantine *(1992) had the Earth cut off from the rest of the solar system by a massive force field whilst* Diaspora *(1997) and* Teranesia *(1999) consider human-kind's next phase of evolution. Egan's short fiction, some of which can be found in* Axiomatic *(1995) and* Luminous *(1998) take no hostages either as the following, about multi-dimensional realities, shows.*

One thing never changes: when some mutant junkie on S starts shuffling reality, it's always me they send into the whirlpool to put things right.

Why? They tell me I'm stable. Reliable. Dependable. After each debriefing, The Company's psychologists (complete strangers, every time) shake their heads in astonishment at their printouts, and tell me that I'm exactly the same person as when "I" went in.

The number of parallel worlds is uncountably infinite– infinite like the real numbers, not merely like the integers – making it difficult to quantify these things without elaborate mathematical definitions, but roughly speaking, it seems that I'm unusually invariant: more alike from world to world than most people are. How alike? In how many worlds? Enough to be useful. Enough to do the job.

How The Company knew this, how they found me, I've never been told. I was recruited at the age of nineteen. Bribed. Trained. Brainwashed, I suppose. Sometimes I wonder if my stability has anything to do with me; maybe the real constant is the way I've been prepared. Maybe an infinite number of different people, put through the same process, would all emerge the same. Have all emerged the same. I don't know.

Detectors scattered across the planet have sensed the faint beginnings of the whirlpool, and pinned down the centre to within a few kilometres, but that's the most accurate fix I can expect by this means. Each version of the Company shares its technology freely with the others, to ensure a uniformly optimal response, but even in the best of all possible worlds, the detectors are too large, and too delicate, to carry in closer for a more precise reading.

A helicopter deposits me on wasteland at the southern edge of the Leightown ghetto. I've never been here before, but the boarded-up shopfronts and grey tower blocks ahead are utterly familiar. Every large city in the world (in every world I know) has a place like this, created by a policy that's usually referred to as *differential enforcement*. Using or possessing S is strictly illegal, and the penalty in most countries is (mostly) summary execution, but the powers that be would rather have the users concentrated in designated areas than risk having them scattered among the community at large. So, if you're caught with S in a nice clean suburb, they'll blow a hole in your skull on the spot, but here, there's no chance of that. Here, there are no cops at all.

I head north. It's just after four a.m., but savagely hot, and once I move out of the buffer zone, the streets are crowded. People are coming and going from nightclubs, liquor stores, pawn shops, gambling houses, brothels. Power for street lighting has been cut off from this part of the city, but someone civic-minded has replaced the normal bulbs with self-contained tritium/phosphor globes, spilling a cool pale light like radioactive milk. There's a popular misconception that most S users do nothing but dream, twenty-four hours a day, but that's ludicrous; not only do they need to eat, drink and earn money like everyone else, but few would waste the drug on the time when their alter egos are themselves asleep.

Intelligence says there's some kind of whirlpool cult in Leightown, who may try to interfere with my work. I've been warned of such groups before, but it's never come to anything; the slightest shift in reality is usually all it takes to make such an aberration vanish. The Company, the ghettos, are the stable responses to S; everything else seems to be highly conditional. Still, I shouldn't be complacent. Even if these cults can have no significant impact on the mission as a whole, no doubt they *have* killed some versions of me in the past, and I don't want it to be my turn, this time. I know that an infinite number of versions of me would survive – some whose only difference from me would be *that they had survived* – so perhaps I ought to be entirely untroubled by the thought of death.

But I'm not.

Wardrobe have dressed me with scrupulous care, in a Fat Single Mothers Must Die World Tour souvenir reflection hologram T-shirt, the right style of jeans, the right model running shoes. Paradoxically, S users tend to be slavish adherents to "local" fashion, as opposed to that of their dreams; perhaps it's a matter of wanting to partition their sleeping and waking lives. For now, I'm in perfect camouflage, but I don't expect that to last; as the whirlpool picks up speed, sweeping different parts of the ghetto into different histories, changes in style will be one of the most sensitive markers. If my clothes don't look out of place before too long, I'll know I'm headed in the wrong direction.

A tall, bald man with a shrunken human thumb dangling from one earlobe collides with me as he runs out of a bar. As we separate, he turns on me, screaming taunts and obscenities. I respond cautiously; he may have friends in the crowd, and I don't have time to waste getting into that kind of trouble. I don't escalate things by replying, but I take care to appear confident, without seeming arrogant or disdainful. This balancing act pays off. Insulting me with impunity for thirty seconds apparently satisfies his pride, and he walks away smirking.

As I move on, though, I can't help wondering how many versions of me didn't get out of it so easily.

I pick up speed to compensate for the delay.

Someone catches up with me, and starts walking beside me. "Hey, I liked the way you handled that. Subtle. Manipulative. Pragmatic. Full marks." A woman in her late twenties, with short, metallic-blue hair.

"Fuck off. I'm not interested."

"In what?"

"In anything."

She shakes her head. "Not true. You're new around here, and you're looking for something. Or someone. Maybe I can help."

"I said, fuck off."

She shrugs and falls behind, but calls after me, "Every hunter needs a guide. Think about it."

A few blocks later, I turn into an unlit side street. Deserted, silent; stinking of half-burnt garbage, cheap insecticide, and piss. And I swear I can *feel it*: in the dark, ruined buildings all around me, people are dreaming on S.

S is not like any other drug. S dreams are neither surreal nor euphoric. Nor are they like simulator trips: empty fantasies, absurd fairy tales of limitless prosperity and indescribable bliss. They're dreams of lives that, literally, *might have been lived* by the dreamers, every bit as solid and plausible as their waking lives.

With one exception: if the dream-life turns sour, the dreamer can abandon it at will, and choose another (without any need to dream of taking S . . . although that's been known to happen). He or she can piece together a second life, in which no mistakes are irrevocable, no decisions absolute. A life without failures, without dead ends. All possibilities remain forever accessible.

S grants dreamers the power to live vicariously in any parallel world in which they have an alter ego – someone with whom they share enough brain physiology to maintain the parasitic resonance of the link. Studies suggest that a perfect genetic match isn't necessary for this – but nor is it sufficient; early childhood development also seems to affect the neural structures involved.

For most users, the drug does no more than this. For one in a hundred thousand, though, dreams are only the beginning. During their third or fourth year on S, they start to move *physically* from world to world, as they strive to take the place of their chosen alter egos.

The trouble is, there's never anything so simple as an infinity of direct exchanges, between all the versions of the mutant users who've gained this power, and all the versions they wish to become. Such transitions are energetically unfavourable; in practice, each dreamer must move gradually, continuously, passing through all the intervening points. But those "points" are occupied by other versions of themselves; it's like motion in a crowd – or a fluid. The dreamers must *flow*.

At first, those alter egos who've developed the skill are distributed too sparsely to have any effect at all. Later, it seems there's a kind of paralysis through symmetry; all potential flows are equally possible, including each one's exact opposite. Everything just cancels out.

The first few times the symmetry is broken, there's usually nothing but a brief shudder, a momentary slippage, an almost imperceptible world-quake. The detectors record these events, but are still too insensitive to localize them.

Eventually, some kind of critical threshold is crossed. Complex, sustained flows develop: vast, tangled currents with the kind of pathological topologies that only an infinite-dimensional space can contain. Such flows are viscous; nearby points are dragged along. That's what creates the whirlpool; the closer you are to the mutant dreamer, the faster you're carried from world to world.

As more and more versions of the dreamer contribute to the flow, it picks up speed – and the faster it becomes, the further away its influence is felt.

The Company, of course, doesn't give a shit if reality is scrambled in the ghettoes. My job is to keep the effects from spreading beyond.

I follow the side street to the top of a hill. There's another main road about four hundred metres ahead. I find a sheltered spot amid the rubble of a half-demolished building, unfold a pair of binoculars, and spend five minutes watching the pedestrians below. Every ten or fifteen seconds, I notice a tiny mutation: an item of clothing changing; a person suddenly shifting position, or vanishing completely, or materializing from nowhere. The binoculars are smart; they count up the number of events which take place in their field of view, as well as computing the map coordinates of the point they're aimed at.

I turn one-hundred-and-eighty degrees, and look back on the crowd that I passed through on my way here. The rate is substantially lower, but the same kind of thing is visible. Bystanders, of course, notice nothing; as yet, the whirlpool's gradients are so shallow that any two people within sight of each other on a crowded street would more or less shift universes together. Only at a distance can the changes be seen.

In fact, since I'm closer to the centre of the whirlpool than the people to the south of me, most of the changes I see in that direction are due to my own rate of shift. I've long ago left the world of my most recent employers behind – but I have no doubt that the vacancy has been, and will continue to be, filled.

I'm going to have to make a third observation to get a fix, some distance away from the north-south line joining the first two points. Over time, of course, the centre will drift, but not very rapidly; the flow runs between worlds where the centres are close together, so its position is the last thing to change.

I head down the hill, westwards.

Among crowds and lights again, waiting for a gap in the traffic, someone taps my elbow. I turn, to see the same blue-haired woman who accosted me before. I give her a stare of mild annoyance, but I keep my mouth shut; I don't know whether or not this version of her has met a version of me, and I don't want to contradict her expectations. By now, at least some of the locals must have noticed what's going on – just listening to an outside radio station, stuttering randomly from song to song, should be enough to give it away – but it's not in my interest to spread the news.

She says, "I can help you find her."

"Help me find who?"

"I know exactly where she is. There's no need to waste time on measurements and calc –"

"Shut up. Come with me."

She follows me, uncomplaining, into a nearby alley. *Maybe I'm being set up for an ambush. By the whirlpool cult?* But the alley is deserted. When I'm sure we're alone, I push her against the wall and put a gun to her head. She doesn't call out, or resist; she's shaken, but I don't think she's surprised by this treatment. I scan her with a hand-held magnetic resonance imager; no weapons, no booby traps, no transmitters.

I say, "Why don't you tell me what this is all about?" I'd swear that nobody could have seen me on the hill, but maybe she saw another version of me. It's not like me to screw up, but it does happen.

She closes her eyes for a moment, then says, almost calmly, "I want to save you time, that's all. I know where the mutant is. I want to help you find her as quickly as possible."

"Why?"

"*Why*? I have a *business* here, and I don't want to see it disrupted. Do you know how hard it is to build up contacts again, after a whirlpool's been through? What do you think – I'm covered by insurance?"

I don't believe a word of this, but I see no reason not to play along; it's probably the simplest way to deal with her, short of blowing her brains out. I put away the gun and take a map from my pocket. "Show me."

She points out a building about two kilometres northeast of where we are. "Fifth floor. Apartment 522."

"How do you know?"

"A friend of mine lives in the building. He noticed the

effects just before midnight, and he got in touch with me." She laughs nervously. "Actually, I don't know the guy all that well . . . but I think the version who phoned me had something going on with another me."

"Why didn't you just leave when you heard the news? Clear out to a safe distance?"

She shakes her head vehemently. "Leaving is the worst thing to do; I'd end up even more out of touch. The outside world doesn't matter. Do you think I care if the government changes, or the pop stars have different names? This is my home. If Leightown shifts, I'm better off shifting with it. Or with part of it."

"So how did you find me?"

She shrugs. "I knew you'd be coming. Everybody knows that much. Of course, I didn't know what you'd look like – but I know this place pretty well, and I kept my eyes open for strangers. And it seems I got lucky."

Lucky. Exactly. Some of my alter egos will be having versions of this conversation, but others won't be having any conversation at all. One more random delay.

I fold the map. "Thanks for the information."

She nods. "Any time."

As I'm walking away, she calls out, "*Every time*."

I quicken my step for a while; other versions of me should be doing the same, compensating for however much time they've wasted. I can't expect to maintain perfect synch, but dispersion is insidious; if I didn't at least try to mini-mize it, I'd end up travelling to the centre by every con-ceivable route, and arriving over a period of days.

And although I can usually make up lost time, I can never entirely cancel out the effects of variable delays. Spending different amounts of time at different distances from the centre means that all the versions of me aren't shifted uniformly. There are theoretical models which show that under certain conditions, this could result in gaps; I could be squeezed into certain portions of the flow, and removed from others – a bit like halving all the numbers between 0 and 1, leaving a hole from 0.5 to 1 . . . squashing one infinity into another which is cardinally identical, but half the geometric size. No versions of me would have been destroyed, and I wouldn't even exist twice in the same world, but nevertheless, a gap would have been created.

As for heading straight for the building where my "informant" claims the mutant is dreaming, I'm not tempted at all. Whether or not the information is genuine, I doubt very much that I've received the tip-off in any but an insignificant portion – technically, a set of measure zero – of the worlds caught up in the whirlpool. Any action taken only in such a sparse set of worlds would be totally ineffectual, in terms of disrupting the flow.

If I'm right, then of course it makes no difference *what* I do; if all the versions of me who received the tip-off simply marched out of the whirlpool, it would have no impact on the mission. A set of measure zero wouldn't be missed. But my actions, as an individual, are *always* irrelevant in that sense; if I, *and I alone*, deserted, the loss would be infinitesimal. The catch is, I could never know that I was acting alone.

And the truth is, versions of me probably have deserted; however stable my personality, it's hard to believe that there are no valid quantum permutations entailing such an action. Whatever the physically possible choices are, my alter egos have made – and will continue to make – every single one of them. My stability lies in the distribution, and the relative density, of all these branches – in the shape of a static, pre-ordained structure. Free will is a rationalization; I can't help making all the right decisions. And all the wrong ones.

But I "prefer" (granting meaning to the word) not to think this way too often. The only sane approach is to think of myself as one free agent of many, and to "strive" for coherence; to ignore short cuts, to stick to procedure, to "do everything I can" to concentrate my presence.

As for worrying about those alter egos who desert, or fail, or die, there's a simple solution: I disown them. It's up to me to define my identity any way I like. I may be forced to accept my multiplicity, but the borders are mine to draw. "I" am those who survive, and succeed. The rest are someone else.

I reach a suitable vantage point and take a third count. The view is starting to look like a half-hour video recording edited down to five minutes – except that the whole scene doesn't change at once; apart from some highly correlated couples, different people vanish and appear independently, suffering their own individual jump cuts. They're still all shifting universes more or less together, but what that means, in terms of where they happen to be physically located at any instant, is so complex that it might as well be random. A few people don't vanish at all; one man loiters consistently on the same street corner – although his haircut changes, radically, at least five times.

When the measurement is over, the computer inside the binoculars flashes up coordinates for the centre's estimated position. It's about sixty metres from the building the blue-haired woman pointed out; well within the margin of error. So perhaps she was telling the truth – but that changes nothing. I must still ignore her.

As I start towards my target, I wonder: Maybe I was ambushed back in that alley, after all. Maybe I was given the mutant's location as a deliberate attempt to distract me, to divide me. Maybe the woman tossed a coin to split the universe: heads for a tip-off, tails for none – or threw dice, and chose from a wider list of strategies.

It's only a theory . . . but it's a comforting idea: if that's the best the whirlpool cult can do to protect the object of their devotion, then I have nothing to fear from them at all.

I avoid the major roads, but even on the side streets it's soon clear that the word is out. People run past me, some hysterical, some grim; some empty-handed, some toting possessions; one man dashes from door to door, hurling bricks through windows, waking the occupants, shouting the news. Not everyone's heading in the same direction; most are simply fleeing the ghetto, trying to escape the whirlpool, but others are no doubt frantically searching for their friends, their families, their lovers, in the hope of reaching them before they turn into strangers. I wish them well.

Except in the central disaster zone, a few hardcore

dreamers will stay put. Shifting doesn't matter to them; they can reach their dream-lives from anywhere – or so they think. Some may be in for a shock; the whirlpool can pass through worlds where there is no supply of S – where the mutant user has an alter ego who has never even heard of the drug.

As I turn into a long, straight avenue, the naked-eye view begins to take on the jump-cut appearance that binoculars produced, just fifteen minutes ago. People flicker, shift, vanish. Nobody stays in sight for long; few travel more than ten or twenty metres before disappearing. Many are flinching and stumbling as they run, baulking at empty space as often as at real obstacles, all confidence in the permanence of the world around them, rightly, shattered. Some run blindly with their heads down and their arms outstretched. Most people are smart enough to travel on foot, but plenty of smashed and abandoned cars strobe in and out of existence on the roadway. I witness one car in motion, but only fleetingly.

I don't see myself anywhere about; I never have yet. Random scatter *should* put me in the same world twice, in some worlds – but only in a set of measure zero. Throw two idealized darts at a dartboard, and the probability of hitting the same point – the same zero-dimensional *point* – twice, is zero. Repeat the experiment in an uncountably infinite number of worlds, and it will happen – but only in a set of measure zero.

The changes are most frantic in the distance, and the blur of activity retreats to some extent as I move – due as it is, in part, to mere separation – but I'm also heading into steeper gradients, so I am, slowly, gaining on the havoc. I keep to a measured pace, looking out for both sudden human obstacles and shifts in the terrain.

The pedestrians thin out. The street itself still endures, but the buildings around me are beginning to be transformed into bizarre chimeras, with mismatched segments from variant designs, and then from utterly different structures, appearing side by side. It's like walking through some holographic architectural identikit machine on overdrive. Before long, most of these composites are collapsing, unbalanced by fatal disagreements on where loads should be borne. Falling rubble makes the footpath dangerous, so I weave my way between the car bodies in the middle of the road. There's virtually no moving traffic now, but it's slow work just navigating between all this "stationary" scrap metal. Obstructions come and go; it's usually quicker to wait for them to vanish than to backtrack and look for another way through. Sometimes I'm hemmed in on all sides, but never for long.

Finally, most of the buildings around me seem to have toppled, in most worlds, and I find a path near the edge of the road that's relatively passable. Nearby, it looks as though an earthquake has levelled the ghetto. Looking back, away from the whirlpool, there's nothing but a grey fog of generic buildings; out there, structures are still moving as one – or near enough to remain standing – but I'm shifting so much faster than they are that the skyline has smeared into an amorphous multiple-exposure of a billion different possibilities.

A human figure, sliced open obliquely from skull to groin, materializes in front of me, topples, then vanishes. My guts squirm, but I press on. I know that the very same thing must be happening to versions of me – but I declare it, I *define* it, to be the death of strangers. The gradient is so high now that different parts of the body can be dragged into different worlds, where the complementary pieces of anatomy have no good statistical reason to be correctly aligned. The rate at which this fatal dissociation occurs, though, is inexplicably lower than calculations predict; the human body somehow defends its integrity, and shifts as a whole far more often that it should. The physical basis for this anomaly has yet to be pinned down – but then, the physical basis for the human brain creating the delusion of a unique history, a sense of time, and a sense of identity, from the multifurcating branches and fans of superspace, has also proved to be elusive.

The sky grows light, a weird blue-grey that no single overcast sky ever possessed. The streets themselves are in a state of flux now; every second or third step is a revelation – bitumen, broken masonry, concrete, sand, all at slightly different levels – and briefly, a patch of withered grass. An inertial navigation implant in my skull guides me through the chaos. Clouds of dust and smoke come and go, and then –

A cluster of apartment blocks, with surface features flickering, but showing no signs of disintegrating. The rates of shift here are higher than ever, but there's a counterbalancing effect: the worlds between which the flow runs are required to be more and more alike, the closer you get to the dreamer.

The group of buildings is roughly symmetrical, and it's perfectly clear which one lies at the centre. None of me would fail to make the same judgement, so I won't need to go through absurd mental contortions to avoid acting on the tip-off.

The front entrance to the building oscillates, mainly between three alternatives. I choose the leftmost door; a matter of procedure, a standard which The Company managed to propagate between itselves before I was even recruited. (No doubt contradictory instructions circulated for a while, but one scheme must have dominated, eventually, because I've never been briefed any differently.) I often wish I could leave (and/or follow) a trial of some kind, but any mark I made would be useless, swept downstream faster than those it was meant to guide. I have no choice but to trust in procedure to minimize my dispersion.

From the foyer, I can see four stairwells – all with stairs converted into piles of flickering rubble. I step into the leftmost, and glance up; the early morning light floods in through a variety of possible windows. The spacing between the great concrete slabs of the floors is holding constant; the energy difference between such large structures in different positions lends them more stability than all the possible, specific shapes of flights of stairs. Cracks must be developing, though, and given time, there's no doubt that even this building would succumb to its discrepancies – killing the dreamer, in world after world, and putting an end to the flow. But who knows how far the whirlpool might have spread by then?

The explosive devices I carry are small, but more than adequate. I set one down in the stairwell, speak the arming sequence, and run. I glance back across the foyer as I retreat, but at a distance, the details among the rubble are nothing but a blur. The bomb I've planted has been swept into another world, but it's a matter of faith – and experience – that there's an infinite line of others to take its place.

I collide with a wall where there used to be a door, step back, try again, pass through. Sprinting across the road, an abandoned car materializes in front of me; I skirt around it, drop behind it, cover my head.

Eighteen. Nineteen. Twenty. Twenty-one. Twenty-two?

Not a sound. I look up. The car has vanished. The building still stands – and still flickers.

I climb to my feet, dazed. Some bombs may have – must have – failed . . . but enough should have exploded to disrupt the flow.

So what's happened? Perhaps the dreamer has survived in some small, but contiguous, part of the flow, and it's closed off into a loop – which it's my bad luck to be a part of. *Survived how?* The worlds in which the bomb exploded should have been spread randomly, uniformly, everywhere dense enough to do the job . . . but perhaps some freak clustering effect has given rise to a gap.

Or maybe I've ended up squeezed out of part of the flow. The theoretical conditions for that have always struck me as far too bizarre to be fulfilled in real life . . . but what if it *has* happened? A gap in my presence, downstream from me, would have left a set of worlds with no bomb planted at all – which then flowed along and caught up with me, once I moved away from the building and my shift rate dropped.

I "return" to the stairwell. There's no unexploded bomb, no sign that any version of me has been here. I plant the backup device, and run. This time, I find no shelter on the street, and I simply hit the ground.

Again, nothing.

I struggle to calm myself, to visualize the possibilities. If the gap without bombs hadn't fully passed the gap without me, when the first bombs went off, then I'd still have been

missing from a part of the surviving flow – allowing exactly
the same thing to happen all over again.

I stare at the intact building, disbelieving. *I am the ones
who succeed. That's all that defines me.* But who, exactly,
failed? If I was absent from part of the flow, there were no
versions of me in those worlds to fail. Who takes the blame?
Who do I disown? Those who successfully planted the
bomb, but "should have" done it in other worlds? *Am I
among them?* I have no way of knowing.

So, what now? How big is the gap? How close am I to it?
How many times can it defeat me?

I have to keep killing the dreamer, until I succeed.

I return to the stairwell. The floors are about three metres
apart. To ascend, I use a small grappling hook on a short
rope; the hook fires an explosive-driven spike into the
concrete floor. Once the rope is uncoiled, its chances of
ending up in separate pieces in different worlds is magnified; it's essential to move quickly.

I search the first storey systematically, following procedure to the letter, as if I'd never heard of Room 522. A blur
of alternative dividing walls, ghostly spartan furniture,
transient heaps of sad possessions. When I've finished, I
pause until the clock in my skull reaches the next multiple
of ten minutes. It's an imperfect strategy – some stragglers
will fall more than ten minutes behind – but that would be
true however long I waited.

The second storey is deserted, too. But a little more
stable; there's no doubt that I'm drawing closer to the
heart of the whirlpool.

The third storey's architecture is almost solid. The
fourth, if not for the abandoned ephemera flickering in
the corners of rooms, could pass for normal.

The fifth –

I kick the doors open, one by one, moving steadily down
the corridor. *502. 504. 506.* I thought I might be tempted to
break ranks when I came this close, but instead I find it
easier than ever to go through the motions, knowing that I'll
have no opportunity to regroup. *516. 518. 520.*

At the far end of Room 522, there's a young woman

stretched out on a bed. Her hair is a diaphanous halo of possibilities, her clothing a translucent haze, but her body looks solid and permanent, the almost-fixed point about which all the night's chaos has spun.

I step into the room, take aim at her skull, and fire. The bullet shifts worlds before it can reach her, but it will kill another version, downstream. I fire again and again, waiting for a bullet from a brother assassin to strike home before my eyes – or for the flow to stop, for the living dreamers to become too few, too sparse, to maintain it.

Neither happens.

"You took your time."

I swing around. The blue-haired woman stands outside the doorway. I reload the gun; she makes no move to stop me. My hands are shaking. I turn back to the dreamer and kill her, another two dozen times. The version before me remains untouched, the flow undiminished.

I reload again, and wave the gun at the blue-haired woman. "What the fuck have you done to me? *Am I alone*? Have you slaughtered all the others?" But that's absurd – and if it were true, how could she see me? I'd be a momentary, imperceptible flicker to each separate version of her, nothing more; she wouldn't even know I was here.

She shakes her head, and says mildly, "We've slaughtered no one. We've mapped you into Cantor dust, that's all. Every one of you is still alive – but none of you can stop the whirlpool."

Cantor dust. A fractal set, uncountably infinite, but with measure zero. There's not one gap in my presence; there's an infinite number, an endless series of ever smaller holes, everywhere. But –

"*How*? You set me up, you kept me talking, but how could you coordinate the delays? And calculate the effects? It would take . . ."

"Infinite computational power? An infinite number of people?" She smiles faintly. "I *am* an infinite number of people. All sleepwalking on S. All dreaming each other. We can act together, in synch, as one – or we can act independently. Or something in between, as now: the versions of me who can see and hear you at any moment are sharing their sense data with the rest of me."

I turn back to the dreamer. "Why defend her? She'll never get what she wants. She's tearing the city apart, and she'll never even reach her destination."

"Not here, perhaps."

"*Not here*? She's crossing all the worlds she lives in! Where else is there?"

The woman shakes her head. "What creates those worlds? Alternative possibilities for ordinary physical processes. But it doesn't stop there; the possibility of motion *between* worlds has exactly the same effect. Superspace *itself* branches out into different versions, versions containing all possible cross-world flows. And there can be higher-level flows, between those versions of superspace, so the whole structure branches again. And so on."

I close my eyes, drowning in vertigo. If this endless ascent into greater infinities is true –

"Somewhere, the dreamer always triumphs? Whatever I do?"

"Yes."

"And somewhere, I always win? Somewhere, you've failed to defeat me?"

"Yes."

Who am I? I'm the ones who succeed. Then who am *I*? I'm nothing at all. A set of measure zero.

I drop the gun and take three steps towards the dreamer. My clothes, already tattered, part worlds and fall away.

I take another step, and then halt, shocked by a sudden warmth. My hair, and outer layers of skin, have vanished; I'm covered in a fine sweat of blood. I notice, for the first time, the frozen smile on the dreamer's face.

And I wonder: in how many infinite sets of worlds will I take one more step? And how many countless versions of me will turn around instead, and walk out of this room? *Who exactly am I saving from shame, when I'll live and die in every possible way?*

Myself.

Anachron

Damon Knight

Damon Knight (b. 1922) is one of the architects of modern science fiction. This is not only through his many anthologies, especially the long-running Orbit *series (1966–80), or his work in co-founding the Milford Science Fiction Writers' Conference, or his work as the main impetus behind creating the Science Fiction Writers of America, or his work as one of the field's major critics, some of which is included in the award-winning* In Search of Wonder *(1956; latest revision 1996). It's also through his own fiction. He's been selling science fiction since 1940 but he really hit his stride in the 1950s with such stories as "Babel II", "To Serve Man", "The Country of the Kind" and "Special Delivery". The best of his early stories was collected as* Far Out *(1961) and there have been several collections since – check out* One Side Laughing *(1991). Amongst his novels his sequence* CV *(1985),* The Observers *(1988) and* A Reasonable World *(1991), where alien parasites try and bring some rationality to humankind, is well worth reading. The following is one of his early stories dealing with one of my favourite subjects, time paradoxes.*

T he body was never found. And for that reason alone, there was no body to find.

It sounds like inverted logic – which, in a sense, it is – but there's no paradox involved. It was a perfectly orderly and explicable event, even though it could only have happened to a Castellare.

Odd fish, the Castellare brothers. Sons of a Scots-English-woman and an expatriate Italian, born in England, educated on the Continent, they were at ease anywhere in the world and at home nowhere.

Nevertheless, in their middle years, they had become settled men. Expatriates like their father, they lived on the island of Ischia, off the Neapolitan coast, in a palace – quattrocento, very fine, with peeling cupids on the walls, a multitude of rats, no central heating, and no neighbors.

They went nowhere; no one except their agents and their lawyers came to them. Neither had ever married. Each, at about the age of thirty, had given up the world of people for an inner world of more precise and more enduring pleasures. Each was an amateur – a fanatical, compulsive amateur.

They had been born out of their time.

Peter's passion was virtu. He collected relentlessly, it would not be too much to say savagely; he collected as some men hunt big game. His taste was catholic, and his acquisitions filled the huge rooms of the palace and half the vaults under them – paintings, statuary, enamel, porcelain, glass, crystal, metalwork. At fifty, he was a round little man with small, sardonic eyes and a careless patch of pinkish goatee.

Harold Castellare, Peter's talented brother, was a scientist. An amateur scientist. He belonged in the nineteenth century, as Peter was a throwback to a still earlier epoch. Modern science is largely a matter of teamwork and drudgery, both impossible concepts to a Castellare. But Harold's intelligence was in its own way as penetrating and original as a Newton's or a Franklin's. He had done respectable work in physics and electronics, and had even, at his lawyer's instance, taken out a few patents. The income from these, when his own purchases of instruments and equipment did not consume it, he gave to his brother, who accepted it without gratitude or rancor.

Harold, at fifty-three, was spare and shrunken, sallow and spotted, with a bloodless, melancholy countenance on whose upper lip grew a neat hedge of pink-and-salt mustache, the companion piece and antithesis of his brother's goatee.

On a certain May morning, Harold had an accident.

Goodyear dropped rubber on a hot stove; Archimedes took a bath; Becquerel left a piece of uranium ore in a drawer with a photographic plate. Harold Castellare, working patiently with an apparatus which had so far consumed a great deal of current without producing anything more spectacular than some rather unusual corona effects, sneezed convulsively and dropped an ordinary bar magnet across two charged terminals.

Above the apparatus a huge, cloudy bubble sprang into being. Harold, getting up from his instinctive crouch, blinked at it in profound astonishment. As he watched, the cloudiness abruptly disappeared and he was looking *through* the bubble at a section of tesselated flooring that seemed to be about three feet above the real floor. He could also see the corner of a carved wooden bench, and on the bench a small, oddly-shaped stringed instrument.

Harold swore fervently to himself, made agitated notes, and then began to experiment. He tested the sphere cautiously with an electroscope, with a magnet, with a Geiger counter. Negative. He tore a tiny bit of paper from his notepad and dropped it toward the sphere. The paper disappeared; he couldn't see where it went.

Speechless, Harold picked up a meter stick and thrust it delicately forward. There was no feeling of contact; the rule went into and through the bubble as if the latter did not exist. Then it touched the stringed instrument, with a solid click. Harold pushed. The instrument slid over the edge of the bench and struck the floor with a hollow thump and jangle.

Staring at it, Harold suddenly recognized its tantalizingly familiar shape.

Recklessly he let go the meter stick, reached in and picked the fragile thing out of the bubble. It was solid and cool in his fingers. The varnish was clear, the color of the wood glowing through it. It looked as if it might have been made yesterday.

Peter owned one almost exactly like it, except for preservation – a viola d'amore of the seventeenth century.

Harold stooped to look through the bubble horizontally.

Gold and rust tapestries hid the wall, fifty feet away, except for an ornate door in the center. The door began to open; Harold saw a flicker of umber.

Then the sphere went cloudy again. His hands were empty; the viola d'amore was gone. And the meter stick, which he had dropped inside the sphere, lay on the floor at his feet.

"Look at that," said Harold simply.

Peter's eyebrows went up slightly. "What is it, a new kind of television?"

"No, no. Look here." The viola d'amore lay on the bench, precisely where it had been before. Harold reached into the sphere and drew it out.

Peter started. "Give me that." He took it in his hands, rubbed the smoothly finished wood. He stared at his brother. "By God and all the saints," he said. "Time travel."

Harold snorted impatiently. "My dear Peter, 'time' is a meaningless word taken by itself, just as 'space' is."

"But, barring that, time travel."

"If you like, yes."

"You'll be quite famous."

"I expect so."

Peter looked down at the instrument in his hands. "I'd like to keep this, if I may."

"I'd be very happy to let you, but you can't."

As he spoke, the bubble went cloudy; the viola d'amore was gone like smoke.

"There, you see?"

"What sort of devil's trick is that?"

"It goes back . . . Later you'll see. I had that thing out once before, and this happened. When the sphere became transparent again, the viola was where I had found it."

"And your explanation for this?"

Harold hesitated. "None. Until I can work out the appropriate mathematics —"

"— Which may take you some time. Meanwhile, in layman's language —?"

Harold's face creased with the effort and interest of

translation. "Very roughly, then – I should say it means that events are conserved. Two or three centuries ago –"

"Three. Notice the soundholes."

"Three centuries ago, then, at this particular time of day, someone was in that room. If the viola were gone, he or she would have noticed the fact. That would constitute an alteration of events already fixed; therefore it doesn't happen. For the same reason, I conjecture, we can't see into the sphere, or –" he probed at it with a fountain pen – "I thought not – or reach into it to touch anything; that would also constitute an alteration. And anything we put into the sphere while it is transparent comes out again when it becomes opaque. To put it very crudely, we cannot alter the past."

"But it seems to me that we did alter it. Just now, when you took the viol out, even if no one of that time saw it happen."

"This," said Harold, "is the difficulty of using language as a means of exact communication. If you had not forgotten all your calculus . . . However. It may be postulated (remembering that everything I say is a lie, because I say it in English) that an event which doesn't influence other events is not an event. In other words –"

"That, since no one saw you take it, it doesn't matter whether you took it or not. A rather dangerous precept, Harold; you would have been burned at the stake for that at one time."

"Very likely. But it can be stated in another way, or indeed, in an infinity of ways which only seem to be different. If someone, let us say God, were to remove the moon as I am talking to you, using zero duration, and substitute an exact replica made of concrete and plaster of paris, with the same mass, albedo, and so on as the genuine moon, it would make no measurable difference in the universe as we perceive it – and therefore we cannot certainly say that it hasn't happened. Nor, I may add, does it make any difference whether it has or not."

"When there's no one about on the quad'," said Peter.

"Yes. A basic, and, as a natural consequence, a meaningless problem of philosophy. Except," he added, "in this one particular manifestation."

He stared at the cloudy sphere. "You'll excuse me, won't you, Peter? I've got to work on this."

"When will you publish, do you suppose?"

"Immediately. That's to say, in a week or two."

"Don't do it till you've talked it over with me, will you? I have a notion about it."

Harold looked at him sharply. "Commercial?"

"In a way."

"No," said Harold. "This is not the sort of thing one patents, or keeps secret, Peter."

"Of course. I'll see you at dinner, I hope?"

"I think so. If I forget, knock on the door, will you?"

"Yes. Until then."

"Until then."

At dinner, Peter asked only two questions.

"Have you found any possibility of changing the time your thing reaches – from the seventeenth century to the eighteenth, for example, or from Monday to Tuesday?"

"Yes, as a matter of fact. Amazing. It's lucky that I had a rheostat already in the circuit; I wouldn't dare turn the current off. Varying the wattage varies the time-set. I've had it up to what I think was Wednesday of last week, at any rate my smock was lying over the workbench where I left it, I remember, Wednesday afternoon. I pulled it out. A curious sensation, Peter – I was wearing the same smock at the time. And then the sphere went opaque and of course the smock vanished. That must have been myself, coming into the room."

"And the future?"

"Yes. Another funny thing, I've had it forward to various times in the near future, and the machine itself is still there, but nothing's been done to it – none of the things I'm thinking I might do. That might be because of the conservation of events, again, but I rather think not. Still farther forward there are cloudy areas, blanks; I can't see anything that isn't in existence now, apparently . . . but here, in the next few days, there's nothing of that.

"It's as if I were going away. Where do you suppose I'm going?"

Harold's abrupt departure took place between midnight and morning. He packed his own grip, it would seem, left unattended, and was seen no more. It was extraordinary, of course, that he should have left at all, but the details were in no way odd. Harold had always detested what he called "the tyranny of the valet." He was, as everyone knew, a most independent man.

On the following day Peter made some trifling experiments with the time-sphere. From the sixteenth century he picked up a scent-bottle of Venetian glass; from the eighteenth, a crucifix of carved rosewood; from the nineteenth, when the palace had been the residence of an Austrian count and his Italian mistress, a hand illuminated copy of de Sade's *La Nouvelle Justine*, very curiously bound in human skin.

They all vanished, naturally, within minutes or hours – all but the scent-bottle. This gave Peter matter for reflection. There had been half a dozen flickers of cloudiness in the sphere just futureward of the bottle; it ought to have vanished, but it hadn't. But then, he had found it on the floor near a wall with quite a large rat-hole in it.

When objects disappeared unaccountably, he asked himself, was it because they had rolled into rat-holes – or because some time fisher had picked them up when they were in a position to do so?

He did not make any attempt to explore the future. That afternoon he telephoned his lawyers in Naples and gave them instructions for a new will. His estate, including his half of the jointly-owned Ischia property, was to go to the Italian government on two conditions: (1) that Harold Castellare would make a similar bequest of the remaining half of the property, and (2) that the Italian government would turn the palace into a national museum to house Peter's collection, using the income from his estate for its administration and for further acquisitions. His surviving relatives, two cousins in Scotland, he cut off with a shilling each.

He did nothing more until after the document had been brought out to him, signed, and witnessed. Only then did he venture to look into his own future.

Events were conserved, Harold had said – meaning, Peter very well understood, events of the present and future as well as of the past. But was there only one pattern in which the future could be fixed? Could a result exist before its cause had occurred?

The Castellare motto was *Audentes fortuna juvat* – into which Peter, at the age of fourteen, had interpolated the word "*prudentesque*": "Fortune favors the bold – and the prudent."

Tomorrow: no change; the room he was looking at was so exactly like this one that the time-sphere seemed to vanish. The next day: a cloudy blur. And the next, and the next . . .

Opacity, straight through to what Peter judged, by the distance he had moved the rheostat handle, to be ten years ahead. Then, suddenly, the room was a long marble hall filled with display cases.

Peter smiled wryly. If you were Harold, obviously you could not look ahead and see Peter working in your laboratory. And if you were Peter, equally obviously, you could not look ahead and know whether the room you saw were an improvement you your-self were going to make, or part of a museum established after your death, eight or nine years from now, or –

No. Eight years was little enough, but he could not even be sure of that. It would, after all, be seven years before Harold could be declared legally dead.

Peter turned the vernier knob slowly forward. A flicker, another, a long series. Forward faster. Now the flickering melted into a grayness; objects winked out of existence and were replaced by others in the showcases; the marble darkened and lightened again, darkened and lightened, darkened and remained dark. He was, Peter judged, looking at the hall as it would be some five hundred years in the future. There was a thick film of dust on every exposed surface; rubbish and the carcass of some small animal had been swept carelessly into a corner.

The sphere clouded.

When it cleared, there was an intricate trial of footprints in the dust, and two of the showcases were empty.

The footprints were splayed, trifurcate, and thirty inches long.

After a moment's deliberation Peter walked around the workbench and leaned down to look through the sphere from the opposite direction. Framed in the nearest of the four tall windows was a scene of picture-postcard banality: the sunsilvered bay and the foreshortened arc of the city, with Vesuvius faintly fuming in the background. But there was something wrong about the colors, even grayed as they were by distance.

Peter went and got his binoculars.

The trouble was, of course, that Naples was green. Where the city ought to have been, a rankness had sprouted. Between the clumps of foliage he could catch occasional glimpses of gray-white that might equally well have been boulders or the wreckage of buildings. There was no movement. There was no shipping in the harbor.

But something rather odd was crawling up the side of the volcano. A rust-orange pipe, it appeared to be, supported on hair-line struts like the legs of a centipede, and ending without rhyme or reason just short of the top.

While Peter watched, it turned slowly blue.

One day farther forward: now all the display cases had been looted; the museum, it would seem, was empty.

Given, that in five centuries the world, or at any rate the department of Campania, has been overrun by a race of Some-things, the human population being killed or driven out in the process; and that the conquerors take an interest in the museum's contents, which they have accordingly removed.

Removed where, and why?

This question, Peter conceded, might have a thousand answers, nine hundred and ninety-nine of which would mean that he had lost his gamble. The remaining answer was: to the vaults, for safety.

With his own hands Peter built a hood to cover the apparatus on the workbench and the sphere above it. It was unaccustomed labor; it took him the better part of two days. Then he called in workmen to break a hole in the stone flooring next to the interior wall, rig a hoist, and cut the power cable that supplied the time-sphere loose from its supports all the way back to the fuse-box, leaving him a single flexible length of cable more than a hundred feet long. They unbolted the workbench from the floor, attached casters to its legs, lowered it into the empty vault below, and went away.

Peter unfastened and removed the hood. He looked into the sphere.

Treasure.

Crates, large and small, racked in rows into dimness.

With pudgy fingers that did not tremble, he advanced the rheostat. A cloudy flicker, another, a leaping blur of them as he moved the vernier faster – and then no more, to the limit of the time-sphere's range.

Two hundred years, Peter guessed – A.D. 2700 to 2900 or thereabout – in which no one would enter the vault. Two hundred years of "unliquidated time".

He put the rheostat back to the beginning of that uninterrupted period. He drew out a small crate and prised it open.

Chessmen, ivory with gold inlay, Florentine, fourteenth century. Superb.

Another, from the opposite rack.

T'ang figurines, horses and men, ten to fourteen inches high. Priceless.

The crates would not burn, Tomaso told him. He went down to the kitchen to see, and it was true. The pieces lay in the roaring stove untouched. He fished one out with a poker; even the feathery splinters of the unplanned wood had not ignited.

It made a certain extraordinary kind of sense. When the moment came for the crates to go back, any physical scrambling that had occurred in the meantime would have no effect; they would simply put themselves together as they had been before, like Thor's goats. But burning was another matter; burning would have released energy which could not be replaced.

That settled one paradox, at any rate. There was another that nagged at Peter's orderly mind. If the things he took out of that vault, seven hundred-odd years in the future, were to become part of the collection bequeathed by him to the museum, preserved by it, and eventually stored in the vault for him to find – then precisely where had they come from in the first place?

It worried him. Peter had learned in life, as his brother in physics, that one never gets anything for nothing.

Moreover this riddle was only one of his perplexities, and that not among the greatest. For another example, there was the obstinate opacity of the time-sphere whenever he attempted to examine the immediate future. However often he tried it the result was always the same: a cloudy blank, all the way forward to the sudden unveiling of the marble gallery.

It was reasonable to expect the sphere to show nothing at times when he himself was going to be in the vault, but this accounted for only five or six hours out of every twenty-four. Again, presumably, it would show him no changes to be made by himself, since foreknowledge would make it possible for him to alter his actions. But he laboriously cleared one end of the vault, put up a screen to hide the rest and made a vow – which he kept – not to alter the clear space or move the screen for a week. Then he tried again – with the same result.

The only remaining explanation was that sometime during the next ten years, something was going to happen which he would prevent if he could; and the clue to it was there, buried in that frustrating unbroken blankness.

As a corollary, it was going to be something which he *could* prevent if only he knew what it was . . . or even when it was supposed to happen.

The event in question, in all probability, was his own death. Peter therefore hired nine men to guard him, three to a shift – because one man alone could not be trusted, two might conspire against him, whereas three, with the very minimum of effort, could be kept in a state of mutual suspicion. He also underwent a thorough medical examination, had new locks installed on every door and window, and took every other precaution ingenuity could suggest. When he had done all these things, the next ten years were as blank as before.

Peter had more than half expected it. He checked through his list of safeguards once more, found it good, and thereafter let the matter rest. He had done all he could; either he would survive the crisis or he would not. In either case, events were conserved; the time-sphere could give him no forewarning.

Another man might have found his pleasure blunted by guilt and fear; Peter's was whetted to a keener edge. If he had been a recluse before, now he was an eremite; he grudged every hour that was not given to his work. Mornings he spent in the vault, unpacking his acquisitions; afternoons and evenings, sorting, cataloguing, examining, and – the word is not too strong – gloating. When three weeks had passed in this way, the shelves were bare as far as the power cable would allow him to reach in every direction, except for crates whose contents were undoubtedly too large to pass through the sphere. These, with heroic self-control, Peter had left untouched.

And still he had looted only a hundredth part of that incredible treasure-house. With grappling hooks he could have extended his reach by perhaps three or four yards, but at the risk of damaging his prizes; and in any case this would have been no solution but only a postponement of the problem. There was nothing for it but to go through the sphere himself, and unpack the crates while on the other "side" of it.

Peter thought about it in a fury of concentration for the rest of the day. So far as he was concerned there was no question that the gain would be worth any calculated risk; the problem was how to measure the risk and if possible reduce it.

Item: he felt a definite uneasiness at the thought of venturing through that insubstantial bubble. Intuition was supported, if not by logic, at least by a sense of the dramatically appropriate. Now, if ever, would be the time for his crisis.

Item: common sense did not concur. The uneasiness had two symbols. One was the white face of his brother Harold just before the water closed over it; the other was a phantasm born of those gigantic, splayed footprints in the dust of the gallery. In spite of himself, Peter had often found himself trying to imagine what the creatures that made them must look like, until his visualization was so clear that he could almost swear he had seen them.

Towering monsters they were, with crested ophidian heads and great unwinking eyes; and they moved in a strutting glide, nodding their heads, like fantastic barnyard fowl.

But, taking these premonitory images in turn; first, it was impossible that he should ever be seriously inconvenienced by Harold's death. There were no witnesses, he was sure; he had struck the blow with a stone; stones also were the weights that had dragged the body down, and the rope was an odd length Peter had picked up on the shore. Second, the three-toed. Somethings might be as fearful as all the world's bogies put together; it made no difference, he could never meet them.

Nevertheless, the uneasiness persisted. Peter was not satisfied; he wanted a lifeline. When he found it, he wondered that he had not thought of it before.

He would set the time-sphere for a period just before one of the intervals of blankness. That would take care of accidents, sudden illnesses, and other unforeseeable contingencies. It would also insure him against one very real and not at all irrational dread: the fear that the mechanism which generated the time-sphere might fail while he was on the other side. For the conservation of events was not a condition created by the sphere but one which limited its operation. No matter what happened, it was impossible for him to occupy the same place-time as any future or past observer; therefore, when the monster entered that vault, Peter would not be there any more.

There was, of course, the scent-bottle to remember. Every rule has its exception; but in this case, Peter thought, the example did not apply. A scent-bottle could roll into a rat-hole; a man could not.

He turned the rheostat carefully back to the last flicker of grayness; past that to the next, still more carefully. The interval between the two, he judged, was something under an hour: excellent.

His pulse seemed a trifle rapid, but his brain was clear and cool. He thrust his head into the sphere and sniffed cautiously. The air was stale and had a faint, unpleasant odor, but it was breathable.

Using a crate as a stepping-stool, he climbed to the top of the workbench. He arranged another crate close to the sphere to make a platform level with its equator. And seven and a half centuries in the future, a third crate stood on the floor directly under the sphere.

Peter stepped into the sphere, dropped, and landed easily, legs bending to take the shock. When he straightened, he was standing in what to all appearances was a large circular hole in the work-bench; his chin was just above the top of the sphere.

He lowered himself, half-squatting, until he had drawn his head through and stepped down from the crate.

He was in the future vault. The sphere was a brightly luminous thing that hung unsupported in the air behind him, its midpoint just higher than his head. The shadows it cast spread black and wedge-shaped in every direction, melting into obscurity.

Peter's heart was pounding miserably. He had an illusory stifling sensation, coupled with the idiotic notion that he ought to be wearing a diver's helmet. The silence was like the pause before a shout.

But down the aisles marched the crated treasures in their hundreds.

Peter set to work. It was difficult, exacting labor, opening the crates where they lay, removing the contents and nailing the crates up again, all without disturbing the positions of the crates themselves, but it was the price he had to pay for his lifeline. Each crate was in a sense a microcosm, like the vault itself – a capsule of unliquidated time. But the vault's term would end some fifty minutes from now, when crested heads nodded down these aisles; those of the crates' interiors, for all that Peter knew to the contrary, went on forever.

The first crate contained lacework porcelain; the second, shakudô sword-hilts; the third, an exquisite fourth-century Greek ornament in repoussé bronze, the equal in every way of the Siris bronzes.

Peter found it almost physically difficult to set the thing down, but he did so; standing on his platform-crate in the future with his head projecting above the sphere in the present – like (again the absurd thought) a diver rising from the ocean – he laid it carefully beside the others on the workbench.

Then down again, into the fragile silence and the gloom. The next crates were too large, and those just beyond were doubtful. Peter followed his shadow down the aisle. He had almost thirty minutes left: enough for one more crate, chosen with care, and an ample margin.

Glancing to his right at the end of the row, he saw a door.

It was a heavy door, rivet-studded, with a single iron step below it. There had been no door there in Peter's time; the whole plan of the building must have been altered. *Of course!*, he realized suddenly. If it had not, if so much as single tile or lintel had remained of the palace as he knew it, then the sphere could never have let him see or enter this particular here-and-now, this – what would Harold have called it? – this nexus in space-time.

For if you saw any now-existing thing as it was going to appear in the future, you could alter it in the present – carve your initials in it, break it apart, chop it down – which was manifestly impossible, and therefore . . .

And therefore the first ten years were necessarily blank when he looked into the sphere, not because anything unpleasant was going to happen to him, but because in that time the last traces of the old palace had not yet been eradicated.

There was no crisis.

Wait a moment, though! Harold had been able to look into the near future . . . But – of course – Harold had been about to die.

In the dimness between Peter and the door he saw a rack of crates that looked promising. The way was uneven; one of the untidy accumulations of refuse that seemed to be characteristic of the Somethings lay in windows across the floor. Peter stepped forward carefully – but not carefully enough.

Harold Castellare had had another accident – and again, if you choose to look at it in that way, a lucky one. The blow stunned him; the old rope slipped from the stones; flaccid, he floated where a struggling man might have drowned. A fishing boat nearly ran him down, and picked him up instead. He was suffering from a concussion, shock, exposure, and asphyxiation and was more than three-quarters dead . . . But he was still alive when he was delivered, an hour later, to a hospital in Naples.

There were of course no identifying papers, labels or monograms in his clothing – Peter had seen to that – and for the first week after his rescue Harold was quite genuinely unable to give any account of himself. During the second week he was mending but uncommunicative, and at the end of the third, finding that there was some difficulty about gaining his release in spite of his physical recovery, he affected to recover his memory, gave a circumstantial but entirely fictitious identification and was discharged.

To understand this as well as all his subsequent actions, it is only necessary to remember that Harold was a Castellare. In Naples, not wishing to give Peter any unnecessary anxiety, he did not approach his bank for funds but cashed a check with an incurious acquaintance, and predated it by four weeks. With part of the money so acquired he paid his hospital bill and rewarded his rescuers. Another part went for new clothing and for four days' residence in an inconspicuous hotel, while he grew used to walking and dressing himself again. The rest, on his last day, he spent in the purchase of a discreetly small revolver and a box of cartridges.

He took the last boat to Ischia, and arrived at his own front door a few minutes before eleven. It was a cool evening, and a most cheerful fire was burning in the central hall.

"Signor Peter is well, I suppose," said Harold, removing his coat.

"Yes, Signor Harold. He is very well, very busy with his collection."

"Where is he? I should like to speak to him."

"He is in the vaults, Signor Harold. But –"

"Yes?"

"Signor Peter sees no one when he is in the vaults. He has given strict orders that no one is to bother him, Signor Harold, when he is in the vaults."

"Oh, well," said Harold. "I dare say he'll see me."

It was a thing something like a bear trap, apparently, except that instead of two semicircular jaws it had four segments that snapped together in the middle, each with a shallow, sharp tooth. The pain was quite unendurable.

Each segment moved at the end of a thin arm, cunningly hinged so that the ghastly thing would close over whichever of the four triggers you stepped on. Each arm had a spring too powerful for Peter's muscles. The whole affair was connected by a chain to a staple solidly embedded in the concrete floor; it left Peter free to move in any direction a matter of some ten inches. Short of gnawing off his own leg, he thought sickly, there was very little he could do about it.

The riddle was, what could the thing possibly be doing here? There were rats in the vaults, no doubt, now as in his own time, but surely nothing larger. Was it conceivable that even the three-toed Somethings would set an engine like this to catch a rat?

Lost inventions, Peter thought irrelevantly, had a way of being rediscovered. Even if he suppressed the time-sphere during his lifetime and it did not happen to survive him, still there might be other time-fishers in the remote future – not here, perhaps, but in other treasure-houses of the world. And that might account for the existence of this metal-jawed horror. Indeed, it might account for the vault itself – a better man-trap – except that it was all nonsense, the trap could only be full until the trapper came to look at it. Events, and the lives of prudent time-travelers, were conserved.

And he had been in the vault for almost forty minutes. Twenty minutes to go, twenty-five, thirty at the most, then the Somethings would enter and their entrance would free him. He had his lifeline; the knowledge was the only thing that made it possible to live with the pain that was the center of his universe just now. It was like going to the dentist, in the bad old days before procaine; it was very bad, sometimes, but you knew that it would end.

He cocked his head toward the door, holding his breath. A distant thud, another, then a curiously unpleasant squeaking, then silence.

But he had heard them. He knew they were there. It couldn't be much longer now.

Three men, two stocky, one lean, were playing cards in the passageway in front of the closed door that led to the vault staircase. They got up slowly.

"Who is he?" demanded the shortest one.

Tomaso clattered at him in furious Sicilian; the man's face darkened, but he looked at Harold with respect.

"I am now," stated Harold, "going down to see my brother."

"No, signor," said the shortest one positively.

"You are impertinent," Harold told him.

"Yes, Signor."

Harold frowned. "You will not let me pass?"

"No, signor."

"Then go and tell my brother I am here."

The shortest one said apologetically but firmly that there were strict orders against this also; it would have astonished Harold very much if he had said anything else.

"Well, at least I suppose you can tell me how long it will be before he comes out?"

"Not long, signor. One hour, no more."

"Oh, very well, then," said Harold pettishly, turning half away. He paused. "One thing more," he said, taking the gun out of his pocket as he turned, "put your hands up and stand against the wall there, will you?"

The first two complied slowly. The third, the lean one, fired through his coat pocket, just like the gangsters in the American movies.

It was not a sharp sensation at all, Harold was surprised

to find; it was more as if someone had hit him in the side with a cricket bat. The racket seemed to bounce interminably from the walls. He felt the gun jolt in his hand as he fired back, but couldn't tell if he had hit anybody. Everything seemed to be happening very slowly, and yet it was astonishingly hard to keep his balance. As he swung around he saw the two stocky ones with their hands half inside their jackets, and the lean one with his mouth open, and Tomaso with bulging eyes. Then the wall came at him and he began to swim along it, paying particular attention to the problem of not dropping one's gun.

As he weathered the first turn in the passageway the roar broke out afresh. A fountain of plaster stung his eyes; then he was running clumsily, and there was a bedlam of shouting behind him.

Without thinking about it he seemed to have selected the laboratory as his destination; it was an instinctive choice, without much to recommend it logically, and in any case, he realized halfway across the central hall, he was not going to get there.

He turned and squinted at the passageway entrance; saw a blur move and fired at it. It disappeared. He turned again awkwardly and had taken two steps nearer an armchair which offered the nearest shelter when something clubbed him between the shoulderblades. One step more, knees buckling, and the wall struck him a second, softer blow. He toppled, clutching at the tapestry that hung near the fireplace.

When the three guards, whose names were Enrico, Alberto and Luca, emerged cautiously from the passage and approached Harold's body, it was already flaming like a Viking's in its impromptu shroud; the dim horses and men and falcons of the tapestry were writhing and crisping into brilliance. A moment later an incertain ring of fire wavered toward them across the carpet.

Although the servants came with fire extinguishers and with buckets of water from the kitchen, and although the fire department was called, it was all quite useless. In five minutes the whole room was ablaze, in ten, as windows

burst and walls buckled, the fire engulfed the second story.
In twenty a mass of flaming timbers dropped into the vault
through the hole Peter had made in the floor of the laboratory, utterly destroying the time-sphere apparatus and
reaching shortly thereafter, as the authorities concerned
were later to agree, an intensity of heat entirely sufficient to
consume a human body without leaving any identifiable
trace. For that reason alone, there was no trace of Peter's
body to be found.

The sounds had just begun again when Peter saw the light
from the time-sphere turn ruddy and then wink out like a
snuffed candle.

In the darkness, he heard the door open.

Firewatch

Connie Willis

*We move from one treatment of time travel to another.
It's hard to believe that Connie Willis (b. 1945) has been
writing sf and fantasy for over thirty years, because her
work remains as fresh as ever. In that time she has won
more Hugo and Nebula Awards for her work than any
other science-fiction writer. This includes one for her
novel,* Doomsday Book *(1992), which shares a common
background with the following story, which won her her
first Hugo and gave its title to her first book,* Fire Watch
(1982).

"History hath triumphed over time, which besides it
nothing but eternity hath triumphed over."
                                    – Sir Walter Raleigh

September 20 – Of course the first thing I looked for was
the firewatch stone. And of course it wasn't there yet. It
wasn't dedicated until 1951, accompanying speech by the
Very Reverend Dean Walter Matthews, and this is only
1940. I knew that. I went to see the firewatch stone only
yesterday, with some kind of misplaced notion that seeing
the scene of the crime would somehow help. It didn't.

The only things that would have helped were a crash
course in London during the Blitz and a little more time. I
had not gotten either.

"Travelling in time is not like taking the tube, Mr

Bartholomew," the esteemed Dunworthy had said, blinking at me through those antique spectacles of his. "Either you report on the twentieth or you don't go at all."

"But I'm not ready," I'd said. "Look, it took me four years to get ready to travel with St Paul. *St Paul*. Not St Paul's. You can't expect me to get ready for London in the Blitz in two days."

"Yes," Dunworthy had said. "We can." End of conversation.

"Two days!" I had shouted at my roommate Kivrin. "All because some computer adds an apostrophe s. And the esteemed Dunworthy doesn't even bat an eye when I tell him. 'Time travel is not like taking the tube, young man,' he says. 'I'd suggest you get ready. You're leaving day after tomorrow.' The man's a total incompetent."

"No," she said. "He isn't. He's the best there is. He wrote the book on St Paul's. Maybe you should listen to what he says."

I had expected Kivrin to be at least a little sympathetic. She had been practically hysterical when she got her practicum changed from fifteenth to fourteenth century England, and how did either century qualify as a practicum? Even counting infectious disease they couldn't have been more than a five. The Blitz is an eight, and St Paul's itself is, with my luck, a ten.

"You think I should go see Dunworthy again?" I said.

"Yes."

"And then what? I've got two days. I don't know the money, the language, the history. Nothing."

"He's a good man," Kivrin said. "I think you'd better listen to him while you can." Good old Kivrin. Always the sympathetic ear.

The good man was responsible for my standing just inside the propped-open west doors, gawking like the country boy I was supposed to be, looking for a stone that wasn't there. Thanks to the good man, I was about as unprepared for my practicum as it was possible for him to make me.

I couldn't see more than a few feet into the church. I could see a candle gleaming feebly a long way off and a closer blur of white moving toward me. A verger, or possibly the Very Reverend Dean himself. I pulled out the letter from my clergyman uncle in Wales that was supposed to gain me access to the Dean, and patted my back pocket to make sure I hadn't lost the microfiche *Oxford English Dictionary, Revised, with Historical Supplements*, I'd smuggled out of the Bodleian. I couldn't pull it out in the middle of the conversation, but with luck I could muddle through the first encounter by context and look up the words I didn't know later.

"Are you from the ayarpee?" he said. He was no older than I am, a head shorter and much thinner. Almost ascetic looking. He reminded me of Kivrin. He was not wearing white, but clutching it to his chest. In other circumstances I would have thought it was a pillow. In other circumstances I would know what was being said to me, but there had been no time to unlearn sub-Mediterranean Latin and Jewish law and learn Cockney and air-raid procedures. Two days, and the esteemed Dunworthy, who wanted to talk about the sacred burdens of the historian instead of telling me what the ayarpee was.

"Are you?" he demanded again.

I considered shipping out the *OED* after all on the grounds that Wales was a foreign country, but I didn't think they had microfilm in 1940. Ayarpee. It could be anything, including a nickname for the fire watch, in which case the impulse to say no was not safe at all. "No," I said.

He lunged suddenly toward and past me and peered out the open doors. "Damn," he said, coming back to me. "Where are they then? Bunch of lazy bourgeois tarts!" And so much for getting by on context.

He looked at me closely, suspiciously, as if he thought I was only pretending not to be with the ayarpee. "The church is closed," he said finally.

I held up the envelope and said, "My name's Bartholomew. Is Dean Matthews in?"

He looked out the door a moment longer, as if he expected the lazy bourgeois tarts at any moment and intended to attack them with the white bundle, then he turned and said, as if he were guiding a tour, "This way, please," and took off into the gloom.

He led me to the right and down the south aisle of the nave. Thank God I had memorized the floor plan or at that moment, heading into total darkness, led by a raving verger, the whole bizarre metaphor of my situation would have been enough to send me out the west doors and back to St John's Wood. It helped a little to know where I was. We should have been passing number twenty-six: Hunt's painting of "The Light of the World" – Jesus with his lantern – but it was too dark to see it. We could have used the lantern ourselves.

He stopped abruptly ahead of me, still raving. "We weren't asking for the bloody Savoy, just a few cots. Nelson's better off than we are – at least he's got a pillow provided." He brandished the white bundle like a torch in the darkness. It was a pillow after all. "We asked for them over a fortnight ago, and here we still are, sleeping on the bleeding generals from Trafalgar because those bitches want to play tea and crumpets with the tommies at Victoria and the Hell with us!"

He didn't seem to expect me to answer his outburst, which was good, because I had understood perhaps one key word in three. He stomped on ahead, moving out of sight of the one pathetic altar candle and stopping again at a black hole. Number twenty-five: stairs to the Whispering Gallery, the Dome, the library (not open to the public). Up the stairs, down a hall, stop again at a medieval door and knock. "I've got to go wait for them," he said. "If I'm not there they'll likely take them over to the Abbey. Tell the Dean to ring them up again, will you?" and he took off down the stone steps, still holding his pillow like a shield against him.

He had knocked, but the door was at least a foot of solid oak, and it was obvious the Very Reverend Dean had not heard. I was going to have to knock again. Yes, well, and the man holding the pinpoint had to let go of it, too, but even knowing it will all be over in a moment and you won't feel a thing doesn't make it any easier to say, "Now!" So I stood in front of the door, cursing the history department and the esteemed Dunworthy and the computer that had made the mistake and brought me here to this dark door with only a letter from a fictitious uncle that I trusted no more than I trusted the rest of them.

Even the old reliable Bodleian had let me down. The batch of research stuff I cross-ordered through Balliol and the main terminal is probably sitting in my room right now, a century out of reach. And Kivrin, who had already done her practicum and should have been bursting with advice, walked around as silent as a saint until I begged her to help me.

"Did you go to see Dunworthy?" she said.

"Yes. You want to know what priceless bit of information he had for me? 'Silence and humility are the sacred burdens of the historian.' He also told me I would love St Paul's. Golden gems from the master. Unfortunately, what I need to know are the times and places of the bombs so one doesn't fall on me." I flopped down on the bed. "Any suggestions?"

"How good are you at memory retrieval?" she said.

I sat up. "I'm pretty good. You think I should assimilate?"

"There isn't time for that," she said. "I think you should put everything you can directly into long-term."

"You mean endorphins?" I said.

The biggest problem with using memory-assistance drugs to put information into your long-term memory is that it never sits, even for a micro-second, in your short-term memory, and that makes retrieval complicated, not to mention unnerving. It gives you the most unsettling sense of *déjà vu* to suddenly know something you're positive you've never seen or heard before.

The main problem, though, is not eerie sensations but retrieval. Nobody knows exactly how the brain gets what it wants out of storage, but short-term is definitely involved. That brief, sometimes microscopic, time information spends in short-term is apparently used for something besides tip-of-the-tongue availability. The whole complex sort-and-file process of retrieval is apparently centered in short-term; and without it, and without the help of the drugs that put it there or artificial substitutes, information can be impossible to retrieve. I'd used endorphins for examinations and never had any difficulty with retrieval, and it looked like it was the only way to store all the information I needed in anything approaching the time I had left, but it also meant that I would *never* have known any of the things I needed to know, even for long enough to have forgotten them. If and when I could retrieve the information, I would know it. Till then I was as ignorant of it as if it were not stored in some cobwebbed corner of my mind at all.

"You can retrieve without artificials, can't you?" Kivrin said, looking skeptical.

"I guess I'll have to."

"Under stress? Without sleep? Low body endorphin levels?" What exactly had her practicum been? She had never said a word about it, and undergraduates are not supposed to ask. Stress factors in the Middle Ages? I thought everybody slept through them.

"I hope so," I said. "Anyway, I'm willing to try this idea if you think it will help."

She looked at me with that martyred expression and said, "Nothing will help." Thank you, St Kivrin of Balliol.

But I tried it anyway. It was better than sitting in Dunworthy's rooms having him blink at me through his historically accurate eyeglasses and tell me I was going to love St Paul's. When my Bodleian requests didn't come, I overloaded my credit and bought out Blackwell's. Tapes on World War II, Celtic literature, history of mass transit, tourist guidebooks, everything I could think of. Then I rented a high-speed recorder and shot up. When I came out of it, I was so panicked by the feeling of not knowing any more than I had when I started that I took the tube to London and raced up Ludgate Hill to see if the firewatch stone would trigger any memories. It didn't.

"Your endorphin levels aren't back to normal yet," I told myself and tried to relax, but that was impossible with the prospect of the practicum looming up before me. And those are real bullets, kid. Just because you're a history major doing his practicum doesn't mean you can't get killed. I read history books all the way home on the tube and right up until Dunworthy's flunkies came to take me to St John's Wood this morning.

Then I jammed the microfiche *OED* in my back pocket and went off feeling as if I would have to survive by my native wit and hoping I could get hold of artificials in 1940. Surely I could get through the first day without mishap, I thought; and now here I was, stopped cold by almost the first word that was spoken to me.

Well, not quite. In spite of Kivrin's advice that I not put anything in short-term, I'd memorized the British money, a map of the tube system, a map of my own Oxford. It had gotten me this far. Surely I would be able to deal with the Dean.

Just as I had almost gotten up the courage to knock, he opened the door, and as with the pinpoint, it really was over quickly and without pain. I handed him my letter, and he shook my hand and said something understandable like, "Glad to have another man, Bartholomew." He looked strained and tired and as if he might collapse if I told him the Blitz had just started. I know, I know: keep your mouth shut. The sacred silence, etc.

He said, "We'll get Langby to show you round, shall we?" I assumed that was my Verger of the Pillow; and I was right. He met us at the foot of the stairs, puffing a little but jubilant.

"The cots came," he said to Dean Matthews. "You'd have thought they were doing us a favor. All high heels and hoity-toity. 'You made us miss our tea, luv,' one of them said to me. 'Yes, well, and a good thing, too,' I said. 'You look as if you could stand to lose a stone or two.'"

Even Dean Matthews looked as though he did not completely understand him. He said, "Did you set them up in the crypt?" and then introduced us. "Mr Bartholomew's just got in from Wales," he said. "He's come to join our volunteers." Volunteers, not fire watch.

Langby showed me around, pointing out various dimnesses in the general gloom and then dragged me down to see the ten folding canvas cots set up among the tombs in the crypt, also in passing Lord Nelson's black marble sarcophagus. He told me I didn't have to stand a watch the first night and suggested I go to bed, since sleep is the most precious commodity in the raids. I could well believe it. He was clutching that silly pillow to his breast like his beloved.

"Do you hear the sirens down here?" I asked, wondering if he buried his head in it.

He looked round at the low stone ceilings. "Some do, some don't. Brinton has to have his Horlich's. Bence-Jones would sleep if the roof fell in on him. I have to have a pillow. The important thing is to get your eight in no matter what. If you don't, you turn into one of the walking dead. And then you get killed."

On that cheering note he went off to post the watches for tonight, leaving his pillow on one of the cots with orders for me to let nobody touch it. So here I sit, waiting for my first air-raid siren and trying to get all this down before I turn into one of the walking or non-walking dead.

I've used the stolen *OED* to decipher a little Langby. Middling success. A tart is either a pastry or a prostitute (I assume the latter, although I was wrong about the pillow). Bourgeois is a catchall term for all the faults of the middle class. A Tommy's a soldier. Ayarpee I could not find under any spelling and I had nearly given up when something in long-term about the use of acronyms and abbreviations in wartime popped forward (bless you, St Kivrin) and I realized it must be an abbreviation. ARP. Air Raid Precautions. Of course. Where else would you get the bleeding cots from?

September 21 – Now that I'm past the first shock of being here, I realize that the history department neglected to tell me what I'm supposed to do in the three-odd months of this practicum. They handed me this journal, the letter from my uncle, and a ten-pound note, and sent me packing into the past. The ten pounds (already depleted by train and tube fares) is supposed to last me until the end of December and get me back to St John's Wood for pickup when the second letter calling me back to Wales to sick uncle's bedside comes. Till then I live here in the crypt with Nelson, who, Langby tells me, is pickled in alcohol inside his coffin.

If we take a direct hit, will he burn like a torch or simply trickle out in a decaying stream onto the crypt floor, I wonder. Board is provided by a gas ring, over which are cooked wretched tea and indescribable kippers. To pay for all this luxury I am to stand on the roofs of St Paul's and put out incendiaries.

I must also accomplish the purpose of this practicum, whatever it may be. Right now the only purpose I care about is staying alive until the second letter from uncle arrives and I can go home.

I am doing makework until Langby has time to "show me the ropes". I've cleaned the skillet they cook the foul little fishes in, stacked wooden folding chairs at the altar end of the crypt (flat instead of standing because they tend to collapse like bombs in the middle of the night), and tried to sleep.

I am apparently not one of the lucky ones who can sleep through the raids. I spent most of the night wondering what St Paul's risk rating is. Practica have to be at least a six. Last night I was convinced this was a ten, with the crypt as ground zero, and that I might as well have applied for Denver.

The most interesting thing that's happened so far is that I've seen a cat. I am fascinated, but trying not to appear so since they seem commonplace here.

September 22 – Still in the crypt. Langby comes dashing through periodically cursing various government agencies (all abbreviated) and promising to take me up on the roofs. In the meantime, I've run out of makework and taught myself to work a stirrup pump. Kivrin was overly concerned about my memory retrieval abilities. I have not had any trouble so far. Quite the opposite. I called up fire-fighting information and got the whole manual with pictures, including instructions on the use of the stirrup pump. If the kippers set Lord Nelson on fire, I shall be a hero.

Excitement last night. The sirens went early and some of the chars who clean offices in the City sheltered in the crypt with us. One of them woke me out of a sound sleep, going like an air raid siren. Seems she'd seen a mouse. We had to go whacking at tombs and under the cots with a rubber boot to persuade her it was gone. Obviously what the history department had in mind: murdering mice.

September 24 – Langby took me on rounds. Into the choir, where I had to learn the stirrup pump all over again, assigned rubber boots and a tin helmet. Langby says Commander Allen is getting us asbestos firemen's coats, but hasn't yet, so it's my own wool coat and muffler and very cold on the roofs even in September. It feels like November and looks it, too, bleak and cheerless with no sun. Up to the dome and onto the roofs which should be flat, but in fact are littered with towers, pinnacles, gutters, and statues, all designed expressly to catch and hold incendiaries out of reach. Shown how to smother an incendiary with sand before it burns through the roof and sets the church on fire. Shown the ropes (literally) lying in a heap at the base of the dome in case somebody has to go up one of the west towers or over the top of the dome. Back inside and down to the Whispering Gallery.

Langby kept up a running commentary through the whole tour, part practical instruction, part church history. Before we went up into the Gallery he dragged me over to the south door to tell me how Christopher Wren stood in the smoking rubble of Old St Paul's and asked a workman to bring him a stone from the graveyard to mark the cornerstone. On the stone was written in Latin, "I shall rise again," and Wren was so impressed by the irony that he had the words inscribed above the door. Langby looked as smug as if he had not told me a story every first-year history student knows, but I suppose without the impact of the firewatch stone, the other is just a nice story.

Langby raced me up the steps and onto the narrow balcony circling the Whispering Gallery. He was already halfway round to the other side, shouting dimensions and acoustics at me. He stopped facing the wall opposite and said softly, "You can hear me whispering because of the shape of the dome. The sound waves are reinforced around the perimeter of the dome. It sounds like the very crack of doom up here during a raid. The dome is one hundred and seven feet across. It is eighty feet above the nave."

I looked down. The railing went out from under me and the black-and-white marble floor came up with dizzying speed. I hung onto something in front of me and dropped to my knees, staggered and sick at heart. The sun had come out, and all of St Paul's seemed drenched in gold. Even the carved wood of the choir, the white stone pillars, the leaden pipes of the organ, all of it golden, golden.

Langby was beside me, trying to pull me free. "Bartholomew," he shouted, "What's wrong? For God's sake, man."

I knew I must tell him that if I let go, St Paul's and all the past would fall in on me, and that I must not let that happen because I was an historian. I said something, but it was not what I intended because Langby merely tightened his grip. He hauled me violently free of the railing and back onto the stairway, then let me collapse limply on the steps and stood back from me, not speaking.

"I don't know what happened in there," I said. "I've never been afraid of heights before."

"You're shaking," he said sharply. "You'd better lie down." He led me back to the crypt.

September 25 – Memory retrieval: ARP manual. Symptoms of bombing victims. Stage one – shock; stupefaction; unawareness of injuries; words may not make sense except to victim. Stage two – shivering; nausea; injuries, losses felt; return to reality. Stage three – talkativeness that cannot be controlled; desire to explain shock behavior to rescuers.

Langby must surely recognize the symptoms, but how does he account for the fact there was no bomb? I can hardly explain my shock behavior to him, and it isn't just the sacred silence of the historian that stops me.

He has not said anything, in fact assigned me my first watches for tomorrow night as if nothing had happened, and he seems no more preoccupied than anyone else. Everyone I've met so far is jittery (one thing I had in short-term was how calm everyone was during the raids) and the raids have not come near us since I got here. They've been mostly over the East End and the docks.

There was a reference tonight to a UXB, and I have been thinking about the Dean's manner and the church being closed when I'm almost sure I remember reading it was open through the entire Blitz. As soon as I get a chance, I'll try to retrieve the events of September. As to retrieving anything else, I don't see how I can hope to remember the right information until I know what it is I am supposed to do here, if anything.

There are no guidelines for historians, and no restrictions either. I could tell everyone I'm from the future if I thought they would believe me. I could murder Hitler if I could get to Germany. Or could I? Time paradox talk abounds in the history department, and the graduate students back from their practica don't say a word one way or the other. Is there a tough, immutable past? Or is there a new past every day and do we, the historians, make it? And what are the consequences of what we do, if there are consequences? And how do we dare do anything without knowing them? Must we interfere boldly, hoping we do not bring about all our downfalls? Or must we do nothing at all, not interfere, stand by and watch St Paul's burn to the ground if need be so that we don't change the future?

All those are fine questions for a late-night study session. They do not matter here. I could no more let St Paul's burn down than I could kill Hitler. No, that is not true. I found that out yesterday in the Whispering Gallery. I could kill Hitler if I caught him setting fire to St Paul's.

September 26 – I met a young woman today. Dean Matthews has opened the church, so the watch have been doing duties as chars and people have started coming in again. The young woman reminded me of Kivrin, though Kivrin is a good deal taller and would never frizz her hair like that. She looked as if she had been crying. Kivrin has looked like that since she got back from her practicum. The Middle Ages were too much for her. I wonder how she would have coped with this. By pouring out her fears to the local priest, no doubt, as I sincerely hoped her lookalike was not going to do.

"May I help you?" I said, not wanting in the least to help. "I'm a volunteer."

She looked distressed. "You're not paid?" she said, and wiped at her reddened nose with a handkerchief. "I read about St Paul's and the fire watch and all and I thought, perhaps there's a position there for me. In the canteen, like, or something. A paying position." There were tears in her red-rimmed eyes.

"I'm afraid we don't have a canteen," I said as kindly as I could, considering how impatient Kivrin always makes me, "and it's not actually a real shelter. Some of the watch sleep in the crypt. I'm afraid we're all volunteers, though."

"That won't do, then," she said. She dabbed at her eyes with the handkerchief. "I love St Paul's, but I can't take on volunteer work, not with my little brother Tom back from the country." I was not reading this situation properly. For all the outward signs of distress, she sounded quite cheerful and no closer to tears than when she had come in. "I've got to get us a proper place to stay. With Tom back, we can't go on sleeping in the tubes."

A sudden feeling of dread, the kind of sharp pain you get sometimes from involuntary retrieval, went over me. "The tubes?" I said, trying to get at the memory.

"Marble Arch, usually," she went on. "My brother Tom saves us a place early and I go –" She stopped, held the handkerchief close to her nose, and exploded into it. "I'm sorry," she said, "this awful cold!"

Red nose, watering eyes, sneezing. Respiratory infection. It was a wonder I hadn't told her not to cry. It's only by luck that I haven't made some unforgivable mistake so far, and this is not because I can't get at the long-term memory. I don't have half the information I need even stored: cats and colds and the way St Paul's looks in full sun. It's only a matter of time before I am stopped cold by something I do not know. Nevertheless, I am going to try for retrieval tonight after I come off watch. At least I can find out whether and when something is going to fall on me.

I have seen the cat once or twice. He is coal-black with a white patch on his throat that looks as if it were painted on for the blackout.

September 27 – I have just come down from the roofs. I am still shaking.

Early in the raid the bombing was mostly over the East End. The view was incredible. Searchlights everywhere, the sky pink from the fires and reflecting in the Thames, the exploding shells sparkling like fireworks. There was a constant, deafening thunder broken by the occasional droning of the planes high overhead, then the repeating stutter of the ack-ack guns.

About midnight the bombs began falling quite near with a horrible sound like a train running over me. It took every bit of will I had to keep from flinging myself flat on the roof, but Langby was watching. I didn't want to give him the satisfaction of watching a repeat performance of my behavior in the dome. I kept my head up and my sandbucket firmly in hand and felt quite proud of myself.

The bombs stopped roaring past about three, and there was a lull of about half an hour, and then a clatter like hail on the roofs. Everybody except Langby dived for shovels and stirrup pumps. He was watching me. And I was watching the incendiary.

It had fallen only a few meters from me, behind the clock tower. It was much smaller than I had imagined, only about thirty centimeters long. It was sputtering violently, throwing greenish-white fire almost to where I was standing. In a minute it would simmer down into a molten mass and begin to burn through the roof. Flames and the frantic shouts of firemen, and then the white rubble stretching for miles, and nothing, nothing left, not even the firewatch stone.

It was the Whispering Gallery all over again. I felt that I had said something, and when I looked at Langby's face he was smiling crookedly.

"St Paul's will burn down," I said. "There won't be anything left."

"Yes," Langby said. "That's the idea, isn't it? Burn St Paul's to the ground? Isn't that the plan?"

"Whose plan?" I said stupidly.

"Hitler's, of course," Langby said. "Who did you think I meant?" and, almost casually, picked up his stirrup pump.

The page of the ARP manual flashed suddenly before me.

I poured the bucket of sand around the still sputtering bomb, snatched up another bucket and dumped that on top of it. Black smoke billowed up in such a cloud that I could hardly find my shovel. I felt for the smothered bomb with the tip of it and scooped it into the empty bucket, then shovelled the sand in on top of it. Tears were streaming down my face from the acrid smoke. I turned to wipe them on my sleeve and saw Langby.

He had not made a move to help me. He smiled. "It's not a bad plan, actually. But of course we won't let it happen. That's what the fire watch is here for. To see that it doesn't happen. Right, Bartholomew?"

I know now what the purpose of my practicum is. I must stop Langby from burning down St Paul's.

September 28 – I try to tell myself I was mistaken about Langby last night, that I misunderstood what he said. Why would he want to burn down St Paul's unless he is a Nazi spy? How can a Nazi spy have gotten on the fire watch? I think about my faked letter of introduction and shudder.

How can I find out? If I set him some test, some fatal thing that only a loyal Englishman in 1940 would know, I fear I am the one who would be caught out. I *must* get my retrieval working properly.

Until then, I shall watch Langby. For the time being at least that should be easy. Langby has just posted the watches for the next two weeks. We stand every one together.

September 30 – I know what happened in September. Langby told me.

Last night in the choir, putting on our coats and boots, he said, "They've already tried once, you know."

I had no idea what he meant. I felt as helpless as that first day when he asked me if I was from the ayarpee.

"The plan to destroy St Paul's. They've already tried once. The tenth of September. A high explosive bomb. But of course you didn't know about that. You were in Wales."

I was not even listening. The minute he had said, "high explosive bomb", I had remembered it all. It had burrowed in under the road and lodged on the foundations. The bomb squad had tried to defuse it, but there was a leaking gas main. They decided to evacuate St Paul's, but Dean Matthews refused to leave, and they got it out after all and exploded it in Barking Marshes. Instant and complete retrieval.

"The bomb squad saved her that time," Langby was saying. "It seems there's always somebody about."

"Yes," I said. "There is," and walked away from him.

October 1 – I thought last night's retrieval of the events of September tenth meant some sort of breakthrough, but I have been lying here on my cot most of the night trying for Nazi spies in St Paul's and getting nothing. Do I have to know exactly what I'm looking for before I can remember it? What good does that do me?

Maybe Langby is not a Nazi spy. Then what is he? An arsonist? A madman? The crypt is hardly conducive to thought, being not at all as silent as a tomb. The chars talk most of the night and the sound of the bombs is muffled, which somehow makes it worse. I find myself straining to hear them. When I did get to sleep this morning, I dreamed about one of the tube shelters being hit, broken mains, drowning people.

October 4 – I tried to catch the cat today. I had some idea of persuading it to dispatch the mouse that has been terrifying the chars. I also wanted to see one up close. I took the water bucket I had used with the stirrup pump last night to put out some burning shrapnel from one of the anti-aircraft guns. It still had a bit of water in it, but not enough to drown the cat, and my plan was to clamp the bucket over him, reach under, and pick him up, then carry him down to the crypt and point him at the mouse. I did not even come close to him.

I swung the bucket, and as I did so, perhaps an inch of water splashed out. I thought I remembered that the cat was a domesticated animal, but I must have been wrong about that. The cat's wide complacent face pulled back into a skull-like mask that was absolutely terrifying, vicious claws extended from what I had thought were harmless paws, and the cat let out a sound to top the chars.

In my surprise I dropped the bucket and it rolled against one of the pillars. The cat disappeared. Behind me, Langby said, "That's no way to catch a cat."

"Obviously," I said, and bent to retrieve the bucket.

"Cats hate water," he said, still in that expressionless voice.

"Oh," I said, and started in front of him to take the bucket back to the choir. "I didn't know that."

"Everybody knows it. Even the stupid Welsh."

October 8 – We have been standing double watches for a week – bomber's moon. Langby didn't show up on the roofs, so I went looking for him in the church. I found him standing by the west doors talking to an old man. The man had a newspaper tucked under his arm and he handed it to Langby, but Langby gave it back to him. When the man saw me, he ducked out. Langby said, "Tourist. Wanted to know where the Windmill Theatre is. Read in the paper the girls are starkers."

I know I looked as if I didn't believe him because he said, "You look rotten, old man. Not getting enough sleep, are you? I'll get somebody to take the first watch for you tonight."

"No," I said coldly. "I'll stand my own watch. I like being on the roofs," and added silently, *where I can watch you*.

He shrugged and said, "I suppose it's better than being down in the crypt. At least on the roofs you can hear the one that gets you."

October 10 – I thought the double watches might be good for me, take my mind off my inability to retrieve. The watched pot idea. Actually, it sometimes works. A few hours of thinking about something else, or a good night's sleep, and the fact pops forward without any prompting, without any artificials.

The good night's sleep is out of the question. Not only do the chars talk constantly, but the cat has moved into the crypt and sidles up to everyone, making siren noises and begging for kippers. I am moving my cot out of the transept and over by Nelson before I go on watch. He may be pickled, but he keeps his mouth shut.

October 11 – I dreamed Trafalgar, ships' guns and smoke and falling plaster and Langby shouting my name. My first waking thought was that the folding chairs had gone off. I could not see for all the smoke.

"I'm coming," I said, limping toward Langby and pulling on my boots. There was a heap of plaster and tangled folding chairs in the transept. Langby was digging in it. "Bartholomew!" he shouted, flinging a chunk of plaster aside. "Bartholomew!"

I still had the idea it was smoke. I ran back for the stirrup pump and then knelt beside him and began pulling on a splintered chair back. It resisted, and it came to me suddenly, There is a body under here. I will reach for a piece of the ceiling and find it is a hand. I leaned back on my heels, determined not to be sick, then went at the pile again.

Langby was going far too fast, jabbing with a chair leg. I grabbed his hand to stop him, and he struggled against me as if I were a piece of rubble to be thrown aside. He picked up a large flat square of plaster, and under it was the floor. I turned and looked behind me. Both chars huddled in the recess by the altar. "Who are you looking for?" I said, keeping hold of Langby's arm.

"Bartholomew," he said, and swept the rubble aside, his hands bleeding through the coating of smoky dust.

"I'm here," I said. "I'm all right." I choked on the white dust. "I moved my cot out of the transept."

He turned sharply to the chars and then said quite calmly, "What's under here?"

"Only the gas ring," one of them said timidly from the shadowed recess, "and Mrs Galbraith's handbag." He dug through the mess until he had found them both. The gas ring was leaking at a merry rate, though the flame had gone out.

"You've saved St Paul's and me after all," I said, standing there in my underwear and boots, holding the useless stirrup pump. "We might all have been asphyxiated."

He stood up. "I shouldn't have saved you," he said.

Stage one: shock, stupefaction, unawareness of injuries, words may not make sense except to victim. He would not know his hand was bleeding yet. He would not remember what he had said. He had said he shouldn't have saved my life.

"I shouldn't have saved you," he repeated. "I have my duty to think of."

"You're bleeding," I said sharply. "You'd better lie down." I sounded just like Langby in the Gallery.

October 13 – It was a high explosive bomb. It blew a hole in the choir roof; and some of the marble statuary is broken; but the ceiling of the crypt did not collapse, which is what I thought at first. It only jarred some plaster loose.

I do not think Langby has any idea what he said. That should give me some sort of advantage, now that I am sure where the danger lies, now that I am sure it will not come crashing down from some other direction. But what good is all this knowing, when I do not know what he will do? Or when?

Surely I have the facts of yesterday's bomb in long-term, but even falling plaster did not jar them loose this time. I am not even trying for retrieval now. I lie in the darkness waiting for the roof to fall in on me. And remembering how Langby saved my life.

October 15 – The girl came in again today. She still has the cold, but she has gotten her paying position. It was a joy to see her. She was wearing a smart uniform and open-toed shoes, and her hair was in an elaborate frizz around her face. We are still cleaning up the mess from the bomb, and Langby was out with Allen getting wood to board up the choir, so I let the girl chatter at me while I swept. The dust made her sneeze, but at least this time I knew what she was doing.

She told me her name is Enola and that she's working for the WVS, running one of the mobile canteens that are sent to the fires. She came, of all things, to thank me for the job. She said that after she told the WVS that there was no proper shelter with a canteen for St. Paul's, they gave her a run in the City. "So I'll just pop in when I'm close and let you know how I'm making out, won't I just?"

She and her brother Tom are still sleeping in the tubes. I asked her if that was safe and she said probably not, but at least down there you couldn't hear the one that got you and that was a blessing.

October 18 – I am so tired I can hardly write this. Nine incendiaries tonight and a land mine that looked as though it was going to catch on the dome till the wind drifted its parachute away from the church. I put out two of the incendiaries. I have done that at least twenty times since I got here and helped with dozens of others, and still it is not enough. One incendiary, one moment of not watching Langby, could undo it all.

I know that is partly why I feel so tired. I wear myself out every night trying to do my job and watch Langby, making sure none of the incendiaries falls without my seeing it. Then I go back to the crypt and wear myself out trying to retrieve something, anything, about spies, fires, St Paul's in the fall of 1940, anything. It haunts me that I am not doing enough, but I do not know what else to do. Without the retrieval, I am as helpless as these poor people here, with no idea what will happen tomorrow.

If I have to, I will go on doing this till I am called home. He cannot burn down St Paul's so long as I am here to put out the incendiaries. "I have my duty," Langby said in the crypt.

And I have mine.

October 21 – It's been nearly two weeks since the blast and I just now realized we haven't seen the cat since. He wasn't in the mess in the crypt. Even after Langby and I were sure there was no one in there, we sifted through the stuff twice more. He could have been in the choir, though.

Old Bence-Jones says not to worry. "He's all right," he said. "The jerries could bomb London right down to the ground and the cats would waltz out to greet them. You know why? They don't love anybody. That's what gets half of us killed. Old lady out in Stepney got killed the other night trying to save her cat. Bloody cat was in the Anderson."

"Then where is he?"

"Someplace safe, you can bet on that. If he's not around St Paul's, it means we're for it. That old saw about the rats deserting a sinking ship, that's a mistake, that is. It's cats, not rats."

October 25 – Langby's tourist showed up again. He cannot still be looking for the Windmill Theatre. He had a newspaper under his arm again today, and he asked for Langby, but Langby was across town with Allen, trying to get the asbestos firemen's coats. I saw the name of the paper. It was *The Worker*. A Nazi newspaper?

November 2 – I've been up on the roofs for a week straight, helping some incompetent workmen patch the hole the bomb made. They're doing a terrible job. There's still a great gap on one side a man could fall into, but they insist it'll be all right because, after all, you wouldn't fall clear through but only as far as the ceiling, and "the fall can't kill you". They don't seem to understand it's a perfect hiding place for an incendiary.

And that is all Langby needs. He does not even have to set a fire to destroy St Paul's. All he needs to do is let one burn uncaught until it is too late.

I could not get anywhere with the workmen. I went down into the church to complain to Matthews, and saw Langby and his tourist behind a pillar, close to one of the windows. Langby was holding a newspaper and talking to the man. When I came down from the library an hour later, they were still there. So is the gap. Matthews says we'll put planks across it and hope for the best.

November 5 – I have given up trying to retrieve. I am so far behind on my sleep I can't even retrieve information on a newspaper whose name I already know. Double watches the permanent thing now. Our chars have abandoned us altogether (like the cat), so the crypt is quiet, but I cannot sleep.

If I do manage to doze off, I dream. Yesterday I dreamed Kivrin was on the roofs, dressed like a saint. "What was the secret of your practicum?" I said. "What were you supposed to find out?"

She wiped her nose with a handkerchief and said, "Two things. One, that silence and humility are the sacred burdens of the historian. Two," she stopped and sneezed into the handkerchief. "Don't sleep in the tubes."

My only hope is to get hold of an artificial and induce a trance. That's a problem. I'm positive it's too early for chemical endorphins and probably hallucinogens. Alcohol is definitely available, but I need something more concentrated than ale, the only alcohol I know by name. I do not dare ask the watch. Langby is suspicious enough of me already. It's back to the *OED*, to look up a word I don't know.

November 11 – The cat's back. Langby was out with Allen again, still trying for the asbestos coats, so I thought it was safe to leave St Paul's. I went to the grocer's for supplies and hopefully, an artificial. It was late, and the sirens sounded before I had even gotten to Cheapside, but the raids do not usually start until after dark. It took awhile to get all the groceries and to get up my courage to ask whether he had any alcohol – he told me to go to a pub – and when I came out of the shop, it was as if I had pitched suddenly into a hole.

I had no idea where St Paul's lay, or the street, or the shop I had just come from. I stood on what was no longer the sidewalk, clutching my brown-paper parcel of kippers and bread with a hand I could not have seen if I held it up before my face. I reached up to wrap my muffler closer about my neck and prayed for my eyes to adjust, but there was no reduced light to adjust to. I would have been glad of the moon, for all St Paul's watch curses it and calls it a fifth columnist. Or a bus, with its shuttered headlights giving just enough light to orient myself by. Or a searchlight. Or the kickback flare of an ack-ack gun. Anything.

Just then I did see a bus, two narrow yellow slits a long way off. I started toward it and nearly pitched off the curb. Which meant the bus was sideways in the street, which meant it was not a bus. A cat meowed, quite near, and rubbed against my leg. I looked down into the yellow lights I had thought belonged to the bus. His eyes were picking up light from somewhere, though I would have sworn there was not a light for miles, and reflecting it flatly up at me.

"A warden'll get you for those lights, old tom," I said, and then as a plane droned overhead, "Or a jerry."

The world exploded suddenly into light, the searchlights and a glow along the Thames seeming to happen almost simultaneously, lighting my way home.

"Come to fetch me, did you, old tom?" I said gaily. "Where've you been? Knew we were out of kippers, didn't you? I call that loyalty." I talked to him all the way home and gave him half a tin of the kippers for saving my life. Bence-Jones said he smelled the milk at the grocer's.

November 13 – I dreamed I was lost in the blackout. I could not see my hands in front of my face, and Dunworthy came and shone a pocket torch at me, but I could only see where I had come from and not where I was going.

"What good is that to them?" I said. "They need a light to show them where they're going."

"Even the light from the Thames? Even the light from the fires and the ack-ack guns?" Dunworthy said.

"Yes. Anything is better than this awful darkness." So he came closer to give me the pocket torch. It was not a pocket torch, after all, but Christ's lantern from the Hunt picture in the south nave. I shone it on the kerb before me so I could find my way home, but it shone instead on the firewatch stone and I hastily put the light out.

November 20 – I tried to talk to Langby today. "I've seen you talking to the old gentleman," I said. It sounded like an accusation. I meant it to. I wanted him to think it was and stop whatever he was planning.

"Reading," he said. "Not talking." He was putting things in order in the choir, piling up sandbags.

"I've seen you reading then," I said belligerently, and he dropped a sandbag and straightened.

"What of it?" he said. "It's a free country. I can read to an old man if I want, same as you can talk to that little WVS tart."

"What do you read?" I said.

"Whatever he wants. He's an old man. He used to come home from his job, have a bit of brandy and listen to his wife read the papers to him. She got killed in one of the raids. Now I read to him. I don't see what business it is of yours."

It sounded true. It didn't have the careful casualness of a lie, and I almost believed him, except that I had heard the tone of truth from him before. In the crypt. After the bomb.

"I thought he was a tourist looking for the Windmill," I said.

He looked blank only a second, and then he said, "Oh, yes, that. He came in with the paper and asked me to tell him where it was. I looked it up to find the address. Clever, that. I didn't guess he couldn't read it for himself. But it was enough. I knew that he was lying."

He heaved a sandbag almost at my feet. "Of course you wouldn't understand a thing like that, would you? A simple act of human kindness?"

"No," I said coldly. "I wouldn't."

None of this proves anything. He gave away nothing, except perhaps the name of an artificial, and I can hardly go to Dean Matthews and accuse Langby of reading aloud.

I waited till he had finished in the choir and gone down to the crypt. Then I lugged one of the sandbags up to the roof and over to the chasm. The planking has held so far, but everyone walks gingerly around it, as if it were a grave. I cut the sandbag open and spilled the loose sand into the bottom. If it has occurred to Langby that this is the perfect spot for an incendiary, perhaps the sand will smother it.

November 21 – I gave Enola some of "uncle's" money today and asked her to get me the brandy. She was more reluctant than I thought she'd be so there must be societal complications I am not aware of, but she agreed.

I don't know what she came for. She started to tell me about her brother and some prank he'd pulled in the tubes that got him in trouble with the guard, but after I asked her about the brandy, she left without finishing the story.

November 25 – Enola came today, but without bringing the brandy. She is going to Bath for the holidays to see her aunt. At least she will be away from the raids for awhile. I will not have to worry about her. She finished the story of her brother and told me she hopes to persuade this aunt to take Tom for the duration of the Blitz but is not at all sure the aunt will be willing.

Young Tom is apparently not so much an engaging scapegrace as a near-criminal. He has been caught twice picking pockets in the Bank tube shelter, and they have had to go back to Marble Arch. I comforted her as best I could, told her all boys were bad at one time or another. What I really wanted to say was that she needn't worry at all, that young Tom strikes me as a true survivor type, like my own tom, like Langby, totally unconcerned with anybody but himself, well-equipped to survive the Blitz and rise to prominence in the future.

Then I asked her whether she had gotten the brandy.

She looked down at her open-toed shoes and muttered unhappily, "I thought you'd forgotten all about that."

I made up some story about the watch taking turns buying a bottle, and she seemed less unhappy, but I am not convinced she will not use this trip to Bath as an excuse to do nothing. I will have to leave St Paul's and buy it myself, and I don't dare leave Langby alone in the church. I made her promise to bring the brandy today before she leaves. But she is still not back, and the sirens have already gone.

November 26 – No Enola, and she said their train left at noon. I suppose I should be grateful that at least she is safely out of London. Maybe in Bath she will be able to get over her cold.

Tonight one of the ARP girls breezed in to borrow half our cots and tell us about a mess over in the East End where a surface shelter was hit. Four dead, twelve wounded. "At least it wasn't one of the tube shelters!" she said. "Then you'd see a real mess, wouldn't you?"

November 30 – I dreamed I took the cat to St John's Wood.

"Is this a rescue mission?" Dunworthy said.

"No, sir," I said proudly. "I know what I was supposed to find in my practicum. The perfect survivor. Tough and resourceful and selfish. This is the only one I could find. I had to kill Langby, you know, to keep him from burning down St Paul's. Enola's brother has gone to Bath, and the others will never make it. Enola wears open-toed shoes in the winter and sleeps in the tubes and puts her hair up on metal pins so it will curl. She cannot possibly survive the Blitz."

Dunworthy said, "Perhaps you should have rescued her instead. What did you say her name was?"

"Kivrin," I said, and woke up cold and shivering.

December 5 – I dreamed Langby had the pinpoint bomb. He carried it under his arm like a brown-paper parcel, coming out of St Paul's Station and up Ludgate Hill to the west doors.

"This is not fair," I said, barring his way with my arm. "There is no fire watch on duty."

He clutched the bomb to his chest like a pillow. "That is your fault," he said, and before I could get to my stirrup pump and bucket, he tossed it in the door.

The pinpoint was not even invented until the end of the twentieth century, and it was another ten years before the dispossessed Communists got hold of it and turned it into something that could be carried under your arm. A parcel that could blow a quarter-mile of the City into oblivion. Thank God that is one dream that cannot come true.

It was a sunlit morning in the dream, and this morning when I came off watch the sun was shining for the first time in weeks. I went down to the crypt and then came up again, making the rounds of the roofs twice more, then the steps and the grounds and all the treacherous alleyways between where an incendiary could be missed. I felt better after that, but when I got to sleep I dreamed again, this time of fire and Langby watching it, smiling.

December 15 – I found the cat this morning. Heavy raids last night, but most of them over towards Canning Town and nothing on the roofs to speak of. Nevertheless the cat was quite dead. I found him lying on the steps this morning when I made my own, private rounds. Concussion. There was not a mark on him anywhere except the white blackout patch on his throat, but when I picked him up, he was all jelly under the skin.

I could not think what to do with him. I thought for one mad moment of asking Matthews if I could bury him in the crypt. Honorable death in war or something. Trafalgar, Waterloo, London, died in battle. I ended by wrapping him in my muffler and taking him down Ludgate Hill to a building that had been bombed out and burying him in the rubble. It will do no good. The rubble will be no protection from dogs or rats, and I shall never get another muffler. I have gone through nearly all of uncle's money.

I should not be sitting here. I haven't checked the alleyways or the rest of the steps, and there might be a dud or a delayed incendiary or something that I missed.

When I came here, I thought of myself as the noble rescuer, the savior of the past. I am not doing very well at the job. At least Enola is out of it. I wish there were some way I could send St Paul's to Bath for safekeeping. There were hardly any raids last night. Bence-Jones said cats can survive anything. What if he was coming to get me, to show me the way home? All the bombs were over Canning Town.

December 16 – Enola has been back a week. Seeing her, standing on the west steps where I found the cat, sleeping in Marble Arch and not safe at all, was more than I could absorb. "I thought you were in Bath," I said stupidly.

"My aunt said she'd take Tom but not me as well. She's got a houseful of evacuation children, and what a noisy lot. Where is your muffler?" she said. "It's dreadful cold up here on the hill."

"I . . ." I said, unable to answer, "I lost it."

"You'll never get another one," she said. "They're going to start rationing clothes. And wool, too. You'll never get another one like that."

"I know," I said, blinking at her.

"Good things just thrown away," she said. "It's absolutely criminal, that's what it is."

I don't think I said anything to that, just turned and walked away with my head down, looking for bombs and dead animals.

December 20 – Langby isn't a Nazi. He's a Communist. I can hardly write this. A Communist.

One of the chars found *The Worker* wedged behind a pillar and brought it down to the crypt as we were coming off the first watch.

"Bloody Communists," Bence-Jones said. "Helping Hitler, they are. Talking against the king, stirring up trouble in the shelters. Traitors, that's what they are."

"They love England same as you," the char said.

"They don't love nobody but themselves, bloody selfish lot. I wouldn't be surprised to hear they were ringing Hitler up on the telephone," Bence-Jones said. "''Ello, Adolf, here's where to drop the bombs.'"

The kettle on the gas ring whistled. The char stood up and poured the hot water into a chipped tea pot, then sat back down. "Just because they speak their minds don't mean they'd burn down old St Paul's, does it now?"

"Of course not," Langby said, coming down the stairs. He sat down and pulled off his boots, stretching his feet in their wool socks. "Who wouldn't burn down St Paul's?"

"The Communists," Bence-Jones said, looking straight at him, and I wondered if he suspected Langby, too.

Langby never batted an eye. "I wouldn't worry about them if I were you," he said. "It's the jerries that are doing their bloody best to burn her down tonight. Six incendiaries so far, and one almost went into that great hole over the choir." He held out his cup to the char, and she poured him a cup of tea.

I wanted to kill him, smashing him to dust and rubble on

the floor of the crypt while Bence-Jones and the char looked on in helpless surprise, shouting warnings to them and the rest of the watch. "Do you know what the Communists did?" I wanted to shout. "Do you? We have to stop him." I even stood up and started toward him as he sat with his feet stretched out before him and his asbestos coat still over his shoulders.

And then the thought of the Gallery drenched in gold, the Communist coming out of the tube station with the package so casually under his arm, made me sick with the same staggering vertigo of guilt and helplessness, and I sat back down on the edge of my cot and tried to think what to do.

They do not realize the danger. Even Bence-Jones, for all his talk of traitors, thinks they are capable only of talking against the king. They do not know, cannot know, what the Communists will become. Stalin is an ally. Communists mean Russia. They have never heard of Karinsky or the New Russia or any of the things that will make "Communist" into a synonym for "monster". They will never know it. By the time the Communists become what they became, there will be no fire watch. Only I know what it means to hear the name "Communist" uttered here, so carelessly, in St Paul's.

A Communist. I should have known. I should have known.

December 22 – Double watches again. I have not had any sleep, and I am getting very unsteady on my feet. I nearly pitched into the chasm this morning, only saved myself by dropping to my knees. My endorphin levels are fluctuating wildly, and I know I must get some sleep soon or I will become one of Langby's walking dead; but I am afraid to leave him alone on the roofs, alone in the church with his Communist party leader, alone anywhere. I have taken to watching him when he sleeps.

If I could just get hold of an artificial, I think I could induce a trance, in spite of my poor condition. But I cannot even go out to a pub. Langby is on the roofs constantly, waiting for his chance. When Enola comes again, I must convince her to get the brandy for me. There are only a few days left.

December 28 – Enola came this morning while I was on the west porch, picking up the Christmas tree. It has been knocked over three nights running by concussion. I righted the tree and was bending down to pick up the scattered tinsel when Enola appeared suddenly out of the fog like some cheerful saint. She stooped quickly and kissed me on the cheek. Then she straightened up, her nose red from her perennial cold, and handed me a box wrapped in colored paper.

"Merry Christmas," she said. "Go on then, open it. It's a gift."

My reflexes are almost totally gone. I knew the box was far too shallow for a bottle of brandy. Nevertheless, I believed she had remembered, had brought me my salvation. "You darling," I said, and tore it open.

It was a muffler. Gray wool. I stared at it for fully half a minute without realizing what it was. "Where's the brandy?" I said.

She looked shocked. Her nose got redder and her eyes started to blur. "You need this more. You haven't any clothing coupons and you have to be outside all the time. It's been so dreadful cold."

"I *needed* the brandy," I said angrily.

"I was only trying to be kind," she started, and I cut her off.

"Kind?" I said. "I asked you for brandy. I don't recall ever saying I needed a muffler." I shoved it back at her and began untangling a string of colored lights that had shattered when the tree fell.

She got that same holy martyr look Kivrin is so wonderful at. "I worry about you all the time up here," she said in a rush. "They're *trying* for St Paul's, you know. And it's so close to the river. I didn't think you should be drinking. I . . . it's a crime when they're trying so hard to kill us all that you won't take care of yourself. It's like you're in it with them. I worry someday I'll come up to St Paul's and you won't be here."

"Well, and what exactly am I supposed to do with a muffler? Hold it over my head when they drop the bombs?"

She turned and ran, disappearing into the gray fog before she had gone down two steps. I started after her, still holding the string of broken lights, tripped over it, and fell almost all the way to the bottom of the steps.

Langby picked me up. "You're off watches," he said grimly.

"You can't do that," I said.

"Oh, yes, I can. I don't want any walking dead on the roofs with me."

I let him lead me down here to the crypt, make me a cup of tea, put me to bed, all very solicitous. No indication that this is what he has been waiting for. I will lie here till the sirens go. Once I am on the roofs he will not be able to send me back without seeming suspicious. Do you know what he said before he left, asbestos coat and rubber boots, the dedicated fire watcher? "I want you to get some sleep." As if I could sleep with Langby on the roofs. I would be burned alive.

December 30 – The sirens woke me, and old Bence-Jones said, "That should have done you some good. You've slept the clock round."

"What day is it?" I said, going for my boots.

"The twenty-ninth," he said, and as I dived for the door, "No need to hurry. They're late tonight. Maybe they won't come at all. That'd be a blessing, that would. The tide's out."

I stopped by the door to the stairs, holding onto the cool stone. "Is St Paul's all right?"

"She's still standing," he said. "Have a bad dream?"

"Yes," I said, remembering the bad dreams of all the past weeks – the dead cat in my arms in St John's Wood, Langby with his parcel and his *Worker* under his arm, the firewatch stone garishly lit by Christ's lantern. Then I remembered I had not dreamed at all. I had slept the kind of sleep I had prayed for, the kind of sleep that would help me remember.

Then I remembered. Not St Paul's, burned to the ground by the Communists. A headline from the dailies. "Marble

Arch hit. Eighteen killed by blast." The date was not clear except for the year. 1940. There were exactly two more days left in 1940. I grabbed my coat and muffler and ran up the stairs and across the marble floor.

"Where the hell do you think you're going?" Langby shouted to me. I couldn't see him.

"I have to save Enola," I said, and my voice echoed in the dark sanctuary. "They're going to bomb Marble Arch."

"You can't leave now," he shouted after me, standing where the firewatch stone would be. "The tide's out. You dirty . . ."

I didn't hear the rest of it. I had already flung myself down the steps and into a taxi. It took almost all the money I had, the money I had so carefully hoarded for the trip back to St. John's Wood. Shelling started while we were still in Oxford Street, and the driver refused to go any farther. He let me out into pitch blackness, and I saw I would never make it in time.

Blast. Enola crumpled on the stairway down to the tube, her open-toed shoes still on her feet, not a mark on her. And when I try to lift her, jelly under the skin. I would have to wrap her in the muffler she gave me, because I was too late. I had gone back a hundred years to be too late to save her.

I ran the last blocks, guided by the gun emplacement that had to be in Hyde Park, and skidded down the steps into Marble Arch. The woman in the ticket booth took my last shilling for a ticket to St Paul's Station. I stuck it in my pocket and raced toward the stairs.

"No running," she said placidly. "To your left, please." The door to the right was blocked off by wooden barricades, the metal gates beyond pulled to and chained. The board with names on it for the stations was X-ed with tape, and a new sign that read, "All trains," was nailed to the barricade, pointing left.

Enola was not on the stopped escalators or sitting against the wall in the hallway. I came to the first stairway and could not get through. A family had set out, just where I wanted to step, a communal tea of bread and butter, a little pot of jam sealed with waxed paper, and a kettle on a ring like the one Langby and I had rescued out of the rubble, all of it spread on a cloth embroidered at the corners with flowers. I stood staring down at the layered tea, spread like a waterfall down the steps.

"I . . . Marble Arch . . ." I said. Another twenty killed by flying tiles. "You shouldn't be here."

"We've as much right as anyone," the man said belligerently, "and who are you to tell us to move on?"

A woman lifting saucers out of a cardboard box looked up at me, frightened. The kettle began to whistle.

"It's you that should move on," the man said. "Go on then." He stood off to one side so I could pass. I edged past the embroidered cloth apologetically.

"I'm sorry," I said. "I'm looking for someone. On the platform."

"You'll never find her in there, mate," the man said, thumbing in that direction. I hurried past him, nearly stepping on the teacloth, and rounded the corner into hell.

It was not hell. Shopgirls folded coats and leaned back against them, cheerful or sullen or disagreeable, but certainly not damned. Two boys scuffled for a shilling and lost it on the tracks. They bent over the edge, debating whether to go after it, and the station guard yelled to them to back away. A train rumbled through, full of people. A mosquito landed on the guard's hand and he reached out to slap it and missed. The boys laughed. And behind and before them, stretching in all directions down the deadly tile curves of the tunnel like casualties, backed into the entrance-ways and onto the stairs, were people. Hundreds and hundreds of people.

I stumbled back into the hall, knocking over a teacup. It spilled like a flood across the cloth.

"I told you, mate," the man said cheerfully. "It's Hell in there, ain't it? And worse below."

"Hell," I said. "Yes." I would never find her. I would never save her. I looked at the woman mopping up the tea, and it came to me that I could not save her either. Enola or the cat or any of them, lost here in the endless stairways and cul-de-sacs of time. They were already dead a hundred years, past saving. The past is beyond saving. Surely that was the lesson the history department sent me all this way to learn. Well, fine, I've learned it. Can I go home now?

Of course not, dear boy. You have foolishly spent all your money on taxicabs and brandy, and tonight is the night the Germans burn the City. (Now it is too late, I remember it all. Twenty-eight incendiaries on the roofs.) Langby must have his chance, and you must learn the hardest lesson of all and the one you should have known from the beginning. You cannot save St Paul's.

I went back out onto the platform and stood behind the yellow line until a train pulled up. I took my ticket out and held it in my hand all the way to St Paul's Station. When I got there, smoke billowed toward me like an easy spray of water. I could not see St Paul's.

"The tide's out," a woman said in a voice devoid of hope, and I went down in a snake pit of limp cloth hoses. My hands came up covered with rank-smelling mud, and I understood finally (and too late) the significance of the tide. There was no water to fight the fires.

A policeman barred my way and I stood helplessly before him with no idea what to say. "No civilians allowed up there," he said. "St Paul's is for it." The smoke billowed like a thundercloud, alive with sparks, and the dome rose golden above it.

"I'm fire watch," I said, and his arm fell away, and then I was on the roofs.

My endorphin levels must have been going up and down like an air raid siren. I do not have any short-term from then on, just moments that do not fit together: the people in the church when we brought Langby down, huddled in a corner playing cards, the whirlwind of burning scraps of wood in the dome, the ambulance driver who wore open-toed shoes like Enola and smeared salve on my burned hands. And in the center, the one clear moment when I went after Langby on a rope and saved his life.

I stood by the dome, blinking against the smoke. The City was on fire and it seemed as if St Paul's would ignite from the heat, would crumble from the noise alone. Bence-Jones was by the northwest tower, hitting at an incendiary with a spade. Langby was too close to the patched place where the bomb had gone through, looking toward me. An incendiary clattered behind him. I turned to grab a shovel, and when I turned back, he was gone.

"Langby!" I shouted, and could not hear my own voice. He had fallen into the chasm and nobody saw him or the incendiary. Except me. I do not remember how I got across the roof. I think I called for a rope. I got a rope. I tied it around my waist, gave the ends of it into the hands of the fire watch, and went over the side. The fires lit the walls of the hole almost all the way to the bottom. Below me I could see a pile of whitish rubble. He's under there, I thought, and jumped free of the wall. The space was so narrow there was nowhere to throw the rubble. I was afraid I would inadvertently stone him, and I tried to toss the pieces of planking and plaster over my shoulder, but there was barely room to turn. For one awful moment I thought he might not be there at all, that the pieces of splintered wood would brush away to reveal empty pavement, as they had in the crypt.

I was numbed by the indignity of crawling over him. If he was dead I did not think I could bear the shame of stepping on his helpless body. Then his hand came up like a ghost's and grabbed my ankle, and within seconds I had whirled and had his head free.

He was the ghastly white that no longer frightens me. "I put the bomb out," he said. I stared at him, so overwhelmed with relief I could not speak. For one hysterical moment I thought I would even laugh, I was so glad to see him. I finally realized what it was I was supposed to say.

"Are you all right?" I said.

"Yes," he said, and tried to raise himself on one elbow. "So much the worse for you."

He could not get up. He grunted with pain when he tried to shift his weight to his right side and lay back, the uneven rubble crunching sickeningly under him. I tried to lift him gently so I could see where he was hurt. He must have fallen on something.

"It's no use," he said, breathing hard. "I put it out."

I spared him a startled glance, afraid that he was delirious, and went back to rolling him onto his side.

"I know you were counting on this one," he went on, not resisting me at all. "It was bound to happen sooner or later with all these roofs. Only I went after it. What'll you tell your friends?"

His asbestos coat was torn down the back in a long gash. Under it his back was charred and smoking. He had fallen on the incendiary. "Oh, my God," I said, trying frantically to see how badly he was burned without touching him. I had no way of knowing how deep the burns went, but they seemed to extend only in the narrow space where the coat had torn. I tried to pull the bomb out from under him, but the casing was as hot as a stove. It was not melting, though. My sand and Langby's body had smothered it. I had no idea if it would start up again when it was exposed to the air. I looked around, a little wildly, for the bucket and stirrup pump Langby must have dropped when he fell.

"Looking for a weapon?" Langby said, so clearly it was hard to believe he was hurt at all. "Why not just leave me here? A bit of overexposure and I'd be done for by morning. Or would you rather do your dirty work in private?"

I stood up and yelled to the men on the roof above us. One of them shone a pocket torch down at us, but its light didn't reach.

"Is he dead?" somebody shouted down to me.

"Send for an ambulance," I said. "He's been burned."

I helped Langby up, trying to support his back without touching the burn. He staggered a little and then leaned against the wall, watching me as I tried to bury the incendiary; using a piece of the planking as a scoop. The rope came down and I tied Langby to it. He had not spoken since I helped him up. He let me tie the rope around his waist, still looking steadily at me. "I should have let you smother in the crypt," he said.

He stood leaning easily, almost relaxed against the wood supports, his hands holding him up. I put his hands on the slack rope and wrapped it once around them for the grip I knew he didn't have. "I've been onto you since that day in the Gallery. I knew you weren't afraid of heights. You came down here without any fear of heights when you thought I'd ruined your precious plans. What was it? An attack of conscience? Kneeling there like a baby, whining, 'What have we done? What have we done?' You made me sick. But you know what gave you away first? The cat. Everybody knows cats hate water. Everybody but a dirty Nazi spy."

There was a tug on the rope. "Come ahead," I said, and the rope tautened.

"That WVS tart? Was she a spy, too? Supposed to meet you in Marble Arch? Telling me it was going to be bombed. You're a rotten spy, Bartholomew. Your friends already blew it up in September. It's open again."

The rope jerked suddenly and began to lift Langby. He twisted his hands to get a better grip. His right shoulder scraped the wall. I put up my hands and pushed him gently so that his left side was to the wall. "You're making a big mistake, you know," he said. "You should have killed me. I'll tell."

I stood in the darkness, waiting for the rope. Langby was unconscious when he reached the roof. I walked past the fire watch to the dome and down to the crypt.

This morning the letter from my uncle came and with it a tenpound note.

December 31 – Two of Dunworthy's flunkies met me in St John's Wood to tell me I was late for my exams. I did not even protest. I shuffled obediently after them without even considering how unfair it was to give an exam to one of the walking dead. I had not slept in – how long? Since yesterday when I went to find Enola. I had not slept in a hundred years.

Dunworthy was at his desk, blinking at me. One of the flunkies handed me a test paper and the other one called time. I turned the paper over and left an oily smudge from the ointment on my burns. I stared uncomprehendingly at them. I had grabbed at the incendiary when I turned Langby over, but these burns were on the backs of my hands. The answer came to me suddenly in Langby's unyielding voice. "They're rope burns, you fool. Don't they teach you Nazi spies the proper way to come up a rope?"

I looked down at the test. It read, "Number of incendiaries that fell on St Paul's. Number of land mines. Number of high explosive bombs. Method most commonly used for extinguishing incendiaries. Land mines. High explosive bombs. Number of volunteers on first watch. Second watch. Casualties. Fatalities." The questions made no sense. There was only a short space, long enough for the writing of a number, after any of the questions. Method most commonly used for extinguishing incendiaries. How would I ever fit what I knew into that narrow space? Where were the questions about Enola and Langby and the cat?

I went up to Dunworthy's desk. "St Paul's almost burned down last night," I said. "What kind of questions are these?"

"You should be answering questions, Mr Bartholomew, not asking them."

"There aren't any questions about the people," I said. The outer casing of my anger began to melt.

"Of course there are," Dunworthy said, flipping to the second page of the test. "Number of casualties, 1940. Blast, shrapnel, other."

"Other?" I said. At any moment the roof would collapse on me in a shower of plaster dust and fury. "Other? Langby put out a fire with his own body. Enola has a cold that keeps getting worse. The cat . . ." I snatched the paper back from him and scrawled "one cat" in the narrow space next to "blast". "Don't you care about them at all?"

"They're important from a statistical point of view," he said, "but as individuals, they are hardly relevant to the course of history."

My reflexes were shot. It was amazing to me that Dunworthy's were almost as slow. I grazed the side of his jaw and knocked his glasses off. "Of course they're relevant!" I shouted. "They *are* the history, not all these bloody numbers!"

The reflexes of the flunkies were very fast. They did not let me start another swing at him before they had me by both arms and were hauling me out of the room.

"They're back there in the past with nobody to save them. They can't see their hands in front of their faces and there are bombs falling down on them and you tell me they aren't important? You call that being an historian?"

The flunkies dragged me out the door and down the hall. "Langby saved St Paul's. How much more important can a person get? You're no historian! You're nothing but a . . ." I wanted to call him a terrible name, but the only curses I could summon up were Langby's. "You're nothing but a dirty Nazi spy!" I bellowed. "You're nothing but a lazy bourgeois tart!"

They dumped me on my hands and knees outside the door and slammed it in my face. "I wouldn't be an historian if you paid me!" I shouted, and went to see the firewatch stone.

December 31 – I am having to write this in bits and pieces. My hands are in pretty bad shape, and Dunworthy's boys didn't help matters much. Kivrin comes in periodically, wearing her St Joan look, and smears so much salve on my hands that I can't hold a pencil.

St Paul's Station is not there, of course, so I got out at Holborn and walked, thinking about my last meeting with Dean Matthews on the morning after the burning of the City. This morning.

"I understand you saved Langby's life," he said "I also understand that between you, you saved St Paul's last night."

I showed him the letter from my uncle and he stared at it as if he could not think what it was. "Nothing stays saved forever," he said, and for a terrible moment I thought he was going to tell me Langby had died. "We shall have to keep on saving St Paul's until Hitler decides to bomb the countryside."

The raids on London are almost over, I wanted to tell him. He'll start bombing the countryside in a matter of weeks. Canterbury, Bath, aiming always at the cathedrals. You and St Paul's will both outlast the war and live to dedicate the firewatch stone.

"I am hopeful, though," he said. "I think the worst is over."

"Yes, sir." I thought of the stone, its letters still readable after all this time. No, sir, the worst is not over.

I managed to keep my bearings almost to the top of

Ludgate Hill. Then I lost my way completely, wandering about like a man in a graveyard. I had not remembered that the rubble looked so much like the white plaster dust Langby had tried to dig me out of. I could not find the stone anywhere. In the end I nearly fell over it, jumping back as if I had stepped on a grave.

It is all that's left. Hiroshima is supposed to have had a handful of untouched trees at ground zero, Denver the capitol steps. Neither of them says, "Remember the men and women of St Paul's Watch who by the grace of God saved this cathedral." The grace of God.

Part of the stone is sheared off. Historians argue there was another line that said, "for all time", but I do not believe that, not if Dean Matthews had anything to do with it. And none of the watch it was dedicated to would have believed it for a minute. We saved St Paul's every time we put out an incendiary, and only until the next one fell. Keeping watch on the danger spots, putting out the little fires with sand and stirrup pumps, the big ones with our bodies, in order to keep the whole vast complex structure from burning down. Which sounds to me like a course description for History Practicum 401. What a fine time to discover what historians are for when I have tossed my chance for being one out the windows as easily as they tossed the pinpoint bomb in! No, sir, the worst is not over.

There are flash burns on the stone, where legend says the Dean of St. Paul's was kneeling when the bomb went off. Totally apocryphal, of course, since the front door is hardly an appropriate place for prayers. It is more likely the shadow of a tourist who wandered in to ask the whereabouts of the Windmill Theatre, or the imprint of a girl bringing a volunteer his muffler. Or a cat.

Nothing is saved forever, Dean Matthews; and I knew that when I walked in the west doors that first day, blinking into the gloom, but it is pretty bad nevertheless. Standing here knee-deep in rubble out of which I will not be able to dig any folding chairs or friends, knowing that Langby died thinking I was a Nazi spy, knowing that Enola came one day and I wasn't there. It's pretty bad.

But it is not as bad as it could be. They are both dead, and Dean Matthews too; but they died without knowing what I knew all along, what sent me to my knees in the Whispering Gallery, sick with grief and guilt: that in the end none of us saved St Paul's. And Langby cannot turn to me, stunned and sick at heart, and say, "Who did this? Your friends the Nazis?" And I would have to say, "No. The Communists." That would be the worst.

I have come back to the room and let Kivrin smear more salve on my hands. She wants me to get some sleep. I know I should pack and get gone. It will be humiliating to have them come and throw me out, but I do not have the strength to fight her. She looks so much like Enola.

January 1 – I have apparently slept not only through the night, but through the morning mail drop as well. When I woke up just now, I found Kivrin sitting on the end of the bed holding an envelope. "Your grades came," she said.

I put my arm over my eyes. "They can be marvelously efficient when they want to, can't they?"

"Yes," Kivrin said.

"Well, let's see it," I said, sitting up. "How long do I have before they come and throw me out?"

She handed the flimsy computer envelope to me. I tore it along the perforation. "Wait," she said. "Before you open it, I want to say something." She put her hand gently on my burns. "You're wrong about the history department. They're very good."

It was not exactly what I expected her to say. "Good is not the word I'd use to describe Dunworthy," I said and yanked the inside slip free.

Kivrin's look did not change, not even when I sat there with the printout on my knees where she could surely see it.

"Well," I said.

The slip was hand-signed by the esteemed Dunworthy. I have taken a first. With honors.

January 2 – Two things came in the mail today. One was Kivrin's assignment. The history department thinks of everything – even to keeping her here long enough to nursemaid me, even to coming up with a prefabricated trial by fire to send their history majors through.

I think I wanted to believe that was what they had done, Enola and Langby only hired actors, the cat a clever android with its clockwork innards taken out for the final effect, not so much because I wanted to believe Dunworthy was not good at all, but because then I would not have this nagging pain at not knowing what had happened to them.

"You said your practicum was England in 1300?" I said, watching her as suspiciously as I had watched Langby.

"1349," she said, and her face went slack with memory. "The plague year."

"My God," I said. "How could they do that? The plague's a ten."

"I have a natural immunity," she said, and looked at her hands.

Because I could not think of anything to say, I opened the other piece of mail. It was a report on Enola. Computer-printed, facts and dates and statistics, all the numbers the history department so dearly loves, but it told me what I thought I would have to go without knowing: that she had gotten over her cold and survived the Blitz. Young Tom had been killed in the Baedaker raids on Bath, but Enola had lived until 2006, the year before they blew up St Paul's.

I don't know whether I believe the report or not, but it does not matter. It is, like Langby's reading aloud to the old man, a simple act of human kindness. They think of everything.

Not quite. They did not tell me what happened to Langby. But I find as I write this that I already know: I saved his life. It does not seem to matter that he might have died in hospital next day; and I find, in spite of all the hard lessons the history department has tried to teach me, I do not quite believe this one: that nothing is saved forever. It seems to me that perhaps Langby is.

January 3 – I went to see Dunworthy today. I don't know what I intended to say – some pompous drivel about my willingness to serve in the firewatch of history, standing guard against the falling incendiaries of the human heart, silent and saintly.

But he blinked at me nearsightedly across his desk, and it seemed to me that he was blinking at that last bright image of St Paul's in sunlight before it was gone forever and that he knew better than anyone that the past cannot be saved, and I said instead, "I'm sorry that I broke your glasses, sir."

"How did you like St Paul's?" he said and, like my first meeting with Enola, I felt I must be somehow reading the signals all wrong, that he was not feeling loss, but something quite different.

"I loved it, sir," I said.

"Yes," he said. "So do I."

Dean Matthews is wrong. I have fought with memory my whole practicum only to find that it is not the enemy at all, and being an historian is not some saintly burden after all. Because Dunworthy is not blinking against the fatal sunlight of the last morning, but into the gloom of that first afternoon, looking in the great west doors of St Paul's at what is, like Langby, like all of it, every moment, in us, saved forever.

At The "Me" Shop

Robert Reed

Robert Reed (b. 1956) is another of those writers, like Greg Egan and Peter Hamilton, whose imagination works on a vast scale. His ninth novel Marrow *(2000) is written on a huge canvas of worlds within worlds.* The Dragons of Springplace *(1999) is an excellent showcase of his mind-expanding short fiction. It does not include the following, which is one of his lesser-known stories. In some ways it's a further aspect of time travel, and though it may seem a very moderate story by Reed's standards, in another way it is of infinite possibilities.*

The first customer was a small man, old but in a lean, muscled way. He wore fluorescent shorts and a self-cooling shirt, gel socks and bright scarlet shoes. He came through the door smiling – like someone familiar with this place, thought the boy – then stopped in front of the counter, the smile brightening.

"Hello, sir," said the boy. "How are you this morning?"

"Warm, thanks."

"I bet." The boy spread his hands on top of the glass counter. "Are you a runner?"

"Sometimes. And I bet you're new here, am I right?"

"This is my first day," the boy agreed. "I came here early, in order to learn –"

"– the particulars."

The boy blinked. "Yes. The particulars."

"Your very first day. Congratulations." The customer nodded with gravity, bright eyes dancing beneath the white sweatband and silver-white hair. Then came a noise from the back – a single wet cough – and the man said, "I've already got an appointment. Actually it's my birthday. Bennett?"

The boy touched the light-sensitive keys on the old terminal, reading what appeared on the yellowed screen. "Mr Willard Bennett?"

"In the flesh."

There were standing appointments for today and the next twenty years. Had the owner mentioned Mr. Bennett? He must have, thought the boy. It seemed familiar – the name; the circumstance – yet he couldn't recall the specifics.

"How's your first day going? Anything eventful?"

Eventful? Not particularly. But these first hours had been pleasant, the boy sitting alone inside a little room next to the workshop, watching old digitals that taught him the basics of this job. The owner had said no more than a dozen words to him. A quiet man, and gruff, he believed. But someone worthy of respect. An eventful first day? Starting now, he told himself. My first customer . . . !

"I've been coming here for thirty-six birthdays," said the old man. "I haven't missed one yet."

"Well . . . congratulations."

"Thank you."

The boy liked Mr Bennett. But then again, he had a cheery, gregarious nature. He liked everyone. An optimist by nature, he took pride in his ceaseless good spirits.

"Oh, and happy birthday," he added.

"Thanks." One eye winked. "I know the routine, so I'll just show myself into the back –"

"Of course, sir. Please do."

For an old man, he had spryness, practically skipping through the swinging door. With a loud voice he called out, "Yates, I'm here. Thought I'd die in the winter, didn't you? Thought I wouldn't make it, am I right?"

Mr Yates, the owner, replied with a growl. Then the door swung shut, and the boy heard nothing but the faint traces of a conversation. Was there anything to do now? He looked

at the front room, bright and populated with simple plastic
chairs, then he looked outside. A flitter was parked in their
lot – the owner's – and the traffic on the old avenue was
sparse. "Prepare to be bored," Mr Yates had warned him.
"This neighborhood is shit, just like the economy."

A negative man, by nature, and the boy couldn't help but
feel sorry for him. The lack of business probably was in
response to his sourness. It was a good thing the boy was
hired. He brought optimism and a fresh outlook. He imagined the next weeks and months, bringing in new customers and winning Mr Yates' approval . . . helping
wherever possible, making The "Me" Shop thrive –

– and now he saw a flitter pull into the parking lot. A
second customer, and they hadn't been open ten minutes!

A middle-aged woman emerged, hands clenched and a
practised kind of wariness showing in her features. She
paused, then entered. "Excuse me?"

"Yes, ma'am. How can I help you?"

She straightened, staring at him for a long moment. "Do
I . . . talk to you?"

"Yes, ma'am."

"Well," she stated, "it's about hiring your service. I've
done it before, elsewhere, but it's been a long time. If I
could ask questions –"

"The process is completely safe," he assured.

"I'm wondering about rates. What will it cost me?"

She was perhaps fifty years old and not well-off. The boy
sensed that from her flitter, dingy and one front fender
crushed, and from the faded clothes that seemed meant for a
smaller woman.

"Do you understand the process?" he inquired.

"I don't understand the *science*, of course."

"I could explain the basics, if you care to hear them."

She shrugged her shoulders, apparently indifferent.

The boy recounted what he had learned this morning.
The mind, he said, was a vast sponge absorbing every
sensory input and every sense of *self*. He told how during
the last century, during primitive surgery, it was found that
weak stimulation of the cortex caused near-perfect memories to emerge. The brain was like a sponge that let nothing

escape, and the technology employed here could extract any portion of any past self. From a week ago, or forty years ago. It was accomplished with a set of glued-on electrodes and sophisticated chips worn on the head. Like a sweatband, he explained. Not at all cumbersome or unattractive.

The woman watched him, her expression distant and subdued.

Something fell in the workshop. *Baam.*

Floating holo projectors created images of a given *self*, said the boy. The product's quality could be enhanced with old photographs or digitals; or, thinking of Mr Bennett, if you were a regular client whose neural maps were on record.

"I want myself as a ten-year-old," she interrupted.

"That's a popular age. People like to meet themselves as –"

"How much?"

The boy touched the keyboard. "For the initial work . . . two hundred new dollars. Then fifty dollars for each hour's use, plus the deposit, refundable and covering the equipment." He knew the rates by heart, but reading them from the screen seemed to give them added validity. "If not a deposit, then a line of credit. After three hours the rates drop, and overnight is a flat fee. Negotiable, it says."

The woman seemed disheartened. "Could my ten year-old self hold anything? An ice cream cone, for instant?"

"I'm sorry. Projections have no substance. However, we could make a projection of an ice cream cone –"

"At the World of Self," she interrupted, "they use robots, not holos. Robots that do anything."

"I wouldn't know about other shops, ma'am."

She blinked and sighed.

She'd already been to World of Self, he realized. Wherever that was. But robots sounded like expensive propositions, complicated and requiring much maintenance. He felt confident, telling her, "You can't do better than our rates, ma'am."

She offered no rebuttal.

"You and your child-self can interact," he assured her. "She'll appear quite normal. A speaker in the projector will give her an authentic voice, and she'll perceive her sur-

roundings. And she'll have the memories you possessed at
her age, too." The process was akin to hypnosis; a past
identity was conjured up from the unconscious. "You can
ask her questions. She'll likely ask you some. She'll even be
able to learn – the chips you wear will learn, actually – and
that way you can return someday and take her out again,
starting where you left off."

"When I was ten," she said, "my mother took me to the
park and bought me a vanilla ice cream cone."

He felt unsure of himself, smiling for lack of better.

"A special day." She made the statement with authority,
then added, "I deserve a nice day. That's what I want."

"Of course," he said.

"I know the precise date."

"That helps."

The woman said, "I don't want her to know who I am.
You can do that, right? Can you make her think of me as an
aunt?"

"Like with hypnosis," he said, "we can implant suggestions. Anything you wish."

She stepped close to the counter, asking, "What now?"

"I'll open an account."

"Thank you." She stared at his hands.

"Name?"

"Susan Markle."

"Age?"

She didn't answer, lifting her eyes. "How old are you?"

"Eighteen," he replied.

She nodded in a vague way. "Do you like working here?"

"Very much. Although it's my first day –"

"Is it?"

"But I'm interested in the business. I'm trying to save
money, actually. I want to buy my own shop –"

"Fifty-three," she interrupted.

"Pardon?"

"That's my age."

The owner emerged from the worship and glanced at the
Susan Markle, his expression moving from surprise to
suspicion. He was an average height, thick-chested with

a broad gut. Save for a solitary twist of brown hair leftover from some long-ago chemical assault, he had gone completely bald. His face was ruddy, red eyes and a puffy nose marred with a lacework of exploded veins. A slender, silverish headband rode his skin – "I wear it for demonstration purposes," he had explained – and his thick abrasive voice seemed to fill the room. "What's the story?" he asked, never looking at the boy.

The boy explained what the woman wanted, her file number and the amount of time paid for. Ms Markle watched them, eyes leaping back and forth. Sometimes the boy felt her gaze, and it made him uneasy.

Suddenly various Mr Bennetts emerged. The authentic one came first, holding the door for the others. Each man was dressed in the same running garb, bright and cheery. The youngest one was perhaps thirty-five and heavyset. Five projections, total. The real Mr Bennett giggled, saying, "Here we are, ladies and gentlemen! The annual Bennett birthday bash!"

Ms Markle shook her head, staring at the odd parade.

"Come on back, lady," said the owner. "We've got to get started."

The boy bristled at his tone. Harshness invited trouble, particularly with a new client, and he did his best to soften the moment. "Ma'am," he said, waving an arm. "Just follow him, and enjoy yourself."

She nodded and went through the doorway.

The various Bennetts jumped out of her way. They seemed equally authentic, except the next-to-oldest one became pale when he stood near the windows, sunshine beaming in on him. The real Bennett approached the counter, asking, "Can you guess the tradition?"

"A birthday run?"

"A race. Ten miles." The old man nodded happily. "Thirty-six years of coming here and racing myself. That fat one? I ran circles around him, and I had such a good time that I made my reservations till the end of the century."

The owner had returned, needing some tool that he'd left beside the keyboard. "You're an idiot, Bennett. It's a furnace out there."

The old man offered an indifferent grin. "We'll manage. Won't we, friends?"

The projections said, "Fine," and "Great!" and "What heat?" The chubby one's voice sputtered, his audio not working properly. The boy made a mental note to suggest doing some general maintenance; then Mr Yates growled:

"Just don't use me when you die!"

Mr Bennett shrugged and glanced at the boy. "Always the grouch. That's another part of the tradition."

The owner gave a forced laugh, then vanished into the back.

"Let's go," said the second-youngest Bennett. He was the leanest of them, legs strong and the skin overly tanned. The mind remembered the fitness of the body, the tautness of the flesh, plus the general mood. This was a cockier, quicker version of the man. "Ten miles," he told the boy. "My PR is sixty minutes, two seconds. And I'm breaking it today."

"I doubt it," the real Bennett laughed. "But you're welcome to try."

The boy wished them luck. It seemed like a lovely idea, racing your one-time selves . . . and the real Mr Bennett opened the outer door for the others. They moved into the parking lot, stretching their calves and hamstrings while talking to each other. It was just like a real race, complete with everyone punching buttons on identical sports watches. Past selves would interface with the current conditions. Weather. Terrain. The lack of water. They lined up on the sidewalk, and the cocky Mr Bennett forced his way to the front. Then after a momentary pause came the collective:

"GO!"

In a tangle of flesh and flesh-colored light, the annual race had begun, streaking up the nearly empty street and out of sight.

"First we'll buy ice cream –"

"*I don't want to!*" The image of a little girl emerged from the back, her face sour and the voice booming. "And who are you? I don't know you!"

Ms Markle muttered, "I'm your aunt . . . dear."

"Where's my mom? I want my mom!"

Mr Yates stood in the doorway, watching without care or even amusement. When the woman glanced at him, he shrugged as if to ask, "What do you want from me?"

"Fix this," she said, pointing to her little-girl self.

"I want to go home. Now!"

She was halfway pretty, and the image was sharp. She almost looked real, down to blood coursing through her face and the whitish knuckles showing within her fists. She was wearing a feminine dress, lacy and colorful, but the dress only made her seem more bratty. The boy felt uneasy, reminding himself that children could be difficult, projected or real.

"I want my mom!"

The owner grudgingly touched buttons on a portable control panel, freezing the little girl with her mouth open, her teeth and tongue showing. "Okay. She thinks you're her aunt?"

"That's what I asked for, isn't it?"

"A family friend would be easier," the man warned.

Easier for the mind to accept, the boy understood. Particularly if the subject hadn't like her aunts –

"Go on. Just make her nice . . . somehow . . ."

The owner paused and looked at her, his expression intense. What was wrong? Taking a deep breath, he said, "I can do anything you want, lady. Except change the past."

It was an attempt to wound, and it worked.

The poor woman stepped backwards, blinked and straightened and then glanced at the boy, something about her expression again making him uneasy. Then with a calm, reasoned voice, she said, "All right. Just please do the best you can."

"Who doesn't?"

The woman said nothing.

"To me," the boy interjected, "the girl seems sensitive. That's all."

Ms Markle turned and asked, "What was that?"

"Sensitive," he repeated, smiling now. "Artistic people

have trouble adjusting through projections. Their old
selves find themselves in a strange place, and because
they're more sensitive . . . well, they respond like this.
Don't they, sir?" He was asking the owner to substantiate
his fabrication. The man almost smiled, then nodded with
careless authority. "Yeah, that's what it is."

The woman watched the interplay between them.

Then Mr Yates pressed a final button, saying, "Try
this."

The little girl blinked and looked about for a moment,
puzzled but not uneasy. Her eyes settled on Ms Markle, and
a less-shrill voice asked, "Where are we, ma'am?"

"On an errand, dear."

The girl nodded soberly.

"Would you like ice cream? It's a warm day."

"What flavor ice cream?"

"Any flavor you want."

"Maybe," she allowed.

"Let's go outside, shall we?" The woman gestured, and
the girl walked to the front door, pausing instinctively
before trying to open it.

Ms Markle pulled on the handle, saying, "There you
go."

"They don't have wheels," the girl observed.

"Flitters don't, dear."

"Which one is yours?"

"This one."

"You've got an ugly flitter."

The woman paused in the doorway, staring at the child
and then the bare floor. Then she followed the child outdoors, her face watery and tired, sad in a tough, accus-
tomed-to-sadness fashion. It occurred to the boy that she
was more transparent than the girl, ready to evaporate in
the sunshine and the heat.

The owner coughed, eyes narrowed and almost looking at
him. He seemed ready to say something, then didn't. He
went back into the workshop without a word.

Quite a day! Two customers already, and six projections!
Maybe this wasn't the best neighborhood, but they did
seem busy. Ms Markle drove off, and the boy watched the

sparse traffic and the buildings across the street – all weathered, some vacant – and to him the world seemed lovely, impossibly and effortlessly beautiful. The beauty came in the quality of the light spilling over him, making him want to sing . . . a song he'd heard just the other day, light and quick and perfect . . .

"Quit it!" the owner shouted through the closed door. "No singing!"

Half a dozen notes into the song, and the boy was already cut off. Somehow he wasn't surprised . . . and that surprised him. Somehow he knew that the old grouch would stop him. Yet he didn't let it ruin his mood, humming the tune under his breath and smiling regardless.

The next customers had an established account. In their early forties, they were a married couple. The man did the talking, knowing what he wanted and speaking with an amused precision. The boy tried to act professional throughout. He made a habit of saying, "Yes, sir." He said, "I understand, sir. Of course." The wife made no sound, standing beside the windows with her arms crossed.

Mr Yates emerged from the workshop once the order was set.

"It seems busy," the boy mentioned. "We've only been open for an hour –"

"A fluke," he was warned. "It'll grind to nothing this afternoon."

The male customer made small talk about the heat, sometimes winking at his wife on the sly.

Mr Yates was trying to appear more friendly. More relaxed. Turning to the boy at one point, he said, "I'll need help here. Come on back." Then he held the door for everyone.

The boy walked behind the woman. She was pretty, he was thinking. Not as old-looking as some forty-plus women. She had heavy breasts and clinging clothes, and he found himself watching her rump as she strolled down the hallway.

Her husband noticed, giving him a little knowing wink.

The couple knew the routine. They sat on old padded

chairs in the middle of the workshop, banks of equipment beside them. The owner set the silverish bands on their heads, then he brought out two holo projectors, setting them on human-high stands. The projectors were heart-sized. They glittered despite age, humming with unequal tones as numbers were fed to them. The boy had the woman's parameters. It was exciting and rather nerve-racking – his first chance with this work – yet it seemed to come naturally to him. At home with this job, he only occasionally referred to the troubleshooting guide.

Mr Yates and the boy sat along one wall, triggering light-sensitive buttons; their subjects remained nearly motion-less, as if they were sitting in an old-fashioned photographic studio, allowing a slow camera to absorb their images. Their younger selves were produced from memory and coherent light. Two figures became four.

Almost done, Mr Yates said, "Hell, it's almost lunch," and pulled open a desk drawer, removing a bottle and pouring liquor into a big coffee cup. "Close enough."

Drinking seemed inappropriate, yet the boy was profes-sional enough to say and show nothing.

The wife seemed uneasy with her younger self. The projection had formed around the stand, then it detached itself. It was dressed exactly like her, and beneath the clinging clothes was the complete illusion of her body. Breasts and nipples; even the brown-blonde pubic hair. Added details cost more money. The entire package was priced under the *Adult* guidelines.

The young couple whispered and cuddled, indifferent to the others.

"Which room?" asked the husband, rising to his feet.

"I don't care." Mr Yates sipped from the coffee cup.

The wife rose and said, "I need to use the bathroom."

"Sure," said her husband. "Go on."

The boy watched her disappear into a tiny room, the door shut and locked. Then her husband told their projections, "Go on back. First room on the right."

The projections giggled and began to walk arm-in-arm.

"And don't wait for us!"

The man had a coarse laugh, almost embarrassing to hear.

Mr Yates sat motionless. He stared at his desk and the cup, even after the husband asked, "How busy are you?"

The boy said, "We've been rather busy," to fill the silence.

He was thinking about the women. He imagined them naked, and he couldn't help but hold his breath, imagining how they would feel and what the younger one must be doing now. That room's door had been left open; he wished he could see around the corner. He thought he heard little gasps, and for an instant, no longer, he saw the smooth teasing shape of a bare leg, shaved and shining under the fluorescent lights.

The husband stared at him. After a moment he laughed, asking, "Hey, why don't you join us? You don't look busy now."

The boy blinked and shuddered.

The man turned. "What do you think, Yates? Let the boy have some fun for a change, why don't you?"

Mr Yates narrowed his eyes, perplexed and then astonished by the request. Then with a quiet, scalding voice, he said, "Shut up."

The woman emerged from the bathroom, water running behind her.

"Hey, it's a joke, for Christ's sake." The man shook his head, telling everyone, "Just a joke."

"What did you say?" asked his wife.

"Just get on with it," said Mr Yates. "You're on the clock."

The wife looked at the boy, somehow understanding. Then she informed her husband, "You're sick —"

"A stupid joke!"

The boy said nothing.

The husband asked, "How long's it been, kid?"

"*Shut up!*"

The shout startled everyone, including Mr Yates. He had shouted, almost rising from behind his desk. His face was full of blood and emotion, dark eyes glaring, big hands closed into fists.

"Hey, all right," said the husband. "Sorry."

Mr Yates said nothing else.

The boy felt embarrassed for him, and saddened.

"Come on," coaxed the wife. "Let's get this over with . . ."

And the husband, following her to the makeshift bed-room, said, "'Let's get this over with'? What kind of attitude is that? Christ Almighty, what's the matter with you?"

More liquor was poured into the cup, then Yates placed the bottle back into its deep drawer. "You need to get up front," said the thick voice.

"Yes, sir."

The man rose, using his arms to steady himself. The boy thought to sniff at the air, searching for the tell-tale stink of alcohol. Yet he couldn't decide what he was smelling, if anything. How odd.

Mr Yates opened the door.

"I hope business stays good," the boy said gamely.

The door swung shut, and from behind it came a bitter, "Yeah, right." All the emotion and life were wrung out of that tired voice.

The boy walked across the sunny room, pausing at a window. Outside, waiting patiently beside the street, was the first Mr Bennett. It had been a little longer than an hour, the boy realized. He saw the glistening of fictional sweat and the strong quick breaths following great exertion. He admired the vibrancy of the figure, the day obviously uncomfortable . . . and he felt a momentary ache, wonder-ing about the real Mr Bennett struggling through such awful weather . . .

A second figure arrived a few minutes later, speaking to the first one while gasping. What was he saying? Both examined their watches, then they shook each other's hands, congratulating themselves.

A third image appeared a little later. The oldest of the projections – Mr Bennett when he was sixty – showed up next, badly winded but otherwise strong. He removed his shirt and wiped himself, sweat continuing to pour out of him. Again the figures congratulated each other, shaking hands, rubbing the oldest man's bright gray hair.

The pudgy Mr Bennett walked the last blocks, on the verge of collapse. Two others shuffled toward him and took him under the arms, light lifting light, and the boy saw the alarming whiteness of the fat puffy face and the trembling of the weak legs.

Where was the real Mr Bennett?

He worried, feeling responsible for some part of this game. What if something had gone wrong? He activated the intercom with a wave of his hand, saying, "There might be a problem. Sir?"

There was no response. Not even a grunt.

The boy turned and started for the workshop. Only he couldn't bring himself to push at the door, standing back from it with both hands raised; and it burst open, the red-faced owner asking him, "What's the matter? What happened?"

The boy turned and saw no one beside the street. "They were there," he began. "Where did they go?"

"*They've extinguished!*"

Could they have? He looked again, recalling that "extinguished" meant two possibilities. The electronics had been dislodged from Mr. Bennett, or he was dead. Mere unconsciousness didn't extinguish projections. But if they had extinguished, he thought, shouldn't the holo projectors be floating in the bright sunshine?

Mr Yates ran as if for the first time in years, charging outdoors. Too late the boy thought to follow him. The door had swung closed . . . and besides, shouldn't someone remain here? In case of a phone call . . .

Mr Yates stopped at the street, hands shielding his eyes from the glare. After a moment he cupped the hands around his mouth and shouted at someone or something, hands muddying the words.

A cluster of Mr Bennetts walked into view. Mr Yates kept shouting at them. Even when they were close, he roared, panic mixed with rage. "What the fuck were you thinking? At your age! In this goddamn furnace! You die and your family sues me blind . . . damn you, you bastard . . ."

The real Mr Bennett was surrounded by projections.

Mr Yates opened the door, letting everyone inside. "Idiot. Trying to kill yourself –!"

"I got tired and walked," said the old man, his voice firm and angry. He wiped his face with his shirt, saying with some dignity, "I'm sorry if I worried you."

"Crazy shit!"

"No," said the old man, "I'm not the crazy one here."

Nobody spoke for a long moment.

Then the boy said, "It was nice of you to go back and find him."

He meant the projections. They nodded simultaneously, with identical motions; and the fastest one said, "It was my idea."

The two men scarcely noticed the conversation. They were staring at the floor beneath each other's feet, faces working, both of them wrestling with their tempers and conflicting emotions.

Finally Mr Bennett reached for his sweatband, removing it and the silvery band beneath it.

"Sorry to worry you," he told Mr Yates.

The projections softened and vanished without complaint.

"I wasn't trying to worry anyone," the old man promised.

"But you did." Mr Yates rocked on his feet, his balance uneven. He looked very much like a man drunk and accustomed to being drunk. The boy knew the symptoms, having seen them in his father.

"Go home," Mr Yates growled.

The holo projectors were floating head-high, humming softly.

Mr Bennett nodded and said, "All right." He set the metal band on the glass countertop, then looked at the boy for a long moment. He was shaking his head, ready to say something. But instead he merely turned and went outdoors, waving his hands in the air as if trying to brush away tensions and anything else that he might remember.

Mr Yates started for the workshop, and the boy slipped after him. He was through the door before it closed, and the man turned, surprised and then angry. But he couldn't speak before the boy told him, "He's an important customer. You can't lose him. I'm sorry, sir, but you're making an awful mistake".

"Shut up." Mr Yates lifted a hand, closing it and opening it, then putting it down again. "Just shut up."

"Sir," said the boy, "I know I shouldn't say anything. But I just think if you –"

"Had a better attitude? Tried to be optimistic and friendly?" He glared at his employee with an intense, indecipherable expression. Both hands lifted, and he laid them on his face, pulling hard while making a low harsh sobbing noise that seemed to linger. "You don't know anything about me. What do you know?"

He was right. The man was a virtual stranger.

"The neighborhood slides, but you wait. You keep thinking it's going to turn around, but then it's too late and you can't afford to pull out and start again. And the business keeps drying up. Year after year."

The boy didn't speak or move.

"There's the chains. House of Self. Mirror, Inc. Fancy places with their fancy mannequins . . . costing fortunes, but they get by through volume. They've got all the whistles and bells."

Yates retreated to his desk and broke the seal on a fresh bottle, halfway filling his coffee cup while the boy lingered nearby. He watched the man drinking, twin rivulets of liquor running down his chin; then he wiped his face with a hand and wiped the hand against his shirt, saying, "You don't know shit. I've lost bigger clients than old Bennett. A whole lot bigger. Don't ever, ever tell *me* what's important."

The boy made a low sound.

"Anyway, Bennett'll be back. Next year, like clockwork." Yates forced a laugh, saying, "If he doesn't blow an artery first . . ."

"Maybe this isn't a good location," the boy allowed, "but if you were to clean up around here –"

"– And clean myself up too? And act optimistic? Like you?" The man didn't quite look at the boy's face, glaring at a point directly beside it. "That's what you were going to say."

He did seem to be reading the boy's thoughts, yes, and the boy felt naive and foolish. And young. Just eighteen, he reminded himself.

There was a noise from the tiny back room. He had forgotten the other clients . . .

Mr Yates poured another drink.

"Success," said the boy, "takes sacrifice and discipline."

Laughing, Mr Yates shook his head. His silver band glittered under the fluorescent lights. "So that's the secret, huh?"

The boy didn't answer.

"I never get tired of you, kid."

What did he mean?

"You're bright, and you'll go far. Believe me."

Why did the words bother him so much?

"You sure will go places." Mr. Yates nodded and turned away, drinking and then setting the cup down. It nearly tipped and spilled. "A smart kid, and popular at school. I bet you're saving for college. Getting ready to conquer the world and all that . . ."

"Sir?"

The man was staring at the banks of machinery.

"Sir? I'm glad that you've given me this chance. And I certainly wish you well in the future. I do." He paused, then said, "But I think it would be best if I left. If I resigned. I hope this won't be too much of an inconvenience for you."

The man was laughing, then the laugh broke down into hard coughs.

"I'm very sorry." The boy turned and walked down the hallway, stopping at the swinging door. He lifted a hand and made himself push, using all of his strength. The door refused to move. He thought he could feel the worn slick wood under his fingers. It was locked, he decided. Who locked it? He turned and started to say, "Could you please –?"

Mr Yates was touching the silver band on his head, a syrupy voice asking, "Who the hell is going to work as cheap as you?"

"Sir?"

"But hey," said the man, "if you've got to quit . . ."

The boy shivered, unable to understand why. He felt perspiration on his face, cold and salty; and like Mr Yates, he wiped his face with a hand and then dried the hand on his shirt . . . watching the man pull at the band . . . thinking what . . . what . . . ?

The owner, a gruff sloppy-voiced man named Mr Yates, took him into a small back room and had him sit on a small bed. He believed he could feel the bed. He believed he was a new employee. Mr Yates plugged a digital into a little television. "Now watch," he grumbled. Mr Yates was in the digital – a younger version of him – and he spoke to the long-ago camera, showing less weight and more hair and acting quite different. Not so gruff, certainly. And his voice was smoother, dressed up in a steady, almost gentle smile.

The boy was to work the rest of the afternoon and into the evening. There might be customers after dark, Mr Yates promised. Customers who would use this room. The flesh-and-blood man said, "Remind me to change the sheets. It smells like a whorehouse in here."

"I don't smell anything," the boy interjected.

Mr Yates stared at the young man on the screen.

"I could change these sheets, sir."

"I doubt it." He shook his head. "No, just go up front. Greet people and set up accounts, then help me if I need you. Soon as you get through this introductory crap."

Which seemed familiar, the boy thought.

Mr Yates left; the digital quit. The boy walked out into the workshop, finding the owner drinking from a coffee cup. "I'm ready to begin, sir."

The man nodded and rose to his feet. For an instant it looked as if he would fall. Should I catch him? thought the boy. Is he ill?

Yet Mr Yates managed to open the swinging door for him – a nice gesture – and he left the boy in charge of the counter, already trusting him. Taking his station, the boy was alert and eager, watching the sporadic traffic and the glare of the lowering sun. What was the date? For a moment he couldn't recall, then he found it displayed on the register. It was Spring, he realized. Yet it appeared quite hot outside . . . and for a moment he was trying to recall coming here. Did he drive here? He couldn't remember being outdoors, yet he must have been and he just wasn't thinking . . . probably nervous, what with the new job . . . and the questions dissolved away, leaving him with a slight sense of unease.

Eventually an old flitter turned into the parking lot, two figures emerging from the driver's side. It was a woman and a little girl, the girl wearing a summery dress. She was a projection, he realized. A very good image, sharp and colorful. The woman held the door for her younger self, and the girl skipped into the room, giggling and saying, "Hello, there. We just came from the park."

"You did?"

"And had a wonderful time," said the woman.

"Yes, yes! We did!"

"I held the ice cream cone for her," the woman reported. "She said it tasted like vanilla —"

"It was good."

"— but of course she wasn't really licking it."

"Yes, I did," the girl protested.

"Yes, you did," said the woman. "I'm teasing, dear."

"I'm glad you had a good time," the boy told them. He began to search for the account, the keyboard responding to his opaque fingertips. "We want everyone to enjoy themselves. Absolutely."

"Well, thank you," said the woman. "For helping to convince me —"

"Excuse me, ma'am?"

"You know, you are a nice person. All day long I kept thinking that really you're . . . well, a lovely young man. I can tell."

"Ma'am?"

The woman blinked, aware that something was wrong.

"I just started working here," the boy explained. "Are you confusing me with another clerk?"

"Perhaps." She nodded, becoming amused and then curious. Then she asked, "Where is Mr Yates?"

"In the back. Shall I call him?"

"No, I'll find him." She glanced at the girl, asking, "Can you stay with this nice young man? For a minute?"

"Hurry back," the girl implored.

"Oh, I will."

The boy and girl spoke for a few moments. The girl described the park – a lagoon sprinkled with toy boats; a flower garden with the "hugest" flowers she'd ever seen. Then the woman, Susan Markle, returned and looked at them for a long interval, finally saying, "Will you follow me, please? Something is wrong."

The owner had fallen asleep with his face down on the desktop. He had spilled coffee, papers soaked and darkened; and he snored with a calm, wet sound.

"The poor man," the woman said, sounding sad and a little angry.

The boy was embarrassed for Mr Yates.

Ms Markle sighed and asked, "Do you know me at all?"

"No, ma'am."

"We've never met?"

"I don't believe so."

"Mr Yates is a good friend of mine," she assured him. "A close friend. Do you know how to use this equipment?"

He had just learned, he explained. But he felt confident.

"Because this is what we'll do." Her face smiled, and her little hands fondled the silver bands both her and Yates were wearing. "I know how it is to have a lousy day."

She was speaking to Mr Yates.

"You're not so awful," she told him, "and you can't fool me."

The little girl played with her new friend – a nine year-old version of the owner – chasing him through the workshop and the back rooms. Ms Markle had turned the CLOSED sign on the front door, locking it. She said it was all right. Mr Yates would approve, and besides, how could he work in his current condition?

The boy had done most of the work himself. Ms Markle had volunteered to position the holo projectors, but setting parameters was his job. The nine year-old boy was easy. (A good thing the man was already wearing the electronics.) The teenage version of Ms Markle was second. She was a slender girl, almost pretty. Why she was needed the boy didn't understand, but Ms. Markle asked him to speak with her, to keep her company. And they discovered common ground, exchanging school stories and the like. The boy admitted that he wanted to open his own place someday; it was a booming technology full of potential. He found himself boasting about his merits – his optimism and drive – and the young Ms Markle never made a negative sound. She didn't even tease him. Nodding, she seemed to absorb everything he said; and sometimes, for moments, it was as if she was a real person. He forgot her origin, some part of him accepting her as a new friend.

Mr Yates woke in the early evening.

By then the little girl and boy were tired, napping in a back room, curling up together like spoons on the rumpled, undented sheets.

Mr Yates growled and sat upright too quickly, his head unsteady. He coughed several times, gunk in his throat, then he spat into a wastecan and blinked, staring at the the three figures.

"What the fuck?"

He reached for the band on his bare head, but Ms Markle slapped his hand. "Now, don't."

"Lady," he muttered, "what're you doing?"

"Having a party," she reported. Her voice was happy, yet beneath it was a warning. A grim intent. "The others are asleep –"

"What others? What do you want?"

She explained the circumstances – how she had found him; how his new assistant had helped; how she had lied, painting them as friends – then she added, "But look at them! They've become fast friends."

"You shut me down? You're putting my equipment through wear-and-tear? What in hell do you want, lady?"

She stood up straight, saying, "A party could do you some good."

"Shit." With both hands, he reached for his headband.

"What if I pay you?" she asked.

"Huh?"

"All of this is my treat. Why not?"

"Because you're dead in the water, lady." Yet his hands paused, then dropped. "I took a risk with your credit as it was . . ."

The boy made a sound. A low soft groan.

Faces turned toward him, and he said, "I can pay. I've saved up quite a bit, and if you want –"

"Shut up," said Mr Yates.

The boy swallowed and glanced at the woman. "Let me help."

She looked ready to laugh.

"Let me," he repeated.

Mr Yates shook his head. He said, "Fuck," and stared straight ahead, his eyes empty. Exhausted.

After a minute, he asked, "If we have a party, can I drink?"

"A little," Ms Markle cautioned.

"Okay, then."

The teenage Ms Markle leaned toward the boy, whispering, "Is there someplace we can go? And talk?"

"Up front?"

She shrugged her shoulders, as if to say, "Good enough."

They rose and walked to the swinging door, pushing and pushing; then a fifth hand joined them, the door opening.

"Behave," warned Ms Markle. She held it for them, laughing to herself.

The boy turned and looked back into the workshop. Mr Yates sat behind his desk, drinking from his coffee cup while looking at the woman. He felt sick, sick and trapped. But the boy sensed a fatigued and slender hopefulness too.

The door swung closed again.

He and the girl began to talk again, then dance, humming some of the same songs as they spun across the dirty floor. In his arms she felt warm and firm and effortlessly alive. Impossible, of course, but he enjoyed the sensation, smiling as he gazed through the windows. Across the street was a line of clean and tall new buildings – *odd, I don't remember*

them – and standing in the little parking lot was an old
couple, holding hands and watching them as they danced, a
soft colored light spilling over the world and the boy closing
his eyes, making one great wish.

Vinland the Dream

Kim Stanley Robinson

*Kim Stanley Robinson (b. 1952) is best known for his
Martian books* Red Mars *(1992),* Green Mars *(1993)
and* Blue Mars *(1996) and the follow-up collection* The
Martians *(1999). He is one of the discoveries of Damon
Knight, with his first two stories appearing in* Orbit #18
in 1975. His first book, The Wild Shore *(1984), was the
start of his Orange County trilogy, and looked at survivors of a world-wide disaster who lived on in an enclave
in California. Other books include* Icehenge *(1984),*
The Memory of Whiteness *(1985) and the wildly
funny* Escape from Kathmandu *(1989). Some of his
early stories were collected as* Remaking History
(1991), including the following.

*A*bstract. It was sunset at L'Anse aux Meadows. The
water of the bay was still, the boggy beach was dark in
the shadows. Flat arms of land pointed to flat islands
offshore; beyond these a taller island stood like a loaf of
stone in the sea, catching the last of the day's light. A stream
gurgled gently as it cut through the beach bog. Above the
bog, on a narrow grassy terrace, one could just make out a
pattern of low mounds, all that remained of sod walls. Next
to them were three or four sod buildings, and beyond the
buildings, a number of tents.

A group of people – archeologists, graduate students,
volunteer laborers, visitors – moved together onto a rocky
ridge overlooking the site. Some of them worked at starting

a campfire in a ring of blackened stones; others began to
unpack bags of food, and cases of beer. Far across the water
lay the dark bulk of Labrador. Kindling caught and their
fire burned, a spark of yellow in the dusk's gloom.

Hot dogs and beer, around a campfire by the sea; and yet
it was strangely quiet. Voices were subdued. The people on
the hill glanced down often at the site, where the head of
their dig, a lanky man in his early fifties, was giving a brief
tour to their distinguished guest. The distinguished guest
did not appear pleased.

Introduction. The head of the dig, an archeology professor from McGill University, was looking at the distinguished guest with the expression he wore when
confronted by an aggressive undergraduate. The distinguished guest, Canada's Minister of Culture, was asking
question after question. As she did, the professor took
her to look for herself, at the forge, and the slag pit, and
the little midden beside Building E. New trenches were
cut across the mounds and depressions, perfect rectangular cuts in the black peat; they could tell the minister
nothing of what they had revealed. But she had insisted
on seeing them, and now she was asking questions that
got right to the point, although they could have been
asked and answered just as well in Ottawa. Yes, the
professor explained, the fuel for the forge was wood
charcoal, the temperature had gotten to around twelve
hundred degrees Celsius, the process was direct reduc-
tion of bog ore, obtaining about one kilogram of iron for
every five kilograms of slag. All was as it was in other
Norse forges – except that the limonites in the bog ore
had now been precisely identified by spectroscopic analysis; and that analysis had revealed that the bog iron
smelted here had come from northern Quebec, near
Chicoutimi. The Norse explorers, who had supposedly
smelted the bog ore, could not have obtained it.

There was a similar situation in the midden; rust migrated in peat at a known rate, and so it could be determined
that the many iron rivets in the midden had only been there
a hundred and forty years, plus or minus fifty.

"So," the minister said, in English with a Francophone lilt. "You have proved your case, it appears?"

The professor nodded wordlessly. The minister watched him, and he couldn't help feeling that despite the nature of the news he was giving her, she was somewhat amused. By him? By his scientific terminology? By his obvious (and growing) depression? He couldn't tell.

The minister raised her eyebrows. "L'Anse aux Meadows, a hoax. Parcs Canada will not like it at all."

"No one will like it," the professor croaked.

"No," the minister said, looking at him. "I suppose not. Particularly as this is part of a larger pattern, yes?"

The professor did not reply.

"The entire concept of Vinland," she said. "A hoax!"

The professor nodded glumly.

"I would not have believed it possible."

"No," the professor said. "But –" he waved a hand at the low mounds around them "– so it appears." He shrugged. "The story has always rested on a very small body of evidence. Three sagas, this site, a few references in Scandinavian records, a few coins, a few cairns. . . ." He shook his head. "Not much." He picked up a chunk of dried peat from the ground, crumbled it in his fingers.

Suddenly the minister laughed at him, then put her hand to his upper arm. Her fingers were warm. "You must remember it is not your fault."

He smiled wanly. "I suppose not." He liked the look on her face; sympathetic as well as amused. She was about his age, perhaps a bit older. An attractive and sophisticated Quebeçois. "I need a drink," he confessed.

"There's beer on the hill."

"Something stronger. I have a bottle of cognac I haven't opened yet . . ."

"Let's get it and take it up there with us."

Experimental Methods. The graduate students and volunteer laborers were gathered around the fire, and the smell of roasting hot dogs filled the air. It was nearly eleven, the sun a half hour gone, and the last light of the summer dusk slowly leaked from the sky. The fire burned like a beacon.

Beer had been flowing freely, and the party was beginning to get a little more boisterous.

The minister and the professor stood near the fire, drinking cognac out of plastic cups.

"How did you come to suspect the story of Vinland?" the minister asked as they watched the students cook hot dogs.

A couple of the volunteer laborers, who had paid good money to spend their summer digging trenches in a bog, heard the question and moved closer.

The professor shrugged. "I can't quite remember." He tried to laugh. "Here I am an archeologist, and I can't remember my own past."

The minister nodded as if that made sense. "I suppose it was a long time ago?"

"Yes." He concentrated. "Now what was it. Someone was following up the story of the Vinland map, to try and figure out who had done it. The map showed up in a bookstore in New Haven in the 1950s – as you may know?"

"No," the minister said. "I hardly know a thing about Vinland, I assure you. Just the basics that anyone in my position would have to know."

"Well, there was a map found in the 1950s called the Vinland map, and it was shown to be a hoax soon after its discovery. But when this investigator traced the map's history, she found that the book it had been in was accounted for all the way back to the 1820s, map and all. It meant the hoaxer had lived longer ago than I had expected." He refilled his cup of cognac, then the minister's. "There were a lot of Viking hoaxes in the nineteenth century, but this one was so early. It surprised me. It's generally thought that the whole phenomenon was stimulated by a book that a Danish scholar published in 1837, containing translations of the Vinland sagas and related material. The book was very popular among the Scandinavian settlers in America, and after that, you know . . . a kind of twisted patriotism, or the response of an ethnic group that had been made fun of too often. . . . So we got the Kensington stone, the halberds, the mooring holes, the coins. But if a hoax predated *Antiquitates Americanae* . . . it made me wonder."

"If the book itself were somehow involved?"

"Exactly," the professor said, regarding the minister with pleasure. "I wondered if the book might not incorporate, or have been inspired by, hoaxed material. Then one day I was reading a description of the field work here, and it occurred to me that this site was a bit too pristine. As if it had been built but never lived in. Best estimates for its occupation were as low as one summer, because they couldn't find any trash middens to speak of, or graves."

"It could have been occupied very briefly," the minister pointed out.

"Yes, I know. That's what I thought at the time. But then I heard from a colleague in Bergen that the *Gronlendinga Saga* was apparently a forgery, at least in the parts referring to the discovery of Vinland. Pages had been inserted that dated back to the 1820s. After that, I had a doubt that wouldn't go away."

"But there are more Vinland stories than that one, yes?"

"Yes. There are three main sources. The *Gronlendinga Saga*, *The Saga of Erik the Red*, and the part of *The Hauksbók* that tells about Thorfinn Karlsefni's expedition. But with one of those questioned, I began to doubt them all. And the story itself. Everything having to do with the idea of Vinland."

"Is that when you went to Bergen?" a graduate student asked.

The professor nodded. He drained his plastic cup, felt the alcohol rushing through him. "I joined Nielsen there and we went over *Erik the Red* and *The Hauksbók*, and damned if the pages in those concerning Vinland weren't forgeries too. The ink gave it away – not its composition, which was about right, but merely how long it had been on that paper. Which was thirteenth-century paper, I might add! The forger had done a super job. But the sagas had been tampered with sometime in the early nineteenth-century."

"But those are masterpieces of world literature," a volunteer laborer exclaimed, round-eyed; the ads for volunteer labor had not included a description of the primary investigator's hypothesis.

"I know," the professor said irritably, and shrugged.

He saw a chunk of peat on the ground, picked it up and threw it on the blaze. After a bit it flared up.

"It's like watching dirt burn," he said absently, staring into the flames.

Discussion. The burnt-garbage smell of peat wafted downwind, and offshore the calm water of the bay was riffled by the same gentle breeze. The minister warmed her hands at the blaze for a moment, then gestured at the bay. "It's hard to believe they were never here at all."

"I know," the professor said. "It looks like a Viking site, I'll give him that."

"Him," the minister repeated.

"I know, I know. This whole thing forces you to imagine a man in the eighteen twenties and thirties, traveling all over – Norway, Iceland, Canada, New England, Rome, Stockholm, Denmark, Greenland . . . Criss-crossing the North Atlantic, to bury all these signs." He shook his head. "It's incredible."

He retrieved the cognac bottle and refilled. He was, he had to admit, beginning to feel drunk. "And so many parts of the hoax were well hidden! You can't assume we've found them all. This place had two butternuts buried in the midden, and butternuts only grow down below the St Lawrence, so who's to say they aren't clues, indicating another site down there? That's where grapevines actually grow, which would justify the name Vinland. I tell you, the more I know about this hoaxer, the more certain I am that other sites exist. The tower in Newport, Rhode Island, for instance – the hoaxer didn't build that, because it's been around since the seventeenth century – but a little work out there at night, in the early nineteenth century . . . I bet if it were excavated completely, you'd find a few Norse artifacts."

"Buried in all the right places," the minister said.

"Exactly." The professor nodded. "And up the coast of Labrador, at Cape Porcupine where the sagas say they repaired a ship. There too. Stuff scattered everywhere, left to be discovered or not."

The minister waved her plastic cup. "But surely this site

must have been his masterpiece. He couldn't have done too many as extensive as this."

"I shouldn't think so." The professor drank deeply, smacked his numbed lips. "Maybe one more like this, down in New Brunswick. That's my guess. But this was surely one of his biggest projects."

"It was a time for that kind of thing," the volunteer laborer offered. "Atlantis, Mu, Lemuria. . . ."

The minister nodded. "It fulfills a certain desire."

"Theosophy, most of that," the professor muttered. "This was different."

The volunteer wandered off. The professor and the minister looked into the fire for a while.

"You are *sure?*" the minister asked.

The professor nodded. "Trace elements show the ore came from upper Quebec. Chemical changes in the peat weren't right. And unclear resonance dating methods show that the bronze pin they found hadn't been buried long enough. Little things like that. Nothing obvious. He was amazingly meticulous, he really thought it out. But the nature of things tripped him up. Nothing more than that."

"But the effort!" the minister said. "This is what I find hard to believe. Surely it must have been more than one man! Burying these objects, building the walls – surely he would have been noticed!"

The professor stopped another swallow, nodded at her as he choked once or twice. A broad wave of the hand, a gasping recovery of breath:

"Fishing village, kilometer north of here. Boarding house in the early nineteenth century. A crew of ten rented rooms in the summer of 1842. Bills paid by a Mr Carlsson."

The minister raised her eyebrows. "Ah."

One of the graduate students got out a guitar and began to play. The other students and the volunteers gathered around her.

"So," the minister said, "Mr Carlsson. Does he show up elsewhere?"

"There was a Professor Ohman in Bergen. A Dr Bergen in Reykjavik. In the right years, studying the sagas. I presume they were all him, but I don't know for sure."

"What do you know about him?"

"Nothing. No one paid much attention to him. I've got him on a couple transatlantic crossings, I think, but he used aliases, so I've probably missed most of them. A Scandinavian-American, apparently Norwegian by birth. Someone with some money – someone with patriotic feelings of some kind – someone with a grudge against a university – who knows? All I have are a few signatures, of aliases at that. A flowery handwriting. Nothing more. That's the most remarkable thing about him! You see, most hoaxers leave clues to their identities, because a part of them wants to be caught. So their cleverness can be admired, or the ones who fell for it embarrassed, or whatever. But this guy didn't want to be discovered. And in those days, if you wanted to stay off the record . . ." He shook his head.

"A man of mystery."

"Yeah. But I don't know how to find out anything more about him."

The professor's face was glum in the firelight as he reflected on this. He polished off another cup of cognac. The minister watched him drink, then said kindly, "There is nothing to be done about it, really. That is the nature of the past."

"I know."

Conclusions. They threw the last big logs on the fire, and flames roared up, yellow licks breaking free among the stars. The professor felt numb all over, his heart was cold, the firelit faces were smeary primitive masks, dancing in the light. The songs were harsh and raucous, he couldn't understand the words. The wind was chilling, and the hot skin of his arms and neck goosepimpled uncomfortably. He felt sick with alcohol, and knew it would be a while before his body could overmaster it.

The minister led him away from the fire, then up the rocky ridge. Getting him away from the students and laborers, no doubt, so he wouldn't embarrass himself. Starlight illuminated the heather and broken granite under their feet. He stumbled. He tried to explain to her what it meant, to be an archeologist whose most important work was the discovery that a bit of their past was a falsehood.

"It's like a mosaic," he said, drunkenly trying to follow the fugitive thought. "A puzzle with most of the pieces gone. A tapestry. And if you pull a thread out . . . it's ruined. So little lasts! We need every bit we can find!"

She seemed to understand. In her student days, she told him, she had waitressed at a café in Montreal. Years later she had gone down the street to have a look, just for nostalgia's sake. The café was gone. The street was completely different. And she couldn't remember the names of any of the people she had worked with. "This was my own past, not all that many years ago!"

The professor nodded. Cognac was rushing through his veins, and as he looked at the minister, so beautiful in the starlight, she seemed to him a kind of muse, a spirit sent to comfort him, or frighten him, he couldn't tell which. Cleo, he thought. The muse of history. Someone he could talk to.

She laughed softly. "Sometimes it seems our lives are much longer than we usually think. So that we live through incarnations, and looking back later we have nothing but . . ." She waved a hand.

"Bronze pins," the professor said. "Iron rivets."

"Yes." She looked at him. Her eyes were bright in the starlight. "We need an archeology for our own lives."

Acknowledgments. Later he walked her back to the fire, now reduced to banked red coals. She put her hand to his upper arm as they walked, steadying herself, and he felt in the touch some kind of portent; but couldn't understand it. He had drunk so much! Why be so upset about it, why? It was his job to find the truth; having found it, he should be happy! Why had no one told him what he would feel?

The minister said goodnight. She was off to bed; she suggested he do likewise. Her look was compassionate, her voice firm.

When she was gone he hunted down the bottle of cognac, and drank the rest of it. The fire was dying, the students and workers scattered – in the tents, or out in the night, in couples.

He walked by himself back down to the site.

Low mounds, of walls that had never been. Beyond the actual site were rounded buildings, models built by the park service, to show tourists what the "real" buildings had looked like. When Vikings had camped on the edge of the new world. Repairing their boats. Finding food. Fighting among themselves, mad with epic jealousies. Fighting the dangerous Indians. Getting killed, and then driven away from this land, so much lusher than Greenland.

A creak in the brush and he jumped, startled. It would have been like that: death in the night, creeping up on you – he turned with a jerk, and every starlit shadow bounced with hidden skraelings, their bows drawn taut, their arrows aimed at his heart. He quivered, hunched over.

But no. It hadn't been like that. Not at all. Instead, a man with spectacles and a bag full of old junk, directing some unemployed sailors as they dug. Nondescript, taciturn, nameless; one night he would have wandered back there into the forest, perhaps fallen or had a heart attack – become a skeleton wearing leathers and swordbelt, with spectacles over the skull's eyesockets, the anachronism that gave him away at last . . . The professor staggered over the low mounds toward the trees, intent on finding that inadvertent grave . . .

But no. It wouldn't be there. The taciturn figure hadn't been like that. He would have been far away when he died, nothing to show what he had spent years of his life doing. A man in a hospital for the poor, the bronze pin in his pocket overlooked by the doctor, stolen by an undertaker's assistant. An anonymous figure, to the grave and beyond. The creator of Vinland. Never to be found.

The professor looked around, confused and sick. There was a waist-high rock, a glacial erratic. He sat on it. Put his head in his hands. Really quite unprofessional. All those books he had read as a child. What would the minister think! Grant money. No reason to feel so bad!

At that latitude midsummer nights are short, and the party had lasted late. The sky to the east was already gray. He could see down onto the site, and its long sod roofs. On the beach, a trio of long narrow high-ended ships. Small figures in furs emerged from the longhouses and went down to the water, and he walked among them and heard their speech, a sort of dialect of Norwegian that he could mostly understand. They would leave that day, it was time to load the ships. They were going to take everything with them, they didn't plan to return. Too many skraelings in the forest, too many quick arrow deaths. He walked among them, helping them load stores. Then a little man in a black coat scurried behind the forge, and he roared and took off after him, scooping up a rock on the way, ready to deal out a skraeling death to that black intruder.

The minister woke him with a touch of her hand. He almost fell off the rock. He shook his head; he was still drunk. The hangover wouldn't begin for a couple more hours, though the sun was already up.

"I should have known all along," he said to her angrily. "They were stretched to the limit in Greenland, and the climate was worsening. It was amazing they got that far. Vinland –" he waved a hand at the site "– was just some dreamer's story."

Regarding him calmly, the minister said, "I am not sure it matters."

He looked up at her. "What do you mean?"

"History is made of stories people tell. And fictions, dreams, hoaxes – they also are made of stories people tell. True or false, it's the stories that matter to us. Certain qualities in the stories themselves make them true or false."

He shook his head. "Some things really happened in the past. And some things didn't."

"But how can you know for sure which is which? You can't go back and see for yourself. Maybe Vinland was the invention of this mysterious stranger of yours; maybe the Vikings came here after all, and landed somewhere else. Either way it can never be anything more than a story to us."

"But . . ." He swallowed. "Surely it matters whether it is a true story or not!"

She paced before him. "A friend of mine once told me something he had read in a book," she said. 'It was by a man who sailed the Red Sea, long ago. He told of a servant boy on one of the dhows, who could not remember ever having been cared for. The boy had become a sailor at age three – before that, he had been a beach-comber." She stopped pacing and looked at the beach below them. "Often I imagined that little boy's life. Surviving alone on a beach, at that age – it astonished me. It made me . . . happy."

She turned to look at him. "But later I told this story to an expert in child development, and he just shook his head. 'It probably wasn't true,' he said. Not a lie, exactly, but a . . ."

"A stretcher," the professor suggested.

"A stretcher, exactly. He supposed that the boy had been somewhat older, or had had some help. You know."

The professor nodded.

"But in the end," the minister said, "I found this judgment did not matter to me. In my mind I still saw that toddler, searching the tidepools for his daily food. And so for me the story lives. And that is all that matters. We judge all the stories from history like that – we value them according to how much they spur our imaginations."

The professor stared at her. He rubbed his jaw, looked around. Things had the sharp-edged clarity they sometimes get after a sleepness night, as if glowing with internal light. He said, "Someone with opinions like yours probably shouldn't have the job that you do."

"I didn't know I had them," the minister said. "I only just came upon them in the last couple of hours, thinking about it."

The professor was surprised. "You didn't sleep?"

She shook her head. "Who could sleep on a night like this?"

"My feeling exactly!" He almost smiled. "So. A *nuit blanche*, you call it?"

"Yes," she said. "A *nuit blanche* for two." And she looked down at him with that amused glance of hers, as if . . . as if she understood him.

She extended her arms toward him, grasped his hands, helped pull him to his feet. They began to walk back toward the tents, across the site of L'Anse aux Meadows. The grass was wet with dew, and very green. "I still think," he said as they walked together, "that we want more than stories from the past. We want something not easily found – something, in fact, that the past doesn't have. Something secret, some secret meaning . . . something that will give our lives a kind of sense."

She slipped a hand under his arm. "We want the Atlantis of childhood. But, failing that . . ." She laughed and kicked at a clump of grass; a spray of dew flashed ahead of them, containing, for just one moment, a bright little rainbow.

A Ticket to Tranai

Robert Sheckley

*I am positive that if there were a poll of the top ten sf
writers who emerged in the 1950s, Robert Sheckley would
be very near the top. (I suspect Philip K. Dick would be
at the top and there's a story by him next.) Sheckley (b.
1928) was immensely prolific in the fifties producing
quality stories with facile gay abandon. He was one of
the Horace Gold school of writers. Gold edited* Galaxy
Magazine, *the leading sf magazine of the fifties that
produced the real Golden Age of science fiction. Gold
didn't go for high-tech sf like John W. Campbell at*
Astounding. *He preferred stories built around people
living in the societies produced by the high-tech stuff that
the guys over at* Astounding *were predicting. Often Gold
published satires of future societies, and the following is
one of the best.*

One fine day in June, a tall, thin, intent, soberly dressed
young man walked into the offices of the Transstellar
Travel Agency. Without a glance, he marched past the
gaudy travel poster depicting the Harvest Feast on Mars.
The enormous photomural of dancing forests on Triga-
nium didn't catch his eye. He ignored the somewhat sug-
gestive painting of dawn-rites on Opiuchus II, and arrived
at the desk of the booking agent.

"I would like to book passage to Tranai," the young man
said.

The agent closed his copy of *Necessary Inventions* and

frowned. "Tranai? Tranai? Is that one of the moons of Kent IV?"

"It is not," the young man said. "Tranai is a planet, revolving around a sun of the same name. I want to book passage there."

"Never heard of it." The agent pulled down a star catalogue, a simplified star chart, and a copy of *Lesser Space Routes*.

"Well, now," he said finally. "You learn something new every day. You want to book passage to Tranai, Mister –"

"Goodman. Marvin Goodman."

"Goodman. Well, it seems that Tranai is about as far from Earth as one can get and still be in the Milky Way. *Nobody* goes there."

"I know. Can you arrange passage for me?" Goodman asked, with a hint of suppressed excitement in his voice.

The agent shook his head. "Not a chance. Even the non-skeds don't go that far."

"How close can you get me?"

The agent gave him a winning smile. "Why bother? I can send you to a world that'll have everything this Tranai place has, with the additional advantages of proximity, bargain rates, decent hotels, tours –"

"I'm going to Tranai," Goodman said grimly.

"But there's no way of getting there," the agent explained patiently. "What is it you expected to find? Perhaps I could help."

"You can help by booking me as far as –"

"Is it adventure?" the agent asked, quickly sizing up Goodman's unathletic build and scholarly stoop. "Let me suggest Africanus II, a dawn-age world filled with savage tribes, sabre-tooths, man-eating ferns, quicksand, active volcanoes, pterodactyls and all the rest. Expeditions leave New York every five days and they combine the utmost in danger with absolute safety. A dinosaur head guaranteed or your money refunded."

"Tranai," Goodman said.

"Hmm." The clerk looked appraisingly at Goodman's set lips and uncompromising eyes. "Perhaps you are tired of the puritanical restrictions of Earth? Then let me suggest a trip to Almagordo III, the Pearl of the Southern Ridge Belt. Our ten day all-expense plan includes a trip through the mysterious Almagordian Casbah, visits to eight night-clubs (first drink on us), a trip to a zintal factory, where you can buy genuine zintal belts, shoes and pocketbooks at phenomenal savings, and a tour through two distilleries. The girls of Almagordo are beautiful, vivacious and re-freshingly naive. They consider the Tourist the highest and most desirable type of human being. Also –"

"Tranai," Goodman said. "How close can you get me?"

Sullenly the clerk extracted a strip of tickets. "You can take the *Constellation Queen* as far as Legis II and transfer to the *Galactic Splendor*, which will take you to Oumé. Then you'll have to board a local, which, after stopping at Machang, Inchang, Pankang, Lekung and Oyster, will leave you at Tung-Bradar IV, if it doesn't break down en route. Then a non-sked will transport you past the Galactic Whirl (if it gets past) to Aloomsridgia, from which the mail ship will take you to Bellismoranti. I believe the mail ship is still functioning. That brings you about half-way. After that, you're on your own."

"Fine," Goodman said. "Can you have my forms made out by this afternoon?"

The clerk nodded. "Mr Goodman," he asked in despair, "just what sort of place is this Tranai supposed to be?"

Goodman smiled a beatific smile. "A utopia," he said.

Marvin Goodman had lived most of his life in Seakirk, New Jersey, a town controlled by one political boss or another for close to fifty years. Most of Seakirk's inhabitants were indifferent to the spectacle of corruption in high places and low, the gambling, the gang wars the teenage drinking. They were used to the sight of their roads crumbling, their ancient water mains bursting, their power plants breaking down, their decrepit old buildings falling apart, while the bosses built bigger homes, longer swimming pools and warmer stables. People were used to it. But not Goodman.

A natural-born crusader, he wrote exposé articles that were never published, sent letters to Congress that were never read, stumped for honest candidates who were never elected, and organized the League for Civic Improvement, the People Against Gangsterism, the Citizen's Union for an Honest Police Force, the Association Against Gambling, the Committee for Equal Job Opportunities for Women, and a dozen others.

Nothing came of his efforts. The people were too apathetic to care. The politicoes simply laughed at him, and Goodman couldn't stand being laughed at. Then, to add to his troubles, his fiancée jilted him for a noisy young man in a loud sports jacket who had no redeeming feature other than a controlling interest in the Seakirk Construction Corporation.

It was a shattering blow. The girl seemed unaffected by the fact that the SCC used disproportionate amounts of sand in their concrete and shaved whole inches from the width of their steel girders. As she put it, "Gee whiz, Marvie, so what? That's how things are. You gotta be realistic."

Goodman had no intention of being realistic. He immediately repaired to Eddie's Moonlight Bar, where, between drinks, he began to contemplate the attractions of a grass shack in the green hell of Venus.

An erect, hawk-faced old man entered the bar. Goodman could tell he was a spacer by his gravity-bound gait, his pallor, his radiation scars and his far-piercing gray eyes.

"A Tranai Special, Sam," the old spacer told the bartender.

"Coming right up, Captain Savage, sir," the bartender said.

"Tranai?" Goodman murmured involuntarily.

"Tranai," the captain said. "Never heard of it, did you, sonny?"

"No, sir," Goodman confessed.

"Well, sonny," Captain Savage said, "I'm feeling a mite wordy tonight, so I'll tell you a tale of Tranai the Blessed, out past the Galactic Whirl."

The captain's eyes grew misty and a smile softened the grim line of his lips.

"We were iron men in steel ships in those days. Me and

Johnny Cavanaugh and Frog Larsen would have blasted to hell itself for half a load of terganium. Aye, and shanghaied Beelzebub for a wiper if we were short of men. Those were the days when space scurvy took every third man, and the ghost of Big Dan McClintock haunted the space-ways. Moll Gann still operated the Red Rooster Inn out on Asteroid 342-AA, asking five hundred Earth dollars for a glass of beer, and getting it too, there being no other place within ten billion miles. In those days, the Scarbies were still cutting up along Star Ridge and ships bound for Prodengum had to run the Swayback Gantlet. So you can imagine how I felt, sonny, when one fine day I came upon Tranai."

Goodman listened as the old captain limned a picture of the great days, of frail ships against an iron sky, ships outward bound, forever outward, to the far limits of the Galaxy.

And there, at the edge of the Great Nothing, was Tranai.

Tranai, where The Way had been found and men were no longer bound to The Wheel! Tranai the Bountiful, a peaceful, creative, happy society, not saints or ascetics, not intellectuals, but ordinary people who had achieved utopia.

For an hour, Captain Savage spoke of the multiform marvels of Tranai. After finishing his story, he complained of a dry throat. Space throat, he called it, and Goodman ordered him another Tranai Special and one for himself. Sipping the exotic, green-gray mixture, Goodman too was lost in the dream.

Finally, very gently, he asked, "Why don't you go back, Captain?"

The old man shook his head. "Space gout. I'm grounded for good. We didn't know much about modern medicine in those days. All I'm good for now is a landsman's job."

"What job do you have?"

"I'm a foreman for the Seakirk Construction Corporation," the old man sighed. "Me, that once commanded a fifty-tube clipper. The way those people make concrete . . . Shall we have another short one in honor of beautiful Tranai?"

They had several short ones. When Goodman left the

bar, his mind was made up. Somewhere in the Universe, the *modus vivendi* had been found, the working solution to Man's old dream of perfection.

He could settle for nothing less.

The next day, he quit his job as designer at the East Coast Robot Works and drew his life savings out of the bank.

He was going to Tranai.

He boarded the *Constellation Queen* for Legis II and took the *Galactic Splendor* to Oumé. After stopping at Machang, Inchang, Pankang, Lekung and Oyster – dreary little places – he reached Tung-Bradar IV. Without incident, he passed the Galactic Whirl and finally reached Bellismoranti, where the influence of Terra ended.

For an exorbitant fee, a local spaceline took him to Dvasta II. From there, a freighter transported him past Seves, Olgo and Mi, to the double planet Mvanti. There he was bogged down for three months and used the time to take a hypnopedic course in the Tranaian language. At last he hired a bush pilot to take him to Ding.

On Ding, he was arrested as a Higastomeritreian spy, but managed to escape in the cargo of an ore rocket bound for g'Moree. At g'Moree, he was treated for frostbite, heat poisoning and superficial radiation burns, and at last arranged passage to Tranai.

He could hardly believe it when the ship slipped past the moons Doé and Ri, to land at Port Tranai.

After the airlocks opened, Goodman found himself in a state of profound depression. Part of it was plain letdown, inevitable after a journey such as his. But more than that, he was suddenly terrified that Tranai might turn out to be a fraud.

He had crossed the Galaxy on the basis of an old spaceman's yarn. But now it all seemed less likely. Eldorado was a more probable place than the Tranai he expected to find.

He disembarked. Port Tranai seemed a pleasant enough town. The streets were filled with people and the shops were piled high with goods. The men he passed looked much like humans anywhere. The women were quite attractive.

But there was something strange here, something subtly yet definitely wrong, something *alien*. It took a moment before he could puzzle it out.

Then he realized that there were at least ten men for every woman in sight. And stranger still, practically all the women he saw apparently were under eighteen or over thirty-five.

What had happened to the nineteen-to-thirty-five age group? Was there a taboo on their appearing in public? Had a plague struck them?

He would just have to wait and find out.

He went to the Idrig Building, where all Tranai's governmental functions were carried out, and presented himself at the office of the Extraterrestrials Minister. He was admitted at once.

The office was small and cluttered, with strange blue blotches on the wallpaper. What struck Goodman at once was a high-powered rifle complete with silencer and telescopic sight, hanging ominously from one wall. He had no time to speculate on this, for the Minister bounded out of his chair and vigorously shook Goodman's hand.

The Minister was a stout, jolly man of about fifty. Around his neck he wore a small medallion stamped with the Tranian seal – a bolt of lightning splitting an ear of corn. Goodman assumed, correctly, that this was an official seal of office.

"Welcome to Tranai," the minister said heartily. He pushed a pile of papers from a chair and motioned Goodman to sit down.

"Mister Minister –" Goodman began, in formal Tranian.

"Den Melith is the name. Call me Den. 'We're all quite informal around here. Put your feet up on the desk and make yourself at home. Cigar?'

"No, thank you," Goodman said, somewhat taken back. "Mister – ah – Den, I have come from Terra, a planet you may have heard of."

"Sure I have," said Melith. "Nervous, hustling sort of place, isn't it? No offense intended, of course."

"Of course. That's exactly how I feel about it. The

reason I came here –" Goodman hesitated, hoping he wouldn't sound too ridiculous. "Well, I heard certain stories about Tranai. Thinking them over now, they seem preposterous. But if you don't mind, I'd like to ask you –"

"Ask anything," Melith said expansively. "You'll get a straight answer."

"Thank you. I heard that there has been no war of any sort on Tranai for four hundred years."

"Six hundred," Melith corrected. "And none in sight."

"Someone told me that there is no crime on Tranai."

"None whatsoever."

"And therefore no police force or courts, no judges, sheriffs, marshals, executioners, truant officers or government investigators. No prisons, reformatories or other places of detention."

"We have no need of them," Melith explained, "since we have no crime."

"I have heard," said Goodman, "that there is no poverty on Tranai."

"None that I ever heard of," Melith said cheerfully. "Are you sure you won't have a cigar?"

"No, thank you." Goodman was leaning forward eagerly now. "I understand that you have achieved a stable economy without resorting to socialistic, communistic, fascistic or bureaucratic practices."

"Certainly," Melith said.

"That yours is, in fact, a free enterprise society, where individual initiative flourishes and governmental functions are kept to an absolute minimum."

Melith nodded. "By and large, the government concerns itself with minor regulatory matters, care of the aged and beautifying the landscape."

"Is it true that you have discovered a method of wealth distribution without resorting to governmental intervention, without even taxation, based entirely upon individual choice?" Goodman challenged.

"Oh, yes, absolutely."

"Is it true that there is no corruption in any phase of the Tranaian government?"

"None," Melith said. "I suppose that's why we have a hard time finding men to hold public office."

"Then Captain Savage was right!" Goodman cried, unable to control himself any longer. "This is utopia!"

"We like it," Melith said.

Goodman took a deep breath and asked, "May I stay here?"

"Why not?" Melith pulled out a form. "We have no restrictions on immigration. Tell me, what is your occupation?"

"On Earth, I was a robot designer."

"Plenty of openings in that." Melith started to fill in the form. His pen emitted a blob of ink. Casually, the minister threw the pen against the wall, where it shattered, adding another blue blotch to the wallpaper.

"We'll make out the paper some other time," he said. "I'm not in the mood now." He leaned back in his chair. "Let me give you a word of advice. Here on Tranai, we feel that we have come pretty close to utopia, as you call it. But ours is not a highly organized state. We have no complicated set of laws. We live by observance of a number of unwritten laws, or customs, as you might call them. You will discover what they are. You would be advised – although certainly not ordered – to follow them."

"Of course I will," Goodman exclaimed. "I can assure you, sir, I have no intention of endangering any phase of your paradise."

"Oh, I wasn't worried about *us*," Melith said with an amused smile. "It was your own safety I was considering. Perhaps my wife has some further advice for you."

He pushed a large red button on his desk. Immediately there was a bluish haze. The haze solidified, and in a moment Goodman saw a handsome young woman standing before him.

"Good morning, my dear," she said to Melith.

"It's afternoon," Melith informed her. "My dear, this young man came all the way from Earth to live on Tranai. I gave him the usual advice. Is there anything else we can do for him?"

Mrs Melith thought for a moment, then asked Goodman, "Are you married?"

"No, ma'am," Goodman answered.

"In that case, he should meet a nice girl," Mrs Melith told her husband. "Bachelordom is not encouraged on Tranai, although certainly not prohibited. Let me see . . . How about that cute Driganti girl?"

"She's engaged," Melith said.

"Really? Have I been in stasis *that* long? My dear, it's not too thoughtful of you."

"I was busy," Melith said apologetically.

"How about Mihna Vensis?"

"Not his type."

"Janna Vley?"

"Perfect!" Melith winked at Goodman. "A most attractive little lady." He found a new pen in his desk, scribbled an address and handed it to Goodman. "My wife will telephone her to be expecting you tomorrow evening."

"And do come around for dinner some night," said Mrs Melith.

"Delighted," Goodman replied, in a complete daze.

"It's been nice meeting you," Mrs Melith said. Her husband pushed the red button. The blue haze formed and Mrs Melith vanished.

"Have to close up now," said Melith, glancing at his watch. "Can't work overtime – people might start talking. Drop in some day and we'll make out those forms. You really should call on Supreme President Borg, too, at the National Mansion. Or possibly he'll call on you. Don't let the old fox put anything over on you. And don't forget about Janna." He winked roguishly and escorted Goodman to the door.

In a few moments, Goodman found himself alone on the side-walk. He had reached utopia, he told himself, a real, genuine, sure-enough utopia.

But there were some very puzzling things about it.

Goodman ate dinner at a small restaurant and checked in at a nearby hotel. A cheerful bellhop showed him to his room, where Goodman stretched out immediately on the bed.

Wearily he rubbed his eyes, trying to sort out his impressions.

So much had happened to him, all in one day! And so much was bothering him. The ratio of men to women, for example. He had meant to ask Melith about that.

But Melith might not be the man to ask, for there were some curious things about him. Like throwing his pen against the wall. Was that the act of a mature, responsible official? And Melith's wife . . .

Goodman knew that Mrs Melith had come out of a derrsin stasis field; he had recognized the characteristic blue haze. The derrsin was used on Terra, too. Sometimes there were good medical reasons for suspending all activity, all growth, all decay. Suppose a patient had a desperate need for a certain serum, procurable only on Mars. Simply project the person into stasis until the serum could arrive.

But on Terra, only a licensed doctor could operate the field. There were strict penalties for its misuse.

He had never heard of keeping one's wife in one.

Still, if all the wives on Tranai *were* kept in stasis, that would explain the absence of the nineteen-to-thirty-five age group and would account for the ten-to-one ratio of men to women.

But what was the reason for this technological purdah?

And something else was on Goodman's mind, something quite insignificant, but bothersome all the same.

That rifle on Melith's wall.

Did he hunt game with it? Pretty big game, then. Target practice? Not with a telescopic sight. Why the silencer? Why did he keep it in his office?

But these were minor matters, Goodman decided, little local idiosyncracies which would become clear when he had lived a while on Tranai. He couldn't expect immediate and complete comprehension of what was, after all, an alien planet.

He was just beginning to doze off when he heard a knock at his door.

"Come in," he called.

A small, furtive, gray-faced man hurried in and closed

the door behind him. "You're the man from Terra, aren't you?" "That's right."

"I figured you'd come here," the little man said, with a pleased smile. "Hit it right the first time. Going to stay on Tranai?"

"I'm here for good."

"Fine," the man said. "How would you like to become Supreme President?"

"Huh?"

"Good pay, easy hours, only a one-year term. You look like a public-spirited type," the man said sunnily. "How about it?"

Goodman hardly knew what to answer. "Do you mean," he asked incredulously, "that you offer the highest office in the land so casually?"

"What do you mean, *casually?*" the little man spluttered. "Do you think we offer the Supreme Presidency to just anybody? It's a great honor to be asked."

"I didn't mean –"

"And you, as a Terran, are uniquely suited."

"Why?"

"Well, it's common knowledge that Terrans derive pleasure from ruling. We Tranians don't, that's all. Too much trouble."

As simple as that. The reformer blood in Goodman began to boil. Ideal as Tranai was, there was undoubtedly room for improvement. He had a sudden vision of himself as ruler of utopia, doing the great task of making perfection even better. But caution stopped him from agreeing at once. Perhaps the man was a crackpot.

"Thank you for asking me," Goodman said. "I'll have to think it over. Perhaps I should talk with the present incumbent and find out something about the nature of the work."

"Well, why do you think I'm here?" the little man demanded. "I'm Supreme President Borg."

Only then did Goodman notice the official medallion around the little man's neck.

"Let me know your decision. I'll be at the National Mansion." He shook Goodman's hand, and left.

Goodman waited five minutes, then rang for the bellhop. "Who was that man?"

"That was Supreme President Borg," the bellhop told him. "Did you take the job?"

Goodman shook his head slowly. He suddenly realized that he had a *great* deal to learn about Tranai.

The next morning, Goodman listed the various robot factories of Port Tranai in alphabetical order and went out in search of a job. To his amazement, he found one with no trouble at all, at the very first place he looked. The great Abbag Home Robot Works signed him on after only a cursory glance at his credentials.

His new employer, Mr Abbag, was short and fierce-looking, with a great mane of white hair and an air of tremendous personal energy.

"Glad to have a Terran on board," Abbag said. "I understand you're an ingenious people and we certainly need some ingenuity around here. I'll be honest with you, Goodman – I'm hoping to profit by your alien viewpoint. We've reached an impasse."

"Is it a production problem?" Goodman asked.

"I'll show you." Abbag led Goodman through the factory, around the Stamping Room, Heat-Treat, X-ray Analysis, Final Assembly and to the Testing Room. This room was laid out like a combination kitchen-living room. A dozen robots were lined up against one wall.

"Try one out," Abbag said.

Goodman walked up to the nearest robot and looked at its controls. They were simple enough; self-explanatory, in fact. He put the machine through a standard repertoire: picking up objects, washing pots and pans, setting a table. The robot's responses were correct enough, but maddeningly slow. On Earth, such sluggishness had been ironed out a hundred years ago. Apparently they were behind the times here on Tranai.

"Seems pretty slow," Goodman commented cautiously.

"You're right," Abbag said. "Damned slow. Personally, I think it's about right. But Consumer Research indicates that our customers want it slower still."

"Huh?"

"Ridiculous, isn't it?" Abbag asked moodily. "We'll lose money if we slow it down any more. Take a look at its guts."

Goodman opened the back panel and blinked at the maze of wiring within. After a moment, he was able to figure it out. The robot was built like a modern Earth machine, with the usual inexpensive high-speed circuits. But special signal-delay relays, impulse-rejection units and step-down gears had been installed.

"Just tell me," Abbag demanded angrily, "how can we slow it down any more without building the thing a third bigger and twice as expensive? I don't know what kind of a disimprovement they'll be asking for next."

Goodman was trying to adjust his thinking to the concept of *disimproving* a machine.

On Earth, the plants were always trying to build robots with faster, smoother, more accurate responses. He had never found any reason to question the wisdom of this. He still didn't.

"And as if that weren't enough," Abbag complained, "the new plastic we developed for this particular model has catalyzed or some damned thing. Watch."

He drew back his foot and kicked the robot in the middle. The plastic bent like a sheet of tin. He kicked again. The plastic bent still further and the robot began to click and flash pathetically. A third kick shattered the case. The robot's innards exploded in spectacular fashion, scattering over the floor.

"Pretty flimsy," Goodman said.

"Not flimsy enough. It's supposed to fly apart on the first kick. Our customers won't get any satisfaction out of stubbing their toes on its stomach all day. But tell me, how am I supposed to produce a plastic that'll take normal wear and tear – we don't want these things falling apart accidentally – and still go to pieces when a customer wants it to?"

"Wait a minute," Goodman protested. "Let me get this straight. You purposely slow these robots down so they will irritate people enough to destroy them?"

Abbag raised both eyebrows. "Of course!"

"Why?"

"You *are* new here," Abbag said. "Any child knows that. It's fundamental."

"I'd appreciate it if you'd explain."

Abbag sighed. "Well, first of all, you are undoubtedly aware that any mechanical contrivance is a source of irritation. Human-kind has a deep and abiding distrust of machines. Psychologists call it the instinctive reaction of life to pseudo-life. Will you go along with me on that?"

Marvin Goodman remembered all the anxious literature he had read about machines revolting, cybernetic brains taking over the world, androids on the march, and the like. He thought of humorous little newspaper items about a man shooting his television set, smashing his toaster against the wall, "getting even" with his car. He remembered all the robot jokes, with their undertone of deep hostility.

"I guess I can go along on that," said Goodman.

"Then allow me to restate the proposition," Abbag said pedantically. "Any machine is a source of irritation. The better a machine operates, the stronger the irritation. So, by extension, a *perfectly operating* machine is a focal point for frustration, loss of self-esteem, undirected resentment –"

"Hold on there!" Goodman objected. "I won't go *that* far!"

"– and schizophrenic fantasies," Abbag continued inexorably. "But machines are necessary to an advanced economy. Therefore the best *human* solution is to have malfunctioning ones."

"I don't see that at all."

"It's obvious. On Terra, your gadgets work close to the optimum, producing inferiority feelings in their operators. But unfortunately you have a masochistic tribal tabu against destroying them. Result? Generalized anxiety in the presence of the sacrosanct and unhumanly efficient Machine, and a search for an aggression-object, usually a wife or friend. A very poor state of affairs. Oh, it's efficient, I suppose, in terms of robot-hour production, but very inefficient in terms of long-range health and well-being."

"I'm not sure –"

"The human is an anxious beast. Here on Tranai, we direct anxiety toward this particular point and let it serve as an outlet for a lot of other frustrations as well. A man's had enough – blam! He kicks hell out of his robot. There's an immediate and therapeutic discharge of feeling, a valuable – and valid – sense of superiority over mere machinery, a lessening of general tension, a healthy flow of adrenin into the bloodstream, and a boost to the industrial economy of Tranai, since he'll go right out and buy another robot. And what, after all, has he done? He hasn't beaten his wife, suicided, declared a war, invented a new weapon, or indulged in any of the other more common modes of aggression-resolution. He has simply smashed an inexpensive robot which he can replace immediately."

"I guess it'll take me a little time to understand," Goodman admitted.

"Of course it will. I'm sure you're going to be a valuable man here, Goodman. Think over what I've said and try to figure out some inexpensive way of disimproving this robot."

Goodman pondered the problem for the rest of the day, but he couldn't immediately adjust his thinking to the idea of producing an inferior machine. It seemed vaguely blasphemous. He knocked off work at five-thirty, dissatisfied with himself, but determined to do better – or worse, depending on viewpoint and conditioning.

After a quick and lonely supper, Goodman decided to call on Janna Vley. He didn't want to spend the evening alone with his thoughts and he was in desperate need of finding something pleasant, simple and uncomplicated in this complex utopia. Perhaps this Janna would be the answer.

The Vley home was only a dozen blocks away and he decided to walk.

The basic trouble was that he had had his own idea of what utopia would be like and it was difficult adjusting his thinking to the real thing. He had imagined a pastoral setting, a planetful of people in small, quaint villages, walking around in flowing robes and being very wise and gentle and understanding. Children who played in the golden sunlight, young folk danced in the village square . . .

Ridiculous! He had pictured a tableau rather than a scene, a series of stylized postures instead of the ceaseless movement of life. Humans could never live that way, even assuming they wanted to. If they could, they would no longer be humans.

He reached the Vley house and paused irresolutely outside. What was he getting himself into now? What alien – although indubitably utopian – customs would he run into?

He almost turned away. But the prospect of a long night alone in his hotel room was singularly unappealing. Gritting his teeth, he rang the bell.

A red-haired, middle-aged man of medium height opened the door. "Oh, you must be that Terran fellow. Janna's getting ready. Come in and meet the wife."

He escorted Goodman into a pleasantly furnished living room and pushed a red button on the wall. Goodman wasn't startled this time by the bluish derrsin haze. After all, the manner in which Tranaians treated their women was their own business.

A handsome woman of about twenty-eight appeared from the haze.

"My dear," Vley said, "this is the Terran, Mr Goodman."

"So pleased to meet you," Mrs Vley said. "Can I get you a drink?"

Goodman nodded. Vley pointed out a comfortable chair. In a moment, Mrs Vley brought in a tray of frosted drinks and sat down.

"So you're from Terra," said Mr Vley. "Nervous, hustling sort of place, isn't it? People always on the go?"

"Yes, I suppose it is," Goodman replied.

"Well, you'll like it here. We know how to live. It's all a matter of –"

There was a rustle of skirts on the stairs. Goodman got to his feet.

"Mr Goodman, this is our daughter Janna," Mrs Vley said.

*   *   *

Goodman noted at once that Janna's hair was the exact color of the supernova in Circe, her eyes were that deep, unbelievable blue of the autumn sky over Algo II, her lips were the tender pink of a Scarsclott-Turner jet stream, her nose –

But he had run out of astronomical comparisons, which weren't suitable anyhow. Janna was a slender and amazingly pretty blonde girl and Goodman was suddenly very glad he had crossed the Galaxy and come to Tranai.

"Have a good time, children," Mrs Vley said.

"Don't come in too late," Mr Vley told Janna.

Exactly as parents said on Earth to their children.

There was nothing exotic about the date. They went to an inexpensive night club, danced, drank a little, talked a lot. Goodman was amazed at their immediate *rapport*. Janna agreed with everything he said. It was refreshing to find intelligence in so pretty a girl.

She was impressed, almost overwhelmed, by the dangers he had faced in crossing the Galaxy. She had always known that Terrans were adventurous (though nervous) types, but the risks Goodman had taken passed all understanding.

She shuddered when he spoke of the deadly Galactic Whirl and listened wide-eyed to his tales of running the notorious Swayback Gantlet, past the bloodthirsty Scarbies who were still cutting up along Star Ridge and infesting the hell holes of Prodengum. As Goodman put it, Terrans were iron men in steel ships, exploring the edges of the Great Nothing.

Janna didn't even speak until Goodman told of paying five hundred Terran dollars for a glass of beer at Moll Gann's Red Rooster Inn on Asteroid 342-AA.

"You must have been very thirsty," she said thoughtfully.

"Not particularly," Goodman said. "Money just didn't mean much out there."

"Oh. But wouldn't it have been better to have saved it? I mean someday you might have a wife and children –" She blushed.

Goodman said coolly, "Well, that part of my life is over. I'm going to marry and settle down right here on Tranai."

"How *nice!*" she cried.

It was a most successful evening.

Goodman returned Janna to her home at a respectable hour and arranged a date for the following evening. Made bold by his own tales, he kissed her on the cheek. She didn't really seem to mind, but Goodman didn't try to press his advantage.

"Till tomorrow then," she said, smiled at him, and closed the door.

He walked away feeling light-headed. Janna! Janna! Was it conceivable that he was in love already? Why not? Love at first sight was a proven psycho-physiological possibility and, as such, was perfectly respectable. Love in utopia! How wonderful it was that here, upon a perfect planet, he had found the perfect girl!

A man stepped out of the shadows and blocked his path. Goodman noted that he was wearing a black silk mask which covered everything except his eyes. He was carrying a large and powerful-looking blaster, and it was pointed steadily at Goodman's stomach.

"Okay, buddy," the man said, "gimme all your money."

"What?" Goodman gasped.

"You heard me. Your money. Hand it over."

"You can't do this," Goodman said, too startled to think coherently. "There's no crime on Tranai!"

"Who said there was?" the man asked quietly. "I'm merely asking you for your money. Are you going to hand it over peacefully or do I have to club it out of you?"

"You can't get away with this! Crime does not pay!"

"Don't be ridiculous," the man said. He hefted the heavy blaster.

"All right. Don't get excited." Goodman pulled out his billfold, which contained all he had in the world, and gave its contents to the masked man.

The man counted it, and he seemed impressed. "Better than I expected. Thanks, buddy. Take it easy now."

He hurried away down a dark street.

Goodman looked wildly around for a policeman, until he remembered that there were no police on Tranai. He saw a

small cocktail lounge on the corner with a neon sign saying
Kitty Kat Bar. He hurried into it.

Inside, there was only a bartender, somberly wiping
glasses.

"I've been robbed!" Goodman shouted at him.

"So?" the bartender said, not even looking up.

"But I thought there wasn't any crime on Tranai."

"There isn't."

"But I was *robbed*."

"You must be new here," the bartender said, finally
looking at him.

"I just came in from Terra."

"Terra? Nervous, hustling sort of —"

"Yes, yes," Goodman said. He was getting a little tired of
that stereotype. "But how can there be no crime on Tranai
if I was robbed?"

"That should be obvious. On Tranai, robbery is no
crime."

"But robbery is *always* a crime!"

"What color mask was he wearing?"

Goodman thought for a moment. "Black. Black silk."

The bartender nodded. "Then he was a government tax
collector."

"That's a ridiculous way to collect taxes," Goodman
snapped.

The bartender set a Tranai Special in front of Goodman.
"Try to see this in terms of the general welfare. The
government has to have *some* money. By collecting it this
way, we can avoid the necessity of an income tax, with all its
complicated legal and legislative apparatus. And in terms of
mental health, it's far better to extract money in a short,
quick, painless operation than to permit the citizen to worry
all year long about paying at a specific date."

Goodman downed his drink and the bartender set up
another.

"But," Goodman said, "I thought this was a society
based upon the concepts of free will and individual initiative."

"It is," the bartender told him. "Then surely the gov-

ernment, what little there is of it, has the same right to free
will as any private citizen, hasn't it?"

Goodman couldn't quite figure that out, so he finished
his second drink. "Could I have another of those? I'll pay
you as soon as I can."

"Sure, sure," the bartender said good-naturedly, pouring another drink and one for himself.

Goodman said, "You asked me what color his mask was.
Why?"

"Black is the government mask color. Private citizens
wear white masks."

"You mean that private citizens commit robbery also?"

"Well, certainly! That's our method of wealth distribution. Money is equalized without government intervention,
without even taxation, entirely in terms of individual initiative." The bar-tender nodded emphatically. "And it
works perfectly, too. Robbery is a great leveler, you know."

"I suppose it is," Goodman admitted, finishing his third
drink. "If I understand correctly, then, any citizen can pack
a blaster, put on a mask, and go out and rob."

"Exactly," the bartender said. "Within limits, of
course."

Goodman snorted. "If that's how it works, I can play that
way. Could you loan me a mask? And a gun?"

The bartender reached under the bar. "Be sure to return
them, though. Family heirlooms."

"I'll return them," Goodman promised. "And when I
come back, I'll pay for my drinks."

He slipped the blaster into his belt, donned the mask and
left the bar. If this was how things worked on Tranai, he
could adjust all right. Rob him, would they? He'd rob them
right back and then some!

He found a suitably dark street corner and huddled in the
shadows, waiting. Presently he heard footsteps and, peering
around the corner, saw a portly, well-dressed Tranaian
hurrying down the street.

Goodman stepped in front of him, snarling, "Hold it,
buddy."

The Tranaian stopped and looked at Goodman's blaster.

"Hmmm. Using a wide-aperture Drog 3, eh? Rather an old-fashioned weapon. How do you like it?"

"It's fine," Goodman said. "Hand over your –"

"Slow trigger action, though," the Tranian mused. "Personally, I recommend a Mils-Sleeven needler. As it happens, I'm a sales representative for Sleeven Arms. I could get you a very good price on a trade-in –"

"Hand over your money," Goodman barked.

The portly Tranaian smiled. "The basic defect of your Drog 3 is the fact that it won't fire at all unless you release the safety lock." He reached out and slapped the gun out of Goodman's hand. "You see? You couldn't have done a thing about it." He started to walk away.

Goodman scooped up the blaster, found the safety lock, released it and hurried after the Tranaian.

"Stick up your hands," Goodman ordered, beginning to feel slightly desperate.

"No, no, my good man," the Tranaian said, not even looking back. "Only one try to a customer. Mustn't break the unwritten law, you know."

Goodman stood and watched until the man turned a corner and was gone. He checked the Drog 3 carefully and made sure that all safeties were off. Then he resumed his post.

After an hour's wait, he heard footsteps again. He tightened his grip on the blaster. This time he was going to rob and nothing was going to stop him.

"Okay, buddy," he said, "hands up!"

The victim this time was a short, stocky Tranaian, dressed in old workman's clothes. He gaped at the gun in Goodman's hand.

"Don't shoot, mister," the Tranaian pleaded.

That was more like it! Goodman felt a glow of deep satisfaction.

"Just don't move," he warned. "I've got all safeties off."

"I can see that," the stocky man said cringing. "Be careful with that cannon, mister. I ain't moving a hair."

"You'd better not. Hand over your money."

"Money?"

"Yes, your money, and be quick about it."

"I don't have any money," the man whined. "Mister, I'm a poor man. I'm poverty-stricken."

"There is no poverty on Tranai," Goodman said sententiously.

"I know. But you can get so close to it, you wouldn't know the difference. Give me a break, mister."

"Haven't you any initiative?" Goodman asked. "If you're poor, why don't you go out and rob like everybody else?"

"I just haven't had a chance. First the kid got the whooping cough and I was up every night with her. Then the derrsin broke down, so I had the wife yakking at me all day long. I say there oughta be a spare derrsin in every house! So she decided to clean the place while the derrsin generator was being fixed and she put my blaster somewhere and she can't remember where. So I was all set to borrow a friend's blaster when –"

"That's enough," Goodman said. "This is a robbery and I'm going to rob you of *something*. Hand over your wallet."

The man snuffled miserably and gave Goodman a worn bill-fold. Inside it, Goodman found one deeglo, the equivalent of a Terran dollar.

"It's all I got," the man snuffled miserably, "but you're welcome to it. I know how it is, standing on a drafty street corner all night –"

"Keep it," Goodman said, handing the billfold back to the man and walking off.

"Gee, thanks, mister!"

Goodman didn't answer. Disconsolately, he returned to the Kitty Kat Bar and gave back the bartender's blaster and mask. When he explained what had happened, the bartender burst into rude laughter.

"Didn't have any money! Man, that's the oldest trick in the books. Everybody carries a fake wallet for robberies – sometimes two or even three. Did you search him?"

"No," Goodman confessed.

"Brother, are you a greenhorn!"

"I guess I am. Look, I really will pay you for those drinks as soon as I can make some money."

"Sure, sure," the bartender said. "You better go home and get some sleep. You had a busy night."

Goodman agreed. Wearily he returned to his hotel room and was asleep as soon as his head hit the pillow.

He reported at the Abbag Home Robot Works and manfully grappled with the problem of disimproving automata. Even in unhuman work such as this, Terran ingenuity began to tell.

Goodman began to develop a new plastic for the robot's case. It was a silicone, a relative of the "silly putty" that had appeared on Earth a long while back. It had the desired properties of toughness, resiliency and long wear; it would stand a lot of abuse, too. But the case would shatter immediately and with spectacular effect upon receiving a kick delivered with an impact of thirty pounds or more.

His employer praised him for this development, gave him a bonus (which he sorely needed), and told him to keep working on the idea and, if possible, to bring the needed impact down to twenty-three pounds. This, the research department told them, was the average frustration kick.

He was kept so busy that he had practically no time to explore further the mores and folkways of Tranai. He did manage to see the Citizen's Booth. This uniquely Tranaian institution was housed in a small building on a quiet back street.

Upon entering, he was confronted by a large board, upon which was listed the names of the present officeholders of Tranai, and their titles. Beside each name was a button. The attendant told Goodman that, by pressing a button, a citizen expressed his disapproval of that official's acts. The pressed button was automatically registered in History Hall and was a permanent mark against the officeholder.

No minors were allowed to press the buttons, of course.

Goodman considered this somewhat ineffectual; but perhaps, he told himself, officials on Tranai were differently motivated from those on Earth.

He saw Janna almost every evening and together they explored the many cultural aspects of Tranai: the cocktail lounges and movies, the concert halls, the art exhibitions, the science museum, the fairs and festivals. Goodman carried a blaster and, after several unsuccessful attempts, robbed a merchant of nearly five hundred deeglo.

Janna was ecstatic over the achievement, as any sensible Tranaian girl would be, and they celebrated at the Kitty Kat Bar. Janna's parents agreed that Goodman seemed to be a good provider.

The following night, the five hundred deeglo – plus some of Goodman's bonus money – was robbed back, by a man of approximately the size and build of the bartender at the Kitty Kat, carrying an ancient Drog 3 blaster.

Goodman consoled himself with the thought that the money was circulating freely, as the system had intended.

Then he had another triumph. One day at the Abbag Home Robot Works, he discovered a completely new process for making a robot's case. It was a special plastic, impervious even to serious bumps and falls. The robot owner had to wear special shoes, with a catalytic agent imbedded in the heels. When he kicked the robot, the catalyst came in contact with the plastic case, with immediate and gratifying effect.

Abbag was a little uncertain at first; it seemed too gimmicky. But the thing caught on like wild-fire and the Home Robot Works went into the shoe business as a subsidiary, selling at least one pair with every robot.

This horizontal industrial development was very gratifying to the plant's stockholders and was really more important than the original catalyst-plastic discovery. Goodman received a substantial raise in pay and a generous bonus.

On the crest of his triumphant wave, he proposed to Janna and was instantly accepted. Her parents favored the match; all that remained was to obtain official sanction from the government, since Goodman was still technically an alien.

Accordingly, he took a day off from work and walked down to the Idrig Building to see Melith. It was a glorious spring day of the sort that Tranai has for ten months out of the year, and Goodman walked with a light and springy step. He was in love, a success in business, and soon to become a citizen of utopia.

Of course, utopia could use some changes, for even Tranai wasn't quite perfect. Possibly he should accept the Supreme Presidency, in order to make the needed reforms. But there was no rush . . .

"Hey, mister," a voice said, "can you spare a deeglo?"

Goodman looked down and saw, squatting on the pavement, an unwashed old man, dressed in rags, holding out a tin cup.

"What?" Goodman asked.

"Can you spare a deeglo, brother?" the man repeated in a wheedling voice. "Help a poor man buy a cup of oglo? Haven't eaten in two days, mister."

"This is disgraceful Why don't you get a blaster and go out and rob someone?"

"I'm too old," the man whimpered. "My victims just laugh at me."

"Are you sure you aren't just lazy?" Goodman asked sternly.

"I'm not, sir!" the beggar said. "Just look how my hands shake!"

He held out both dirty paws; they trembled.

Goodman took out his billfold and gave the old man a deeglo. "I thought there was no poverty on Tranai. I understood that the government took care of the aged."

"The government does," said the old man. "Look." He held out his cup. Engraved on its side was: *Government Authorized Beggar, Number DB*-43241–3.

"You mean the government makes you do this?"

"The government *lets* me do it," the old man told him. "Begging is a government job and is reserved for the aged and infirm."

"Why, that's disgraceful!"

"You must be a stranger here."

"I'm a Terran."

"Aha! Nervous, hustling sort of people, aren't you?"

"*Our* government does not let people beg," Goodman said.

"No? What do the old people do? Live off their children? Or sit in some home for the aged and wait for death by boredom? Not here, young man. On Tranai, every old man is assured of a government job, and one for which he needs no particular skill, although skill helps. Some apply for indoor work, within the churches and theatres. Others like the excitement of fairs and carnivals. Personally, I like it outdoors. My job keeps me out in the sunlight and fresh air, gives me mild exercise, and helps me meet many strange and interesting people, such as yourself."

"But *begging!*"

"What other work would I be suited for?"

"I don't know. But – but look at you! Dirty, unwashed, in filthy clothes –"

"These are my working clothes," the government beggar said. "You should see me on Sunday."

"You have other clothes?"

"I certainly do, and a pleasant little apartment, and a season box at the opera, and two Home Robots, and probably more money in the bank than you've seen in your life. It's been pleasant talking to you, young man, and thanks for your contribution. But now I must return to work and suggest you do likewise."

Goodman walked away, glancing over his shoulder at the government beggar. He observed that the old man seemed to be doing a thriving business.

But *begging!*

Really, that sort of thing should be stopped. If he ever assumed the Presidency – and quite obviously he should – he would look into the whole matter more carefully.

It seemed to him that there had to be a more dignified answer.

At the Idrig Building, Goodman told Melith about his marriage plans.

The immigrations minister was enthusiastic.

"Wonderful, absolutely wonderful," he said. "I've known the Vley family for a long time. They're splendid people. And Janna is a girl any man would be proud of."

"Aren't there some formalities I should go through?" Goodman asked. "I mean being an alien and all –"

"None whatsoever. I've decided to dispense with the formalities. You can become a citizen of Tranai, if you wish, by merely stating your intention verbally. Or you can retain Terran citizenship, with no hard feelings. Or you can do both – be a citizen of Terra *and* Tranai. If Terra doesn't mind, we certainly don't."

"I think I'd like to become a citizen of Tranai," Goodman said.

"It's entirely up to you. But if you're thinking about the Presidency, you can retain Terran status and still hold office. We aren't at all stuffy about that sort of thing. One of our most successful Supreme Presidents was a lizard-evolved chap from Aquarella XI."

"What an enlightened attitude!"

"Sure, give everybody a chance, that's our motto. Now as to your marriage – any government employee can perform the ceremonies. Supreme President Borg would be happy to do it, this afternoon if you like." Melith winked. "The old codger likes to kiss the bride. But I think he's genuinely fond of you."

"This afternoon?" Goodman said. "Yes, I *would* like to be married this afternoon, if it's all right with Janna."

"It probably will be," Melith assured him. "Next, where are you going to live after the honeymoon? A hotel room is hardly suitable." He thought for a moment. "Tell you what – I've got a little house on the edge of town. Why don't you move in there, until you find something better? Or stay permanently, if you like it."

"Really," Goodman protested, "you're too generous –"

"Think nothing of it. Have you ever thought of becoming the next immigrations minister? You might like the work. No red tape, short hours, good pay – No? Got your eye on the Supreme Presidency, eh? Can't blame you, I suppose."

Melith dug in his pockets and found two keys. "This is for the front door and this is for the back. The address is stamped right on them. The place is fully equipped, including a brand-new derrsin field generator."

"A derrsin?"

"Certainly. No home on Tranai is complete without a derrsin stasis field generator."

Clearing his throat, Goodman said carefully, "I've been meaning to ask you – exactly what is the stasis field used for?"

"Why, to keep one's wife in," Melith answered. "I thought you knew."

"I did," said Goodman. "But *why?*"

"Why?" Melith frowned. Apparently the question had never entered his head. "Why does one do anything? It's the custom, that's all. And very logical, too. You wouldn't want a woman chattering around you all the time, night and day."

Goodman blushed, because ever since he had met Janna, he had been thinking how pleasant it would be to have her around him all the time, night and day.

"It hardly seems fair to the women," Goodman pointed out.

Melith laughed. "My dear friend, are you preaching the doctrine of equality of the sexes? Really, it's a completely disproved theory. Men and women just aren't the same. They're different, no matter what you've been told on Terra. What's good for men isn't necessarily – or even usually – good for women."

"Therefore you treat them as inferiors," Goodman said, his reformer's blood beginning to boil.

"Not at all. We treat them in a *different* manner from men, but not in an *inferior* manner. Anyhow, they don't object."

"That's because they haven't been allowed to know any better. Is there any law that requires me to keep my wife in the derrsin field?"

"Of course not. The custom simply suggests that you keep her *out* of stasis for a certain minimum amount of time every week. Not fair incarcerating the little woman, you know."

"Of course not," Goodman said sarcastically. "Must let her live *some* of the time."

"Exactly," Melith said, seeing no sarcasm in what Goodman said. "You'll catch on."

Goodman stood up. "Is that all?"

"I guess that's about it. Good luck and all that."

"Thank you," Goodman said stiffly, turned sharply and left.

That afternoon, Supreme President Borg performed the simple Tranaian marriage rites at the National Mansion and afterward kissed the bride with zeal. It was a beautiful ceremony and was marred by only one thing.

Hanging on Borg's wall was a rifle, complete with telescopic sight and silencer. It was a twin to Melith's and just as inexplicable.

Borg took Goodman to one side and asked, "Have you given any further thought to the Supreme Presidency?"

"I'm still considering it," Goodman said. "I don't really want to hold public office –"

"No one does."

"– but there are certain reforms that Tranai needs badly. I think it may be my duty to bring them to the attention of the people."

"That's the spirit," Borg said approvingly. "We haven't had a really enterprising Supreme President for some time. Why don't you take office right now? Then you could have your honeymoon in the National Mansion with complete privacy."

Goodman was tempted. But he didn't want to be bothered by affairs of state on his honeymoon, which was all arranged anyhow. Since Tranai had lasted so long in its present near-utopian condition, it would undoubtedly keep for a few weeks more.

"I'll consider it when I come back," Goodman said.

Borg shrugged. "Well, I guess I can bear the burden a while longer. Oh, here." He handed Goodman a sealed envelope.

"What's this?"

"Just the standard advice," Borg said. "Hurry, your bride's waiting for you!"

"Come on, Marvin!" Janna called. "We don't want to be late for the spaceship."

Goodman hurried after her, into the spaceport limousine.

"Good luck!" her parents cried.

"Good luck!" Borg shouted.

"Good luck!" added Melith and his wife, and all the guests.

On the way to the spaceport, Goodman opened the envelope and read the printed sheet within:

ADVICE TO A NEW HUSBAND

You have just been married and you expect, quite naturally, a lifetime of connubial bliss. This is perfectly proper, for a happy marriage is the foundation of good government. But you must do more than merely wish for it. Good marriage is not yours by divine right. A good marriage must be worked for!

Remember that your wife is a human being. She should be allowed a certain measure of freedom as her inalienable right. We suggest you take her out of stasis at least once a week. Too long in stasis is bad for her orientation. Too much stasis is bad for her complexion and this will be your loss as well as hers.

At intervals, such as vacations and holidays, it's customary to let your wife remain out of stasis for an entire day at a time, or even two or three days. It will do no harm and the novelty will do wonders for her state of mind.

Keep in mind these few common-sense rules and you can be assured of a happy marriage.

– By the Government Marriage Council

Goodman slowly tore the card into little bits, and let them drop to the floor of the limousine. His reforming spirit was now thoroughly aroused. He had known that Tranai was too good to be true. Someone had to pay for perfection. In this case, it was the women.

He had found the first serious flaw in paradise.

"What was that, dear?" Janna asked, looking at the bits of paper.

"That was some very foolish advice." Goodman said. "Dear, have you ever thought – really thought – about the marriage customs of this planet of yours?"

"I don't think I have. Aren't they all right?"

"They are wrong, completely wrong. They treat women like toys, like little dolls that one puts away when one is finished playing. Can't you see that?"

"I never thought about it."

"Well, you can think about it now," Goodman told her, "because some changes are going to be made and they're going to start in our home."

"Whatever you think best, darling," Janna said dutifully. She squeezed his arm. He kissed her.

And then the limousine reached the spaceport and they got aboard the ship.

Their honeymoon on Doé was like a brief sojourn in a flawless paradise. The wonders of Tranai's little moon had been built for lovers, and for lovers only. No businessman came to Doé for a quick rest; no predatory bachelor prowled the paths. The tired, the disillusioned, the lewdly hopeful all had to find other hunting grounds. The single rule on Doé, strictly enforced, was two by two, joyous and in love, and in no other state admitted.

This was one Tranaian custom that Goodman had no trouble appreciating.

On the little moon, there were meadows of tall grass and deep, green forests for walking and cool black lakes in the forests and jagged, spectacular mountains that begged to be climbed. Lovers were continually getting lost in the forests, to their great satisfaction; but not too lost, for one could circle the whole moon in a day. Thanks to the gentle gravity, no one could drown in the black lakes, and a fall from a mountaintop was frightening, but hardly dangerous.

There were, at strategic locations, little hotels with dimly lit cocktail lounges run by friendly, white-haired bartenders. There were gloomy caves which ran deep (but never too deep) into phosphorescent caverns glittering with ice, past sluggish underground rivers in which swam great luminous fish with fiery eyes.

The Government Marriage Council had considered these simple attractions sufficient and hadn't bothered putting in a golf course, swimming pool, horse track or shuffleboard court. It was felt that once a couple desired these things, the honeymoon was over.

Goodman and his bride spent an enchanted week on Doé and at last returned to Tranai.

After carrying his bride across the threshold of their new home, Goodman's first act was to unplug the derrsin generator.

"My dear," he said, "up to now, I have followed all the customs of Tranai, even when they seemed ridiculous to me. But this is one thing I will not sanction. On Terra, I was the founder of the Committee for Equal Job Opportunities for Women. On Terra, we treat our women as equals, as companions, as partners in the adventure of life."

"What a strange concept," Janna said, a frown clouding her pretty face.

"Think about it," Goodman urged. "Our life will be far more satisfying in this companionable manner than if I shut you up in the purdah of the derrsin field. Don't you agree?"

"You know far more than I, dear. You've traveled all over the Galaxy, and I've never been out of Port Tranai. If you say it's the best way, then it must be."

Past a doubt, Goodman thought, she was the most perfect of women.

He returned to his work at the Abbag Home Robot Works and was soon deep in another disimprovement project. This time, he conceived the bright idea of making the robot's joints squeak and grind. The noise would increase the robot's irritation value, thereby making its destruction more pleasing and psychologically more valuable. Mr Abbag was overjoyed with the idea, gave him another pay raise, and asked him to have the disimprovement ready for early production.

Goodman's first plan was simply to remove some of the lubrication ducts. But he found that friction would then wear out vital parts too soon. That naturally could not be sanctioned.

He began to draw up plans for a built-in squeak-and-grind unit. It had to be absolutely life-like and yet cause no real wear. It had to be inexpensive and it had to be small, because the robot's interior was already packed with dis-improvements.

But Goodman found that small squeak-producing units sounded artificial. Larger units were too costly to manu-facture or couldn't be fitted inside the robot's case. He began working several evenings a week, lost weight, and his temper grew edgy.

Janna became a good, dependable wife. His meals were always ready on time and she invariably had a cheerful word for him in the evenings and a sympathetic ear for his difficulties. During the day, she supervised the cleaning of the house by the Home Robots. This took less than an hour and afterward she read books, baked pies, knitted, and destroyed robots.

Goodman was a little alarmed at this, because Janna destroyed them at the rate of three or four a week. Still, everyone had to have a hobby. He could afford to indulge her, since he got the machines at cost.

Goodman had reached a complete impasse when another designer, a man named Dath Hergo, came up with a novel control. This was based upon a counter-gyroscopic prin-ciple and allowed a robot to enter a room at a ten-degree list. (Ten degrees, the research department said, was the most irritating angle of list a robot could assume.) Moreover, by employing a random selection principle, the robot would *lurch*, drunkenly, annoyingly, at irregular intervals – never dropping anything, but always on the verge of it.

This development was, quite naturally, hailed as a great advance in disimprovement engineering. And Goodman found that he could center his built-in squeak-and-grind unit right in the lurch control. His name was mentioned in the engineering journals next to that of Dath Hergo.

The new line of Abbag Home Robots was a sensation.

At this time, Goodman decided to take a leave of absence from his job and assume the Supreme Presidency of Tranai. He felt he owed it to the people. If Terran ingenuity and know-how could bring out improvements in disimprove-ments, they would do even better improving improvements. Tranai was a near-utopia. With his hand on the reins, they could go the rest of the way to perfection.

He went down to Melith's office to talk it over.

"I suppose there's always room for change," Melith said thoughtfully. The immigration chief was seated by the window, idly watching people pass by. "Of course, our present system has been working for quite some time and working very well. I don't know what you'd improve. There's no crime, for example –"

"Because everybody steals. And there's no trouble with old people because the government turns them into beggars. Really, there's plenty of room for change and improvement."

"Well, perhaps," Melith said. "But I think –" he stopped suddenly, rushed over to the wall and pulled down the rifle. "There he is!"

Goodman looked out the window. A man, apparently no different from anyone else, was walking past. He heard a muffled click and saw the man stagger, then drop to the pavement.

Melith had shot him with the silenced rifle.

"What did you do that for?" Goodman gasped.

"Potential murderer," Melith said.

"What?"

"Of course. We don't have any out-and-out crime here, but, being human, we have to deal with the potentiality."

"What did he do to make him a potential murderer?"

"Killed five people," Melith stated.

"But – damn it, man, this isn't fair! You didn't arrest him, give him a trial, the benefit of counsel –"

"How could I?" Melith asked, slightly annoyed. "We don't have any police to arrest people with and we don't have any legal system. Good Lord, you didn't expect me to just let him go on, did you? Our definition of a murderer is a killer of ten and he was well on his way. I couldn't just sit idly by. It's my duty to protect the people. I can assure you, I made careful inquiries."

"It isn't just!" Goodman shouted.

"Who ever said it was?" Melith shouted back. "What has *justice* got to do with utopia?"

"Everything!" Goodman had calmed himself with an effort. "Justice is the basis of human dignity, human desire –"

"Now you're just using words," Melith said, with his usual good-natured smile. "Try to be realistic. We have created a utopia for *human beings*, not for saints who don't need one. We must accept the deficiencies of the human character, not pretend they don't exist. To our way of thinking, a police apparatus and a legal-judicial system all tend to create an atmosphere for crime and an acceptance of crime. It's better, believe me, not to accept the possibility of crime at all. The vast majority of the people will go along with you."

"But when crime does turn up, as it inevitably does –"

"Only the potentiality turns up," Melith insisted stubbornly. "And even that is much rarer than you would think. When it shows up, we deal with it, quickly and simply."

"Suppose you get the wrong man?"

"We can't get the wrong man. Not a chance of it."

"Why not?"

"Because," Melith said, "anyone disposed of by a government official is, by definition and by unwritten law, a potential criminal."

Marvin Goodman was silent for a while. Then he said, "I see that the government has more power than I thought at first."

"It does," Melith said. "But not as much as you now imagine."

Goodman smiled ironically. "And is the Supreme Presidency still mine for the asking?"

"Of course. And with no strings attached. Do you want it?"

Goodman thought deeply for a moment. Did he really want it? Well, someone had to rule. Someone had to protect the people. Someone had to make a few reforms in this utopian madhouse.

"Yes, I want it," Goodman said.

The door burst open and Supreme President Borg rushed in. "Wonderful! Perfectly wonderful! You can move into the National Mansion today. I've been packed for a week, waiting for you to make up your mind."

"There must be certain formalities to go through –"

"No formalities," Borg said, his face shining with perspiration. "None whatsoever. All we do is hand over the Presidential Seal; then I'll go down and take my name off the rolls and put yours on."

Goodman looked at Melith. The immigration minister's round face was expressionless.

"All right," Goodman said.

Borg reached for the Presidential Seal, started to remove it from his neck –

It exploded suddenly and violently.

Goodman found himself staring in horror at Borg's red, ruined head. The Supreme President tottered for a moment, then slid to the floor.

Melith took off his jacket and threw it over Borg's head. Goodman backed to a chair and fell into it. His mouth opened, but no words came out.

"It's really a pity," Melith said. "He was so near the end of his term. I warned him against licensing that new spaceport. The citizens won't approve, I told him. But he was sure they would like to have two spaceports. Well, he was wrong."

"Do you mean – I mean – how – what –"

"All government officials," Melith explained, "wear the badge of office, which contains a traditional amount of tessium, an explosive you may have heard of. The charge is radio-controlled from the Citizens Booth. Any citizen has access to the Booth, for the purpose of expressing his disapproval of the government." Melith sighed. "This will go down as a permanent black mark against poor Borg's record."

"You let the people express their disapproval by blowing up officials?" Goodman croaked, appalled.

"It's the only way that means anything," said Melith. "Check and balance. Just as the people are in our hands, so we are in the people's hands."

"And *that's* why he wanted me to take over his term. Why didn't anyone tell me?"

"You didn't ask," Melith said, with the suspicion of a smile. "Don't look so horrified. Assassination is always possible, you know, on any planet, under any government. We try to make it a constructive thing. Under this system, the people never lose touch with the government, and the government never tries to assume dictatorial powers. And, since everyone knows he can turn to the Citizens Booth, you'd be surprised how sparingly it's used. Of course, there are always hotheads –"

Goodman got to his feet and started to the door, not looking at Borg's body.

"Don't you still want the Presidency?" asked Melith.

"No!"

"That's so like you Terrans," Melith remarked sadly. "You want responsibility only if it doesn't incur risk. That's the wrong attitude for running a government."

"You may be right," Goodman said. "I'm just glad I found out in time."

He hurried home.

His mind was in a complete turmoil when he entered his house. Was Tranai a utopia or a planetwide insane asylum? Was there much difference? For the first time in his life, Goodman was wondering if utopia was worth having. Wasn't it better to strive for perfection than to possess it? To have ideals rather than to live by them? If justice was a fallacy, wasn't the fallacy better than the truth?

Or was it? Goodman was a sadly confused young man when he shuffled into his house and found his wife in the arms of another man.

The scene had a terrible slow-motion clarity in his eyes. It seemed to take Janna forever to rise to her feet, straighten her disarranged clothing and stare at him open-mouthed. The man – a tall, good-looking fellow whom Goodman had never before seen – appeared too startled to speak. He made small, aimless gestures, brushing the lapel of his jacket, pulling down his cuffs.

Then, tentatively, the man smiled.

"Well!" Goodman said. It was feeble enough, under the circumstances, but it had its effect. Janna started to cry.

"Terribly sorry," the man murmured. "Didn't expect you home for hours. This must come as a shock to you. I'm terribly sorry."

The one thing Goodman hadn't expected or wanted was sympathy from his wife's lover. He ignored the man and stared at the weeping Janna.

"Well, what did you expect?" Janna screamed at him suddenly. "I had to! You didn't love me!"

"Didn't love you! How can you say that?"

"Because of the way you treated me."

"I loved you very much, Janna," he said softly.

"You didn't!" she shrilled, throwing back her head. "Just look at the way you treated me. You kept me around all day, every day, doing *housework, cooking, sitting*. Marvin, I could *feel* myself aging. Day after day, the same weary, stupid routine. And most of the time, when you came home, you were too tired to even notice me. All you could talk about was your stupid robots! I was being wasted, Marvin, *wasted*!"

It suddenly occurred to Goodman that his wife was unhinged. Very gently he said, "But, Janna, that's how life is. A husband and wife settle into a companionable situation. They age together side by side. It can't all be high spots –"

"But of course it can! Try to understand, Marvin. It can, on Tranai – for a woman!"

"It's impossible," Goodman said.

"On Tranai, a woman expects a life of enjoyment and pleasure. It's her right, just as men have their rights. She expects to come out of stasis and find a little party prepared, or a walk in the moonlight, or a swim, or a movie." She began to cry again. "But *you* were so smart. *You* had to change it. I should have known better than to trust a Terran."

The other man sighed and lighted a cigarette.

"I know you can't help being an alien, Marvin," Janna said. "But I do want you to understand. Love isn't everything. A woman must be practical, too. The way things were going, I would have been an old woman while all my friends were still young."

"Still young?" Goodman repeated blankly.

"Of course," the man said. "A woman doesn't age in the derrsin field."

"But the whole thing is ghastly," said Goodman. "My wife would still be a young woman when I was old."

"That's just when you'd appreciate a young woman," Janna said.

"But how about you?" Goodman asked. "Would you appreciate an old man?"

"He still doesn't understand," the man said.

"Marvin, *try*. Isn't it clear yet? Throughout your life, you would have a young and beautiful woman whose only desire would be to please you. And when you died – don't look shocked, dear; everybody dies – when you died, I would still be young, and by law I'd inherit all your money."

"I'm beginning to see," Goodman said. "I suppose that's another accepted phase of Tranaian life – the wealthy young widow who can pursue her own pleasures."

"Naturally. In this way, everything is for the best for everybody. The man has a young wife whom he sees only when he wishes. He has his complete freedom and a nice home as well. The woman is relieved of all the dullness of ordinary living and, while she can still enjoy it, is well provided for."

"You should have told me," Goodman complained.

"I thought you knew," Janna said, "since you thought you had a better way. But I can see that you would never have understood, because you're so naive – though I must admit it's one of your charms." She smiled wistfully. "Besides, if I told you, I would never have met Rondo."

The man bowed slightly. "I was leaving samples of Greah's Confections. You can imagine my surprise when I found this lovely young woman *out of stasis*. I mean it was like a storybook tale come true. One never expects old legends to happen, so you must admit that there's a certain appeal when they do."

"Do you love him?" Goodman asked heavily.

"Yes," said Janna. "Rondo cares for me. He's going to keep me in stasis long enough to make up for the time I've lost. It's a sacrifice on his part, but Rondo has a generous nature."

"If that's how it is," Goodman said glumly, "I certainly won't stand in your way. I am a civilized being, after all. You may have a divorce."

He folded his arms across his chest, feeling quite noble. But he was dimly aware that his decision stemmed not so much from nobility as from a sudden, violent distaste for all things Tranaian.

"We have no divorce on Tranai," Rondo said.

"No?" Goodman felt a cold chill run down his spine.

A blaster appeared in Rondo's hand. "It would be too unsettling, you know, if people were always swapping around. There's only one way to change a marital status."

"But this is revolting!" Goodman blurted, backing away. "It's against all decency!"

"Not if the wife desires it. And that, by the by, is another excellent reason for keeping one's spouse in stasis. Have I your permission, my dear?"

"Forgive me, Marvin," Janna said. She closed her eyes. "Yes!"

Rondo leveled the blaster. Without a moment's hesitation, Goodman dived head-first out the nearest window. Rondo's shot fanned right over him.

"See here!" Rondo called. "Show some spirit, man. Stand up to it!"

Goodman had landed heavily on his shoulder. He was up at once, sprinting, and Rondo's second shot scorched his arm. Then he ducked behind a house and was momentarily safe. He didn't stop to think about it. Running for all he was worth, he headed for the spaceport.

Fortunately, a ship was preparing for blastoff and took him to g'Moree. From there he wired to Tranai for his funds and bought passage to Higastomeritreia, where the authorities accused him of being a Ding spy. The charge couldn't stick, since the Dingans were an amphibious race, and Goodman almost drowned proving to everyone's satisfaction that he could breathe only air.

A drone transport took him to the double planet Mvanti, past Seves, Olgo and Mi. He hired a bush pilot to take him to Bellismoranti, where the influence of Terra began. From there, a local spaceline transported him past the Galactic Whirl and, after stopping at Oyster, Lekung, Pankang, Inchang and Machang, arrived at Tung-Bradar IV.

His money was now gone, but he was practically next door to Terra, as astronomical distances go. He was able to work his passage to Oumé, and from Oumé to Legis II. There the Interstellar Travelers Aid Society arranged a berth for him and at last he arrived back on Earth.

Goodman has settled down in Seakirk, New Jersey, where a man is perfectly safe as long as he pays his taxes. He holds the post of Chief Robotic Technician for the Seakirk Construction Corporation and has married a small, dark, quiet girl, who obviously adores him, although he rarely lets her out of the house.

He and old Captain Savage go frequently to Eddie's Moonlight Bar, drink Tranai Specials, and talk of Tranai the Blessed, where The Way has been found and Man is no longer bound to The Wheel. On such occasions, Goodman complains of a touch of space malaria – because of it, he can never go back into space, can never return to Tranai.

There is always an admiring audience on these nights.

Goodman has recently organized, with Captain Savage's help, the Seakirk League to Take the Vote from Women. They are its only members, but as Goodman puts it, when did that ever stop a crusader?

The Exit Door Leads In

Philip K. Dick

I can still remember quite clearly a period, back in the mid-sixties, during which the work of Philip K. Dick (1928–82), which up until then had been appreciated by only a small core within the sf world, suddenly began to be appreciated not only by all those others in the sf world, who hitherto hadn't quite cottoned on to what he was raving about, but by the wider world. And that appreciation grew throughout the seventies, as he acquired a cult status, and into the eighties, especially with the film Blade Runner *(1982) based on his 1968 book* Do Androids Dream of Electric Sheep? *After his death he was held up as the major sf writer of his generation. Well there were plenty of major sf writers in the sixties and seventies and Dick was one of them, but what made his work unique was his total paranoia and the neurotic stories and novels that tumbled out of that. Dick's work was a product of the Cold War era and McCarthyism and by the time he had recycled that fifties paranoia society had turned full circle into the upheaval following Vietnam, Watergate and the many conspiracy theories that fuelled the seventies. The following is one of Dick's last stories and, with his wonderfully absurdist view of a totalitarian society, I thought the story a perfect match for Sheckley's apparent utopia.*

B ob Bibleman had the impression that robots wouldn't look you in the eye. And when one had been in the vicinity small valuable objects disappeared. A robot's idea of order was to stack everything into one pile. Nonetheless, Bibleman had to order lunch from robots, since vending ranked too low on the wage scale to attract humans.

"A hamburger, fries, strawberry shake, and –" Bibleman paused, reading the printout. "Make that a supreme double cheeseburger, fries, a chocolate malt –"

"Wait a minute," the robot said. 'I'm already working on the burger. You want to buy into this week's contest while you're waiting?"

"I don't get the royal cheeseburger," Bibleman said.

"That's right."

It was hell living in the twenty-first century. Information transfer had reached the velocity of light. Bibleman's older brother had once fed a ten-word plot outline into a robot fiction machine, changed his mind as to the outcome, and found that the novel was already in print. He had had to program a sequel in order to make his correction.

"What's the prize structure in the contest?" Bibleman asked.

At once the printout posted all the odds, from first prize down to last. Naturally, the robot blanked out the display before Bibleman could read it.

"What is first prize?" Bibleman said.

"I can't tell you that," the robot said. From its slot came a hamburger, french fries, and a strawberry shake. "That'll be one thousand dollars in cash."

"Give me a hint," Bibleman said as he paid.

"It's everywhere and nowhere. It's existed since the seventeenth century. Originally it was invisible. Then it became royal. You can't get it unless you're smart, although cheating helps and so does being rich. What does the word 'heavy' suggest to you?"

"Profound."

"No, the literal meaning."

"Mass." Bibleman pondered. "What is this, a contest to see who can figure out what the prize is? I give up."

"Pay the six dollars," the robot said, "to cover our costs, and you'll receive an –"

"Gravity," Bibleman broke in. "Sir Isaac Newton. The Royal College of England. Am I right?"

"Right," the robot said. "Six dollars entitles you to a chance to go to college – a statistical chance, at the posted odds. What's six dollars? Pratfare."

Bibleman handed over a six-dollar coin.

"You win," the robot said. "You get to go to college. You beat the odds, which were two trillion to one against. Let me be the first to congratulate you. If I had a hand, I'd shake hands with you. This will change your life. This has been your lucky day."

"It's a setup," Bibleman said, feeling a rush of anxiety.

"You're right," the robot said, and it looked Bibleman right in the eye. "It's also mandatory that you accept your prize. The college is a military college located in Buttfuck, Egypt, so to speak. But that's no problem; you'll be taken there. Go home and start packing."

"Can't I eat my hamburger and drink –"

"I'd suggest you start packing right away."

Behind Bibleman a man and woman had lined up; reflexively he got out of their way, trying to hold on to his tray of food, feeling dizzy.

"A charbroiled steak sandwich," the man said, "onion rings, root beer, and that's it."

The robot said, "Care to buy into the contest? Terrific prizes." It flashed the odds on its display panel.

When Bob Bibleman unlocked the door of his one-room apartment, his telephone was on. It was looking for him.

"There you are," the telephone said.

"I'm not going to do it," Bibleman said.

"Sure you are," the phone said. "Do you know who this is? Read over your certificate, your first-prize legal form. You hold the rank of shavetail. I'm Major Casals. You're under my jurisdiction. If I tell you to piss purple, you'll piss purple. How soon can you be on a transplan rocket? Do you have friends you want to say goodbye to? A sweetheart, perhaps? Your mother?"

"Am I coming back?" Bibleman said with anger. "I mean, who are we fighting, this college? For that matter, what college is it? Who is on the faculty? Is it a liberal arts college or does it specialize in the hard sciences? Is it government-sponsored? Does it offer –"

"Just calm down," Major Casals said quietly.

Bibleman seated himself. He discovered that his hands were shaking. To himself he thought, I was born in the wrong century. A hundred years ago this wouldn't have happened and a hundred years from now it will be illegal. What I need is a lawyer.

His life had been a quiet one. He had, over the years, advanced to the modest position of floating-salesman. For a man twenty-two years old, that wasn't bad. He almost owned his one-room apartment; that is, he rented with an option to buy. It was a small life, as lives went; he did not ask too much and he did not complain – normally – at what he received. Although he did not understand the tax structure that cut through his income, he accepted it; he accepted a modified state of penury the same way he accepted it when a girl would not go to bed with him. In a sense this defined him; this was his measure. He submitted to what he did not like, and he regarded this attitude as a virtue. Most people in authority over him considered him a good person. As to those over whom *he* had authority, that was a class with zero members. His boss at Cloud Nine Homes told him what to do and his customers, really, told him what to do. The government told everyone what to do, or so he assumed. He had very few dealings with the government. That was neither a virtue nor a vice; it was simply good luck.

Once he had experienced vague dreams. They had to do with giving to the poor. In high school he had read Charles Dickens and a vivid idea of the oppressed had fixed itself in his mind to the point where he could see them: all those who did not have a one-room apartment and a job and a high school education. Certain vague place names had floated through his head, gleaned from TV, places like India, where heavy-duty machinery swept up the dying. Once a teaching machine had told him, *You have a good heart*. That amazed him – not that a machine would say so, but that it would say it to him. A girl had told him the same thing. He marveled at this. Vast forces colluding to tell him that he was not a bad person! It was a mystery and a delight.

But those days had passed. He no longer read novels, and the girl had been transferred to Frankfurt. Now he had been set up by a robot, a cheap machine, to shovel shit in the boonies, dragooned by a mechanical scam that was probably pulling citizens off the streets in record numbers. This was not a college he was going to; he had won nothing. He had won a stint at some kind of forced-labor camp, most likely. The exit door leads in, he thought to himself. Which is to say, when they want you they already have you; all they need is the paperwork. And a computer can process the forms at the touch of a key. The H key for hell and the S key for slave, he thought. And the Y key for you.

Don't forget your toothbrush, he thought. You may need it.

On the phone screen Major Casals regarded him, as if silently estimating the chances that Bob Bibleman might bolt. Two trillion to one I will, Bibleman thought. But the one will win, as in the contest; I'll do what I'm told.

"Please," Bibleman said, "let me ask you one thing, and give me an honest answer."

"Of course," Major Casals said.

"If I hadn't gone up to the Earl's Senior robot and –"

"We'd have gotten you anyhow," Major Casals said.

"Okay," Bibleman said, nodding. "Thanks. It makes me feel better. I don't have to tell myself stupid stuff like, If only I hadn't felt like a hamburger and fries. If only – " He broke off. "I'd better pack."

Major Casals said, "We've been running an evaluation on you for several months. You're overly endowed for the kind of work you do. And undereducated. You need more education. You're *entitled* to more education."

Astonished, Bibleman said, "You're talking about it as if it's a genuine college!"

"It is. It's the finest in the system. It isn't advertised; something like this can't be. No one selects it; the college selects you. Those were not joke odds that you saw posted. You can't really imagine being admitted to the finest college in the system by this method, can you, Mr Bibleman? You have a lot to learn."

"How long will I be at the college?" Bibleman said.

Major Casals said, "Until you have learned."

They gave him a physical, a haircut, a uniform, and a place to bunk down, and many psychological tests. Bibleman suspected that the true purpose of the tests was to determine if he were a latent homosexual, and then he suspected that his suspicions indicated that he *was* a latent homosexual, so he abandoned the suspicions and supposed instead that they were sly intelligence and aptitude tests, and he informed himself that he was showing both: intelligence and aptitude. He also informed himself that he looked great in his uniform, even though it was the same uniform that everyone else wore. That is why they call it a uniform, he reminded himself as he sat on the edge of his bunk reading his orientation pamphlets.

The first pamphlet pointed out that it was a great honor to be admitted to the College. That was its name – the one word. How strange, he thought, puzzled. It's like naming your cat Cat and your dog Dog. This is my mother, Mrs Mother, and my father, Mr Father. Are these people working right? he wondered. It had been a phobia of his for years that someday he would fall into the hands of madmen – in particular, madmen who seemed sane up until the last moment. To Bibleman this was the essence of horror.

As he sat scrutinizing the pamphlets, a red-haired girl, wearing the College uniform, came over and seated herself beside him. She seemed perplexed.

"Maybe you can help me," she said. "What is a syllabus? It says here that we'll be given a syllabus. This place is screwing up my head."

Bibleman said, "We've been dragooned off the streets to shovel shit."

"You think so?"

"I know so."

"Can't we just leave?"

"You leave first," Bibleman said. "And I'll wait and see what happens to you."

The girl laughed. "I guess you don't know what a syllabus is."

"Sure I do. It's an abstract of courses or topics."

"Yes, and pigs can whistle."

He regarded her. The girl regarded him.

"We're going to be here forever," the girl said.

Her name, she told him, was Mary Lorne. She was, he decided, pretty, wistful, afraid, and putting up a good front. Together they joined the other new students for a showing of a recent Herbie the Hyena cartoon which Bibleman had seen; it was the episode in which Herbie attempted to assassinate the Russian monk Rasputin. In his usual fashion, Herbie the Hyena poisoned his victim, shot him, blew him up six times, stabbed him, tied him up with chains and sank him in the Volga, tore him apart with wild horses, and finally shot him to the moon strapped to a rocket. The cartoon bored Bibleman. He did not give a damn about Herbie the Hyena or Russian history and he wondered if this was a sample of the College's level of pedagogy. He could imagine Herbie the Hyena illustrating Heisenberg's indeterminacy principle. Herbie – in Bibleman's mind – chased after by a subatomic particle fruitlessly, the particle bobbing up at random here and there . . . Herbie making wild swings at it with a hammer; then a whole flock of subatomic particles jeering at Herbie, who was doomed as always to fuck up.

"What are you thinking about?" Mary whispered to him.

The cartoon ended; the hall lights came on. There stood Major Casals on the stage, larger than on the phone. The fun is over, Bibleman said to himself. He could not imagine Major Casals chasing subatomic particles fruitlessly with wild swings of a sledgehammer. He felt himself grow cold and grim and a little afraid.

The lecture had to do with classified information. Behind Major Casals a giant hologram lit up with a schematic diagram of a homeostatic drilling rig. Within the hologram the rig rotated so that they could see it from all angles. Different stages of the rig's interior glowed in various colors.

"I asked what you were thinking," Mary whispered.

"We have to listen," Bibleman said quietly.

Mary said, equally quietly, "It finds titanium ore on its own. Big deal. Titanium is the ninth most abundant element in the crust of the planet. I'd be impressed if it could seek out and mine pure wurtzite, which is found only at Potosi, Bolivia; Butte, Montana; and Goldfield, Nevada."

"Why is that?" Bibleman said.

"Because," Mary said, "wurtzite is unstable at temperatures below one thousand degrees centigrade. And further –" She broke off. Major Casals had ceased talking and was looking at her.

"Would you repeat that for all of us, young woman?" Major Casals said.

Standing, Mary said, "Wurtzite is unstable at temperatures below one thousand degrees centigrade." Her voice was steady.

Immediately the hologram behind Major Casals switched to a readout of data on zinc-sulfide minerals.

"I don't see 'wurtzite' listed," Major Casals said.

"It's given on the chart in its inverted form," Mary said, her arms folded. "Which is sphalerite. Correctly, it is ZnS, of the sulfide group of the AX type. It's related to greenockite."

"Sit down," Major Casals said. The readout within the hologram now showed the characteristics of greenockite.

As she seated herself, Mary said, "I'm right. They don't have a homeostatic drilling rig for wurtzite because there is no –"

"Your name is?" Major Casals said, pen and pad poised.

"Mary Wurtz." Her voice was totally without emotion. "My father was Charles-Adolphe Wurtz."

"The discoverer of wurtzite?" Major Casals said uncertainly; his pen wavered.

"That's right," Mary said. Turning toward Bibleman, she winked.

"Thank you for the information," Major Casals said. He made a motion and the hologram now showed a flying buttress and, in comparison to it, a normal buttress.

"My point," Major Casals said, "is simply that certain information such as architectural principles of long-standing –"

"Most architectural principles are long-standing," Mary said.

Major Casals paused.

"Otherwise they'd serve no purpose," Mary said.

"Why not?" Major Casals said, and then he colored.

Several uniformed students laughed.

"Information of that type," Major Casals continued, "is not classified. But a good deal of what you will be learning is classified. This is why the college is under military charter. To reveal or transmit or make public classified information given you during your schooling here falls under the jurisdiction of the military. For a breach of these statutes you would be tried by a military tribunal."

The students murmured. To himself Bibleman thought, Banged, ganged, and then some. No one spoke. Even the girl beside him was silent. A complicated expression had crossed her face, however; a deeply introverted look, somber and – he thought – unusually mature. It made her seem older, no longer a girl. It made him wonder just how old she really was. It was as if in her features a thousand years had surfaced before him as he scrutinized her and pondered the officer on the stage and the great information hologram behind him. What is she thinking? he wondered. Is she going to say something more? How can she be not afraid to speak up? We've been told we are under military law.

Major Casals said, "I am going to give you an instance of a strictly classified cluster of data. It deals with the Panther Engine." Behind him the hologram, surprisingly, became blank.

"Sir," one of the students said, "the hologram isn't showing anything."

"This is not an area that will be dealt with in your studies here," Major Casals said. "The Panther Engine is a two-rotor system, opposed rotors serving a common main shaft. Its main advantage is a total lack of centrifugal torque in the housing. A cam chain is thrown between the opposed rotors, which permits the main shaft to reverse itself without hysteresis."

Behind him the big hologram remained blank. Strange, Bibleman thought. An eerie sensation: information without information, as if the computer had gone blind.

Major Casals said, "The College is forbidden to release any information about the Panther Engine. It cannot be programmed to do otherwise. In fact, it knows nothing about the Panther Engine; it is programmed to destroy any information it receives in that sector."

Raising his hand, a student said, "So even if someone fed information into the College about the Panther –"

"It would eject the data," Major Casals said.

"Is this a unique situation?" another student asked.

"No," Major Casals said.

"Then there're a number of areas we can't get printouts for," a student murmured.

"Nothing of importance," Major Casals said. "At least as far as your studies are concerned."

The students were silent.

"The subjects which you will study," Major Casals said, "will be assigned to you, based on your aptitude and personality profiles. I'll call off your names and you will come forward for your allocation of topic assignment. The College itself has made the final decision for each of you, so you can be sure no error has been made."

What if I get proctology? Bibleman asked himself. In panic he thought, Or podiatry. Or herpetology. Or suppose the College in its infinite computeroid wisdom decides to ram into me all the information in the universe pertaining to or resembling herpes labialis . . . or things even worse. If there is anything worse.

"What you want," Mary said, as the names were read alphabetically, "is a program that'll earn you a living. You have to be practical. I know what I'll get; I know where my strong point lies. It'll be chemistry."

His name was called; rising, he walked up the aisle to Major Casals. They looked at each other, and then Casals handed him an unsealed envelope.

Stiffly, Bibleman returned to his seat.

"You want me to open it?" Mary said.

Wordlessly, Bibleman passed the envelope to her. She opened it and studied the printout.

"Can I earn a living with it?" he said.

She smiled. "Yes, it's a high-paying field. Almost as good

as – well, let's just say that the colony planets are really in need of this. You could go to work anywhere."

Looking over her shoulder, he saw the words on the page.

COSMOLOGY COSMOGONY PRE-SOCRATICS

"Pre-Socratic philosophy," Mary said. "Almost as good as structural engineering." She passed him the paper. "I shouldn't kid you. No, it's not really something you can make a living at, unless you teach . . . but maybe it interests you. Does it interest you?"

"No," he said shortly.

"I wonder why the College picked it, then," Mary said.

"What the hell," he said, "is cosmogony?"

"How the universe came into being. Aren't you interested in how the universe –?" She paused, eyeing him. "You certainly won't be asking for printouts of any classified material," she said meditatively. "Maybe that's it," she murmured, to herself. "They won't have to watchdog you."

"I can be trusted with classified material," he said.

"Can you? Do you know yourself? But you'll be getting into that when the College bombards you with early Greek thought. 'Know thyself.' Apollo's motto at Delphi. It sums up half of Greek philosophy."

Bibleman said, "I'm not going up before a military tribunal for making public classified military material." He thought, then, about the Panther Engine and he realized, fully realized, that a really grim message had been spelled out in that little lecture by Major Casals. "I wonder what Herbie the Hyena's motto is," he said.

"'I am determined to prove a villain,'" Mary said. "'And hate the idle pleasures of these days. Plots have I laid.'" She reached out to touch him on the arm. "Remember? The Herbie the Hyena cartoon version of *Richard the Third*."

"Mary Lorne," Major Casals said, reading off the list.

"Excuse me." She went up, returned with her envelope, smiling. "Leprology," she said to Bibleman. "The study and treatment of leprosy. I'm kidding; it's chemistry."

"You'll be studying classified material." Bibleman said.

"Yes," she said. "I know."

On the first day of his study program, Bob Bibleman set his College input-output terminal on AUDIO and punched the proper key for his coded course.

"Thales of Miletus," the terminal said. "The founder of the Ionian school of natural philosophy."

"What did he teach?" Bibleman said.

"That the world floated on water, was sustained by water, and originated in water."

"That's really stupid," Bibleman said.

The College terminal said, "Thales based this on the discovery of fossil fish far inland, even at high altitudes. So it is not as stupid as it sounds." It showed on its holoscreen a great deal of written information, no part of which struck Bibleman as very interesting. Anyhow, he had requested AUDIO. "It is generally considered that Thales was the first rational man in history," the terminal said.

"What about Ikhnaton?" Bibleman said.

"He was strange."

"Moses?"

"Likewise strange."

"Hammurabi?"

"How do you spell that?"

"I'm not sure. I've just heard the name."

"Then we will discuss Anaximander," the College terminal said. "And, in a cursory initial survey, Anaximenes, Xenophanes, Paramenides, Melissus – wait a minute; I forgot Heraclitus and Cratylus. And we will study Empedocles, Anaxagoras, Zeno –"

"Christ," Bibleman said.

"That's another program," the College terminal said.

"Just continue," Bibleman said.

"Are you taking notes?"

"That's none of your business."

"You seem to be in a state of conflict."

Bibleman said, "What happens to me if I flunk out of the College?"

"You go to jail."

"I'll take notes."

"Since you are so driven –"

"What?"

"Since you are so full of conflict, you should find Empedocles interesting. He was the first dialectical philosopher. Empedocles believed that the basis of reality was an antithetical conflict between the forces of Love and Strife. Under Love the whole cosmos is a duly proportioned mixture, called a *krasis*. This *krasis* is a spherical deity, a single perfect mind which spends all its time –"

"Is there any practical application to any of this?" Bibleman interrupted.

"The two antithetical forces of Love and Strife resemble the Taoist elements of Yang and Yin with their perpetual interaction from which all change takes place."

"Practical application."

"Twin mutually opposed constituents." On the holoscreen a schematic diagram, very complex, formed. "The two-rotor Panther Engine."

"What?" Bibleman said, sitting upright in his seat. He made out the large words PANTHER HYDRODRIVE SYSTEM TOP SECRET above the schematic comprising the readout. Instantly he pressed the PRINT key; the machinery of the terminal whirred and three sheets of paper slid down into the RETRIEVE slot.

They overlooked it, Bibleman realized, this entry in the College's memory banks relating to the Panther Engine. Somehow the cross-referencing got lost. No one thought of pre-Socratic philosophy – who would expect an entry on an engine, a modern-day top-secret engine, under the category PHILOSOPHY, PRE-SOCRATIC, subheading EMPEDOCLES?

I've got it in my hands, he said to himself as he swiftly lifted out the three sheets of paper. He folded them up and stuck them into the notebook the College had provided.

I've hit it, he thought. Right off the bat. Where the hell am I going to put these schematics? Can't hide them in my locker. And then he thought, Have I committed a crime already, by asking for a written printout?

"Empedocles," the terminal was saying, "believed in

four elements as being perpetually rearranged: earth, water, air, and fire. These elements eternally –"

Click. Bibleman had shut the terminal down. The holoscreen faded to opaque gray.

Too much learning doth make a man slow, he thought as he got to his feet and started from the cubicle. Fast of wit but slow of foot. Where the hell am I going to hide the schematics? he asked himself again as he walked rapidly down the hall toward the ascent tube. Well, he realized, they don't know I have them; I can take my time. The thing to do is hide them at a random place, he decided, as the tube carried him to the surface. And even if they find them they won't be able to trace them back to me, not unless they go to the trouble of dusting for fingerprints.

This could be worth billions of dollars, he said to himself. A great joy filled him and then came the fear. He discovered that he was trembling. Will they ever be pissed, he said to himself. When they find out, *I* won't be pissing purple, *they'll* be pissing purple. The College itself will, when it discovers its error.

And the error, he thought, is on its part, not mine. The College fucked up and that's too bad.

In the dorm where his bunk was located, he found a laundry room maintained by a silent robot staff, and when no robot was watching he hid the three pages of schematics near the bottom of a huge pile of bed sheets. As high as the ceiling, this pile. They won't get down to the schematics this year. I have plenty of time to decide what to do.

Looking at his watch, he saw that the afternoon had almost come to an end. At five o'clock he would be seated in the cafeteria, eating dinner with Mary.

She met him a little after five o'clock; her face showed signs of fatigue.

"How'd it go?" she asked him as they stood in line with their trays.

"Fine," Bibleman said.

"Did you get to Zeno? I always like Zeno; he proved that motion is impossible. So I guess I'm still in my mother's womb. You look strange." She eyed him.

"Just sick of listening to how the earth rests on the back of a giant turtle."

"Or is suspended on a long string," Mary said. Together they made their way among the other students to an empty table. "You're not eating much."

"Feeling like eating," Bibleman said as he drank his cup of coffee, "is what got me here in the first place."

"You could flunk out."

"And go to jail."

Mary said, "The College is programmed to say that. Much of it is probably just threats. Talk loudly and carry a small stick, so to speak."

"I have it," Bibleman said.

"You have what?" She ceased eating and regarded him.

He said, "The Panther Engine."

Gazing at him, the girl was silent.

"The schematics," he said.

"Lower your goddam voice."

"They missed a citation in the memory storage. Now that I have them I don't know what to do. Just start walking, probably. And hope no one stops me."

"They don't know? The College didn't self-monitor?"

"I have no reason to think it's aware of what it did."

"Jesus Christ," Mary said softly. "On your first day. You had better do a lot of slow, careful thinking."

"I can destroy them," he said.

"Or sell them."

He said, "I looked them over. There's an analysis on the final page. The Panther –"

"Just say *it*," Mary said.

"It can be used as a hydroelectric turbine and cut costs in half. I couldn't understand the technical language, but I did figure out that. Cheap power source. Very cheap."

"So everyone would benefit."

He nodded.

"They really screwed up," Mary said. "What was it Casals told us? 'Even if someone fed data into the College about the – about it, the College would eject the data'." She began eating slowly, meditatively. "And they're withholding it from the public. It must be industry pressure. Nice."

"What should I do?" Bibleman said.

"I can't tell you that."

"What I was thinking is that I could take the schematics to one of the colony planets where the authorities have less control. I could find an independent firm and make a deal with them. The government wouldn't know how –"

"They'd figure out where the schematics came from," Mary said. "They'd trace it back to you."

"Then I better burn them."

Mary said, "You have a very difficult decision to make. On the one hand, you have classified information in your possession which you obtained illegally. On the other –"

"I didn't obtain it illegally. The College screwed up."

Calmly, she continued, "You broke the law, military law, when you asked for a written transcript. You should have reported the breach of security as soon as you discovered it. They would have rewarded you. Major Casals would have said nice things to you."

"I'm scared," Bibleman said, and he felt the fear moving around inside him, shifting about and growing; as he held his plastic coffee cup it shook, and some of the coffee spilled onto his uniform.

Mary, with a paper napkin, dabbed at the coffee stain.

"It won't come off," she said.

"Symbolism," Bibleman said. "Lady Macbeth. I always wanted to have a dog named Spot so I could say, 'Out, out, damned Spot'."

"I am not going to tell you what to do," Mary said. "This is a decision that you will make alone. It isn't ethical for you even to discuss it with me; that could be considered conspiracy and put us both in prison."

"Prison," he echoed.

"You have it within your – Christ, I was going to say, 'You have it within your power to provide a cheap power source to human civilization'." She laughed and shook her head. "I guess this scares me, too. Do what you think is right. If you think it's right to publish the schematics –"

"I never thought of that. Just publish them. Some magazine or newspaper. A slave printing construct could print it and distribute it all over the solar system in fifteen minutes." All I have to do, he realized, is pay the fee and then feed in the three pages of schematics. As simple as that. And then spend the rest of my life in jail or anyhow in court. Maybe the adjudication would go in my favor. There are precedents in history where vital classified material – military classified material – was stolen and published, and not only was the person found innocent but we now realize that he was a hero; he served the welfare of the human race itself, and risked his life.

Approaching their table, two armed military security guards closed in on Bob Bibleman; he stared at them, not believing what he saw but thinking, *Believe it*.

"Student Bibleman?" one of them said.

"It's on my uniform," Bibleman said.

"Hold out your hands, Student Bibleman." The larger of the two security guards snapped handcuffs on him.

Mary said nothing; she continued slowly eating.

In Major Casal's office Bibleman waited, grasping the fact that he was being – as the technical term had it – "detained". He felt glum. He wondered what they would do. He wondered if he had been set up. He wondered what he would do if he were charged. He wondered why it was taking so long. And then he wondered what it was all about really and he wondered whether he would understand the grand issues if he continued with his course in COSMOLOGY COSMOGONY PRE-SOCRATICS.

Entering the office, Major Casals said briskly, "Sorry to keep you waiting."

"Can these handcuffs be removed?" Bibleman said. They hurt his wrists; they had been clapped on to him as tightly as possible. His bone structure ached.

"We couldn't find the schematics," Casals said, seating himself behind his desk.

"What schematics?"

"For the Panther Engine."

"There aren't supposed to be any schematics for the Panther Engine. You told us that in orientation."

"Did you program your terminal for that deliberately? Or did it just happen to come up?"

"My terminal programmed itself to talk about water," Bibleman said. "The universe is composed of water."

"It automatically notified security when you asked for a written transcript. All written transcripts are monitored."

"Fuck you," Bibleman said.

Major Casals said, "I tell you what. We're only interested in getting the schematics back; we're not interested in putting you in the slam. Return them and you won't be tried."

"Return what?" Bibleman said, but he knew it was a waste of time. "Can I think it over?"

"Yes."

"Can I go? I feel like going to sleep. I'm tired. I feel like having these cuffs off."

Removing the cuffs, Major Casals said, "We made an agreement, with all of you, an agreement between the College and the students, about classified material. You entered into the agreement."

"Freely?" Bibleman said.

"Well, no. But the agreement was known to you. When you discovered the schematics for the Panther Engine encoded in the College's memory and available to anyone who happened for any reason, any reason whatsoever, to ask for a practical application of pre-Socratic –"

"I was as surprised as hell," Bibleman said. "I still am."

"Loyalty is an ethical principle. I'll tell you what; I'll waive the punishment factor and put it on the basis of loyalty to the College. A responsible person obeys laws and agreements entered into. Return the schematics and you can continue your courses here at the College. In fact, we'll give you permission to select what subjects you want; they won't be assigned to you. I think you're good college material. Think it over and report back to me tomorrow morning, between eight and nine, here in my office. Don't talk to anyone; don't try to discuss it. You'll be watched. Don't try to leave the grounds. Okay?"

"Okay," Bibleman said woodenly.

He dreamed that night that he had died. In his dream vast spaces stretched out, and his father was coming toward him, very slowly, out of a dark glade and into the sunlight. His father seemed glad to see him, and Bibleman felt his father's love.

When he awoke, the feeling of being loved by his father remained. As he put on his uniform, he thought about his father and how rarely, in actual life, he had gotten that love. It made him feel lonely, now, his father being dead and his mother as well. Killed in a nuclear power accident, along with a whole lot of other people.

They say someone important to you waits for you on the other side, he thought. Maybe by the time I die Major Casals will be dead and he will be waiting for me, to greet me gladly. Major Casals and my father combined as one.

What am I going to do? he asked himself. They have waived the punitive aspects; it's reduced to essentials, a matter of loyalty. Am I a loyal person? Do I qualify?

The hell with it, he said to himself. He looked at his watch. Eight-thirty. My father would be proud of me, he thought. For what I am going to do.

Going into the laundry room, he scoped out the situation. No robots in sight. He dug down in the pile of bed sheets, found the pages of schematics, took them out, looked them over, and headed for the tube that would take him to Major Casal's office.

"You have them," Casals said as Bibleman entered. Bibleman handed the three sheets of paper over to him.

"And you made no other copies?" Casals asked.

"No."

"You give me your word of honor?"

"Yes," Bibleman said.

"You are herewith expelled from the College," Major Casals said.

"What?" Bibleman said.

Casals pressed a button on his desk. "Come in."

The door opened and Mary Lorne stood there.

"I do not represent the College," Major Casals said to Bibleman. "You were set up."

"I am the College," Mary said.

Major Casals said, "Sit down, Bibleman. She will explain it to you before you leave."

"I failed?" Bibleman said.

"You failed me," Mary said. "The purpose of the test was to teach you to stand on your own feet, even if it meant challenging authority. The covert message of institutions is: 'Submit to that which you psychologically construe as an authority.' A good school trains the whole person; it isn't a matter of data and information; I was trying to make you morally and psychologically complete. But a person can't be commanded to disobey. You can't order someone to rebel. All I could do was give you a model, an example."

Bibleman thought, When she talked back to Casals at the initial orientation. He felt numb.

"The Panther Engine is worthless," Mary said, "as a technological artifact. This is a standard test we use on each student, no matter what study course he is assigned."

"They *all* got a readout on the Panther Engine?" Bibleman said with disbelief. He stared at the girl.

"They will, one by one. Yours came very quickly. First you are told that it is classified; you are told the penalty for releasing classified information; then you are leaked the information. It is hoped that you will make it public or at least try to make it public."

Major Casals said, "You saw on the third page of the printout that the engine supplied an economical source of hydroelectric power. That was important. You knew that the public would benefit if the engine design was released."

"And legal penalties were waived," Mary said. "So what you did was not done out of fear."

"Loyalty," Bibleman said. "I did it out of loyalty."

"To what?" Mary said.

He was silent; he could not think.

"To a holoscreen?" Major Casals said.

"To you," Bibleman said.

Major Casals said, "I am someone who insulted you and derided you. Someone who treated you like dirt. I told you that if I ordered you to piss purple, you —"

"Okay," Bibleman said. "Enough."

"Goodbye," Mary said.

"What?" Bibleman said, startled.

"You're leaving. You're going back to your life and job, what you had before we picked you."

Bibleman said, "I'd like another chance."

"But," Mary said, "you know how the test works now.

So it can never be given to you again. You know what is really wanted from you by the College. I'm sorry."

"I'm sorry, too," Major Casals said.

Bibleman said nothing.

Holding out her hand, Mary said, "Shake?"

Blindly, Bibleman shook hands with her. Major Casals only stared at him blankly; he did not offer his hand. He seemed to be engrossed in some other topic, perhaps some other person. Another student was on his mind, perhaps. Bibleman could not tell.

Three nights later, as he wandered aimlessly through the mixture of lights and darkness of the city, Bob Bibleman saw ahead of him a robot food vendor at its eternal post. A teenage boy was in the process of buying a taco and an apple turnover. Bob Bibleman lined up behind the boy and stood waiting, his hands in his pockets, no thoughts coming to him, only a dull feeling, a sense of emptiness. As if the inattention which he had seen on Casal's face had taken him over, he thought to himself. He felt like an object, an object among objects, like the robot vendor. Something which, as he well knew, did not look you directly in the eye.

"What'll it be, sir?" the robot asked.

Bibleman said, "Fries, a cheeseburger, and a strawberry shake. Are there any contests?"

After a pause the robot said, "Not for you, Mr Bibleman."

"Okay," he said, and stood waiting.

The food came, on its little throwaway plastic tray, in its little throwaway cartons.

"I'm not paying," Bibleman said, and walked away.

The robot called after him, "Eleven hundred dollars. Mr Bibleman. You're breaking the law!"

He turned, got out his wallet.

"Thank you, Mr Bibleman," the robot said. "I am very proud of you."

What Have I Done?

Mark Clifton

Mark Clifton (1906–63) didn't live long enough to discover how much his work was appreciated. He died unheralded aged only 57 with the view that many regarded his work as bitter, acerbic and misanthropic. He, of course, maintained it wasn't. Clifton had been a personnel officer and his experiences dealing with thousands and thousands of people gave him a pessimistic view of humankind as a whole but a fairly positive one of the capabilities of individuals. He firmly believed that it was only individuals acting as individuals that could overturn the mess that governments and conglomerates had caused. This fuelled all of his science fiction, which includes the early award-winning They'd Rather be Right *(Astounding, 1954) and* Eight Keys to Eden *(1960). It was not until 1980 that a collection of his short fiction was made,* The Science Fiction of Mark Clifton, *compiled and championed by Barry Malzberg. The following is Clifton's first published story and they don't come much more downbeat than this.*

I t had to be I. It would be stupid to say that the burden should have fallen to a great statesman, a world leader, a renowned scientist. With all modesty, I think I am one of the few who could have caught the problem early enough to avert disaster. I have a peculiar skill. The whole thing hinged on that. I have learned to know human beings.

The first time I saw the fellow, I was at the drugstore

counter buying cigarettes. He was standing at the magazine rack. One might have thought from the expression on his face that he had never seen magazines before. Still, quite a number of people get that rapt and vacant look when they can't make up their minds to a choice.

The thing which bothered me in that casual glance was that I couldn't recognize him.

There are others who can match my record in taking case histories. I happened to be the one who came in contact with this fellow. For thirty years I have been listening to, talking with, counseling people – over two hundred thousand of them. They have not been routine interviews. I have brought intelligence, sensitivity and concern to each of them.

Mine has been a driving, burning desire to know people. Not from the western scientific point of view of devising tools and rules to measure animated robots and ignoring the man beneath. Nor from the eastern metaphysical approach to painting a picture of the soul by blowing one's breath upon a fog to be blurred and dispersed by the next breath.

Mine was the aim to know the man by making use of both. And there was some success.

A competent geographer can look at a crude sketch of a map and instantly orient himself to it anywhere in the world – the bend of a river, the angle of a lake, the twist of a mountain range. And he can mystify by telling in finest detail what is to be found there.

After about fifty thousand studies where I could predict and then observe and check, with me it became the lift of a brow, the curve of a mouth, the gesture of a hand, the slope of a shoulder. One of the universities became interested, and over a long controlled period they rated me 92 per cent accurate. That was fifteen years ago. I may have improved some since.

Yet standing there at the cigarette counter and glancing at the young fellow at the magazine rack, I could read nothing. Nothing at all.

If this had been an ordinary face, I would have catalogued it and forgotten it automatically. I see them by the thousands. But this face would not be catalogued nor forgotten, because there was nothing in it.

I started to write that it wasn't even a face, but of course it was. Every human being has a face – of one sort or another.

In build he was short, muscular, rather well proportioned. The hair was crew cut and blond, the eyes were blue, the skin fair. All nice and standard Teutonic – only it wasn't.

I finished paying for my cigarettes and gave him one more glance, hoping to surprise an expression which had some meaning. There was none. I left him standing there and walked out on the street and around the corner. The street, the store fronts, the traffic cop on the corner, the warm sunshine were all so familiar I didn't see them. I climbed the stairs to my office in the building over the drugstore. My employment agency waiting room was empty. I don't cater to much of a crowd because it cuts down my opportunity to talk with people and further my study.

Margie, my receptionist, was busy making out some kind of a report and merely nodded as I passed her desk to my own office. She is a good conscientious girl who can't understand why I spend so much time working with bums and drunks and other psychos who obviously won't bring fees into the sometimes too small bank account.

I sat down at my desk and said aloud to myself, "The guy is a fake! As obvious as a high school boy's drafting of a dollar bill."

I heard myself say that and wondered if I was going nuts, myself. What did I mean by fake? I shrugged. So I happened to see a bird I couldn't read, that was all.

Then it struck me. But that would be unique. I hadn't had that experience for twenty years. Imagine the delight, after all these years, of exploring an unreadable!

I rushed out of my office and back down the stairs to the street. Hallahan, the traffic cop, saw me running up the street and looked at me curiously. I signaled to him with a wave of a hand that everything was all right. He lifted his cap and scratched his head. He shook his head slowly and settled his cap back down. He blew a whistle at a woman driver and went back to directing traffic.

I ran into the drugstore. Of course the guy wasn't there. I looked all around, hoping he was hiding behind the pots and pans counter, or something. No guy.

I walked quickly back out on the street and down to the next corner. I looked up and down the side streets. No guy.

I dragged my feet reluctantly back toward the office. I called up the face again to study it. It did no good. The first mental glimpse of it told me there was nothing to find. Logic told me there was nothing to find. If there had been, I wouldn't be in such a stew. The face was empty – completely void of human feelings or character.

No, those weren't the right words. Completely void of human – being!

I walked on past the drugstore again and looked in curiously, hoping I would see him. Hallahan was facing my direction again, and he grinned crookedly at me. I expect around the neighborhood I am known as a character. I ask the queerest questions of people, from a layman's point of view. Still, applicants sometimes tell me that when they asked a cop where was an employment agent they could trust they were sent to me.

I climbed the stairs again, and walked into my waiting room. Margie looked at me curiously, but she only said, "There's an applicant. I had him wait in your office." She looked like she wanted to say more, and then shrugged. Or maybe she shivered. I knew there was something wrong with the bird, or she would have kept him in the waiting room.

I opened the door to my office, and experienced an overwhelming sense of relief, fulfillment. It was he. Still, it was logical that he should be there. I run an employment agency. People come to me to get help in finding work. If others, why not he?

My skill includes the control of my outward reactions. That fellow could have no idea of the delight I felt at the opportunity to get a full history. If I had found him on the street, the best I might have done was a stock question about what time is it, or have you got a match, or where is the city hall. Here I could question him to my heart's content.

I took his history without comment, and stuck to routine questions. It was all exactly right.

He was ex-G.I., just completed college, major in astronomy, no experience, no skills, no faintest idea of what he wanted to do, nothing to offer an employer – all perfectly normal for a young grad.

No feeling or expression either. Not so normal. Usually they're petulantly resentful that business doesn't swoon at the chance of hiring them. I resigned myself to the old one-two of attempting to steer him toward something practical.

"Astronomy?" I asked. "That means you're heavy in math. Frequently we can place a strong math skill in statistical work." I was hopeful I could get a spark of something.

It turned out he wasn't very good at math. "I haven't yet reconciled my math to –" he stopped. For the first time he showed a reaction – hesitancy. Prior to that he had been a statue from Greece – the rounded expressionless eyes, the too perfect features undisturbed by thought.

He caught his remark and finished, "I'm just not very good at math, that's all."

I sighed to myself. I'm used to that, too. They give degrees nowadays to get rid of the guys, I suppose. Sometimes I'll go for days without uncovering any usable knowledge. So in a way, that was normal.

The only abnormal part of it was he seemed to think it didn't sound right. Usually the lads don't even realize they should know something. He seemed to think he'd pulled a boner by admitting that a man can take a degree in astronomy without learning math. Well, I wouldn't be surprised to see them take their degree without knowing how many planets there are.

He began to fidget a bit. That was strange, also. I thought I knew every possible combination of muscular contractions and expansions. This fidget had all the reality of a puppet activated by an amateur. And the eyes – still completely blank.

I led him up one mental street and down the next. And of all the false-fronted stores and cardboard houses and paper lawns, I never saw the like. I get something of that once in a while from a fellow who has spent a long term in prison and comes in with a manufactured past – but never anything as phony as this one was.

Interesting aspect to it. Most guys, when they realize you've spotted them for a phony, get out as soon as they can. He didn't. It was almost as though he were – well, testing; to see if his answers would stand up.

I tried talking astronomy, of which I thought I knew a little. I found I didn't know anything, or he didn't. This bird's astronomy and mine had no point of reconciliation.

And then he had a slip of the tongue – yes, he did. He was talking, and said, "The ten planets –"

He caught himself, "Oh, that's right. There's only nine."

Could be ignorance, but I didn't think so. Could be he knew of the existence of a planet we hadn't yet discovered.

I smiled. I opened a desk drawer and pulled out a couple science-fiction magazines. "Ever read any of these?" I asked.

"I looked through several of them at the newsstand a while ago," he answered.

"They've enlarged my vision," I said. "Even to the point where I could believe that some other star system might hold intelligence." I lit a cigarette and waited. If I was wrong, he would merely think I was talking at random.

His blank eyes changed. They were no longer Greek statue eyes. They were no longer blue. They were black, deep bottomless black, as deep and cold as space itself.

"Where did I fail in my test?" he asked. His lips formed a smile which was not a smile – a carefully painted-on-canvas sort of smile.

Well, I'd had my answer. I'd explored something unique, all right. Sitting there before me, I had no way of determining whether he was benign or evil. No way of knowing his motive. No way of judging – anything. When it takes a lifetime of learning how to judge even our own kind, what standards have we for judging an entity from another star system?

At that moment I would like to have been one of those space-opera heroes who, in similar circumstances, laugh casually and say, "What ho! So you're from Arcturus. Well,

well. It's a small universe after all, isn't it?" And then with linked arms they head for the nearest bar, bosom pals.

I had the almost hysterical thought, but carefully suppressed, that I didn't know if this fellow would like beer or not. I will not go through the intermuscular and visceral reactions I experienced. I kept my seat and maintained a polite expression. Even with humans, I know when to walk carefully.

"I couldn't feel anything about you," I answered his question. "I couldn't feel anything but blankness."

He looked blank. His eyes were nice blue marble again. I liked them better that way.

There should be a million questions to be asked, but I must have been bothered by the feeling that I held a loaded bomb in my hands. And not knowing what might set it off, or how, or when. I could think of only the most trivial.

"How long have you been on Earth?" I asked. Sort of a when did you get back in town, Joe, kind of triviality.

"For several of your weeks," he was answering. "But this is my first time out among humans."

"Where have you been in the meantime?" I asked.

"Training." His answers were getting short and his muscles began to fidget again.

"And where do you train?" I kept boring in.

As an answer he stood up and held out his hand, all quite correctly. "I must go now," he said. "Naturally you can cancel my application for employment. Obviously we have more to learn."

I raised an eyebrow. "And I'm supposed to just pass over the whole thing? A thing like this?"

He smiled again. The contrived smile which was a symbol to indicate courtesy. "I believe your custom on this planet is to turn your problems over to your police. You might try that." I could not tell whether it was irony or logic.

At that moment I could think of nothing else to say. He walked out of my door while I stood beside my desk and watched him go.

Well, what was I supposed to do? Follow him?

I followed him.

Now I'm no private eye, but I've read my share of mystery stories. I knew enough to keep out of sight. I followed him about a dozen blocks into a quiet residential section of small homes. I was standing behind a palm tree, lighting a cigarette, when he went up the walk of one of these small houses. I saw him twiddle with the door, open it, and walk in. The door closed.

I hung around a while and then went up to the door. I punched the doorbell. A motherly gray-haired woman came to the door, drying her hands on her apron. As she opened the door she said, "I'm not buying anything today."

Just the same, her eyes looked curious as to what I might have.

I grinned my best grin for elderly ladies. "I'm not selling anything, either," I answered. I handed her my agency card. She looked at it curiously and then looked a question at me.

"I'd like to see Joseph Hoffman," I said politely.

She looked puzzled. "I'm afraid you've got the wrong address, sir," she answered.

I got prepared to stick my foot in the door, but it wasn't necessary. "He was in my office just a few minutes ago," I said. "He gave that name and this address. A job came in right after he left the office, and since I was going to be in this neighborhood anyway, I thought I'd drop by and tell him in person. It's sort of rush," I finished. It had happened many times before, but this time it sounded lame.

"Nobody lives here but me and my husband," she insisted. "He's retired."

I didn't care if he hung by his toes from trees. I wanted a young fellow.

"But I saw the young fellow come in here," I argued. "I was just coming around the corner, trying to catch him. I saw him."

She looked at me suspiciously. "I don't know what your racket is," she said through thin lips, "but I'm not buying anything. I'm not signing anything. I don't even want to talk to you." She was stubborn about it.

I apologized and mumbled something about maybe making a mistake.

"I should say you have," she rapped out tartly and shut the door in righteous indignation. Sincere, too. I could tell.

An employment agent who gets the reputation of being a right guy makes all kinds of friends. That poor old lady must have thought a plague of locusts had swept in on her for the next few days.

First the telephone repair man had to investigate an alleged complaint. Then a gas service man had to check the plumbing. An electrician complained there was a power short in the block and he had to trace their house wiring. We kept our fingers crossed hoping the old geezer had never been a construction man. There was a mistake in the last census, and a guy asked her a million questions.

That house was gone over rafter by rafter and sill by sill, attic and basement. It was precisely as she said. She and her husband lived there; nobody else.

In frustration, I waited three months. I wore out the sidewalks haunting the neighborhood. Nothing.

Then one day my office door opened and Margie ushered a young man in. Behind his back she was radiating heart throbs and fluttering her eyes.

He was the traditionally tall, dark and handsome young fellow, with a ready grin and sparkling dark eyes. His personality hit me like a sledge hammer. A guy like that never needs to go to an employment agency. Any employer will hire him at the drop of a hat, and wonder later why he did it.

His name was Einar Johnson. Extraction, Norwegian. The dark Norse strain, I judged. I took a chance on him thinking he had walked into a booby hatch.

"The last time I talked with you," I said, "your name was Joseph Hoffman. You were Teutonic then. Not Norse."

The sparkle went out of his eyes. His face showed exasperation and there was plenty of it. It looked real, too, not painted on.

"All right. Where did I flunk this time?" he asked impatiently.

"It would take me too long to tell you," I answered. "Suppose you start talking." Strangely, I was at ease. I knew that underneath he was the same incomprehensible entity, but his surface was so good that I was lulled.

He looked at me levelly for a long moment. Then he said, "I didn't think there was a chance in a million of being recognized. I'll admit that other character we created was crude. We've learned considerably since then, and we've concentrated everything on this personality I'm wearing."

He paused and flashed his teeth at me. I felt like hiring him myself. "I've been all over Southern California in this one," he said. "I've had a short job as a salesman. I've been to dances and parties. I've got drunk and sober again. Nobody, I say nobody, has shown even the slightest suspicion."

"Not very observing, were they?" I taunted.

"But you are," he answered. "That's why I came back here for the final test. I'd like to know where I failed." He was firm.

"We get quite a few phonies," I answered. "The guy drawing unemployment and stalling until it is run out. The geezik whose wife drives him out and threatens to quit her job if he doesn't go to work. The plainclothes detail smelling around to see if maybe we aren't a cover for a bookie joint or something. Dozens of phonies."

He looked curious. I said in disgust, "We know in the first two minutes they're phony. You were phony also, but not of any class I've seen before. And," I finished dryly, "I've been waiting for you."

"Why was I phony?" he persisted.

"Too much personality force," I answered. "Human beings just don't have that much force. I felt like I'd been knocked flat on my . . . well . . . back."

He sighed. "I've been afraid you would recognize me one way or another. I communicated with home. I was advised that if you spotted me, I was to instruct you to assist us."

I lifted a brow. I wasn't sure just how much authority they had to instruct me to do anything.

"I was to instruct you to take over the supervision of our final training, so that no one could ever spot us. If we are going to carry out our original plan that is necessary. If not, then we will have to use the alternate." He was almost didactic in his manner, but his charm of personality still radiated like an infrared lamp.

"You're going to have to tell me a great deal more than that," I said.

He glanced at my closed door.

"We won't be interrupted," I said. "A personnel history is private."

"I come from one of the planets of Arcturus," he said.

I must have allowed a smile of amusement to show on my face, for he asked, "You find that amusing?"

"No," I answered soberly, and my pulses leaped because the question confirmed my conclusion that he could not read my thoughts. Apparently we were as alien to him as he to us. "I was amused," I explained, "because the first time I saw you I said to myself that as far as recognizing you, you might have come from Arcturus. Now it turns out that accidentally I was correct. I'm better than I thought."

He gave a fleeting polite smile in acknowledgment. "My home planet," he went on, "is similar to yours. Except that we have grown overpopulated."

I felt a twinge of fear.

"We have made a study of this planet and have decided to colonize it." It was a flat statement, without any doubt behind it.

I flashed him a look of incredulity. "And you expect me to help you with that?"

He gave me a worldly wise look – almost an ancient look. "Why not?" he asked.

"There is the matter of loyalty to my own kind, for one thing," I said. "Not too many generations away and we'll be overpopulated also. There would hardly be room for both your people and ours on Earth."

"Oh that's all right," he answered easily. "There'll be plenty of room for us for quite some time. We multiply slowly."

"We don't," I said shortly. I felt this conversation should be taking place between him and some great statesman – not me.

"You don't seem to understand," he said patiently. "Your race won't be here. We have found no reason why your race should be preserved. You will die away as we absorb."

"Now just a moment," I interrupted. "I don't want our race to die off." The way he looked at me I felt like a spoiled brat who didn't want to go beddie time.

"Why not?" he asked.

I was stumped. That's a good question when it is put logically. Just try to think of a logical reason why the human race should survive. I gave him at least something.

"Mankind," I said, "has had a hard struggle. We've paid a tremendous price in pain and death for our growth. Not to have a future to look forward to, would be like paying for something and never getting the use of it."

It was the best I could think of, honest. To base argument on humanity and right and justice and mercy would leave me wide open. Because it is obvious that man doesn't practice any of these. There is no assurance he ever will.

But he was ready for me, even with that one. "But if we are never suspected, and if we absorb and replace gradually, who is to know there is no future for humans?"

And as abruptly as the last time, he stood up suddenly. "Of course," he said coldly, "we could use our alternative plan: destroy the human race without further negotiation. It is not our way to cause needless pain to any life form. But we can.

"If you do not assist us, then it is obvious that we will eventually be discovered. You are aware of the difficulty of even blending from one country on Earth to another. How much more difficult it is where there is no point of contact at all. And if we are discovered, destruction would be the only step left."

He smiled and all the force of his charm hit me again. "I know you will want to think it over for a time. I'll return."

He walked to the door, then smiled back at me. "And don't bother to trouble that poor little woman in that house again. Her doorway is only one of many entrances we have opened. She doesn't see us at all, and merely wonders why her latch doesn't work sometimes. And we can open another, anywhere, anytime. Like this –"

He was gone.

I walked over and opened the door. Margie was all prettied up and looking expectant and radiant. When she didn't see him come out she got up and peeked into my office. "But where did he go?" she asked with wide eyes.

"Get hold of yourself, girl," I answered. "You're so dazed you didn't even see him walk right by you."

"There's something fishy going on here," she said.

"Well, I had a problem. A first rate, genuine, dyed in the wool dilemma.

What was I to do? I could have gone to the local authorities and got locked up for being a psycho. I could have gone to the college professors and got locked up for being a psycho. I could have gone to maybe the FBI and got locked up for being a psycho. That line of thinking began to get monotonous.

I did the one thing which I thought might bring help. I wrote up the happenings and sent it to my favorite science-fiction magazine. I asked for help and sage counsel from the one place I felt awareness and comprehension might be reached.

The manuscript bounced back so fast it might have had rubber bands attached to it, stretched from California to New York. I looked the little rejection slip all over, front and back, and I did not find upon it those sage words of counsel I needed. There wasn't even a printed invitation to try again some time.

And for the first time in my life I knew what it was to be alone – genuinely and irrevocably alone.

Still, I could not blame the editor. I could see him cast the manuscript from him in disgust, saying, "Bah! So another evil race comes to conquer Earth. If I gave the fans one more of those, I'd be run out of my office." And like the deacon who saw the naughty words written on the fence, saying, "And misspelled, too."

The fable of the boy who cried "Wolf! Wolf!" once too often came home to me now. I was alone with my problem. The dilemma was my own. On one hand was immediate extermination. I did not doubt it. A race which can open doors from one star system to another, without even visible means of mechanism, would also know how to – disinfect.

On the other hand was extinction, gradual, but equally certain, and none the less effective in that it would not be perceived. If I refused to assist, then acting as one lone judge of all the race, I condemned it. If I did assist, I would be arch traitor, with an equal final result.

For days I sweltered in my miasma of indecision. Like many a man before me, uncertain of what to do, I temporized. I decided to play for time. To play the role of traitor in the hopes I might learn a way of defeating them.

Once I had made up my mind, my thoughts raced wildly through the possibilities. If I were to be their instructor on how to walk unsuspected among men, then I would have them wholly in my grasp. If I could build traits into them, common ordinary traits which they could see in men all about them, yet which would make men turn and destroy them, then I would have my solution.

And I knew human beings. Perhaps it was right, after all, that it became my problem. Mine alone.

I shuddered now to think what might have happened had this being fallen into less skilled hands and told his story. Perhaps by now there would be no man left upon Earth.

Yes, the old and worn-out plot of the one little unknown guy who saved Earth from outer evil might yet run its course in reality.

I was ready for the Arcturan when he returned. And he did return.

Einar Johnson and I walked out of my office after I had sent a tearful Margie on a long vacation with fancy pay. Einar had plenty of money, and was liberal with it. When a fellow can open some sort of fourth-dimensional door into a bank vault and help himself, money is no problem.

I had visions of the poor bank clerks trying to explain things to the examiners, but that wasn't my worry right now.

We walked out of the office and I snapped the lock shut behind me. Always conscious of the cares of people looking for work, I hung a sign on the door saying I was ill and didn't know when I would be back.

We walked down the stairs and into the parking lot. We got into my car, my own car, please note, and I found myself sitting in a sheltered patio in Beverly Hills. Just like that. No awful wrenching and turning my insides out. No worrisome nausea and emptiness of space. Nothing to dramatize it at all. Car – patio, like that.

I would like to be able to describe the Arcturans as having long snaky appendages and evil slobbering maws, and stuff like that. But I can't describe the Arcturans, because I didn't see any.

I saw a gathering of people, rougly about thirty of them, wandering around the patio, swimming in the pool, going in and out of the side doors of the house. It was a perfect spot. No one bothers the big Beverly Hills home without invitation.

The natives wouldn't be caught dead looking toward a star's house. The tourists see the winding drive, the trees and grass, and perhaps a glimpse of a gabled roof. If they can get any thrill out of that then bless their little spending money hearts, they're welcome to it.

Yet if it should become known that a crowd of strange acting people are wandering around in the grounds, no one would think a thing about it. They don't come any more zany than the Hollywood crowd.

Only these were. These people could have made a fortune as life-size puppets. I could see now why it was judged that the lifeless Teutonic I had first interviewed was thought adequate to mingle with human beings. By comparison with these, he was a snappy song and dance man.

But that is all I saw. Vacant bodies wandering around, going through human motions, without human emotions. The job looked bigger than I had thought. And yet, if this was their idea of how to win friends and influence people, I might be successful after all.

There are dozens of questions the curious might want answered – such as how did they get hold of the house and how did they get their human bodies and where did they learn to speak English, and stuff. I wasn't too curious. I had important things to think about. I supposed they were able to do it, because here it was.

I'll cut the following weeks short. I cannot conceive of

what life and civilization on their planet might be like. Yardsticks of scientific psychology are used to measure a man, and yet they give no indication at all of the inner spirit of him, likewise, the descriptive measurements of their civilization are empty and meaningless. Knowing about a man, and knowing a man are two entirely different things.

For example, all those thalamic urges and urgencies which we call emotion were completely unknown to them, except as they saw them in antics on TV. The ideals of man were also unknown – truth, honor, justice, perfection – all unknown. They had not even a division of sexes, and the emotion we call love was beyond their understanding. The TV stories they saw must have been like watching a parade of ants.

What purpose can be gained by describing such a civilization to man? Man cannot conceive accomplishment without first having the dream. Yet it was obvious that they accomplished, for they were here.

When I finally realized there was no point of contact between man and these, I knew relief and joy once more. My job was easy. I knew how to destroy them. And I suspected they could not avoid my trap.

They could not avoid my trap because they had human bodies. Perhaps they conceived them out of thin air, but the veins bled, the flesh felt pain and heat and pressure, the glands secreted.

Ah yes, the glands secreted. They would learn what emotion could be. And I was a master at wielding emotion. The dream of man has been to strive toward the great and immortal ideals. His literature is filled with admonishments to that end. In comparison with the volume of work which tells us what we should be, there is very little which reveals us as we are.

As part of my training course, I chose the world's great literature, and painting, and sculpture, and music – those mediums which best portray man lifting to the stars. I gave them first of all, the dream.

And with the dream, and with the pressure of the glands as kicker, they began to know emotion. I had respect for the superb acting of Einar when I realized that he, also, had still known no emotion.

They moved from the puppet to the newborn babe – a newborn babe in training, with an adult body, and its matured glandular equation.

I saw emotions, all right. Emotions without restraint, emotions unfettered by taboos, emotions uncontrolled by ideals. Sometimes I became frightened and all my skill in manipulating emotions was needed. At other times they became perhaps a little too Hollywood, even for Hollywood. I trained them into more ideal patterns.

I will say this for the Arcturans. They learned – fast. The crowd of puppets to the newborn babes, to the boisterous boys and girls to the moody and unpredictable youths, to the matured and balanced men and women. I watched the metamorphosis take place over the period of weeks.

I did more.

All that human beings had ever hoped to be, the brilliant, the idealistic, the great in heart, I made of these. My little 145 I.Q. became a moron's level. The dreams of the greatness of man which I had known became the vaguest wisps of fog before the reality which these achieved.

My plan was working.

Full formed, they were almost like gods. And training these things into them, I trained their own traits out. One point I found we had in common. They were activated by logic, logic carried to heights of which I had never dreamed. Yet my poor and halting logic found point of contact.

They realized at last that if they let their own life force and motivation remain active they would carry the aura of strangeness to defeat their purpose. I worried, when they accepted this. I felt perhaps they were laying a trap for me, as I did for them. Then I realized that I had not taught them deceit.

And it was logical, to them, that they follow my training completely. Reversing the position, placing myself upon their planet, trying to become like them, I must of necessity follow my instructor without question. What else could they do?

At first they saw no strangeness that I should assist them to destroy my race. In their logic the Arcturan was most fit to survive, therefore he should survive. The human was less fit, therefore he should perish.

I taught them the emotion of compassion. And when they began to mature their human thought and emotion, and their intellect was blended and shaded by such emotion, at last they understood my dilemma.

There was irony in that. From my own kind I could expect no understanding. From the invaders I received sympathy and compassion. They understand at last my traitorous action to buy a few more years for Man.

Yet their Arcturan logic still prevailed. They wept with me, but there could be no change of plan. The plan was fixed, they were merely instruments by which it was to be carried out.

Yet, through their compassion, I did get the plan modified.

This was the conversation which revealed that modification. Einar Johnson, who as the most fully developed had been my constant companion, said to me one day, "To all intents and purposes we have become human beings." He looked at me and smiled with fondness, "You have said it is so, and it must be so. For we begin to realize what a great and glorious thing a human is."

The light of nobility shone from him like an aura as he told me this, "Without human bodies, and without the emotion-intelligence equation which you call soul, our home planet cannot begin to grasp the growth we have achieved. We know now that we will never return to our own form, for by doing that we would lose what we have gained.

"Our people are logical, and they must of necessity accept our recommendation, as long as it does not abandon the plan entirely. We have reported what we have learned, and it is conceived that both our races can inhabit the Universe side by side.

"There will be no more migration from our planet to yours. We will remain, and we will multiply, and we will live in honor, such as you have taught us, among you. In time perhaps we may achieve the greatness which all humans now have.

"And we will assist the human kind to find their destiny among the stars as we have done."

I bowed my head and wept. For I knew that I had won.

Four months had gone. I returned to my own neighborhood. On the corner Hallahan left the traffic to shift for itself while he came over to me with the question, "Where have you been?"

"I've been sick," I said.

"You look it," he said frankly. "Take care of yourself, man. Hey – Lookit that fool messing up traffic." He was gone, blowing his whistle in a temper.

I climbed the stairs. They still needed repainting as much as ever. From time to time I had been able to mail money to Margie, and she had kept the rent and telephone paid. The sign was still on my door. My key opened the lock.

The waiting room had that musty, they've-gone-away look about it. The janitor had kept the windows tightly closed and there was no freshness in the air. I half hoped to see Margie sitting at her desk, but I knew there was no purpose to it. When a girl is being paid for her time and has nothing to do, the beach is a nice place to spend it.

There was dust on my chair, and I sank down into it without bothering about the seat of my pants. I buried my head in my arms and I looked into the human soul.

Now the whole thing hinged on that skill. I know human beings. I know them as well as anyone in the world, and far better than most.

I looked into the past and I saw a review of the great and fine and noble and divine torn and burned and crucified by man.

Yet my only hope of saving my race was to build these qualities, the fine, the noble, the splendid, into these thirty beings. To create the illusion that all men were likewise great. No less power could have gained the boom of equality for man with them.

I look into the future. I see them, one by one, destroyed. I gave them no defense. They are totally unprepared to meet man as he genuinely is – and they are incapable of understanding.

For these things which man purports to admire the most

– the noble, the brilliant, the splendid – these are the very things he cannot tolerate when he finds them.

Defenseless, because they cannot comprehend, these thirty will go down beneath the ravening fury of rending and destroying man always displays whenever he meets his ideal face to face.

I bury my head in my hands.

What have I done?

Two Apocalyptic Classics: Finis

Frank Lillie Pollock

I wanted to include in this anthology one or two really old stories that demonstrated not only that science fiction has been around a long time but also that writers of a hundred years ago were writing at their cutting edge. The progress in science and technology was every bit as amazing to the Victorians as recent progress has been to us and it was this that gave added impetus to the growth of science fiction during the 1890s, pioneered by writers like H.G. Wells, George Griffith and Grant Allen. The fear of progress had also inspired a number of "end of the world" stories – in fact they'd been around already for a century. The manic-depressive Cousin de Grainville had written The Last Man *as early as 1806. In "The Star" (1897), H.G. Wells tells how the Earth narrowly survives conflict with a heavenly body, whilst in* The Time Machine *(1895) he describes a desolate scene in the far distant future when the sun has cooled and most life is extinct. The famous French astronomer, Camille Flammarion, combined these two ideas in* Omega *(1897) where the Earth survives a near collision with a comet but in the distant future cools and dies. This thinking was thus very prevalent around the start of the last century and doubtless influenced the following two stories.*

Frank Lillie Pollock (1876–1957) is pretty much forgotten these days and if he's remembered for anything it's for this story, which was published in the American pulp magazine The Argosy *in June 1906. He was a*

Canadian writer who produced a number of offtrail stories and maybe someday he'll be rediscovered.

"**I**'m getting tired," complained Davis, lounging in the window of the Physics Building, "and sleepy. It's after eleven o'clock. This makes the fourth night I've sat up to see your new star, and it'll be the last. Why, the thing was billed to appear three weeks ago."

"Are *you* tired, Miss Wardour?" asked Eastwood, and the girl glanced up with a quick flush and a negative murmur.

Eastwood made the reflection anew that she was certainly painfully shy. She was almost as plain as she was shy, though her hair had an unusual beauty of its own, fine as silk and colored like palest flame.

Probably she had brains; Eastwood had seen her reading some extremely "deep" books, but she seemed to have no amusements, few interests. She worked daily at the Art Students' League, and boarded where he did, and he had thus come to ask her with the Davises to watch for the new star from the laboratory windows on the Heights.

"Do you really think that it's worth while to wait any longer, professor?" inquired Mrs Davis, concealing a yawn.

Eastwood was somewhat annoyed by the continued failure of the star to show itself, and he hated to be called "professor," being only an assistant professor of physics.

"I don't know," he answered somewhat curtly. "This is the twelfth night that I have waited for it. Of course, it would have been a mathematical miracle if astronomers should have solved such a problem exactly, though they've been figuring on it for a quarter of a century."

The new Physics Building of Columbia University was about twelve stories high. The physics laboratory occupied the ninth and tenth floors, with the astronomical rooms above it, an arrangement which would have been impossible before the invention of the oil vibration cushion, which practically isolated the instrument-rooms from the Earth.

Eastwood had arranged a small telescope at the window, and below them spread the illuminated map of Greater New York, sending up a faintly musical roar. All the streets were crowded, as they had been every night since the fifth of the month, when the great new star, or sun, was expected to come into view.

Some error had been made in the calculations, though, as Eastwood said, astronomers had been figuring on them for twenty-five years.

It was, in fact, nearly forty years since Professor Adolphe Bernier first announced his theory of a limited universe at the International Congress of Sciences in Paris, where it was counted as little more than a masterpiece of imagination.

Professor Bernier did not believe that the universe was infinite. Somewhere, he argued, the universe must have a center, which is the pivot for its revolution.

The moon revolves around the Earth, the planetary system revolves about the sun, the solar system revolves about one of the fixed stars, and this whole system in its turn undoubtedly revolves around some distant point. But this sort of progression must stop somewhere.

Somewhere there must be a central sun, a vast incandescent body which does not move at all. And as a sun is always larger and hotter than its satellites, therefore the body at the center of the universe must be of an immensity and temperature beyond anything known or imagined.

It was objected that this hypothetical body should then be large enough to be visible from Earth, and Professor Bernier replied that some day it undoubtedly would be visible. Its light had simply not yet had time to reach the Earth.

The passage of light from the nearest of the fixed stars is a matter of three years, and there must be many stars so distant that their rays have not yet reached us. The great central sun must be so inconceivably remote that perhaps hundreds, perhaps thousands of years would elapse before its light should burst upon the solar system.

All this was contemptuously classed as "newspaper science," till the extraordinary mathematical revival a little after the middle of the twentieth century afforded the means of verifying it.

Following the new theorems discovered by Professor Burnside, of Princeton, and elaborated by Dr Taneka, of Tokyo, astronomers succeeded in calculating the art of the sun's movements through space, and its ratio to the orbit of its satellites. With this as a basis, it was possible to follow the widening circles, the consecutive systems of the heavenly bodies and their rotations.

The theory of Professor Bernier was justified. It was demonstrated that there really was a gigantic mass of incandescent matter, which, whether the central point of the universe or not, appeared to be without motion.

The weight and distance of this new sun were approximately calculated, and, the speed of light being known, it was an easy matter to reckon when its rays would reach the Earth.

It was then estimated that the approaching rays would arrive at the Earth in twenty-six years, and that was twenty-six years ago. Three weeks had passed since the date when the new heavenly body was expected to become visible, and it had not yet appeared.

Popular interest had risen to a high pitch, stimulated by innumerable newspaper and magazine articles, and the streets were nightly thronged with excited crowds armed with opera-glass and star maps, while at every corner a telescope man had planted his tripod instrument at a nickel a look.

Similar scenes were taking place in every civilized city on the globe.

It was generally supposed that the new luminary would appear in size about midway between Venus and the moon. Better informed persons expected something like the sun, and a syndicate quietly leased large areas on the coast of Greenland in anticipation of a great rise in temperature and a northward movement in population.

Even the business situation was appreciably affected by the public uncertainty and excitement. There was a decline in stocks, and a minor religious sect boldly prophesied the end of the world.

"I've had enough of this," said Davis, looking at his watch again. "Are you ready to go, Grace? By the way, isn't it getting warmer?"

It had been a sharp February day, but the temperature was certainly rising. Water was dripping from the roofs, and from the icicles that fringed the window ledges, as if a warm wave had suddenly arrived.

"What's that light?" suddenly asked Alice Wardour, who was lingering by the open window.

"It must be moonrise," said Eastwood, though the illumination of the horizon was almost like daybreak.

Davis abandoned his intention of leaving, and they watched the east grow pale and flushed till at last a brilliant white disc heaved itself above the horizon.

It resembled the full moon, but as if trebled in luster, and the streets grew almost as light as by day.

"Good heavens, that must be the new star, after all!" said Davis in an awed voice.

"No, it's only the moon. This is the hour and minute for her rising," answered Eastwood, who had grasped the cause of the phenomenon. "But the new sun must have appeared on the other side of the Earth. Its light is what makes the moon so brilliant. It will rise here just as the sun does, no telling how soon. It must be brighter than was expected – and maybe hotter," he added with a vague uneasiness.

"Isn't it getting very warm in here?" said Mrs. Davis, loosening her jacket. "Couldn't you turn off some of the heat?"

Eastwood turned it all off, for, in spite of the open window, the room was really growing uncomfortably close. But the warmth appeared to come from without; it was like a warm spring evening, and the icicles cornices.

For half an hour they leaned from the windows with but desultory conversation, and below them the streets were black with people and whitened with upturned faces. The brilliant moon rose higher, and the mildness of the night sensibly increased.

It was after midnight when Eastwood first noticed the

reddish flush tinging the clouds low in the east, and he pointed it out to his companions.

"That must be it at last," he exclaimed, with a thrill of vibrating excitement at what he was going to see, a cosmic event unprecedented in intensity.

The brightness waxed rapidly.

"By Jove, see it redden!" Davis ejaculated. "It's getting lighter than day – and hot! Whew!"

The whole eastern sky glowed with a deepening pink that extended half round the horizon. Sparrows chirped from the roofs, and it looked as if the disc of the unknown star might at any moment be expected to lift above the Atlantic, but it delayed long.

The heavens continued to burn with myriad hues, gathering at last to a fiery furnace glow on the sky line.

Mrs Davis suddenly screamed. An American flag blowing freely from its staff on the roof of the tall building had all at once burst into flame.

Low in the east lay a long streak of intense fire which broadened as they squinted with watering eyes. It was as if the edge of the world had been heated to whiteness.

The brilliant moon faded to a feathery white film in the glare. There was a confused outcry from the observatory overhead, and a crash of something being broken, and as the strange new sunlight fell through the window the onlookers leaped back as if a blast furnace had been opened before them.

The glass cracked and fell inward. Something like the sun, but magnified fifty times in size and hotness, was rising out of the sea. An iron instrument-table by the window began to smoke with an acrid smell of varnish.

"What the devil is this, Eastwood?" shouted Davis accusingly.

From the streets rose a sudden, enormous wail of fright and pain, the outcry of a million throats at once, and the roar of a stampede followed. The pavements were choked with struggling, panic-stricken people in the fierce glare, and above the din arose the clanging rush of fire-engines and trucks.

Smoke began to rise from several points below Central Park, and two or three church chimes pealed crazily.

The observers from overhead came running down the stairs with a thunderous trampling, for the elevator man had deserted his post.

"Here, we've got to get out of this," shouted Davis, seizing his wife by the arm and hustling her toward the door. "This place'll be on fire directly."

"Hold on. You can't go down into that crush on the street," Eastwood cried, trying to prevent him.

But Davis broke away and raced down the stairs, half carrying his terrified wife. Eastwood got his back against the door in time to prevent Alice from following them.

"There's nothing in this building that will burn, Miss Wardour," he said as calmly as he could. "We had better stay here for the present. It would be sure death to get involved in that stampede below. Just listen to it."

The crowds on the street seemed to sway to and fro in contending waves, and the cries, curses, and screams came up in a savage chorus.

The heat was already almost blistering to the skin, though they carefully avoided the direct rays, and instruments of glass in the laboratory cracked loudly one by one.

A vast cloud of dark smoke began to rise from the harbor, where the shipping must have caught fire, and something exploded with a terrific report. A few minutes later half a dozen fires broke out in the lower part of the city, rolling up volumes of smoke that faded to a thin mist in the dazzling light.

The great new sun was now fully above the horizon, and the whole east seemed ablaze. The stampede in the streets had quieted all at once, for the survivors had taken refuge in the nearest houses, and the pavements were black with motionless forms of men and women.

"I'll do whatever you say," said Alice, who was deadly pale, but remarkably collected. Even at that moment Eastwood was struck by the splendor of her ethereally brilliant hair that burned like pale flame above her pallid face. "But we can't stay here, can we?"

"No," replied Eastwood, trying to collect his faculties in

the face of this catastrophe revolution of nature. "We'd better go to the basement, I think."

In the basement were deep vaults used for the storage of delicate instruments, and these would afford shelter for a time at least. It occurred to him as he spoke that perhaps temporary safety was the best that any living thing on Earth could hope for.

But he led the way down the well staircase. They had gone down six or seven flights when a gloom seemed to grow upon the air, with a welcome relief.

It seemed almost cool, and the sky had clouded heavily, with the appearance of polished and heated silver.

A deep but distant roaring arose and grew from the southeast, and they stopped on the second landing to look from the window.

A vast black mass seemed to fill the space between sea and sky, and it was sweeping toward the city, probably from the harbor, Eastwood thought, at a speed that made it visibly grow as they watched it.

"A cyclone – and a water-spout!" muttered Eastwood, appalled.

He might have foreseen it from the sudden, excessive evaporation and the heating of the air. The gigantic black pillar drove toward them swaying and reeling, and a gale came with it, and a wall of impenetrable mist behind.

As Eastwood watched its progress he saw its cloudy bulk illumined momentarily by a dozen lightning-like flashes, and a moment later, above its roar, came the tremendous detonations of heavy cannon.

The forts and the warships were firing shells to break the waterspout, but the shots seemed to produce no effect. It was the city's last and useless attempt at resistance. A moment later forts and ships alike must have been engulfed.

"Hurry! This building will collapse!" Eastwood shouted.

They rushed down another flight, and heard the crash with which the monster broke over the city. A deluge of water, like the emptying of a reservoir, thundered upon the street, and the water was steaming hot as it fell.

There was a rending crash of falling walls, and in another

instant the Physics Building seemed to be twisted around by a powerful hand. The walls blew out, and the whole structure sank in a chaotic mass.

But the tough steel frame was practically unwreekable, and, in fact, the upper portion was simply bent down upon the lower stories peeling off most of the shell of masonry and stucco.

Eastwood was stunned as he was hurled to the floor, but when he came to himself he was still upon the landing, which was tilted at an alarming angle. A tangled mass of steel rods and beams hung a yard over his head, and a huge steel girder had plunged down perpendicularly from above, smashing everything in its way.

Wreckage choked the well of the staircase, a mass of plaster, bricks, and shattered furniture surrounded him, and he could look out in almost every direction through the rent iron skeleton.

A yard away Alice was sitting up, mechanically wiping the mud and water from her face, and apparently uninjured. Tepid water was pouring through the interstices of the wreck in torrents, though it did not appear to be raining.

A steady, powerful gale had followed the whirlwind, and it brought a little coolness with it. Eastwood inquired perfunctorily of Alice if she were hurt, without being able to feel any degree of interest in the matter. His faculty of sympathy seemed paralyzed.

"I don't know. I thought – I thought that we were all dead!" the girl murmured in a sort of daze. "What was it? Is it all over?"

"I think it's only beginning," Eastwood answered dully.

The gale had brought up more cloud, and the skies were thickly overcast, but shining white-hot. Presently the rain came down in almost scalding floods, and as it fell upon the hissing streets it steamed again into the air.

In three minutes all the world was choked with hot vapor, and from the roar and splash the streets seemed to be running rivers.

The downpour seemed too violent to endure, and after an hour it did cease, while the city reeked with mist. Through the whirling fog Eastwood caught glimpses of ruined buildings, vast heaps of debris, all the wreckage of the greatest city of the twentieth century.

Then the torrents fell again like a cataract, as if the waters of the Earth were shuttlecocking between sea and heaven. With a jarring tremor of the ground a landslide went down into the Hudson.

The atmosphere was like a vapor bath, choking and sickening. The physical agony of respiration aroused Alice from a sort of stupor, and she cried out pitifully that she would die.

The strong wind drove the hot spray and steam through the shattered building till it seemed impossible that human lungs could extract life from the semi-liquid that had replaced the air, but the two lived.

After hours of this parboiling, the rain slackened, and, as the clouds parted, Eastwood caught a glimpse of a familiar form half way up the heavens. It was the sun, the old sun, looking, small and watery.

But the intense heat and brightness told that the enormous body still blazed behind the clouds. The rain seemed to have ceased definitely, and the hard, shining whiteness of the sky grew rapidly hotter.

The heat of the air increased to an oven-like degree; the mists were dissipated, the clouds licked up, and the earth seemed to dry itself almost immediately. The heat from the two suns beat down simultaneously till it became a monstrous terror, unendurable.

An odor of smoke began to permeate the air; there was a dazzling shimmer, over the streets, and great clouds of mist arose from the bay, but these appeared to evaporate before they could darken the sky.

The piled wreck of the building sheltered the two refugees from the direct rays of the new sun, now almost overhead, but not from the penetrating heat of the air. But the body will endure almost anything, short of tearing asunder, for a time at least; it is the finer mechanism of the nerves that suffers most.

* * *

Alice lay face down among the bricks, gasping and moaning. The blood hammered in Eastwood's brain, and the strangest mirages flickered before his eyes.

Alternately he lapsed into heavy stupors, and awoke to the agony of the day. In his lucid moments he reflected that this could not last long, and tried to remember what degree of heat would cause death.

Within an hour after the drenching rains he was feverishly thirsty, and the skin felt as if peeling from his whole body.

This fever and horror lasted until he forgot that he had ever known another state; but at last the west reddened, and the flaming sun went down. It left the familiar planet high in the heavens, and there was no darkness until the usual hour, though there was a slight lowering of the temperature.

But when night did come it brought life-giving coolness, and though the heat was still intense it seemed temperate by comparison. More than all, the kindly darkness seemed to set a limit to the cataclysmic disorders of the day.

"Ouf! This is heavenly!" said Eastwood, drawing long breaths and feeling mind and body revived in the gloom.

"It won't last long," replied Alice, and her voice sounded extraordinarily calm through the darkness. "The heat will come again when the new sun rises in a few hours."

"We might find some better place in the meanwhile – a deep cellar – or we might get into the Subway," Eastwood suggested.

"It would be no use. Don't you understand? I have been thinking it all out. After this, the new sun will always shine, and we could not endure it even another day. The wave of heat is passing round the world as it revolves, and in a few hours the whole Earth will be a burnt-up ball. Very likely we are the only people left alive in New York, or perhaps America."

She seemed to have taken the intellectual initiative, and spoke with an assumption of authority that amazed him.

"But there must be others," said Eastwood, after thinking for a moment. "Other people have found sheltered places, or miners, or men underground."

"They would have been drowned by the rain. At any rate, there will be none left alive by tomorrow night.

"Think of it," she went on dreamily. "For a thousand years this wave of fire has been rushing toward us, while life has been going on so happily in the world, so unconscious, that the world was doomed all the time. And now this is the end of life."

"I don't know," Eastwood said slowly. "It may be the end of human life, but there must be some forms that will survive – some micro-organisms perhaps capable of resisting high temperatures, if nothing higher. The seed of life will be left at any rate, and that is everything. Evolution will begin over again, producing new types to suit the changed conditions. I only wish I could see what creatures will be here in a few thousand years.

"But I can't realize it at all – this thing!" he cried passionately, after a pause. "Is it real? Or have we gone mad? It seems too much like a bad dream."

The rain crashed down again as he spoke, and the earth steamed, though not with the dense reek of the day. For hours the waters roared and splashed against the Earth in hot billows till the streets were foaming yellow rivers, dammed by the wreck of fallen buildings.

There was a continual rumble as earth and rock slid into the East River, and at last the Brooklyn Bridge collapsed with a thunderous crash and splash that made all Manhattan vibrate. A gigantic billow like a tidal wave swept up the river from its fall.

The downpour slackened and ceased soon after the moon began to shed an obscured but brilliant light through the clouds.

Presently the east commenced to grow luminous, and this time there could be no doubt as to what was coming.

Alice crept closer to the man as the gray light rose upon the watery air.

"Kiss me!" she whispered suddenly, throwing her arms around his neck. He could feel her trembling. "Say you love me. Hold me in your arms. I want you to love me – now – now. There is only an hour."

"Don't be afraid. Try to face it bravely," stammered Eastwood.

"I don't fear it – not death. But I have never lived. I have never had love. I have never felt or known anything. I have always been timid and wretched and afraid – afraid to speak – and I've almost wished for suffering and misery or anything rather than to be stupid and dumb and dead, as I've always been.

"I've never dared to tell anyone what I was, what I wanted. I've been afraid all my life, but I'm not afraid now. I have never lived. I have never been happy, and now we must die together!"

It seemed to Eastwood the cry of the perishing world. He held her in his arms and kissed her wet, tremulous face that was strained to his.

In that terrible desolation his heart turned toward her, and a strange passion intoxicated him as his lips met hers, an intoxication and passion more poignant for the certainty of coming death.

"You must love me – you must!" whispered Alice. "Let us live, a little, at the very last!"

The twilight was gone before he knew it. The sky was blue already, with crimson flakes mounting to the zenith, and the heat was growing once more intense.

"This is the end, Alice," said Eastwood, and his voice trembled.

She looked at him, her eyes shining with an unearthly softness and brilliancy, and turned her face to the east.

There, in crimson and orange, flamed the last dawn that human eyes would ever see.

The Last Days of Earth

George C. Wallis

George C. Wallis (1871–1956) wrote extensively for the British magazines and the boys' story papers at the start of the last century. He became a cinema manager in Sheffield but continued to write into the 1940s. The following story, which takes the complete opposite premise to the previous one, is rather more dated, though it is a wonderful example of Victorian values and attitude. It comes from The Harmsworth Magazine *for July 1901. I wanted to reprint it not only for its fascinating imagery but also for its climax, which is very unusual for its day.*

A man and a woman sat facing each other across a table in a large room. They were talking slowly, and eating – eating their last meal on earth. The end was near; the sun had ceased to warm, was but a red-hot cinder outwardly; and these two, to the best of their belief, were the last people left alive in a world-wilderness of ice and snow and unbearable cold.

The woman was beautiful – very fair and slight, but with the tinge of health upon her delicate skin and the fire of intellect in her eyes. The man was of medium height, broad-shouldered, with wide, bald head and resolute mien – a man of courage, dauntless purpose, strenuous life. Both were dressed in long robes of a thick, black material, held in at the waist by a girdle.

As they talked, their fingers were busy with a row of small white knobs let into the surface of the table, and marked with various signs. At the pressure of each knob a flap in the middle of the table opened, and a small glass vessel, with a dark, semi-liquid compound steaming in it, was pushed up. As these came, in obedience to the tapping of their fingers, the two ate their contents with the aid of tiny spoons. There was no other dining apparatus or dinner furniture upon the table, which stood upon a single but massive pedestal of grey metal.

The meal over, the glasses and spoons replaced, the table surface clean and clear, a silence fell between them. The man rested his elbows upon his knees and his chin upon his upturned palms. He did not look at his fair companion, but beyond her, at a complicated structure projecting from the wall. This was the Time Indicator, and gave, on its various discs, the year, the month, the day, the hour and the instant, all corrected to mean astronomical time and to the exact latitude and longitude of the place. He read the well-known symbols with defiant eyes. He saw that it was just a quarter to thirteen in the afternoon of Thursday, July 18th, 13,000,085 A.D. He reflected that the long association of the place with time-recording had been labour spent in vain. The room was in a great building on the site of ancient Greenwich. In fact, the last name given to the locality by its now dead and cold inhabitants had been Grenijia.

From the time machine, the man's gaze went round the room. He noted, with apparently keen interest, all the things that were so familiar to him – the severely plain walls, transparent on one side, but without window-frame or visible door in their continuity; the chilling prospect of a faintly-lit expanse of snow outside; the big telescope that moved in an airtight slide across the ceiling, and the little motor that controlled its motions; the electric radiators that heated the place, forming an almost unbroken dado round the walls; the globe of pale brilliance that hung in the middle of the room and assisted the twilight glimmer of the day; the neat library of books and photo-phono cylinders, and the tier of speaking machines beneath it; the bed in the further corner, surrounded by yet more radiators; the two ventilating valves; the great dull disc of the Pictorial Telegraph; and the thermometer let into a vacant space of floor. On this last his glance rested for some time, and the woman's also. It registered the degrees from absolute zero, and stood at a figure equivalent to 42° Fahrenheit. From this tell-tale instrument the eyes of the two turned to each other, a common knowledge shining in each face. The man was the first to speak again.

"A whole degree, Celia, since yesterday. And the dynamos are giving out a current at a pressure of 6,000 volts. I can't run them at any higher efficiency. That means that any further fall of temperature will close the drama of this planet. Shall we go tonight?"

There was no quiver of fear nor hint of resentment in his voice, nor in the voice that answered him. Long ages of mental evolution had weeded all the petty vices and unreasoning passions out of the mind of man.

"I am ready any time, Alwyn. I do not like to go; I do not like the risk of going: but it is our last duty to the humanity behind us – and I must be with you to the end."

There was another silence between them: a silence in which the humming of the dynamos in the room below seemed to pervade the whole place, thrilling through everything with annoying audibility. Suddenly the man leaned forward, regarding his companion with a puzzled expression.

"Your eyelashes are damp, Celia. You are not crying? That is too archaic."

"I must plead guilty," she said, banishing the sad look with an effort. "We are not yet so thoroughly adjusted to our surroundings as to be able to crush down every weak impulse. Wasn't it the day before yesterday that you said the sun had begun to cool about five million years too soon for man? But I will not give way again. Shall we start at once?"

"That is better; that sounds like Celia. Yes, if you wish, at once; but I had thought of taking a last look round the world – at least, as far as the telegraph system is in order. We have three hours' daylight yet."

For answer, Celia came and sat beside him on the couch facing the disc of the Pictorial Telegraph. His left hand clasped her right; both were cold. With his right hand he pulled over and held down a small lever under the disc – one of many, each bearing a distinctive name and numeral.

The side wall became opaque; the globe above ceased to be luminous. A moving scene grew out of the dullness of the disc, and a low, moaning sound stole into the room. They looked upon a telegraphically-transmitted view of a place near which had once been Santiago, Chili. There were the ruins of an immense white city there now, high on the left of the picture. Down on the right, far below the well-defined marks of six successive beach-lines, a cold sea moaned over an icy bar, and dashed in semi-frozen spray under the bluff of an over-hanging glacier's edge.

Out to sea great bergs drifted slowly, and the distant horizon was pale with the ice-blink from vast floes. The view had scarcely lasted a moment, when a great crack appeared on the top of the ice-front, and a huge fragment fell forward into the sea. It overturned on the bar, churning up a chaos of foam, and began to drift away. At the same instant came the deafening report of the breakage. There was no sign of life, neither of man nor beast, nor bird nor fish, in that cold scene. Polar bears and Arctic foxes, blubber-eating savages and hardy seals, had all long since passed away, even from the tropic zone.

Another lever pressed down, and the Rock of Gibraltar appeared on the disc. It rose vast and grim from the ice-arched waters of a shallow strait, with a vista of plain and mountain and glacier stretching behind it to the hazy distance – a vista of such an intolerable whiteness that the two watchers put on green spectacles to look at it. On the flat top of the Rock – which ages ago had been levelled to make it an alighting station for the Continental aerial machines – rose, gaunt and frost-encrusted, the huge skeleton framework of one of the last flying conveyances used by man.

Another lever, and Colombo, Ceylon, glared lifeless on the disc. Another, and Nagasaki, Japan, the terminal front of a vast glacier, frowned out over a black, ice-filling sea. Yet more levers, and yet more scenes; and everywhere ice and snow, and shallow, slowly-freezing seas, or countries here black and plantless, and there covered with glaciers from the crumbling hills. No sign of life, save the vestiges of man's now-ended reign, and of his long fight with the relentless cold – here ruins, on the ice-free levels, of his Cities of Heat; here gigantic moats, excavated to retard the glaciers; here canals, to connect the warmer seas; here the skeletons of huge metallic floating palaces jettisoned on some ice-bound coast; and everywhere that the ice had not overcome, the tall masts of the Pictorial Telegraph, sending to the watchers at Greenwich, by reflected Marconi waves, a presentment of each sight and sound impinging on the speculums and drums at their summits. And in every daylight scene, the pale ghost of a dim, red sun hung in a clear sky.

In the more northern and southern views the magnetic lights were as brilliant as ever, but there were no views of the extreme Polar Regions. These were more inaccessible than in the remote past, for there cakes and patches of liquid and semi-solid air were slowly settling and spreading on land and sea.

Yet more levers, and yet more; and the two turned away from the disc; and the room grew light again.

"It appears just as we have seen it these last two years," said the man, "yet today the tragedy of it appals me as it has never done before. I did not think, after all the years of expectation and mental schooling, that it would seem like this at the last. I feel tempted to do as our parents did – to seek the safety of the Ultimate Silence."

"Not that, Alwyn – not that. From generation to generation this day has been foreseen and prepared for, and we promised, after we were chosen to remain, that we would not die until all the devices of our science failed. Let us go down and get ready to leave at once."

Celia's face had a glow upon it, a glow that Alwyn's caught.

"I only said 'tempted,' Celia. Were I alone, I do not think I should break my word. And I am also curious. And the old, strange desire for life has come to me. And you are here. Let me kiss you, Celia. That . . . at least, is not archaic."

They walked hand-in-hand to a square space marked out

on the floor in a corner of the room, and one of them pressed a button on the wall. The square sank with them, lowering them into a dimmer room, where the ceaseless, humming of the dynamos became a throbbing roar. They saw, with eyes long used to faint light, the four great alternators spinning round the armatures; felt the fanning of the rapid revolutions upon their faces. By the side of each machine they saw the large, queer-shaped chemical engines that drove them, that were fed from dripping vats, and from many actions and re-actions supplied the power that stood between their owners and the cold that meant the end. Coal had long been exhausted, along with peat and wood and all inflammable oils and gases; no turbines could be worked from frozen streams and seas; no air wheels would revolve in an atmosphere but slightly stirred by a faded sun. The power in chemical actions and re-actions, in transmutations and compoundings of the elements, was the last great source of power left to man in the latter days.

After a brief glance round the room, they pressed another button, and the lift went down to a still lower floor. Here a small glow-lamp was turned on, and they stood before a sphere of bright red metal that filled the greater part of the room. They had not seen this many times in their lives. Its meaning was too forcible a reminder of a prevision for the time that had at last arrived.

The Red Sphere was made of a manufactured element, unknown except within the last million years, and so costly and trouble-some to produce that only two Red Spheres had ever been built. It had been made 500 years before Alwyn and Celia were born. It was made for the purpose of affording the chosen survivors of humanity a means of escaping from the earth when the chemical power proved incapable of resisting the increasing cold. In the Red Sphere Alwyn and Celia intended to leave the earth, to plunge into space – not to seek warmth and light on any other member of the Solar System, for that would be useless – but to gain the neighbourhood of some yet young and fiery star. It was a terrible undertaking – as much more terrible than mere interplanetary voyages as the attempt of a savage to cross the Atlantic in his dugout after having learned to navigate his own narrow creek. It had been left undared until the last, when, however slight the chance of life in it, the earth could only offer instead the choice of soon and certain death.

"It appears just as it did the day I first saw it and was told its purpose," said Celia, with a shudder she could not repress. "Are you sure, Alwyn, that it will carry us safely – that you can follow out the Instructions?"

For generations the Red Sphere and all appertaining to it had been mentioned with a certain degree of awe.

"Don't trouble yourself on that point. The Instructions are simple. The necessary apparatus, and the ten years' supply of imperishable nutriment, are already inside and fixed. We have only to subject the Red Metal to our 6,000-volt current for an hour, get inside, screw up the inlet, and cut ourselves adrift. The Red Metal, thus electrified, becomes, as you know, repulsive to gravitation, and will so continue for a year and a half. By that time, as we shall travel, according to calculation, at twice the speed of light, we should be more than half-way to one of the nearer stars, and so become subject to its gravitation. With the earth in its present position, if we start in a couple of hours, we should make F. 188, mag. 2, of the third order of spectra. Our sun, according to the records, belonged to the same order. And we know that it has at least two planets."

"But if we fall right into F. 188, instead of just missing it, as we hope? Or if we miss, but so closely as to be fused by its heat? Or if we miss it too widely and are thrown back into space on a parabolic or hyperbolic orbit? Or if we should manage the happy medium and find there be no life, nor any chance of life, upon the planets of that system? Or if there be life, but it be hostile to us?"

"Those are the inevitable dangers of our plunge, Celia. The balance of probabilities is in favour of either the first or second of those things befalling us. But that is not the same as absolute certainty, and the improbable *may* happen."

"Quite so, Alwyn; but – do you recollect if the Instructions make any reference to these possibilities?"

"To –? Yes. There is enough fulminate of sterarium packed in the Sphere to shiver it and us to fine dust in the thousandth part of a second – if we wish. We shall always have that resource. Now I'll attach the dynamo leads to the Sphere. Get your little items of personal property together, and we shall be ready."

Celia went up the lift again, and Alwyn, after fixing the connections to several small switches on the surface of the Sphere, followed her. They sat together in the darkening twilight of the dim room above, waiting for the first hour to pass. They spoke at intervals, and in fragmentary phrases.

"It will be cold while the Sphere is being prepared," said Alwyn.

"Yes, but we shall be together, dear, as we have been so long now. I remember how miserable I felt when I first knew my destiny; but when I learned that you were chosen to share it with me, I was glad. But you were not, Alwyn – you loved Amy?"

"Yes."

"And you love her still, but you love me, too? Do you know why she was not chosen?"

"Yes; I love you, Celia, though not so much as I loved Amy. They chose you instead of her, they said, because you had a stronger will and greater physical vigour. The slight curve we shall describe on rising will bring us over the Heat-house she and her other lover retired to after the Decision, and we shall perhaps see whether they are really dead, as we believe. Amy, I remember, had an heretical turn of mind."

"If they are not dead, it is strange that they should not have answered our Marconi and telepathic messages after the first year – unless, of course, as you have so often suggested, they have retired to the interior of the other Red Sphere. How strange that it should have been left there! If they have only enough food, they may live in it till old age intervenes, secure from all the rigours that approach, but what a tame end – what a prisonment!"

"Terrible. I could not endure the Red Sphere except as we shall endure it – travelling."

So the hour passed. They switched the electric current into the framework of the vehicle that was to bear them into space. All the radiators ceased to glow and all the lights went out, leaving them, in that lower room, in absolute darkness and intense cold. They sat huddled together against the wall, where they could feel the thrill of the humming dynamos, embracing each other, silent and re-solute; waiting for the end of the cold hour. They could find few words to speak now, but their thoughts were the busier.

They thought of the glorious, yet now futile past, with all its promises shattered, its ideals valueless, its hopes un-fulfilled; and seemed to feel in themselves the concentration and culmination of the woes and fears of the ages. They saw, as in one long vista, the history of the millions of vanished years – "from earth's nebulous origin to its final ruin"; from its days of four hours to its days of twenty-six and a half: from its germinating specks of primal proto-plasm to its last and greatest, and yet most evil creature, Man. They saw, in mental perspective, the uneven periods of human progress; the long stages of advance and retro-gression, of failure and success. They saw the whole long struggle between the tendencies of Egoism and Altruism, and knew how these had merged at last into an automatic equilibration of Duty and Desire. They saw the climax of this equilibration, the Millennium of Man – and they knew how the inevitable decay had followed.

They saw how the knowledge of the sureness and nature of life's end had come to Man; slowly at first, and not influencing him much, but gaining ever more and more power as the time grew nearer and sympathy and intellect more far-sighted and acute; how, when the cold itself began, and the temperate zone grew frigid, and the tropic temperate, and Man was compelled to migrate, and his sources of heat and power failed one after the other, the knowledge of the end reacted on all forms of mental activity, throwing all thought and invention into one groove. They saw the whole course of the long fight; the ebb and flow of the struggle against the cold, in which, after each long period, it was seen that Man was the loser; how men, armed with powers that to their ancestors would have made them seem as gods, had migrated to the other planets of the system, only to find that there, even on Mercury himself, the dying sun had made all life a fore-known lost battle; how many men, whole nations, had sought a pre-mature refuge from the Fear in the Ultimate Silence called Death. They saw how all the old beliefs, down to the tiniest shreds of mysticism, had fallen from Man as a worn-out garment, leaving him spiritually naked to face the terrors of a relentless Cosmos: how, in the slow dissolving of the ideal Future, man's duties and thoughts were once more moulded with awe and reverence to the wishes of the Past.

They saw the closing centuries of the struggle; the dis-covery of the Red Metal the building of the Spheres that none dare venture to use, but which each succeeding and lessening generation handed down to the next as a sacred heritage only to be put to test in the last resort: they remembered, in their own childhood, the Conference, of the Decision, when they two had been chosen, as the only pair of sufficient vigour and health and animal courage to accept the dread legacy and dare the dread adventure of seeking a fresh home in the outer vastness, so that haply the days of Man might not be ended; and they remembered, only too well, how the rest of humanity, retiring to their last few houses, had one and all pledged each other to seek the Silence and trouble the chilly earth no more. They knew how well that pledge had been kept, and in the darkness and silence of the room clutched each other closer and closer.

And at last they heard the Time Indicator in the upper-most room ring the peal of the completed hour, and knew that in their own lives they must act the final scene in the long life-tragedy of the earth.

Alwyn's hand reached out and touched the switch, and the glow-lamp sprang into radiance again. In silence he handed Celia into the Sphere – which shone a deeper red now and coruscated strangely in the light – and then followed her, drawing the screw section in after him and making it secure. Within, the Sphere was spacious and comfortable, and, save where thickly padded, transparent, even to the weak incandescence of the lamp. It was also pleasantly warm, for the Red Metal was impervious to heat. The man's hand went to the lever that worked through the shell, and pushed aside the strong jaws of the spring clamp that held the Sphere down; and as it went, he looked into the woman's eyes. He hesitated. There was a light in her eyes and his, a feeling in her heart and his, that neither had seen nor experienced before.

"It's madness, Celia," he said, slowly. "It's not too late yet. The moment I pull this lever over the Sphere will tear its way up through the building like an air-bubble through water, but until then it is not too late."

This was not a question in phrase, but it was in fact. Celia did not answer.

"Isn't it a miserable folly – this deference to the past? Don't we know perfectly well that death is as certain out there as here?" the man went on.

Then Celia answered: "Yes, Alwyn; Man, life, everything, is a most miserable folly. But we have nothing to do with that; we can't help it. We don't know, until we try, what fortune may yet meet us. We should be untrue to our ancestors, cowards and recreants to ourselves, if we drew back now. Even in face of the unconscious enmity of the whole Universe of Matter, let us remember that we are living and conscious yet."

As so often in the past, the woman was the man's strengthener in the time of need. Alwyn pulled over the lever, and cried, with antique impulsiveness –

"Forgive me, Celia! We will not give in, not even against a hostile universe! She moves! – we go!"

There was a sudden shock that threw them staggering against each other for a moment; a rending, tearing, rolling crash of masonry and metal, and the Red Sphere rose through the falling ruins of the house and soared up into the night, slanting slightly to the west as it rose. One brief glimpse they had of the dials of the Time Indicator falling across a gap of the ruin; and then their eyes were busy with the white face of earth beneath and the clear brilliance of the starry dome above.

They were still clinging to each other, when both caught sight of a small dark object approaching them from beneath. It came, apparently, from a black spot on the chill whiteness of the landscape to the west of their abandoned home, and it was travelling faster than themselves.

They gazed down at it with sudden interest, that, as they

gazed, turned into acute apprehension, and then to a numb horror.

"The other Sphere!"

"Amy and her lover!"

While they spoke it grew definitely larger, and they saw that a collision was unavoidable. By what caprice of fate it had so fallen out that the helpless paths of the two Red Spheres should thus come to coincide in point of space and time, they could not imagine. The idea of leaving the earth might, by magnetic sympathy, have occurred to both couples at about the same time, but the rest of the unlucky coincidence was inexplicable. They turned from looking at the second Sphere and sought each other's eyes and hands, saying much by look and pressure that words could not convey.

"They did not mean to keep the pledge of the Decision," said Alwyn. "The desire for life must have come to them as it came to me today, and Amy must have remembered the Instructions. I can understand them coming up faster than us, because their Sphere was in a sheet-metal shed in the open, and so would start with less opposition and greater initial velocity. But it is strange that their path should be so nearly ours. It can only be a matter of minutes, at the rate they are gaining, before the end comes for all of us. It will be before we get through the atmosphere and gather our full speed. And it will be the end of Humanity's troubled dream . . . And Amy is in that . . ."

The thought of possible malice, impulsive or premeditated, on the part of the occupants of the second Red Sphere, never entered into the minds of those of the first.

"The responsibility of action rests upon us," said Celia. "They evidently cannot see us, against the background of the black sky. They are coming up swiftly, dear."

"It will have to be that: there is no other way. Better one than both," said the man.

"Be what, Alwyn?"

"The fulminate of sterarium."

"It will not injure them?"

"No; not if we fire the fuse within – about – three minutes. It must seem hard to you, Celia, to know that my hand will send you to the Silence so that Amy may have the last desperate chance of life. Somehow, these last few hours, I have felt the ancient emotions surging back."

The hand that clasped his gave a gentle pressure.

"And I, too, Alwyn; but their reign will be brief. I would rather die with you now than live without you. I am ready. Do not be too late with the fulminate, Alwyn."

They swayed together; their arms were about each other; their lips met in the last kiss. While their faces were yet very near. Alwyn's disengaged right hand touched a tiny white button that was embedded in the padding of the interior.

There was an instantaneous flash of light and roar of sound, and the man and woman in the second sphere were startled by the sudden glare and concussion of it, as their metal shell drove upwards through the cloud of elemental dust that was all that remained of the first Red Sphere and its occupants.

The silence and clear darkness that had been round them a moment before, had returned when they recovered their balance, and in that silence and clear darkness, the man and woman who had not been chosen passed out into the abyss of the Beyond, ignorant of the cause and meaning of that strange explosion in the air, and knew that they were alone in Space, bound they knew not whither.

Approaching Perimelasma

Geoffrey A. Landis

*Now let's leap ahead a hundred years to the cutting edge of current scientific thinking. We're all fascinated by the concept of black holes in space and this story brings all the current thinking together as to how someone might attempt to approach one. I wonder how this story will be perceived in a hundred years time. Geoffrey A. Landis (b. 1955) is on permanent assignment to the NASA Lewis Research Centre. He has written hundreds of scientific papers and began writing science fiction with "Elemental" (*Analog, *December 1984). Soon after he won a Nebula award for "Ripples in the Dirac Sea" (*Asimov's, *October 1988) and a Hugo for "A Walk in the Sun" (*Asimov's, *October 1991). Some of his early stories were collected as* Myths, Legends and True History *(1991). His latest book* Mars Crossing *(2000) won the Locus Award for the year's best first novel.*

T here is a sudden frisson of adrenaline, a surge of something approaching terror (if I could still feel terror), and I realize that this is it, this time I am the one who is doing it.

I'm the one who is going to drop into a black hole.

Oh, my God. This time I'm not you.

This is real.

Of course, I have experienced this exact feeling before. We both know exactly what it feels like.

*   *   *

My body seems weird, too big and at once too small. The feel of my muscles, my vision, my kinesthetic sense, everything is wrong. Everything is strange. My vision is fuzzy, and colors are oddly distorted. When I move, my body moves unexpectedly fast. But there seems to be nothing wrong with it. Already I am getting used to it. "It will do," I say.

There is too much to know, too much to be all at once. I slowly coalesce the fragments of your personality. None of them are you. All of them are you.

A pilot, of course, you must have, you must be, a pilot. I integrate your pilot persona, and he is me. I will fly to the heart of a darkness far darker than any mere unexplored continent. A scientist, somebody to understand your experience, yes. I synthesize a persona. You are him, too, and I understand.

And someone to simply *experience* it, to tell the tale (if any of me will survive to tell the tale) of how you dropped into a black hole, and how you survived. If you survive. *Me*. I will call myself Wolf, naming myself after a nearby star, for no reason whatsoever, except maybe to claim, if only to myself, that I am not you.

All of we are me are you. But, in a real sense, you're not here at all. None of me are you. You are far away. Safe.

Some black holes, my scientist persona whispers, are decorated with an accretion disk, shining like a gaudy signal in the sky. Dust and gas from the interstellar medium fall toward the hungry singularity, accelerating to nearly the speed of light in their descent, swirling madly as they fall. It collides; compresses; ionizes. Friction heats the plasma millions of degrees, to emit a brilliant glow of hard X-rays. Such black holes are anything but black; the incandescence of the infalling gas may be the most brilliantly glowing thing in a galaxy. Nobody and nothing would be able to get near it; nothing would be able to survive the radiation.

The Virgo hole is not one of these. It is ancient, dating from the very first burst of star-formation when the universe was new, and has long ago swallowed or ejected all the interstellar gas in its region, carving an emptiness far into the interstellar medium around it.

The black hole is fifty-seven light years from Earth. Ten billion years ago, it had been a supermassive star, and exploded in a supernova that for a brief moment had shone brighter than the galaxy, in the process tossing away half its mass. Now there is nothing left of the star. The burned-out remnant, some thirty times the mass of the sun, has pulled in space itself around it, leaving nothing behind but gravity.

Before the download, the psychologist investigated my – your – mental soundness. We must have passed the test, obviously, since I'm here. What type of man would allow himself to fall into a black hole? That is my question. Maybe if I can answer that, I would understand ourself.

But this did not seem to interest the psychologist. She did not, in fact, even look directly at me. Her face had the focusless abstract gaze characteristic of somebody hotlinked by the optic nerve to a computer system. Her talk was perfunctory. To be fair, the object of her study was not the flesh me, but my computed reflection, the digital maps of my soul. I remember the last thing she said.

"We are fascinated with black holes because of their depth of metaphor," she said, looking nowhere. "A black hole is, literally, the place of no return. We see it as a metaphor for how we, ourselves, are hurled blindly into a place from which no information ever reaches us, the place from which no one ever returns. We live our lives falling into the future, and we will all inevitably meet the singularity." She paused, expecting, no doubt, some comment. But I remained silent.

"Just remember this," she said, and for the first time her eyes returned to the outside world and focused on me. "This is a real black hole, not a metaphor. Don't treat it like a metaphor. Expect reality." She paused, and finally added, "Trust the math. It's all we really know, and all that we have to trust."

Little help.

Wolf versus the black hole! One might think that such a contest is an unequal one, that the black hole has an over-whelming advantage.

Not quite so unequal.

On my side, I have technology. To start with, the wormhole, the technological sleight-of-space which got you fifty-seven light years from Earth in the first place.

The wormhole is a monster of relativity no less than the black hole, a trick of curved space allowed by the theory of general relativity. After the Virgo black hole was discovered, a wormhole mouth was laboriously dragged to it, slower than light, a project that took over a century. Once the wormhole was here, though, the trip became only a short one, barely a meter of travel. Anybody could come here and drop into it.

A wormhole – a far too cute name, but one we seem to be stuck with – is a shortcut from one place to another. Physically, it is nothing more than a loop of exotic matter. If you move through the hoop on this side of the wormhole, you emerge out the hoop on that side. Topologically, the two sides of the wormhole are pasted together, a piece cut out of space glued together elsewhere.

Exhibiting an excessive sense of caution, the proctors of Earthspace refused to allow the other end of the Virgo wormhole to exit at the usual transportation nexus, the wormhole swarm at Neptune-Trojan 4. The far end of the wormhole opens instead to an orbit around Wolf-562, an undistinguished red dwarf sun circled by two airless planets that are little more than frozen rocks, twenty-one light-years from Earthspace. To get here we had to take a double wormhole hop: Wolf, Virgo.

The black hole is a hundred kilometers across. The wormhole is only a few meters across. I would think that they were overly cautious.

The first lesson of relativity is that time and space are one. For a long time after the theoretical prediction that such a thing as a traversable wormhole ought to be possible, it was believed that a wormhole could also be made to traverse time as well. It was only much later, when wormhole travel was tested, that it was found that the Cauchy instability makes it impossible to form a wormhole that leads backward in time. The theory was correct – space and time are indeed just aspects of the same reality, spacetime –

but any attempt to move a wormhole in such a way that it becomes a timehole produces a vacuum polarization to cancel out the time effect.

After we – the spaceship I am to pilot, and myself/ yourself – come through the wormhole, the wormhole engineers go to work. I have never seen this process close up, so I stay nearby to watch. This is going to be interesting.

A wormhole looks like nothing more than a circular loop of string. It is, in fact, a loop of exotic material, negative-mass cosmic string. The engineers, working telerobotically via vacuum manipulator pods, spray charge onto the string. They charge it until it literally glows with Paschen discharge, like a neon light in the dirty vacuum, and then use the electric charge to manipulate the shape. With the application of invisible electromagnetic fields, the string starts to twist. This is a slow process. Only a few meters across, the wormhole loop has a mass roughly equal to that of Jupiter. Negative to that of Jupiter, to be precise, my scientist persona reminds me, but either way, it is a slow thing to move.

Ponderously, then, it twists further and further, until at last it becomes a lemniscate, a figure of eight. The instant the string touches itself, it shimmers for a moment, and then suddenly there are two glowing circles before us, twisting and oscillating in shape like jellyfish.

The engineers spray more charge onto the two wormholes, and the two wormholes, arcing lightning into space, slowly repel each other. The vibrations of the cosmic string are spraying out gravitational radiation like a dog shaking off water – even where I am, floating ten kilometers distant, I can feel it, like the swaying of invisible tides – and as they radiate energy, the loops enlarge. The radiation represents a serious danger. If the engineers lose control of the string for even a brief instant, it might enter the instability known as "squiggle mode", and catastrophically enlarge. The engineers damp out the radiation before it gets critical, though – they are, after all, well practised at this – and the loops stabilize into two perfect circles. On the other side, at Wolf, precisely the same scene has played out, and two loops of exotic string now circle Wolf-562 as well. The wormhole has been cloned.

All wormholes are daughters of the original wormhole, found floating in the depths of interstellar space eleven hundred years ago, a natural loop of negative cosmic string as ancient as the Big Bang, invisible to the eyes save for the distortion of spacetime. That first one led from nowhere interesting to nowhere exciting, but from that one we bred hundreds, and now we casually move wormhole mouths from star to star, breeding new wormholes as it suits us, to form an ever-expanding network of connections.

I should not have been so close. Angry red lights have been flashing in my peripheral vision, warning blinkers that I have been ignoring. The energy radiated in the form of gravitational waves had been prodigious, and would have, to a lesser person, been dangerous. But in my new body, I am nearly invulnerable, and if I can't stand a mere wormhole cloning, there is no way I will be able to stand a black hole. So I ignore the warnings, wave briefly to the engineers – though I doubt that they can even see me, floating kilometers away – and use my reaction jets to scoot over to my ship.

The ship I will pilot is docked to the research station, where the scientists have their instruments and the biological humans have their living quarters. The wormhole station is huge compared to my ship, which is a tiny ovoid occupying a berth almost invisible against the hull. There is no hurry for me to get to it.

I'm surprised that any of the technicians can even see me, tiny as I am in the void, but a few of them apparently do, because in my radio I hear casual greetings called out: how's it, *ohayo gozaimasu*, hey glad you made it, how's the bod? It's hard to tell from the radio voices which ones are people I know, and which are only casual acquaintances. I answer back: how's it, *ohayo*, yo, surpassing spec. None of them seem inclined to chat, but then, they're busy with their own work.

They are dropping things into the black hole.

Throwing things in, more to say. The wormhole station

orbits a tenth of an astronomical unit from the Virgo black hole, closer to the black hole than Mercury is to the sun. This is an orbit with a period of a little over two days, but, even so close to the black hole, there is nothing to see. A rock, released to fall straight downward, takes almost a day to reach the horizon.

One of the scientists supervising, a biological human named Sue, takes the time to talk with me a bit, explaining what they are measuring. What interests me most is that they are measuring whether the fall deviates from a straight line. This will let them know whether the black hole is rotating. Even a slight rotation would mess up the intricate dance of the trajectory required for my ship. However, the best current theories predict that an old black hole will have shed its angular momentum long ago, and, as far as the technicians can determine, their results show that the conjecture holds.

The black hole, or the absence in space where it is located, is utterly invisible from here. I follow the pointing finger of the scientist, but there is nothing to see. Even if I had a telescope, it is unlikely that I would be able to pick out the tiny region of utter blackness against the irregular darkness of an unfamiliar sky.

My ship is not so different from the drop probes. The main difference is that I will be on it.

Before boarding the station, I jet over in close to inspect my ship, a miniature egg of perfectly reflective material. The hull is made of a single crystal of a synthetic material so strong that no earthly force could even dent it.

A black hole, though, is no earthly force.

Wolf versus the black hole! The second technological trick I have in my duel against the black hole is my body.

I am no longer a fragile, fluid-filled biological human. The tidal forces at the horizon of a black hole would rip a true human apart in mere instants; the accelerations required to hover would squash one into liquid. To make this journey, I have downloaded your fragile biological mind into a body of more robust material. As important as the strength of my new body is the fact that it is tiny. The force produced by the curvature of gravity is proportional to the size of the object. My new body, a millimeter tall, is millions of times more resistant to being stretched to spaghetti.

The new body has another advantage as well. With my mind operating as software on a computer the size of a pinpoint, my thinking and my reflexes are thousands of times faster than biological. In fact, I have already chosen to slow my thinking down, so that I can still interact with the biologicals. At full speed, my microsecond reactions are lightning compared to the molasses of neuron speeds in biological humans. I see far in the ultraviolet now, a necessary compensation for the fact that my vision would consist of nothing but a blur if I tried to see by visible light.

You could have made my body any shape, of course, a tiny cube or even a featureless sphere. But you followed the dictates of social convention. A right human should be recognizably a human, even if I am to be smaller than an ant, and so my body mimics a human body, although no part of it is organic, and my brain faithfully executes your own human brain software. From what I see and feel, externally and internally, I am completely, perfectly human.

As is right and proper. What is the value of experience to a machine?

Later, after I return – *if* I return – I can upload back. I can become you. But return is, as they say, still somewhat problematical.

You, my original, what do you feel? Why did I think I would do it? I imagine you laughing hysterically about the trick you've played, sending me to drop into the black hole while you sit back in perfect comfort, in no danger. Imagining your laughter comforts me, for all that I know that it is false. I've been in the other place before, and never laughed.

I remember the first time I fell into a star.

We were hotlinked together, that time, united in online-realtime, our separate brains reacting as one brain. I remember what I thought, the incredible electric feel: ohmigod, am I really going to do this? Is it too late to back out?

The idea had been nothing more than a whim, a crazy idea, at first. We had been dropping probes into a star, Groombridge 1830B, studying the dynamics of a flare star. We were done, just about, and the last-day-of-project party was just getting in swing. We were all fuzzed with neurotransmitter randomizers, creativity spinning wild and critical thinking nearly zeroed. Somebody, I think it was Jenna, said, we could ride one *down*, you know. Wait for a flare, and then plunge through the middle of it. Helluva ride!

Helluva *splash* at the end, too, somebody said, and laughed.

Sure, somebody said. It might have been me. What do you figure? Download yourself to temp storage and then uplink frames from yourself as you drop?

That works, Jenna said. Better: we copy our bodies first, then link the two brains. One body drops; the other copy hotlinks to it.

Somehow, I don't remember when, the word "we" had grown to include me.

"Sure," I said. "And the copy on top is in null-input suspension; experiences the whole thing realtime!"

In the morning, when we were focused again, I might have dismissed the idea as a whim of the fuzz, but for Jenna the decision was already immovable as a droplet of neutronium. *Sure* we're dropping, let's start now!

We made a few changes. It takes a long time to fall into a star, even a small one like Bee, so the copy was reengineered to a slower thought-rate, and the original body in null-input was frame-synched to the drop copy with impulse-echoers. Since the two brains were molecule by molecule identical, the uplink bandwidth required was minimal.

The probes were reworked to take a biological, which meant mostly that a cooling system had to be added to hold the interior temperature within the liquidus range of water. We did that by the simplest method possible: we surrounded the probes with a huge block of cometary ice. As it sublimated, the ionized gas would carry away heat. A secondary advantage of the ice was that our friends, watching from orbit, would have a blazing cometary trail to cheer on. When the ice was used up, of course, the body would slowly vaporize. None of us would actually survive to hit the star.

But that was no particular concern. If the experience turned out to be too undesirable, we could always edit the pain part of it out of the memory later.

It would have made more sense, perhaps, to have simply recorded the brain-uplink from the copy onto a local high-temp buffer, squirted it back, and linked to it as a memory upload. But Jenna would have none of that. She wanted to experience it in realtime, or at least in as close to realtime as speed-of-light delays allow.

Three of us – Jenna, Martha, and me – dropped. Something seems to be missing from my memory here; I can't remember the reason I decided to do it. It must have been something about a biological body, some a-rational consideration that seemed normal to my then-body, that I could never back down from a crazy whim of Jenna's.

And I had the same experience, the same feeling then, as I, you, did, always do, the feeling that my God *I* am the copy and I am going to die. But that time, of course, thinking every thought in synchrony, there was no way at all to tell the copy from the original, to split the me from you.

It is, in its way, a glorious feeling.

I dropped.

You felt it, you remember it. Boring at first, the long drop with nothing but freefall and the chatter of friends over the radio-link. Then the ice shell slowly flaking away, ionizing and beginning to glow, a diaphanous cocoon of pale violet, and below the red star getting larger and larger, the surface mottled and wrinkled, and then suddenly we fell into and through the flare, a huge luminous vault above us, dwarfing our bodies in the immensity of creation.

An unguessable distance beneath me, the curvature of the star vanished, and, still falling at three hundred kilometers per second, I was hanging motionless over an infinite plane stretching from horizon to horizon.

And then the last of the ice vaporized, and I was suddenly suspended in nothing, hanging nailed to the burning sky over endless crimson horizons of infinity, and pain came like the inevitability of mountains – I didn't edit it – pain like infinite oceans, like continents, like a vast, airless world.

Jenna, now I remember. The odd thing is, I never did really connect in any significant way with Jenna. She was already in a quadrad of her own, a quadrad she was fiercely loyal to, one that was solid and accepting to her chameleon character, neither needing nor wanting a fifth for completion.

Long after, maybe a century or two later, I found out that Jenna had disassembled herself. After her quadrad split apart, she'd downloaded her character to a mainframe, and then painstakingly cataloged everything that made her Jenna: all her various skills and insights, everything she had experienced, no matter how minor, each facet of her character, every memory and dream and longing: the myriad subroutines of personality. She indexed her soul, and she put the ten thousand pieces of it into the public domain for download. A thousand people, maybe a million people, maybe even more, have pieces of Jenna, her cleverness, her insight, her skill at playing antique instruments.

But nobody has her sense of self. After she copied her subroutines, she deleted herself.

And who am I?

Two of the technicians who fit me into my spaceship and who assist in the ten thousand elements of the preflight check are the same friends from that drop, long ago; one of them even still in the same biological body as he had then, although eight hundred years older, his vigor undiminished by biological reconstruction. My survival, if I am to survive, will be dependent on microsecond timing, and I'm embarrassed not to be able to remember his name.

He was, I recall, rather stodgy and conservative even back then.

We joke and trade small talk as the checkout proceeds.

I'm still distracted by my self-questioning, the implications of my growing realization that I have no understanding of why I'm doing this.

Exploring a black hole would be no adventure if only we had faster-than-light travel, but of the thousand technological miracles of the third and fourth millennia, this one miracle was never realized. If I had the mythical FTL motor, I could simply drive out of the black hole. At the event horizon, space falls into the black hole at the speed of light; the mythical motor would make that no barrier.

But such a motor we do not have. One of the reasons I'm taking the plunge – not the only one, not the main one, but one – is in the hope that scientific measurements of the warped space inside the black hole will elucidate the nature of space and time, and so I myself will make one of the innumerable small steps to bring us closer to an FTL drive.

The spaceship I am to pilot has a drive nearly – but not quite – as good. It contains a microscopic twist of spacetime inside an impervious housing, a twist that will parity-reverse ordinary matter into mirror-matter. This total conversion engine gives my ship truly ferocious levels of thrust. The gentlest nudge of my steering rockets will give me thousands of gravities of acceleration. Unthinkable acceleration for a biological body, no matter how well cushioned. The engine will allow the rocket to dare the unthinkable, to hover at the very edge of the event horizon, to maneuver where space itself is accelerating at nearly light-speed. This vehicle, no larger than a peanut, contains the engines of an interstellar probe.

Even with such an engine, most of the ship is reaction mass.

The preflight checks are all green. I am ready to go. I power up my instruments, check everything out for myself, verify what has already been checked three times, and then check once again. My pilot persona is very thorough. Green.

"You still haven't named your ship," comes a voice to me. It is the technician, the one whose name I have forgotten. "What is your call sign?"

One way journey, I think. Maybe something from Dante?

No, Sartre said it better: no exit. "*Huis Clos*," I say, and drop free.

Let them look it up.

Alone.

The laws of orbital mechanics have not been suspended, and I do not drop into the black hole. Not yet. With the slightest touch of my steering engines – I do not dare use the main engine this close to the station – I drop into an elliptical orbit, one with a perimelasma closer to, but still well outside, the dangerous zone of the black hole. The black hole is still invisible, but inside my tiny kingdom I have enhanced senses of exquisite sensitivity, spreading across the entire spectrum from radio to gamma radiation. I look with my new eyes to see if I can detect an X-ray glow of interstellar hydrogen being ripped apart, but if there is any such, it is too faint to be visible with even my sensitive instruments. The interstellar medium is so thin here as to be essentially nonexistent. The black hole is invisible.

I smile. This makes it better, somehow. The black hole is pure, unsullied by any outside matter. It consists of gravity and nothing else, as close to a pure mathematical abstraction as anything in the universe can ever be.

It is not too late to back away. If I were to choose to accelerate at a million gravities, I would reach relativistic velocities in about thirty seconds. No wormholes would be needed for me to run away; I would barely even need to slow down my brain to cruise at nearly the speed of light to anywhere in the colonized galaxy.

But I know I won't. The psychologist knew it too, damn her, or she would never have approved me for the mission. Why? What is it about me?

As I worry about this with part of my attention, while the pilot persona flies the ship, I flash onto a realization, and at this realization another memory hits. It is the psychologist, and in the memory I'm attracted to her sexually, so much so that you are distracted from what she is saying.

I feel no sexual attraction now, of course. I can barely remember what it is. That part of the memory is odd, alien.

"We can't copy the whole brain to the simulation, but we

can copy enough that, to yourself, you will still feel like yourself," she said. She is talking to the air, not to you. "You won't notice any gaps."

I'm brain-damaged. This is the explanation.

You frowned. "How could I not notice that some of my memories are missing?"

"The brain makes adjustments. Remember, at any given time, you never even use one per cent of one per cent of your memories. What we'll be leaving out will be stuff that you will never have any reason to think about. The memory of the taste of strawberries, for example; the floor-plan of the house you lived in as a teenager. Your first kiss."

This bothered you somewhat – you want to remain yourself. I concentrate, hard. What do strawberries taste like? I can't remember. I'm not even certain what color they are. Round fruits, like apples, I think, only smaller. And the same color as apples, or something similar, I'm sure, except I don't remember what color that is.

You decided that you can live with the editing, as long as it doesn't change the essential you. You smiled. "Leave in the first kiss."

So I can never possibly solve the riddle: what kind of a man is it that would deliberately allow himself to drop into a black hole. I cannot, because I don't have the memories of you. In a real sense, I am *not* you at all.

But I do remember the kiss. The walk in the darkness, the grass wet with dew, the moon a silver sliver on the horizon, turning to her, and her face already turned up to meet my lips. The taste indescribable, more feeling than taste (not like strawberries at all), the small hardness of her teeth behind the lips – all there. Except the one critical detail: I don't have any idea at all who she *was*.

What else am I missing? Do I even know what I don't know?

I was a child, maybe nine, and there was no tree in the neighborhood that you could not climb. I was a careful, meticulous, methodical climber. On the tallest of the trees, when you reached toward the top, you were above the forest canopy (did I live in a forest?) and, out of the dimness of the forest floor, emerged into brilliant sunshine. Nobody else could climb like you; nobody ever suspected how high I climbed. It was your private hiding place, so high that the world was nothing but a sea of green waves in the valley between the mountains.

It was my own stupidity, really. At the very limit of the altitude needed to emerge into sunlight, the branches were skinny, narrow as your little finger. They bent alarmingly with your weight, but I knew exactly how much they would take. The bending was a thrill, but I was cautious, and knew exactly what I was doing.

It was further down, where the branches were thick and safe, that I got careless. Three points of support, that was the rule of safety, but I was reaching for one branch, not paying attention, when one in my other hand broke, and I was off balance. I slipped. For a prolonged instant I was suspended in space, branches all about me, I reached out and grasped only leaves, and I fell and fell and fell, and all I could think as leaves and branches fell upward past me was, oh my, I made a miscalculation; I was really stupid.

The flash memory ends with no conclusion. I must have hit the ground, but I cannot remember it. Somebody must have found me, or else I wandered or crawled back, perhaps in a daze, and found somebody, but I cannot remember it.

Half a million kilometers from the hole. If my elliptical orbit were around the sun instead of a black hole, I would already have penetrated the surface. I now hold the record for the closest human approach. There is still nothing to see with unmagnified senses. It seems surreal that I'm in the grip of something so powerful that is utterly invisible. With my augmented eyes used as a telescope, I can detect the black hole by what isn't there, a tiny place of blackness nearly indistinguishable from any other patch of darkness except for an odd motion of the stars near it.

My ship is sending a continuous stream of telemetry back to the station. I have an urge to add a verbal commentary – there is plenty of bandwidth – but I have nothing to say. There is only one person I have any interest in talking to, and you are cocooned at absolute zero, waiting for me to upload myself and become you.

My ellipse takes me inward, moving faster and faster. I am still in Newton's grip, far from the sphere where Einstein takes hold.

A tenth of a solar radius. The blackness I orbit is now large enough to see without a telescope, as large as the sun seen from Earth, and swells as I watch with time-distorted senses. Due to its gravity, the blackness in front of the star pattern is a bit larger than the disk of the black hole itself. Square root of twenty-seven over two – about two and a half times larger, the physicist persona notes. I watch in fascination.

What I see is a bubble of purest blackness. The bubble pushes the distant stars away from it as it swells. My orbital motion makes the background stars appear to sweep across the sky, and I watch them approach the black hole and then, smoothly pushed by the gravity, move off to the side, a river of stars flowing past an invisible obstacle. It is a gravitational lensing effect, I know, but the view of flowing stars is so spectacular that I cannot help but watch it. The gravity pushes each star to one side or the other. If a star were to pass directly behind the hole, it would appear to split and for an instant become a perfect circle of light, an Einstein ring. But this precise alignment is too rare to see by accident.

Closer, I notice an even odder effect. The sweeping stars detour smoothly around the bubble of blackness, but very close to the bubble, there are other stars, stars that actually move in the opposite direction, a counterflowing river of stars. It takes me a long time (microseconds perhaps) before my physicist persona tells me that I am seeing the image of the stars in the Einstein mirror. The entire external universe is mirrored in a narrow ring outside the black hole, and the mirror image flows along with a mirror of my own motion.

In the center of the ring there is nothing at all.

Five thousand kilometers, and I am moving fast. The gravitational acceleration here is over ten million gees, and I am still fifty times the Schwarzschild radius from the black hole. Einstein's correction is still tiny, though, and if I were to do nothing, my orbit would whip around the black hole and still escape into the outside world.

One thousand kilometers. Perimelasma, the closest point of my elliptical orbit. Ten times the Schwarzschild radius, close enough that Einstein's correction to Newton now makes a small difference to the geometry of space. I fire my engines. My speed is so tremendous that it takes over a second of my engine firing at a million gravities to circularize my orbit.

My time sense has long since speeded up back to normal, and then faster than normal. I orbit the black hole about ten times per second.

My God, this is why I exist, this is why I'm here!

All my doubts are gone in the rush of naked power. No biological could have survived this far; no biological could have even survived the million-gee circularization burn, and I am only at the very beginning! I grin like a maniac, throb with a most unscientific excitement that must be the electronic equivalent of an adrenaline high.

Oh, this ship is good. This ship is sweet. A million-gee burn, smooth as magnetic levitation, and I barely cracked the throttle. I should have taken it for a spin before dropping in, should have hot-rodded *Huis Clos* around the stellar neighborhood. But it had been absolutely out of the question to fire the main engine close to the wormhole station. Even with the incredible efficiency of the engine, that million-gee perimelasma burn must have lit up the research station like an unexpected sun.

I can't wait to take *Huis Clos* in and see what it will *really* do.

My orbital velocity is a quarter of the speed of light.

The orbit at nine hundred kilometers is only a parking orbit, a chance for me to configure my equipment, make final measurements, and, in principle, a last chance for me to change my mind. There is nothing to reconnoiter that the probes have not already measured, though, and there is no chance that I will change my mind, however sensible that may seem.

The river of stars swirls in a dance of counterflow around the blackness below me. The horizon awaits.

The horizon below is invisible, but real. There is no

barrier at the horizon, nothing to see, nothing to feel. I will even be unable to detect it, except for my calculations.

An event horizon is a one-way membrane, a place you can pass into but neither you nor your radio signals can pass out of. According to the mathematics, as I pass through the event horizon, the directions of space and time change identity. Space rotates into time; time rotates into space. What this means is that the direction to the center of the black hole, after I pass the event horizon, will be the future. The direction out of the black hole will be the past. This is the reason that no one and nothing can ever leave a black hole; the way inward is the one direction we always must go, whether we will it or not: into the future.

Or so the mathematics says.

The future, inside a black hole, is a very short one.

So far the mathematics has been right on. Nevertheless, I go on. With infinitesimal blasts from my engine, I inch my orbit lower.

The bubble of blackness gets larger, and the counterflow of stars around it becomes more complex. As I approach three times the Schwarzschild radius, 180 kilometers, I check all my systems. This is the point of no rescue: inside three Schwarzschild radii, no orbits are stable, and my automatic systems will be constantly thrusting to adjust my orbital parameters to keep me from falling into the black hole or being flung away to infinity. My systems are all functional, in perfect form for the dangerous drop. My orbital velocity is already half the speed of light. Below this point, centrifugal force will decrease toward zero as I lower my orbit, and I must use my thrusters to increase my velocity as I descend, or else plunge into the hole.

When I grew up, in the last years of the second millennium, nobody thought that they would live forever. Nobody would have believed me if I told them that by my thousandth birthday, I would have no concept of truly dying.

Even if all our clever tricks fail, even if I plunge through the event horizon and am stretched into spaghetti and crushed by the singularity, I will not die. You, my original, will live on, and if *you* were to die, we have made dozens of back-ups and spin-off copies of myselves in the past, some versions of which must surely still be living on. My individual life has little importance. I can, if I chose, uplink my brain-state to the orbiting station right at this instant, and reawake, whole, continuing this exact thought, unaware (except on an abstract intellectual level) that I and you are not the same.

But we are not the same, you and I. I am an edited-down version of you, and the memories that have been edited out, even if I never happen to think them, make me different, a new individual. Not *you*.

On a metaphorical level, a black hole stands for death, the blackness that is sucking us all in. But what meaning does death have in a world of matrix back-ups and modular personality? Is my plunge a death wish? Is it thumbing my nose at death? Because I intend to survive. Not you. *Me*.

I orbit the black hole over a hundred times a second now, but I have revved my brain processing speed accordingly, so that my orbit seems to me leisurely enough. The view here is odd. The black hole has swollen to the size of a small world below me, a world of perfect velvet darkness, surrounded by a belt of madly rotating stars.

No engine, no matter how energetic, can put a ship into an orbit at 1.5 times the Schwarzschild radius; at this distance, the orbital velocity is the speed of light, and not even my total-conversion engine can accelerate me to that speed. Below that, there are no orbits at all. I stop my descent at an orbit just sixty kilometers from the event horizon, when my orbital velocity reaches 85 per cent of the speed of light. Here I can coast, ignoring the constant small adjustments of the thrusters that keep my orbit from sliding off the knife-edge. The velvet blackness of the black hole is almost half of the universe now, and if I were to trust the outside view, I am diving at a slant downward into the black hole. I ignore my pilot's urge to override the automated navigation and manually even out the trajectory. The downward slant is only relativistic aberration, nothing more, an illusion of my velocity.

And 85 per cent of the speed of light is as fast as I dare

orbit; I must conserve my fuel for the difficult part of the plunge to come.

In my unsteady orbit sixty kilometers above the black hole, I let my ship's computer chat with the computer of the wormhole station, updating and downloading my sensors' observations.

At this point, according to the mission plan, I am supposed to uplink my brain state, so that should anything go wrong further down the well, you, my original, will be able to download my state and experiences to this point. To hell with that, I think, a tiny bit of rebellion. I am not you. If you awaken with my memories, I will be no less dead.

Nobody at the wormhole station questions my decision not to upload.

I remember one other thing now. "You're a type N personality," the psychologist had said, twitching her thumb to leaf through invisible pages of test results. The gesture marked her era; only a person who had grown up before computer hotlinks would move a physical muscle in commanding a virtual. She was twenty-first century, possibly even twentieth. "But I suppose you already know that."

"Type N?" you asked.

"Novelty-seeking," she said. "Most particularly, one not prone to panic at new situations."

"Oh," you said. You did already know that. "Speaking of novelty seeking, how do you feel about going to bed with a type N personality?"

"That would be unprofessional." She frowned. "I think."

"Not even one who is about to jump down a black hole?"

She terminated the computer link with a flick of her wrist, and turned to look at you. "Well —"

From this point onward, microsecond timing is necessary for the dance we have planned to succeed. My computer and the station computer meticulously compare clocks, measuring Doppler shifts to exquisite precision. My clocks are running slow, as expected, but half of the slowness is relativistic time dilation due to my velocity. The gravitational redshift is still modest. After some milliseconds – a long wait for me, in my hyped-up state – they declare that they agree. The station has already done their part, and I begin the next phase of my descent.

The first thing I do is fire my engine to stop my orbit. I crack the throttle to fifty million gees of acceleration, and the burn takes nearly a second, a veritable eternity, to slow my flight.

For a moment I hover, and start to drop. I dare not drop too fast, and I ramp my throttle up, to a hundred megagee, five hundred, a billion gravities. At forty billion gravities of acceleration, my engine thrust equals the gravity of the black hole, and I hover.

The blackness has now swallowed half of the universe. Everything beneath me is black. Between the black below and the starry sky above, a spectacularly bright line exactly bisects the sky. I have reached the altitude at which orbital velocity is just equal to the speed of light, and the light from my rocket exhaust is in orbit around the black hole. The line I see around the sky is my view of my own rocket, seen by light that has traveled all the way around the black hole. All I can see is the exhaust, far brighter than anything else in the sky.

The second brightest thing is the laser beacon from the wormhole station above me, shifted from the original red laser color to a greenish blue. The laser marks the exact line between the station and the black hole, and I maneuver carefully until I am directly beneath the orbiting station.

At forty billion gravities, even my ultrastrong body is at its limits. I cannot move, and even my smallest finger is pressed against the form-fitting acceleration couch. But the controls, hardware-interfaced to my brain, do not require me to lift a finger to command the spacecraft. The command I give *Huis Clos* is: down.

My engine throttles down slightly, and I drop inward from the photon sphere, the bright line of my exhaust vanishes. Every stray photon from my drive is now sucked downward.

Now my view of the universe has changed. The black hole has become the universe around me, and the universe itself, all the galaxies and stars and the wormhole station, is a shrinking sphere of sparkling dust above me.

Sixty billion gravities. Seventy. Eighty.

Eighty billion gravities is full throttle. I am burning fuel at an incredible rate, and only barely hold steady. I am still twenty kilometers above the horizon.

There is an unbreakable law of physics: incredible accelerations require incredible fuel consumption. Even though my spaceship is, by mass, comprised mostly of fuel, I can maintain less than a millisecond worth of thrust at this acceleration. I cut my engine and drop.

It will not be long now. This is my last chance to uplink a copy of my mind back to the wormhole station to wake in your body, with my last memory the decision to upload my mind.

I do not.

The stars are blueshifted by a factor of two, which does not make them noticeably bluer. Now that I have stopped accelerating, the starlight is falling into the hole along with me, and the stars do not blueshift any further. My instruments probe the vacuum around me. The theorists say that the vacuum close to the horizon of a black hole is an exotic vacuum, abristle with secret energy. Only a ship plunging through the event horizon would be able to measure this. I do, recording the results carefully on my ship's on-board recorders, since it is now far too late to send anything back by radio.

There is no sign to mark the event horizon, and there is no indication at all when I cross it. If it were not for my computer, there would be no way for me to tell that I have passed the point of no return.

Nothing is different. I look around the tiny cabin, and can see no change. The blackness below me continues to grow, but is otherwise not changed. The outside universe continues to shrink above me; the brightness beginning to concentrate into a belt around the edge of the glowing sphere of stars, but this is only an effect of my motion. The only difference is that I have only a few hundred microseconds left.

From the viewpoint of the outside world, the light

from my spacecraft has slowed down and stopped at the horizon. But I have far outstripped my lagging image, and am falling toward the center at incredible speed. At the exact center is the singularity, far smaller than an atom, a mathematical point of infinite gravity and infinite mystery.

Whoever I am, whether or not I survive, I am now the first person to penetrate the event horizon of a black hole. That's worth a cheer, even with nobody to hear. Now I have to count on the hope that the microsecond timing of the technicians above me had been perfect for the second part of my intricate dance, the part that might, if all goes well, allow me to survive.

Above me, according to theory, the stars have already burned out, and even the most miserly red dwarf has sputtered the last of its hydrogen fuel and grown cold. The universe has already ended, and the stars have gone out. I still see a steady glow of starlight from the universe above me, but this is fossil light, light that has been falling down into the black hole with me for eons, trapped in the infinitely stretched time of the black hole.

For me, time has rotated into space, and space into time. Nothing feels different to me, but I cannot avoid the singularity at the center of the black hole any more than I can avoid the future. Unless, that is, I have a trick.

Of course, I have a trick.

At the center of the spherical universe above me is a dot of bright blue-violet; the fossil light of the laser beacon from the orbiting station. My reaction jets have kept on adjusting my trajectory to keep me centered in the guidance beam, so I am directly below the station. Anything dropped from the station will, if everything works right, drop directly on the path I follow.

I am approaching close to the center now, and the tidal forces stretching my body are creeping swiftly toward a billion gees per millimeter. Much higher, and even my tremendously strong body will be ripped to spaghetti. There are only microseconds left for me. It is time.

I hammer my engine, full throttle. Far away, and long ago, my friends at the wormhole station above dropped a wormhole into the event horizon. If their timing was perfect –

From a universe that has already died, the wormhole cometh.

Even with my enhanced time sense, things happen fast. The laser beacon blinks out, and the wormhole sweeps down around me like the vengeance of God, far faster than I can react. The sparkle-filled sphere of the universe blinks out like a light, and the black hole – and the tidal forces stretching my body – abruptly disappears. For a single instant I see a black disk below me, and then the wormhole rotates, twists, stretches, and then silently vanishes.

Ripped apart by the black hole.

My ship is vibrating like a bell from the abrupt release of tidal stretching. "I did it," I shout. "It worked! God damn it, it really worked!"

This was what was predicted by the theorists, that I would be able to pass through the wormhole before it was shredded by the singularity at the center. The other possibility, that the singularity itself, infinitesimally small and infinitely powerful, might follow me through the wormhole, was laughed at by everyone who had any claim to understand wormhole physics. This time, the theorists were right.

But where am I?

There should be congratulations pouring into my radio by now, teams of friends and technicians swarming over to greet me, cheering and shouting.

"*Huis Clos*," I say, over the radio. "I made it! *Huis Clos* here. Is anybody there?"

In theory, I should have reemerged at Wolf-562. But I do not see it. In fact, what I see is not recognizably the universe at all.

There are no stars.

Instead of stars, the sky is filled with lines, parallel lines of white light by the uncountable thousands. Dominating the sky, where the star Wolf-562 should have been, is a glowing red cylinder, perfectly straight, stretching to infinity in both directions.

Have I been transported into some other universe? Could

the black hole's gravity sever the wormhole, cutting it loose from our universe entirely, and connect it into this strange new one?

If so, it has doomed me. The wormhole behind me, my only exit from this strange universe, is already destroyed. Not that escaping through it could have done me any good – it would only have brought me back to the place I escaped, to be crushed by the singularity of the black hole.

I could just turn my brain off, and I will have lost nothing, in a sense. They will bring you out of your suspended state, tell you that the edition of you that dropped into the black hole failed to upload, and they lost contact after it passed the event horizon. The experiment failed, but you had never been in danger.

But, however much you think we are the same, *I am not you*. I am a unique individual. When they revive you, without your expected new memories, I will still be gone.

I want to survive. I want to return.

A universe of tubes of light! Brilliant bars of an infinite cage. The bright lines in the sky have slight variations in color, from pale red to plasma-arc blue. They must be similar to the red cylinder near me, I figure, but light-years away. How could a universe have lines of light instead of stars?

I am amazingly well equipped to investigate that question, with senses that range from radio through X-ray, and I have nothing else to do for the next thousand years or so. So I take a spectrum of the light from the glowing red cylinder.

I have no expectation that the spectrum will reveal anything I can interpret, but oddly, it looks normal. Impossibly, it looks like the spectrum of a star.

The computer can even identify, from its data of millions of spectra, precisely which star. The light from the cylinder has the spectral signature of Wolf-562.

Coincidence? It cannot possibly be coincidence, out of billions of possible spectra, that this glowing sword in the sky has exactly the spectrum of the star that should have been there. There can be no other conclusion but that the cylinder *is* Wolf-562.

I take a few more spectra, this time picking at random

three of the lines of light in the sky, and the computer analyzes them for me. A bright one: the spectrum of 61 Virginis. A dimmer one: a match to Wolf-1061. A blue-white streak: Vega.

The lines in the sky are stars.

What does this mean?

I'm not in another universe. I am in *our* universe, but the universe has been transformed. Could the collision of a wormhole with a black hole destroy our entire universe, stretching suns like taffy into infinite straight lines? Impossible. Even if it had, I would still see far-away stars as dots, since the light from them has been traveling for hundreds of years.

The universe cannot have changed. Therefore, by logic, it must be *me* who has been transformed.

Having figured out this much, the only possible answer is obvious.

When the mathematicians describe the passage across the event horizon of a black hole, they say that the space and time directions switch identity. I had always thought this only a mathematical oddity, but if it were true, if I had rotated when I passed the event horizon, and was now perceiving time as a direction in space, and one of the space axes as time – this would explain everything. Stars extend from billions of years into the past to long into the future; perceiving time as space, I see lines of light. If I were to come closer and find one of the rocky planets of Wolf 562, it would look like a braid around the star, a helix of solid rock. Could I land on it? How would I interact with a world where what I perceive as time is a direction in space?

My physicist persona doesn't like this explanation, but is at a loss to find a better one. In this strange sideways existence, I must be violating the conservation laws of physics like mad, but the persona could find no other hypothesis and must reluctantly agree: time is rotated into space.

To anybody outside, I must look like a string, a knobby long rope with one end at the wormhole and the other at my death, wherever that might be. But nobody could see me fast enough, since with no extension in time I must only be a transient event that bursts everywhere into existence and vanishes at the same instant. There is no way I can signal, no way I can communicate –

Or? Time, to me, is now a direction I can travel in as simply as using my rocket. I could find a planet, travel parallel to the direction of the surface –

But, no, all I could do would be to appear to the inhabitants briefly as a disk, a cross-section of myself, infinitely thin. There is no way I could communicate.

But I can travel in time, if I want. Is there any way I can use this?

Wait. If I have rotated from space into time, then there is one direction in space that I cannot travel. Which direction is that? The direction that used to be away from the black hole.

Interesting thoughts, but not ones which help me much. To return, I need to once again flip space and time. I could dive into a black hole. This would again rotate space and time, but it wouldn't do me any good: once I left the black hole – if I could leave the black hole – nothing would change.

Unless there were a wormhole inside the black hole, falling inward to destruction just at the same instant I was there? But the only wormhole that has fallen into a black hole was already destroyed. Unless, could I travel forward in time? Surely some day the research team would drop a new wormhole into the black hole –

Idiot. Of course there's a solution. Time is a spacelike dimension to me, so I can travel either direction in time now, forward or back. I need only to move back to an instant just after the wormhole passed through the event horizon, and, applying full thrust, shoot through. The very moment that my original self shoots through the wormhole to escape the singularity, I can pass through the opposite direction, and rotate myself back into the real universe.

The station at Virgo black hole is forty light years away, and I don't dare use the original wormhole to reach it. My spacetime-rotated body must be an elongated snake in this version of space-time, and I do not wish to find out what a wormhole passage will do to it until I have no other choice.

Still, that is no problem for me. Even with barely enough fuel to thrust for a few microseconds, I can reach an appreciable fraction of light-speed, and I can slow down my brain to make the trip appear only an instant.

To an outside observer, it takes literally no time at all.

"No," says the psych tech, when I ask her. "There's no law that compels you to uplink back into your original. You're a free human being. Your original can't force you."

"Great," I say. Soon I'm going to have to arrange to get a biological body built for myself. This one is superb, but it's a disadvantage in social intercourse being only a millimeter tall.

The transition back to real space worked perfectly. Once I figured out how to navigate in time-rotated space, it had been easy enough to find the wormhole and the exact instant it had penetrated the event horizon.

"Are you going to link your experiences to public domain?" the tech asks. "I think he would like to see what you experienced. Musta been pretty incredible."

"Maybe," I said.

"For that matter," the psych tech added, "I'd like to link it, too."

"I'll think about it."

So I am a real human being now, independent of you, my original.

There had been cheers and celebrations when I had emerged from the wormhole, but nobody had an inkling quite how strange my trip had been until I told them. Even then, I doubt that I was quite believed until the sensor readings and computer logs of *Huis Clos* confirmed my story with hard data.

The physicists had been ecstatic. A new tool to probe time and space. The ability to rotate space into time will open up incredible capabilities. They were already planning new expeditions, not the least of which was a trip to probe right to the singularity itself.

They had been duly impressed with my solution to the problem, although, after an hour of thinking it over, they all agreed it had been quite obvious. "It was lucky," one of them remarked, "that you decided to go through the wormhole from the opposite side, that second time."

"Why?" I asked.

"If you'd gone through the same direction, you'd have rotated an additional ninety degrees, instead of going back."

"So?"

"Reversed the time vector. Turns you into antimatter. First touch of the interstellar medium – Poof."

"Oh," I said. I hadn't thought of that. It made me feel a little less clever.

Now that the mission is over, I have no purpose, no direction for my existence. The future is empty, the black hole that we all must travel into. I will get a biological body, yes, and embark on the process of finding out who I am. Maybe, I think, this is a task that everybody has to do.

And then I will meet you. With luck, perhaps I'll even like you.

And maybe, if I should like you enough, and I feel confident, I'll decide to upload you into myself, and once more, we will again be one.

The Pen and the Dark

Colin Kapp

From one seemingly impossible journey to another. Colin Kapp is not as well known a writer as he should be. His first sf appeared in New Worlds *back in 1958 and throughout the sixties and seventies he produced some of the most technologically stunning stories of the period. His best novel remains* The Dark Mind *(1963) about a psychic superbeing who attempts to take over control of alternate dimensions. My favourite of his stories were those that featured the "unorthodox" engineers. These were a group of lateral-thinking problem solvers who were called in whenever something insuperable arose. They first appeared in "The Railways Up on Cannis" (*New Worlds, *October 1959) and the stories were collected as* The Unorthodox Engineers *(1979). The following was one of the most intriguing.*

The scudder slid through candy-floss clouds of cirrus and strato-cumulus so extremely Earthlike in formation that even the scudder's well-travelled occupants felt a twinge of nostalgia for home. Far below, the green and gilded fields proudly displayed the rich bust of the planet Ithica ripening in the rays of the G-type primary. The occasional sprawl of town or metropolis betrayed the Terran origin of Ithica's inhabitants and the results of their desire to recreate the image of a far-off homeworld. With a little imagination this could easily have been mistaken for one of the rarer spots on Earth.

But when the scudder cleared the haze of the cloud formation, the black and fearsome thing which reared above them was decidedly not of Earth.

Caught on a sudden and curious down-draught, the scudder dived steeply and then went into a mammoth power-climb that took it soaring into a wide and safe helical orbit around and finally above the hideous patch of darkness.

"So that's it!" said Lieutenant Fritz Van Noon.

Dr Maxwell Courtney nodded. "That's it. That's what we call the Dark. What you see now is the mushroom dome. It's all of twenty-five kilometres across, and as near indestructible as anything we've ever encountered. We put a nuclear Hell-raiser down on to it and nothing happened at all."

Van Noon raised a swift eyebrow. "Nothing?"

"We know the device exploded, because we were able to detect the start of the priming flash. After that – nothing. The Dark absorbed every quantum of energy released. It swallowed the whole damn lot and never so much as flickered."

"And you say that aliens put it there?"

"So the records read. About two hundred terrayears ago – long before we re-established contact with Ithica. It would seem some sort of alien vessel made a touchdown on the edge of the city, stayed a night, then vanished as abruptly as it had come. But in its place it left this pillar of darkness, and nobody has ever found out why they left it or what it's supposed to do. There's a great many theories about it, but none which completely explains the facts. Some think that it soaks up energy and transmits it elsewhere. Some think it's contra-terrene. It's even suggested that an alien colony lives inside it."

"And what's your own opinion?" asked Van Noon.

Courtney shrugged. "After three years of scientific examination I still don't know what to think. At some time or another I've held most of the current physical theories only to discard them for another."

"Is it uniform right the way down?"

"It's really shaped like a bolt," said Courtney. "The

shaft proper is about seven kilometres in diameter and about thirty kilometres high. It is capped by the mushroom head here which extends out to about twenty-five kilometres in diameter and apparently defines the region of the Pen."

"The Pen?" Van Noon looked up from his notes. "What's that?"

Courtney smiled fleetingly. "Sorry! That's local terminology. I mean the apparent penumbral shadow of reduced effects which surrounds the pillar of Dark. It's a twilight region about nine kilometres average depth, the outer reaches of which are easily penetrable, and the inner regions connect with the Dark. It has an interesting subclimate too – but you'll see that for yourself later."

Van Noon scowled. "And you have no idea at all what the Dark is made of?"

Courtney spread his hands. "It's commonly assumed to be contra-terrene, as I said, but I don't think the hypothesis holds water in the face of all the evidence. But God-alone knows what it really is. Even the Pen raises some nice problems in physics which don't have answers in any of the textbooks we know."

"All right," said Van Noon. "I'd like to take a closer look at it first and come back to you when I've some idea of what questions to ask."

"I rather hoped you'd do it that way," Courtney said. "We've assembled such a mass of data on the Dark that we don't know if we've lost our way in our own erudition. That's why we asked for some of you Unorthodox Engineering chaps to come out to Ithica to supply a fresh approach. The answer may be so damned obvious that we can't see it for the weight of the maths intervening."

"And the primary object of the exercise is what?"

Courtney glanced from the window at the monstrous column of darkness which reared its head high over the landscape. "I don't know. Study it, use it, get rid of it – it's an alien paradox, Fritz, and I don't think anyone with an ounce of science in his makeup can let it rest there doing nothing but soaking up the sun."

*   *   *

"What's the general topography of the Dark area, Jacko?"

Jacko Hine of the Unorthodox Engineers unrolled his sheaf of maps. "This is the position of the Dark, and the area I've coloured shows the extent of the Pen. As you can see, the whole is centred on the edge of what used to be the city of Bethlem."

"Is the city still there?"

"Its ruins are. The present city of New Bethlem has moved southwards, but in and around the Pen the remains of the old city still exist. Nobody lives there now. If you'd been into the Pen you'd understand why."

"You've been in, then? What's it like?"

"Weird," said Jacko. "It's cold and dull, but the sensations aren't the usual ones of coldness and dullness. This is a different feeling entirely. I can't quite explain it, but there's something wrong with the physics of the place."

"Then I think I'd better start there. Where's the rest of the U.E. squad?"

"Doing some preliminary fact-finding at the edge of the Pen. I suggest we can contact them as we go in, and see what they've found."

"No," said Van Noon. "I'd sooner contact them on the way out. I want my first impressions of the Pen to be a direct personal experience. I need to get the 'feel' of the thing – because I have a suspicion that this problem is going to be cracked by intuition rather than by observation. Maxwell Courtney's no fool, and he and his team have been gathering facts for three years now. There's no sense in repeating what they've already done, so I'm going to play it my way."

"I was rather afraid of that," said Jacko, following in his wake.

The edgeland was an area dominated by the ruins of the old city. The transport took them to the very perimeter of the Pen, and here they dismounted. Van Noon surveyed the phenomenon thoughtfully.

The termination of the Pen was sharp, precise, and unwavering. At one point the magnificent sunshine of Ithica baked the dust golden and ripened dark berries on the hanks of hackberry-like scrub. A centimetre away the summer changed abruptly to a dark winter, shadowed and uninviting, and such scrub as grew within its bounds was thin and gnarled and bore no fruit at all.

Above them the wall of shade rose vertically until it disappeared into the cloud-ring which clung stubbornly round the sombre column. Looking into the Pen, Van Noon gained the impression of gradually increasing coldness and bleakness and gloom until, in the centre, he could just detect the absolute blackness of the great pillar of the Dark. Cautiously he extended a hand into the boundary of the Pen and withdrew it, experiencing the strange chill on his skin.

"Very curious," he said. "What strikes you most about this, Jacko?"

"Lack of interaction between the warmth outside and the cold inside."

"Precisely. At a guess there's a temperature fall of fifteen degrees centigrade over a distance of one centimetre. Now there's plenty of heat capacity available out here, so why doesn't the warmth penetrate farther into the Pen?"

"There's only one answer. The heat is being removed."

"Yes, but I don't see how. Even if you postulate that in the centre of the Pen is an area of absolute zero temperature you would still expect to get a graduated temperature rise at the boundary and not a sharp transition such as you have here."

"So?" Jacko looked at him expectantly.

"So I can see how to achieve the inverse of this situation using, for instance, a collimated beam of infra-red heat. But a collimated shaft of coldness is something very new indeed. As you remarked, Jacko, there's something wrong with the physics of this place."

With swift resolution Van Noon stepped through the perimeter and into the Pen. Jacko pulled up his collar and followed him in. The contrast was staggering. Whereas a few seconds previously the Ithican warmth had been sufficient to bring them to a gentle sweat, they now stood shivering with the curious chill which inhabited the Pen. Van Noon was looking with amazement at the dreary landscape and sub-climate of the Pen interior.

The bright Ithican sunlight did not penetrate. The

internal winter continued sheer up to the outer wall, and such light as there was filtered downwards from a dirty, leaden cloudbase trapped within the Pen itself. Even looking sunward, no sign of the Ithican primary could be seen, though it should have been clearly visible, and its apparent loss was not explicable in terms of haze or diffraction.

The sun-toasted ruins which stood outside the Pen continued inside as a depressing waste of rotting bricks and slimed timbers, forming forgotten streets on which even the sparse and miserable vegetation had not much cared to grow. A few furred rodents scattered at their approach, with an attitude of resignation, as if self-preservation here was a matter about which one thought twice.

Van Noon was sampling his surroundings with the detachment of a scientist, yet using his own body in lieu of instrumentation. The process went on for several minutes before he came to a conclusion.

"What do you feel, Jacko?"

"Cold."

"Anything else?"

"Yes, dull. I don't know if it's physical or psychological, but every action seems to demand too much effort."

"You're right there," said Fritz. "I found the same thing myself, and I don't think it's psychological. It's almost as if every form of energy here was negated or opposed."

He picked up a stone. "Watch! I want to throw it through the window in the old wall over there."

He threw the stone with practised ease, having judged its weight to a nicety. But the stone lost speed rapidly and fell in a limp trajectory to the muddied soil several metres short of its intended target.

"See what I mean?" said Van Noon. "That stone, accelerated to the velocity at which I released it, should at least have hit the wall. But it didn't. It acted as a lighter body might have done on travelling through these conditions – or as a body of its actual weight might have done had it somehow lost kinetic energy during flight. How do you lose kinetic energy from a body in flight, Jacko?"

"You can't *lose* it," said Jacko. "You can only react it against something – friction, air-resistance, and so on – in which case the energy leaves the system in some other form, usually heat. The energy itself is never lost, only converted."

"But here it wasn't," said Van Noon. "I wasn't throwing against a headwind, and the air in here is no more dense than outside after allowing for temperature and humidity differences. So whatever stopped that stone wasn't a normal reaction to flight. And I can find no evidence of abnormal gravity or coriolis effects. That stone just progressively lost energy. Mass times velocity doesn't seem to equal momentum in the Pen – and that's a hell of a smack at the textbooks you and I were raised on."

"Working outside the textbooks never worried you before," said Jacko. "Let's get out of this place, Fritz. It's giving me the creeps."

"In a minute, Jacko. I'd like to explore a bit farther in first."

They walked together down the remains of a long-forgotten road, treading wearily on the slimed cobbles of the surface. The environment was desolate and forlorn, with an air of perpetual dampness and slow rot and reluctant fungus. As they penetrated to greater depths the gloom grew perceptibly greater, and the cold chill reached a degree where it would have been unwise to remain too long without the protection of additional clothing. Vegetable and animal life were here almost completely absent, and the slime and fungus showed plainly that even the lower life-forms were maintaining their hold only with the greatest difficulty. Even organic decay had not progressed far after two centuries of perpetual winter.

"What are we looking for, Fritz?"

"I don't know, Jacko. It's the feel of this cold that has me puzzled. I don't feel I'm cold just because the environment is cold. I feel I'm cold because my body is radiating more heat than it should at these temperatures. To judge from the feel of my skin it's about five degrees below freezing point here."

"Agreed," said Jacko. "Well below freezing, certainly."

"Then just an observation," said Van Noon. "Why aren't the puddles of water frozen? It's my guess that a thermometer wouldn't give much below ten centigrade. It's the same effect that we encountered at the perimeter of the Pen – radiant heat being opposed by something only explicable as radiant cold."

"I don't understand that, Fritz. After all, cold is only the absence of heat."

"I wonder," said Van Noon, "if that isn't a limitation to thinking which we've imposed upon ourselves. What happens if we postulate a phenomenon called contra-heat, which we treat as the conventional electromagnetic heat radiation but with the signs reversed?"

"There's no such animal," objected Jacko.

"No? Fetch some equipment in here and compare the radiant heat loss against temperature and I think you'll find there is. There has to be. There's nothing else you could set up in an equation which would go half way to meeting all the facts."

Something crackled and spat unexpectedly behind them with a sound like a multiple pistol shot. They whirled round and stopped in quick amazement. Between them and their path out of the Pen was quite the smallest and darkest and lowest thundercloud they had ever seen. The bottom of the cloud hung probably not more than thirty metres above the ground, and its inky-black consistency made them think of vapours other than those of the air, though this was probably a trick of light and circumstance.

But it was the lightning which gave them pause to think: vicious arcs between ground and cloud which started to stab with all the anticipated brilliance and fire but which were curiously extinguished by some constrictive phenomenon which pinched the plasma and quenched the arc. The result was a staccato "pop" instead of a thunderclap, and a rate of lightning repetition which occasionally generated a continuous tearing noise rather than the usual sounds of storm. But there was no doubting the destructive potential of the lightning bolts.

Moved by unfelt winds, the thundercloud was drawing rapidly nearer, and Van Noon was more than a little apprehensive.

"Better find some shelter, Jacko. This could be dangerous."

They looked about them. The ruins of a hovel, partly roofed with sloped and perilous slates, provided the nearest offer of sanctuary. This they accepted, and squatted within the miserable, damp, boxlike walls while the cloud moved overhead. Lightning stabbed at the path outside with a viciousness which seemed to contain some element of personal malice, but finally it passed. The cloud went spitting and snarling on towards the pillar of the Dark, and Van Noon and Jacko emerged to watch its progress.

"I'll teach Maxwell Courtney to speak of 'interesting subclimate'," said Van Noon ominously. "Let's get out of here Jacko."

"You know, Fritz, I was just about to suggest the self-same thing myself."

"That was what they call a rogue storm," said Courtney. "In the Pen you meet them quite a lot. They seem to form and disperse almost spontaneously, but while they last they can be very dangerous. They always travel fast, and always in straight lines. If caught in the open we avoid them by simply running out of the way."

They were seated in Courtney's office in New Bethlem, and the broad windows of the room opened to a distant view of the Pen and its core of Dark. Courtney's desk faced the window as if to give him a constant reminder of the broad enigma to which his life was currently dedicated. The attitude of his visitors' chairs showed that they were no less aware of the dominating influence of the looming column of shades.

"Well," said Van Noon. "We've gathered a little data of our own on a preliminary survey, and I'm told you have acquired data by the ton. That puts you in a good position for answering questions, and me for asking them."

"Ask away," said Courtney. "I don't pretend to have all the answers, but I can do you a nice line in inexplicable facts."

"What can you tell me about anti-energy or contra-energy effects?"

Courtney whistled softly. "That's a piece of fast think-ing, Fritz. It took us two years before we could bring ourselves to consider the hypothesis seriously. But I know what you're thinking. Most of the physical effects observed in the Pen can be satisfactorily explained only by thinking in terms of polar opposition – negation by precisely defined effects of exactly opposite character. The fact that these opposite effects are completely unknown to nature outside the Pen doesn't necessarily invalidate the case for their existence inside the Pen. The very nature of the Pen and the Dark is obviously extra-physical, or we'd not have a problem in the first place."

"Precisely!" said Van Noon. "But you do admit the possibility of contra-energy?"

Courtney spread his hands. "I admit it as a possibility. It's certainly a basic premise which fits all the observed facts in the Pen. But it's only one premise among many, and it doesn't have much to commend it when you consider it a little deeper."

"Go on," said Van Noon.

"Let's take an extreme case," said Courtney. "You can prove it for yourself, or take my word for it, that the difference between the Pen and the dark is purely one of degree. Whereas energy negation in the Pen is only partial, that of the Dark is absolute."

"I'll take your word for it. I'd guessed it anyway."

"Good. Now consider this: no matter what intensity, character, or type of energy we have applied to the Dark, we have had no discernible effect upon it, nor have we been able to pass any energy through even a thin sector of it. We have encountered absolute negation, Fritz, of any energy applied in any way. If you stick to your contra theory the implications are too complex to be true, and rather frightening."

"I think I understand you," said Van Noon, "but I'd rather hear it your way."

"I'll put it as simply as I can. If we fire a projectile at it, according to your theory that projectile needs to be met precisely at the perimeter of the Dark by what is effectively a counter projectile of identical mass travelling at an identical velocity to a precisely identical point. That makes too many coincidences for my orthodox-type stomach. And again, suppose we use X-ray bombardment or any other form of radiation. For precise negation this would need to be met at the identical point by contra radiation of the same intensity, wavelength, and phase as that which we apply. Either the Dark is an extremely broadband transmitter capable of producing any type of force, energy, intensity, and phase of radiation at any point on its perimeter at any instant without prior notice – accurately and instantaneously – or else the Dark is full of little green men with an uncanny knack of anticipating our test programme and arranging their contra facilities to suit."

"I get the point," said Fritz. "How do you arrange to fire a projectile to meet an unexpected projectile head-on with precisely matched mass and velocity and to an impact position predetermined to an accuracy of plus or minus a few microns? It can't be done. You've shaken some of my confidence, but you still haven't encompassed the impossible."

"No? Then I'll do so right away. For your contra theory to be true, the Dark would need to be a dynamic entity. It must necessarily give out exactly as much energy as it receives, for the negation to be complete. It's been here for two hundred years, Fritz. Now calculate two hundred years of radiant energy from the Ithican sun alone and then add what we've flung at it in the last three years of experiment. You'll see that it would need the energy resources of a small star in order to have the reserves to meet any demand. We dropped a nuclear Hell-raiser on it, and a Hell-raiser is a planet-buster, remember. What sort of power supply could conceivably meet a demand like that instantaneously?"

"I don't know," said Van Noon, "but we can't yet claim to know the ultimate in power sources. But very soon I intend to find a way into the Dark, and then perhaps we'll find out."

"You can't do it, Fritz. There isn't a ghost of a chance of penetrating into the Dark."

"I think there is. And I think I know the very way in which it might be done."

"Whatever made you say that?" asked Jacko anxiously, as they left the room.

"It's a feeling I have," said Van Noon. "I said I was going to play this by intuition, and right now my intuition tells me that the Pen and the Dark *are* contra-energy effects."

"In spite of what Courtney said?"

"Certainly. I must admit he had a nice point about the projectile needing to be met effectively by a contra projectile if the contra-energy theory was to be maintained. It wouldn't actually need to be met by a contra projectile, but merely by an opposing force of the right sort applied in the right place at the right time. I don't doubt that Courtney's correct that such a negation is necessary to substantiate the contra theory. But I do suspect that his data on absolute negation is not quite as complete as he imagines."

"In what way, Fritz?"

"Well, I can't conceive of a continuous pattern of negative energy which could deal with any sort of force or radiation applied at any point at any time. I can, however, conceive of a pattern of contra radiation or effect which is selectively produced in response to a particular stimulus at a particular point. But you see what this involves?"

"No," said Jacko.

"It involves detection, analysis, and synthesis of a contra effect. Three steps – which must necessitate some sort of time-lag. Courtney has established that any applied energy is negated – but I doubt if it can be negated instantaneously. The three steps may be completed in nano-seconds, but I'm quite sure that a time-lag must exist. Now I want to go into the Pen, right up to the Dark perimeter, and see if we can prove or disprove this."

"And if we prove it?"

"Then I think we'll have a way to drive a tunnel into the Dark and see what's inside."

Jacko lost his power of speech as his mind strove to contain the enormity of the project. Fritz shot him an amused glance, and continued.

"There's a particular reason I want to go in, Jacko. There's a second principle involved in this detection, analysis, contra-synthesis set-up which you might not have thought of. Something else is implied . . . and that something is some form of guiding intelligence.''

They had chosen heavy caterpillar crawlers for their transport into the Pen. The choice was determined not only by the fact that a tracked vehicle was an advantage over the broken terrain but also for the reason that the vehicles possessed magnificently powerful engines and an ample reserve of power. Three crawlers were obtained for the expedition; one to run well ahead, one to act as reserve, and one to stay well in the rear with sufficient rescue equipment to recover either of the leading crawlers should the deeper Pen effects exceed the capacity of the engines to keep the vehicles in motion.

Clothing for the party had been chosen for a simple property-thermal insulation. Although the actual temperature of the deep Pen probably did not reach freezing point it was essential to insulate the radiant heat of a man's body against the contra-heat effect which would otherwise have striven to reduce the temperature of a man to the ambient point, with lethal effect. In this way the cold of the Pen differed from normal cold, and the expeditionary figures were clad as though for a journey to the arctic.

Once clear into the outer perimeter of the Pen and out of the strong Ithican sunshine, the expedition began to appreciate the clothing which up to that point had caused them a barely tolerable condition of overheating. Now, as the light faded and the chill of the perpetual winter closed around them, they grew more comfortable. But the underlying seriousness of the venture was pointed-up by a change in the engine note to a more laboured level as both the functioning of the engine and the momentum of the vehicle were affected by the contra elements of the Pen.

The leading crawler carried the bulk of the equipment, especially the precious lasers with which it was hoped to establish the existence of a time lag in the Dark phenomena. Van Noon was captaining the vehicle. Jacko was driving, and Pederson, an observer sent by Courtney, completed the party. Van Noon had intended their route to follow a road indicated on the old maps as running for nearly two kilometers straight in the direction of the axis of the Dark. The intention was abandoned quickly on finding that a building of considerable proportions had collapsed, turning part of the road into an unnavigable pile of masonry. The maps were forgotten and a new route was improvised as the situation demanded, having regard to the abilities of the crawler and taking advantage of the opportunities presented by the slow erosion of the Pen environment on the fabric of the old town.

The light from the trapped cloudbase became increasingly leaden and dull until, at about five kilometers in from the perimeter of the Pen, Jacko was forced to switch on the headlamps. Their effect was negligible. Such light as they produced was robbed by some contra effect in the Pen environment and did little to disperse the muddy gloom. Van Noon had anticipated this and had a searchlight mounted on the roof of the crawler. The intensity of light from this was sufficient to permit their passage through the damp, dilapidated, ghost-like streets of Bethlem to within two kilometres of the Dark itself. Then that illumination too became inadequate.

"Better get out, Jacko, and let's estimate the situation," said Van Noon.

They descended, conscious of the acute contra-heat coldness which searched at their shrouded faces and probed at their wrists and ankles. They were conscious too, now, of contra-momentum, which gave an entirely false impression of the density of the air, since the effect was remarkably like trying to move under water.

Pederson joined them, and they made a brief survey of the situation. Whereas from a greater distance the column of the Dark had been clearly visible, it was now merged into the claylike blankness of scene which made it scarcely distinguishable as a separate entity. Jacko tried the radio communicator; but the instrument was dead save for some rare static from a distant rogue-storm. The magnetic compass also had become nonfunctional much earlier, and though the gyro compass still purred unhappily in its box its readings were questionable in view of the conditions under which it was operating.

The quality of light from the cloudbase was curious and unreal. Effectively the light from above should have given them far greater incident and reflected illumination than they actually experienced. This drastic attenuation of the light should have been explicable in terms of fog or haze, but nothing such existed, and their inexpressibly dreary state of near-night had no explanation save for that of an alien opposition to the fundamental laws of physics.

"What are we going to do, Fritz?" Jacko's own attempt to resolve the situation had reached an impasse.

Van Noon looked back, hoping for an indication as to whether or not the second crawler had been able to follow their tortuous route to the spot. No evidence was forthcoming, so he shrugged his shoulders.

"You two can vote me down if you want to, but I propose that we choose the most likely direction for the Dark and just drive blind until we hit it or stop."

"I'm with you," said Jacko. "What about you, Pederson?"

"Count me in. I've no ambition to walk back on my own."

They re-entered the crawler. Having decided on the most probable direction of the Dark, Jacko orientated the vehicle, locked the tracks on synchronization, and proceeded to drive straight into the unknown.

The journey was a driver's conception of Hell, a nightmare route across unfamiliar territory, effectively blind, and with no warning of what obstacle might halt or jolt them. Added to this was the rising resistance to movement, both on the part of the vehicle and of its occupants. Inside the driving cab even the instrument lights had become impossible to see, and the penetrating coldness finalized the depression which was settling over the spearhead of the expedition. Once or twice Jacko questioned whether they ought to attempt to turn back. Van Noon chided him gently and looked only ahead to the point where the darkness ought to terminate in a meeting with the absolute of the Dark.

Constantly the vehicle rolled and bucked, and canted at dangerous angles as it encountered broken walls or piles of debris in its path. Sometimes it stopped with a bruising shock against some obstacle beyond its power to move. Jacko was skilful in such emergencies and withdrew the vehicle from each such predicament without stalling the engine, knowing that a stopped engine this far into the Pen would never be restarted. Bruised, and in constant danger from masonry from grazed walls crushing the cab, they endured the journey patiently; although with various deviations from the course which the presence of unsurmountable obstacles forced on Jacko, they had no certain idea if they were still headed towards the Dark at all.

Then came the moment they had been dreading. In pitch darkness now, the crawler came to a sudden halt against something immovable. The tracks churned the soft floor uselessly for a half second, and then the engine stalled before Jacko could throw the vehicle in reverse. He tried the ignition cycle in vain, but the contra effects were too powerful to permit the heavy engine to be restarted. The silence grew absolute save for the tick-tick of metal cooling rapidly and Fritz's voice cursing in a strangely muted way.

"End of the line," said Jacko finally.

Van Noon opened the door. "As we've managed to get here we may as well see where we are," he said.

They climbed out. Their powerful torches were about as useful as glow-worms, and permitted an examination of no object more distant than about a quarter of a metre. Beyond this was darkness in all directions except directly vertical, where a muddied stain across the sky mocked them with its inability to provide any useful illumination on the ground. Van Noon searched around him and picked up a short length of rotting timber with which he cast about in the darkness on all sides. Then he called urgently.

"Jacko, are you near the crawler?"

"I am," said Pederson. "Just by the cab door." He banged the metal, which returned a dull and unrewarding thud. Like their voices, the sound was strangely attenuated.

"Good! Now, Jacko, can you place yourself by sound in a line between our two voices?"

Jacko moved somewhere in the darkness. "I think I'm there."

"Right. Now we're three in a line, with Pederson on the right, you central, and myself on the left. As far as I can make out, about three paces ahead of us is the Dark. Find something to probe it with, and don't touch it even with your gloves. Maintain your orientation carefully so that you don't lose direction and walk into it. It could be very dangerous to touch."

They advanced slowly, Pederson tapping the side of the crawler for identification, and Fritz and Jacko talking so that the sound of voices gave their relative positions. Even so, Jacko got there first. His probe was a shard of splintered ceramic with which he was striking before him as though at some anticipated enemy. Contra-momentum made this a difficult movement to achieve, and the darkness added to the soup-like resistance to movement, giving the whole situation a dream-like character without the visual qualities of the conventional nightmare.

Then Jacko hit the Dark. It was detectable by its complete negation of the force with which he struck it. And it returned no sound, and in this way was distinguishable from any ordinary obstacle struck with force.

"Got it," said Jacko. "But that knocking sound you hear is my knees. I admit I'm frightened of this thing, Fritz."

"I'm not exactly keen on it, either," said Van Noon. "But this is what we came to see. It's a pity we can't see it now we've got here. Have you any suggestions, Pederson?"

"I've just discovered the Dark is what we ran the crawler into. No wonder it didn't move."

An ominous and familiar staccato rattle made them turn. A rogue storm, travelling towards them and parallel to the wall of the Dark, was making its passage known by its peculiarly pinched lightning. Because of attenuation, the lightning and thunder had been undetectable even from a short distance, and the storm was almost upon them before they were aware it existed. There was no time to seek shelter. They flung themselves down on the damp earth at the foot of the Dark and waited for it to pass. It sprayed the area with quenched fire as it went, doing no damage to them, but the intensity of the arcs was such that momentarily they had a clear picture of their situation.

The Dark was just in front of them, a sheer wall of unblemished black-velvet nothingness, impossibly perfect. The crawler had nosed head-on up to the black wall, and its tracks were pressed hard against the exterior. On all other sides of them lay the ghost-suburb of desolate ruins, the reflecting white teeth of broken masonry contrasting with the wet, black, soilstones of the earth.

As soon as the worst of the storm was over, they climbed back to their feet.

"What are you going to do, Fritz? Try the lasers?"

"I don't know." Fritz had moved back to the crawler and was examining the tracks in contact with the Dark by the spasmodic light of the rapidly waning storm. "I don't think we need to, Jacko. I think I've got my answer. You see, it did take time for the Dark to analyse and apply a counter-force to stop the crawler. But that fraction of a second was sufficient for something significant to happen. The crawler tracks have penetrated very slightly into the Dark."

It was impossible for the others to verify Van Noon's statement since the light from the storm had rapidly become eclipsed by the strength of the contra effects. The combined output of searchlight and torches failed to re-establish the point, and the lasers refused to function from the crawler's emergency power supply. But Van Noon was sufficiently convinced of what he had seen to regard the expedition as a success.

"All we have to do now is to get back to tell the tale," said Jacko, unhappily.

They started back by the only means available – they walked. For the first half kilometre they stumbled blindly through the darkness and the nightmare of contra-momentum. The coldness, too, was becoming serious now that they were exposed for a long period without the protection of the crawler cab. But gradually their eyes, accustomed to complete darkness, began to discern light like the first touch of dawn, and with the returning ability to see, they no longer blundered into blind paths in the ruins from which they had to retreat by sense of touch alone. And the contra-effects grew slightly less, so that their pace progressively improved as they made their way out of the deep Pen regions.

Two kilometres away from the Dark they came across the crushed path that their own crawler had made on its way in, and this they followed gratefully. Shortly they found the second crawler, abandoned, and with its engine stalled and cold. The third crawler was patrolling a broad front along a road about three kilometres radius from the Dark perimeter. They were hailed and taken aboard for the last part of the journey through the growing light and finally out into the unbearably bright gold sunset of an Ithican evening.

Courtney was there to greet them. His team had spent the day re-running exploratory tests, but this time with particular reference to the onset-time of negation. His results amply confirmed Van Noon's experience. There was a time-lag on the introduction of any energy phenomenon to the Dark or the Pen before negation set in. The exact period of the lag varied with the type of phenomenon, but was greatest for applied physical force.

The Ithican government, sensing promise in the issue, had already granted almost unlimited facilities to aid any practical application of the idea. On Van Noon's behalf Courtney had accepted the challenge, and the party rode with buoyant spirits back to New Bethlem where work on the next phase of Fritz's plans against the Dark were just about to begin.

"A tunnel?" said Jacko.

"Strictly speaking," said Van Noon, "I had in mind something more in the nature of a horizontal well, but I think a tunnel is a fair description."

"And just how do you propose to sink a horizontal well into the Dark?"

"Frankly, I don't see much difficulty. We take an ordinary iron pipe of sufficient dimension to permit the passage of a man – and just knock it in."

"Crazy like a fox!" said Jacko. "We're talking about the Dark – the great energy negator. In the name of Moses, how do you just knock a pipe into that?"

"I thought I'd already demonstrated that," said Fritz. "There's a time-lag before the onset of negation. Apply a pile driver or something to your pipe and hit it once and it will penetrate the Dark just a little before the detection, analysis, contra synthesis has a chance to stop it. Then the negation will be applied and stop the tube going in any farther, and the system will reach stasis. The contra-force obviously cannot continue to be applied after the original force has ceased to operate, so the force, contra-force balance will then relax."

"So?"

"So then you hit your pipe again and drive it in a little more. And so on. And providing you work on a completely random and non-predictable basis there's no chance of the contra-force being applied in anticipation. I suspect that only if we set up a standard repetition rate will we meet with complete and instantaneous negation of the force that we apply."

"So we knock in our tube. Then what?"

"It depends on what we find. The Dark may be a solid or it may be a thin-wall phenomenon. If it's a solid we shall not gain much except for a little knowledge. But if it's thin-wall, then we might have a chance to look inside."

"From which you're assuming that the Dark effect won't penetrate inside the pipe."

"I think it may to some extent, but take any physical phenomenon and place an inch of steel in front of it and you always get some modification or attenuation, if not a complete shutoff. I don't see that the situation should be materially different for contra-physical phenomena. With a bit of luck we should be able to get through."

"What do you think's inside there, Fritz?"

"As I see it, Jacko, some form of intelligence, but I wouldn't like to guess any closer than that. Whether the Dark is some cosmic amoeba or has inside it a complex of little green men is something I intend to find out. Are you with me?"

"I'm right behind you," said Jacko. "But don't ask me to be the first man through that ruddy pipe."

By the time that Courtney returned to the base camp a few days later Van Noon's plans were fairly well advanced.

Fritz described the scheme briefly. Courtney was intrigued but doubtful.

"I don't see," he said, "how you're going to drive a pipe of that diameter into the Dark – remembering that the driving has to be done in the deep Pen area where the contra-momentum is killing. You'd never get a horizontal pile driver to work under those conditions."

"No. We've already taken care of that point by taking a new line entirely. We're going to fire it in."

"Fire it?"

"Yes. Attach the free end of the pipe to what is effectively a large-bore gun or reaction chamber with an open muzzle pointing away from the Dark. In the gun we fire a high-explosive charge and let the recoil of the apparatus drive the pipe against the Dark. According to my calculations, a series of explosive shocks should have the right sort of driving characteristics for the job. How does it sound as an idea?"

"It could work," admitted Courtney. "Unless we're up against something we don't know about yet. How far have you got with the project."

"We've managed to get the lengths of pipe into the Dark area, and the gun chamber is there also. There's trouble keeping handling equipment working so far into the Pen, but we've managed somehow. We should be ready to start firing sometime tomorrow. Have you been able to get the extra stuff I asked for?"

"Most of it's outside on the carriers, and the generators will arrive in the morning. Here's the radiation monitor, trolley-mounted as specified. I only hope it fits into the pipe."

"I'll try it out," said Van Noon. "I can run it through our test length and if it doesn't fit we can modify it before it goes into the Pen."

He wheeled the small apparatus-laden trolley to the length of pipe that ran down the workshop where they had been fabricating the gun chamber. The trolley fitted easily into the interior of the pipe and, to give himself a little practice, he crawled in after it and pushed it before him. The iron confines of the pipe returned the roar of the small casters with a noise like a train speeding through a tunnel. When Van Noon reached the far end he found that Jacko had returned and was peering anxiously down the pipe.

"Why the sound effects, Fritz?"

"Eh? Oh, this? It's the radiation detector. It's obvious that even the iron of the pipe can't do more than attenuate some wavelengths of the electromagnetic spectrum – and the same presumably applies to the contra spectrum. So just to be on the safe side Courtney has knocked up a combined range monitor which should cover anything likely to be dangerous but not detectable by our own senses. I don't expect that we'll encounter any such radiation, but it's better to be safe than sterile."

"Agreed," said Jacko. "We're taking enough chances with the unknown already. I've just come back out of the Pen, and we're right on schedule. The first firing can take place at mid-day tomorrow."

"I'll be there," said Fritz. "I'm particularly interested in knowing what happens to the core which we leave in the pipe. If the Dark is true radiation-type phenomena, there won't be any core material. But if it's something else, we may have to think again."

The null-pressure suits obtained from Space Command were far more suitable for working under deep Pen conditions than the expeditionary clothing had been. Specifically designed for work on asteroids and similar bodies under a pressure dome but exposed to extremes of stellar heat and cold, the suits were the finest flexibilized radiation foils that had yet been devised. In the Pen, of course, no pressurized dome was needed, but the suits ensured that the searching fingers of contra-heat were no longer a danger or of major discomfort to the U.E. squad.

But the drag of the contra-momentum was not so easily avoided. Close to the wall of the Dark it exhibited an almost treacle-like resistance to movement which was common to both men and machines alike. The adaptations of technique needed for working in an environment possessing such a high quasi-viscosity were numerous, but the combined ingenuity of the Unorthodox Engineering squad was equal to the challenge. Somehow the impossible had been accomplished, and the structural components of Van Noon's tunnel had been patiently sworn into place ready for the projected penetration of the Dark.

"Ready to fire?"

Jacko nodded. "First shot in thirty seconds."

They were watching the scene by the light of two large, continuously operating lasers which Courtney had managed to obtain. These were directed on the point where the leading end of the pipe was pressed hard against the Dark perimeter. The illumination, spread slightly by deliberate diffusion with mesh screens, was adequate despite the contra-radiation loss. The backscatter illumination was also quite useful around the working area, but was attenuated sharply and unnaturally with distance. The power for the lasers had to be derived from outside the Pen via cable, and the contra-electrical loss was such that two large generators were needed to drive sufficient energy in to keep the lasers in operation.

The first shot was fired. The sound of the explosion was incredibly muted, and the tongue of flame from the reaction chamber was quickly quenched and drained. Van Noon examined the junction between the pipe and the Dark.

"I think it's working, Jacko. Only millimetres so far, but it's definitely going in. Keep firing rapidly but erratically. Let me know when you're in about a metre. Then I want to go down inside the pipe and see if any sort of core is left."

By reason of good organization on Jacko's part they had penetrated a metre by late afternoon. Then the gun chamber was removed to allow access to the free end of the pipe. Van Noon had a line measured to pipe's length minus one metre, and one end he left clamped to the free end of the pipe while he took the rest of the line inside to give him an indication of his position. Ten minutes later he came out jubilant.

"No core material, Jacko. The pipe is clear to the very end, and then the Dark begins again. That means we've got a metre of clear tunnel already and no complications so far. Now I want firings to continue right round the clock, as close-spaced as possible without setting up a standard repetition rate. If you scatter the charges round the area a bit so that each has to be fetched from a slightly different distance, that should be sufficient. But I want the depth of penetration per shot carefully watched, and if it varies very much from the existing rate, cease firing and let me know."

It took forty hours to drive the first length of pipe into the Dark. By this time a second length had been added to the first and there were indications that the depth of penetration per shot was increasing. The second was driven home in twenty-five hours, partly due to the decreasing resistance it encountered, and partly due to the increasing proficiency of the shot-firers.

The third pipe was inserted in seventeen hours, and the fourth, in twelve. The time for subsequent pipes decreased in rough proportion. The tenth went half way, and then the indications were that no great resistance was being offered to it by the Dark since the assembly of pipes now moved forward the full theoretical distance per shot that they would have moved in the Pen itself. Jacko brought his charts to Van Noon.

"I think we're through, Fritz. These seem to show that the Dark is a relatively thin-wall phenomenon with its effects decreasing with depth of penetration and reaching virtually zero at about ninety-five metres. God alone knows what's at the other end."

"Take the gun chamber off, Jacko, but be careful in case something unexpected comes out of the pipe. If nothing happens in half an hour then I'm going through to have a look."

Nothing did happen. The end of the pipe protruding from the Dark remained empty, silent and cold; and there was no way of telling what lay at the far end. A laser directed down the pipe returned nothing but light-scatter from walls and motes of dust. The only factor of note was a strong current of air entering the pipe as though to equalize some unexplained deficiency in pressure.

Finally Van Noon hoisted the radiation trolley into the pipe and followed it in.

"I'm going down a bit, Jacko, for a preliminary survey. Stand by with some weapons in case I come out fast with something after me."

"Nothing doing!" said Jacko. "If you're going down that pipe, then I'm coming too."

"That's what I hoped you'd say," said Fritz. "Let's get on with it. The situation won't improve itself by waiting."

He crawled into the pipe. With some misgivings, Jacko followed him in. Ahead of Fritz the radiation trolley clattered on the iron and raised a multitude of clamorous echoes which engulfed them in a tide of sound. Inside the pipe the contra-sound attenuation apparently did not operate to anything like the same degree as that encountered in the Pen. The radiation monitor gave no indication of any increase in rate above the slow background count, and they considered it safe to continue.

Occasionally Van Noon stopped and let the echoes die, but nothing else disturbed the silence except their own breathing and their own awkward movements in the confines of the pipe. Then after what seemed an eternity of crawling the clatter of the trolley ceased again and Van Noon stopped and half twisted himself to look back.

"Jacko," he said urgently, "think very carefully. Are you absolutely sure how many lengths of pipe we drove into the Dark?"

"A ruddy fine time to be concerned about the economics of the project."

"Hang the economics! Are you sure?"

"Certainly. Ten in all. Why?"

"I've been counting the joins. I'm now in the twelfth pipe, that's why."

"Don't make jokes like that, Fritz. You'll give me heart failure."

"I wasn't joking. The casters on the trolley drop into the flange gap at every join, and I have to ease them over. That's what made me start counting how many joins I'd passed."

"So you're now in the twelfth pipe out of the original ten," said Jacko, still not fully convinced. "That's quite a trick! How do you explain it, Fritz?"

"Contra-iron pipe," said Van Noon. "Lord! I thought it was a joke when Courtney suggested that they stopped a projectile with a contra projectile. But it appears it wasn't.

They do just that. They tried to stop our pipe with a length of contra-iron pipe so precisely similar that I'd not have noticed the difference had I not been counting. What type of creatures could do that, Jacko – almost instantaneously?"

"I don't know," said Jacko. "But I'm afraid of them."

"You and me both. To work a trick like that must demand a technology centuries ahead of ours. But even so, I've a feeling we've got them worried."

"Why's that?"

"Because if they were still operating at full efficiency there's something we'd logically have met in this pipe before now – a contra-radiation monitoring trolley pushed by a contra Fritz Van Noon."

"We're way out of our depth, Fritz," said Jacko finally. "Are you still going on?"

"If you're still following."

"I'm still behind you, but I'm darned if I know why. I've followed you into some crazy situations before, but this has the lot beaten."

They moved on, the roar of the trolley casters echoing and reverberating around them and occasionally stopping as Fritz eased the little wheels over a flange gap.

"Just entering pipe nineteen," said Van Noon finally. "If they provided as many as we did them there's only one to go."

"See anything yet?"

"Not an atom."

"I was just thinking, Fritz. It'd be a neat trick if they'd connected an infinity of pipes together. We could go on crawling through here till Judgment Day."

"Good point, Jacko. We'll reconsider the position when we get to the end of number twenty."

Again the trolley roared and stopped.

"Just entering pipe twenty," said Van Noon.

"Let's get it over with," said Jacko. "I feel like a godevil working overtime."

"right. This is it!"

The trolley was moving slowly now, with Fritz concentrating on every centimetre of its progress, using the feel of the iron instead of eyes. There was no way to measure distance in the darkness. The only way was to crawl and to hope that one remembered the feeling of crawling a length of pipe. Then a sudden cessation of noise, with the echoes slowly sinking around them.

"End of pipe," said Van Noon. "But there's no resistance. The trolley is half way out of the end but I still can't see a thing. I'm going to let the trolley go and see what happens."

There was a brief scrape of metal on metal, and the thump of something on the pipe.

"It fell down," said Van Noon, "but not very far. I can still feel it with my hand. And something else . . . There's no contra-momentum out here. I can move quite freely. It isn't even very cold. It must mean we're well inside the wall of the Dark. I wonder if the torch will work."

The torch did work. In the darkness the light touched the interior of the pipe with an intensity that was momentarily dazzling. Projected outwards, the beam was clearly visible but it contacted nothing that reflected except the wet, brown stones of the earth, and the radiation trolley fallen on its side. Ostensibly they were looking into night, bare and empty, but Fritz was not convinced.

"This isn't darkness," said Van Noon. "It's more like veils of darkness . . . thin layers of contra-light. See how the torch beam falls off in discrete quanta. I'm going out there, Jacko, to see if I can make head or tail of this. You stay by the pipe with a torch ready to guide me back. I'd very much like to find out who or what it was that put ten pipes on the end of ours."

"And I'm going to wish you luck," Jacko said. "I'm not at all sure I want to know."

Van Noon dropped to the ground. The soil underfoot was an obvious continuation of the old town terrain. His torch illuminated the stony earth for many metres in front of him, but it was useless when directed horizontally in any direction because of the apparent lack of anything to reflect the light.

But he was right in his observation that the intensity of the light was stepped-down by curtaining veils of something. As he approached a veil he could see a distinct drop in the brightness of the beam as it was intercepted by something dark and nebulous. He reached the veil and touched it, curiously. His fingers encountered nothing, and he walked through it without sensation. Looking back, he was glad still to be able to see the light from Jacko's torch, but he knew that if he passed through many veils even that would be lost to him.

But the situation changed without warning. The fifth veil was not insubstantial at all. It was a film of something like dark, thin-blown glass, and he shattered it with his torch because he had not known of its solidity. And as it shattered, light from beyond spilled out through the broken edges and he had the briefest glimpse of the scene of gold-hazed wonder . . . and then the air exploded in his face.

And even the explosion was unreal. The blast caught him not from in front but from behind and above, moving towards the explosion rather than from it. It tumbled him forward and pinned his body to the ground with a great pressure. Desperately he fought to raise his neck and shoulders for a further glimpse of the creatures who lived in their sanctuary deep inside the hollow Dark. He wanted a better look at the godlike machines they controlled, now rising high like gossamer and congregating in the golden light as they swept magnificently upwards almost faster than the eye could follow. But a sheet of flame crackled and tore across the vastness of the area and whipped high in an angry, explosive tide.

A shockfront of pressure tore him from the ground, then dropped him cruelly. Despite the hurt he fought to retain consciousness and turn and watch the exodus of the gods. But the forces acting on him were too great. Instead he was swamped by darkness.

His next impression was that of Courtney's face and the sense of lapsed hours. He felt bruised and shaken, but not seriously hurt. He was lying in the open, and the Ithican sky above was broadly trailed with the colours of the sunset.

Courtney came up and put a folded coat beneath his head and a blanket over his body.

"Take it easy, Fritz. There's a doctor on his way."

Van Noon smiled wanly. He tried to sit up, then thought better of it. "Is this where the Dark was, or did you get me out."

Courtney sat down beside him. "The Dark's gone, Fritz. I don't know what you did, but you certainly made a good job of it. The whole darn thing imploded. It was a fantastic sight. The Dark and the Pen drew up together, then spiralized like a whirlwind. There was a blast which broke every window in New Bethlem . . . and then the whole complex just disappeared."

"I know what did it," said Van Noon. "Our atmosphere reacted with theirs with a sort of mutual destructiveness. It was the total reaction of mass with mass – complete consumption of both and no by-product. It was our tunnel let the air through, and I broke the last seal by accident. And once the reaction started, nothing could stop it."

"So it was contra-terrene!" said Courtney.

"Deep inside, yes. And I'd guess that the purpose of the Dark was to act as a form of barrier against the contra world outside – an insulator separating the opposed atomic conditions. They must have tried to maintain it against penetration by every trick they knew. But what damned them was a simple slip of logic. They stopped a hollow object with a hollow object . . . and forgot the hole inside. But even so, we were lucky to get through."

"Lucky?"

"Yes," said Fritz. "We were operating on the wrong principle. There was no detection, analysis, synthesis reaction involved. There didn't need to be, not the way they did it."

"I don't follow, Fritz."

"I missed the point myself at first, but there's only one logical answer to the detection and negation of any phenomena applied anywhere at any time . . . They did it with mirrors."

"Mirrors?"

"Yes. Not ordinary mirrors, of course, but using a reflecting principle capable of producing the exact and true physical inverse of whatever comes into its field – a mirror that works not only with light but over the entire region of physical and force phenomena, including matter itself."

"My God!" said Courtney. "It's a fascinating concept."

"I'd give anything to know the mechanics of it," said Van Noon. "The reflector wasn't a simple plane, it was a three-dimensional cavity about ninety metres deep between the inner and outer walls. And somehow in that space were reproduced contra-physical objects rather than mere images. And in our innocence we had the temerity to bore right through the 'glass' to the back."

"That's where you have me puzzled by this mirror hypothesis, Fritz. It doesn't seem to fit the facts. Your breakthrough was dependent on the assumed detection–analysis–synthesis trinity, and it worked. But the theory assumed a delay time was inherent. But a mirror has no time-lag. Its returned image is instantaneous."

"That's not true," objected Van Noon. "The image returned by a mirror is never instantaneous. Light travels from the object to the glass at a finite velocity, and through the glass at a different but also finite velocity. So the image returned to the object is always delayed in time by just twice the time it takes light to reach the reflector. We were lucky in that in their contra mirror the effect was even more pronounced for the type of phenomenon in which we were interested."

Courtney absorbed this in silence for a moment or two. Then: "What put you on to the idea, Fritz?"

"Primarily your point about their power output having to match the total power input from all sources. It seemed improbable they would have chosen such a dynamic and wasteful method of maintaining a long-term defence. But a reflection principle has no such disadvantage. A mirror returns only when it receives. It needs no power to return the image. And when I got into the cavity and found nothing there but the image-iron pipes by which we'd just arrived, I knew that reflection was the only answer. But like a damn fool I went and blundered through the 'silvering' on the back of this mirror."

He leaned back momentarily and closed his eyes, trying

to recapture an image in his own head. "What happened to *them*, Maxwell? Did they get away?"

Courtney turned his head to look at the sunset.

"No. They didn't make it, Fritz. They reached the stratosphere in those machines of theirs, but then they exploded. Thank God the power release was too high to do much damage!"

"It's a pity," said Fritz. "I'd sooner have got to know them than have destroyed them. We could have learnt an awful lot from people who could build mirrors like that."

"Had they been inclined to teach," said Courtney, "but in two hundred years they never attempted even to make a contact. I think that they were so far ahead of us that we were merely as ants to them."

Van Noon sat up painfully and looked around. "By the way, what happened to Jacko?"

"He's a little bruised and dazed, but nothing serious. Apparently the implosive blast shot him out of the pipe like a cork out of a bottle. He swears you did it on purpose."

"I saw them go," said Van Noon, "and they were like golden gods flying back to Olympus. I would never have done a thing like that on purpose. Do you suppose we'll ever know why they were here?"

"I doubt it," said Courtney. "And even if they'd tried to tell us, I doubt our capacity to have understood. Try explaining the uses and construction of a Dewar flask to an ant – and see who gets tired first."

Inanimate Objection

H. Chandler Elliott

I do like stories that take the simplest of ideas and then develop it to the ultimate extreme. That's what happens here. Harry Chandler Elliott (1907–78) is another of those authors now pretty much forgotten. He was a Canadian physicist who worked in the US. He wrote one novel, Reprieve from Paradise *(1955) and a handful of short stories in the mid-to-late fifties, of which this was his first, and then stopped.*

Dr Carl Wahl (intern) skimmed over the highlights of the Worksheet, Mental Status, as it strove presumptuously to fix the outlines of a human personality – and an off-beat one at that:

PATIENT'S NAME: (Maj.) Angus G. Burnside. AGE: 57. DOCTOR: Wm. Svindorff, Dr Matthew Loftus in attendance.
GENERAL HISTORY: Army Engineers, specialist electric communications. Retired small Catskill estate 1949. No record of major trauma or disease. KIN: Married, Ruth Elvira, née Barker, aged 35, she says. Relationship amicable but somewhat distant.
ATTITUDE: Quiet, cooperative. Personal habits meticulous. Permitted unlimited access to books and electronic materials. Coherent outside limits of his mania. EMOTIONAL REACTION, AFFECT: Calm, amused at his own situation. NATURE OF ABERRA-

TION: Believes inanimate objects display active hostility. This is not directed at himself personally. In fact, he believes he can circumvent it more readily than most, but expresses concern for safety of the human race. Discusses this belief with scholarship and detachment. EXAMPLES: Said to nurse (Miss Clements): "Your apron-bow is waiting to pick something off that tray." Said to me (Loftus): "I'd fix that loose heel if I were you. If it hasn't thrown you yet, it's just waiting for an opportunity to really break your neck."

"Well, hell!" said Dr Carl Wahl. "That's just a picturesque way of expressing commonplace facts. He sees something that's liable to cause an accident, and personifies it. Why put a mild eccentric like that in here, when we can't accommodate urgent cases?"

Dr Matthew Loftus (resident) grimaced: "Since you ask, I'll agree it stinks. Of course, those excerpts don't give you any real idea. He's as psychotic as a jay-bird, no doubt at all. He conducts himself entirely according to this fixation. And he's got it all worked out in theory, too; damnedest stuff you ever heard, plausible as only a complete psychotic can be – half convinces you, till you get away from his spell and have a chance to think. But I agree . . . he certainly shouldn't be here."

Wahl put the Worksheet on Matt Loftus's desk, looking interested. "You *would* draw the only ripsnorter with big ideas in this grab-bag of catatonics and dements."

"Not to mention dipsos and plain stumblebums," Matt Loftus grinned. "And that old lady who makes immoral paper dolls." He looked at the sheet almost fondly. "A little old-fashioned, poetic madness *is* rather refreshing, isn't it? And Angus Burnside is a gentleman and scholar of some old school, and a most engaging conversationalist. I frequent his lair considerably more than is strictly required. Tell you what, Carl . . . I'll take you on as consultant, if you're interested. You could get next to him on music; he's got a terrific audio system up there, and he actually plays it as much as he tinkers with it. Best company in the institute."

"That," said Carl Wahl, "is a deal."

* * *

That afternoon, after a non-institutional knock and a polite summons from within, the two men entered the Major's room. Large by local standards, it could have been a good hotel-room-with-bath, except for the barred windows and general starkness. The chintzy curtains, cheery rugs, and optimistic pictures usually found in high-class mental wards were absent, replaced with dialed cabinets, a long shelf of records and tape spools, and an electrician's workbench of impressive resources.

The occupant, rising from the bench to face his visitors, would have dominated a much more distracting environment – say, an amphibious retreat under enemy fire. He was a lean, brown man; his hair was silver but thick; his white mustache was clipped with extreme precision. His gray eyes were merry and kind, however: in that amphibious debacle, he would be the type to rescue men physically by diving in, or mentally with acrid jests. Carl's practiced glance could note none of the little tics or rigidities that often betray underlying dislocation of nerves or mind.

The Major immediately put everybody on terms of informal equality by displaying the wireless relay he was arranging between his phonograph amplifier and speaker. Then, with the smartness of a precision-drill squad, he clicked back into racks and drawers the few tools and bits of material in use, and turned to Carl with disconcerting candor: "I suppose you want to hear my theory – or mania? Fine! Make yourselves comfortable."

Matt draped himself on the bed and Carl took an armchair. The two were a complete contrast: Matt, behind a youthful face and mild voice, kept in ambush a mind as incisive as an electric scalpel; Carl, raw-boned and lankhaired, was a very reliable citizen, but he harbored a quiet mysticism that was often invaluable in establishing rapport with the mentally unconventional.

"I'll ask you," the Major began, "to consider my thesis as dispassionately as our relative positions will allow. For a start, perhaps you'll admit that any notion, however apparently fantastic, that has been held by many ages and cultures is worth scientific investigation, if only to explain it away."

They nodded.

"Good," said the Major. "Now, few notions have been so universally held as the one I shall discuss: that what we call inanimate objects have a will of their own. The ancients endowed them with spirits – lares, oreads and so on. Medieval alchemists described an elaborate, if largely arbitrary, system of sympathies and antipathies – *not* personification, but something far subtler. Modern science simply shrugs: fantasies of dawning reason. An opinion without proof, I submit. In the last war our fliers, the flower of the mechanical age, devised the Gremlins – whole fun and half earnest – for they sensed something more than a chance mechanical failure . . . some Thing malicious and aggressive."

Carl was attentively analyzing manner as well as matter: The Major's logic was certainly off the gold standard – the case built on random gleanings, the disregard for alternative possibilities. Yet certain psychotic qualities were lacking: the grandiose seriousness, the touchiness, the air of knock-down argument. And, an inner mentor reminded, the ability to select significant detail was often the trademark of genius: "great wits are oft to madness near allied . . ."

"Of course," the Major continued, "the idea flouts sacred axioms. But, after all . . . sacred? Science is study of *evidence*, not recitation of a creed. And aren't the axioms being badly strained? '*If* you knew all the physical factors, you could explain everything.' Safe enough, since you never will know them. But your axioms work to a high approximation in certain carefully selected and managed cases, so you reject all other explanations for everything, in the name of a spurious unity."

So he *did* consider alternatives, Carl thought. Aloud, he asked, "What evidence exists for any other explanations?"

"Ha! That's exactly my 'mania'. By the theory of probability, you get a straight flush in every-so-many poker hands. But what if straight flushes crop up all over?"

Matt objected: "We've already discussed how easily you can prove dreams are prophetic if you record the ones that turn out and disregard the rest, and so on."

"True enough. And you can prove tigers' claws or 17-

desoxybethylene are miracle-drugs, *if* you stress the cures and explain away the regrettable fatalities."

"Touché," said Matt. "Fire ahead."

"Also, I've already admitted that my weak point *is* getting things on a statistical basis. I've been collecting data for years –" he gestured toward a row of fat notebooks beside his records – but things like poker hands, which you can tabulate easily, are obviously least likely to illustrate my point – they're too simple, mechanically, to enjoy much freedom of action. Besides . . ." He smiled faintly.

"Go on," said Matt. "You think this is a weak link . . . sounds irrational. Seriously, it impressed me as genuine observation."

"Glad to know it, Doctor. Well, you know that the presence of an observer changes conditions so you can't know what would have happened with no observer. That won't perceptibly affect motion of a falling body, or other such elementary cases. But in complex, versatile systems, I believe the effect increases enormously. I believe physical processes *know* they're being observed and evade analysis – I'm using 'know' as engineers do when they use the expression 'How does the valve *know* force is applied?'"

Carl was drawn off guard: "There's a traffic light at Tenth and Capitol I swear goes red just as I reach it – oh, four times in five. I tried keeping count once, and I'm certain the frequency changed while I was doing it."

"More likely your car than the light. Anyway, there you are. If you can't get statistics, you have to fall back on intuition, and that isn't science."

"Well, then," Carl made amends to his professional conscience, "there isn't much point bothering with it, is there?"

"Sometimes I fear not. But if enough people were thinking along those lines, someone might hit on a way to fool the resistance. Anyway, amuse yourself applying my theory and see how it fits." The Major dismissed the topic and talked electronics for the rest of the visit.

"Well," Matt grinned afterward, "isn't that a honey of a mania? His science is top-drawer stuff, too. Tell you what:

I'll lay you a dollar even that you'll be taking him 'whole fun and half earnest,' as he puts it, by Christmas. I know you won't cheat for that little: in fact, knowing you, it'll make you confess if you weaken."

Carl laughed and took him up. Which meant that he had to take the Major's suggestion at least in half earnest. But he needed amusement. In addition to a merciless load of work at an institute half destaffed by flu, he had worries: his wife Clare, of whom he was somewhat fond, had the flu too, followed by pneumonia and complicated by allergic reaction to the antibiotics applied. Having had a fortnight off during the emergency, he could not decently get down to their little apartment more than once or twice in the next fortnight, and he was a type who worried quietly but effectively. He found Major Burnside's fantasy a distraction, and even hoped it would later appeal to Clare's lively sense of humor.

So he collected instances: The dollar pencil that dropped on its rubber and vaulted into the plumbless depths of a hot-air register; the tiny rip in the sleeve of his white jacket that snagged on the tap of a coffee-urn, causing him to slop a cup of scalding coffee over trousers and ankle; the page of vital report that blew off his worktable and slid craftily behind a newspaper in the wastebasket; and a dozen more commonplace acts of malice by familiar objects.

He had to convince himself that the laws of chance adequately covered each incident; but also he had to grapple with underlying implications. So Sunday afternoon he seized a breathing-space to go up, armed with a clearance from Matt, to reason with the Major.

"Look here, sir," he began. "Gathering data is the first step, but you've got to have some general theory. Ruling out literal Gremlins, why *should* objects be actively hostile?"

The Major looked up from a soldering job, with a twinkle: "If I give you a theory, will you be the least bit more persuaded? All right: why do *we* like organization, control, applied power?"

Carl reflected: "Oh . . . I suppose it's the nature of life to extend itself by organization of the environment – tools and so on."

"Excellent. Well, the mass of the Universe behaves in exactly the opposite way – *disorganizing*, devolving. Any reason why this much vaster process shouldn't have – well, a sort of counter-life? Well, then, to *it*, our organizing activities would be equivalent to fires, contrary winds, rust. Up to a few thousand years ago, the effects of life were trivial – a little photosynthesis and burrowdigging that mattered no more to counter-life than geological erosion matters to us. But now Man is organizing matter and energy on an expanding scale – a regular epidemic of natural disasters to counter-life. So, of course, it resists and fights back."

"Hold on!" Carl protested. "After all, our activities cause increased breakdown of material, on the whole. That should be gratifying to it, not disconcerting."

"Yes – but we organize *some* matter very highly, and might eventually reverse the whole trend. Anyway, the further we go, the more opposition we generate."

"Pretty trivial opposition. Guerilla warfare."

The Major smiled. "Napoleon and Hitler were softened up for the real counter-offensive by guerilla warfare. How much of *your* life does it waste, for example?"

Carl thought that over. That morning, he had lost half an hour over a broken shoelace, a shaving-cream cap that escaped down the sink, a shirt-collar loop that refused to hitch over its button, and a handful of money that scattered jubilantly when his trouser pocket snared a finger. He had accordingly breakfasted on peanuts and, on ward rounds, had covered himself with mediocrity in the eyes of Dr Svindorff.

He changed his point of attack – or perhaps fell back on his own second line?

"But how does it work?" he asked. "I mean, we know the laws of mechanics, and they don't leave scope for free action."

"Oh, don't they? *We* operate by chemistry, and yet we feel we have plenty of freedom. Simple mechanical systems made of docile materials don't have much freedom, true. But we can't extrapolate that fact to cover all cases."

"Docile materials?"

"Metals, for example. Passive, like plant life. And we cast them in geometric forms. And even then they trick us. We get endless amusement out of games played with the simplest geometric form of all, the sphere, from billiards to baseball. What do we know of possibilities in really subtle systems of matter – fabrics, paper, rubber, ready to rebound from the almost organic forms forced on them?"

"Hm! Aren't those organic materials?"

"*Ex*organic. What populations are more fanatical for liberty than those that have just been liberated from obnoxious control? And note this: we organize matter only for special purposes; matter tries to waste our energies out of systematic hostility. The aspirin tablet that eludes you and wastes two minutes of your time has won a victory in a battle we're not even consciously fighting yet."

Carl rationed himself one last question – the topper: "Do you consider that individual objects have personality – that soldering iron, for instance?"

"I have an impression they enjoy a sort of merged or cooperative mentality – but certain forms have more or less individuality too. This iron –" He reached for it backhanded; his cuff touched a kink in the cord and the iron swiveled in its cradle to graze his wrist. He snatched his hand away, sending the iron clattering across the bench; but he caught it neatly before it had singed the wood, and set it in the cradle as if he were handling a cobra. "Yes! That soldering iron – or its cord – has plenty of personality; one of the most treacherous tools I've ever owned. And you'll notice how they use our very actions to thwart us, just as we use mechanical laws to make them act constructively. Of course, clumsiness gives them opportunity. I should have switched that off."

Carl attributed the little accident to autosuggestion, a Freudian slip, and went away shaking his head. He had never met so well-integrated a delusion. By heaven, he hadn't found the flaw yet! He hoped it would amuse Clare – she was often mighty sharp at analyzing such things.

The following evening was his night off. He entered the apartment house with two large shopping bags of staples and Clare's favorite delicacies, to find that he would have to heft them up six flights, the elevator being out of order.

He set them, panting, on the floor of the seventh flight while he opened the door. The door-check resisted sullenly, and he had to put his heel in the opening while he scooped up the groceries.

As he turned, something jerked violently at the small of his back – the belt of his trenchcoat somehow, impossibly, had snubbed over the doorknob.

Surprise, as much as the jerk, unbalanced him. His other heel slipped on the waxed linoleum of the landing. He lurched against the door, which now yielded like a swooning maiden, and he dove into the living room, frantically trying to save the toppling bags. The belt let go with the timing of a trained athlete, and everything went flying. He snatched at the top of one bag, and the sturdy paper ripped like tissue. With his other hand he came down solidly on a carton of cream that had rolled to the precise spot requisite, like an outfielder intercepting a fly.

Clare, in her bathrobe, came scurrying to the bedroom door, to find him arising from among the debris. The door had closed decisively on a bag of eggs; a small sack of flour, disgorging at one corner, smirked raffishly against a sofa-leg.

"Gracious!" Clare said, between mirth and peevishness. "*Must* you be clumsy?"

Through Carl's mind, before he realized it, flashed, *Well, they're not going to make trouble between me and Clare!* And he gave the soft answer that turneth away wrath.

After supper, he tried to turn the episode to account by using it to introduce the Major's fantasy.

At the end, Clare said languidly, "Well, anyone who ever kept house wouldn't think he was so crazy!"

They spent the next hour swapping instances: the row of books that always toppled the way you didn't want them; the garment that slid silkily to the floor if one arm hung over an edge; the drawerful of articles that restacked themselves to wedge it shut; the ball of paper that avoided the gaping waste-basket and dove easily into the narrow cranny behind; the balcony door that normally refused to latch and banged in every breeze, but that had swung shut and smartly locked her out; and so on.

It was fun and did amuse Clare; but afterward he wondered if he should have put such fantastic ideas into her still feverish mind. Also, he worried about having humored the Major quite so far; it was really very unprofessional!

Next day, however, Matt eased the latter burden considerably by saying, "Dr Svindorff is working on the Major's case – at my instigation. We can't prove that Ruth Elvira wants to enjoy his worldly goods in his absence; but there's no more reason to keep him here than a million other harmless cranks. Let him exercise his persuasive powers on the public along with Flat-Earthers, telekineticists, and prophets of Judgment Day come Jan. 19 . . . though, personally, I'll be sorry to lose him. I find him a diversion."

Carl felt the same. Candidly, he was itching to lick the Major's theory, over and above liking the man. But the odd hours they spent with the Major in his ward-cell-laboratory were devoted to mere yarns:

"– The wind snagged his parka on this one stub of branch, and there he was haltered over a five-hundred-foot drop, with the blizzard settling down . . . The jeep door knocked his glasses onto the one bit of rock within yards – thirty miles from town, dozens of hairpin bends, and the hills full of Huks –"

Amusing, but . . . against violent backgrounds of far outposts, violent accidents seemed natural enough; while by contrast, the freaks of civilized life grew pale and trifling. The magnificent phantasmagoria seemed to be sinking in a swamp of believe-it-or-not curiosities.

Half wishing to rescue things from anticlimax, Carl finally demanded, "You called all this just so much guerilla action. What shape would the real offensive take?"

The Major racked his tools and turned, as if the matter demanded his full attention: "Isn't it obvious? When we think of atomic war, we're afraid of the blast and fires and secondary radiation. But, to my mind, the big danger comes *afterward* . . . Ever drive down the Hudson, past those endless cliffs of apartment blocks, and wonder what would happen if a few power lines and water mains were cut, with no repair in sight? Lord! Those millions would be strangled, thrown back on techniques they'd utterly forgotten, pitted against materials that had learned to – defend themselves."

"Yes," Carl said slowly, "that would be an opportunity."

The Major sat down and clasped his hands over a knee.

"Look, Doctor, this may sound fantastic, but I'm mad anyway according to you. It's calculated that there must be millions of habitable planets, of which many have had ample time to develop space travel. Yet we've never had a certified visitor. Why?"

"I've heard it discussed. We're just a minor unit on the outskirts, for one thing."

"Quite true," the Major nodded. "Yet, if there were no more than a few hundred exploring races, surely *one* would have gotten around to us. Isn't it just possible that something deadlocks all life at a certain stage – some universal feed-back mechanism? And, on my theory, you can see what it would be – progress piling up resistance from counter-life. Past a crucial point, you might tip the balance in favor of life – but we're not nearly so close to that stage yet as we are to a blow-up. One slip, and we're done."

"Well, wouldn't thinkers on other worlds have seen the danger, if it's real?"

"Oh, I'm not so conceited – or mad – as to suppose I'm the only mind in the Universe to notice the obvious. But one is likely to see it too late, or not be able to persuade his contemporaries. *I'm* not making much headway, am I?"

Carl departed considerably relieved. You might come to take Gremlins half seriously, as personifying an active principle behind freak accidents; but as a cosmic threat engulfing the world and myriads of populated planets, they were merely silly. Carl suddenly felt himself back in daylight, free of the insidious suspicion that after all there might be something in what the old boy said. He knew once more that mechanics explained all accidents, if you only had time and patience to analyze them.

He said as much to Matt in the cafeteria.

"So I lose my bet, do I?" Matt smiled wistfully: "Well,

the bet's off anyway . . . Dr Svindorff says that Angus G. will be leaving before Christmas. But I thought you *were* drifting toward his siren song. Weren't you, honestly?"

"Out of idle amusement. It's lost its fascination."

That afternoon, a phone call from Clare wiped out all other concerns. Clare had been out the day before and gotten caught in the rain – now she had a misery and a temperature of 102. Carl felt a nasty qualm of apprehension; even a poor psychiatrist knew that in these cases the real danger was in relapse. He mortgaged his free time for the month ahead, and got the evening off.

He arrived at the apartment to find Clare in bed with their electric blanket huddled around her, not even trying to read. She greeted him with an anxiety that showed she too knew about relapses: "Do you think I'm going to be *very* sick?"

"Not if we keep you warm and quiet." He fixed the best light snacks he knew and fed her by hand.

At the end, she suddenly asked, "How's that old man with the theory about objects?" and hastened on, not waiting for a reply, "He's perfectly right."

She looked about fourteen, and valuable, bundled up with her brindled hair loose and her face worried. Carl scored himself for having filled her head with nonsense; though, of course, her fever would just have fastened on something else.

He jollied her seriously: "Well, I think bacteria are more dangerous than objects, in your case."

"*These* bacteria wouldn't have had a chance at me," she said firmly, "without some mighty funny coincidences. I got wet because I dropped my last carfare money, and it rolled like mad, and when it came to a crack, I'll swear it just swiveled and eased itself in. And I wouldn't have dropped it if my finger hadn't been hurt from when the window-cord broke and the window came down on my hand. And I wouldn't have gotten so wet if I'd had my slicker – but you remember how that went all funny when that bottle of cleaner on the shelf came uncorked and spilled over it."

Carl sighed. "You wouldn't have gotten wet at all if you hadn't tried to be noble and get back into harness before you were ready. Now, take this, and you'll sleep ten hours and wake up feeling fine."

But the last thing she said as she drowsed off was, "Shouldn've given'm chance. They know when you can't fight'm, 'n they pile on you."

He pulled the sofa to the bedroom door, so he could hear the least murmur, made himself a bed and turned in. He knew he was exhausted, and was determined to avoid being a soft target for either germs or Gremlins by getting overfatigued . . .

He woke in the dead of night, with an extra-sensory perception of something wrong. He rolled to his elbow. The air was abnormally chilly, even for a low-cost apartment in December.

Clare stirred, and he called softly, "You all right?"

She mumbled feverishly, "No. I'm coooold."

His hand found the floor-lamp without actually knocking it over. Naturally, the switch was in the one position where he had to flounder to reach it, and when it did click, nothing happened.

Oh, fine, he thought. Electricity's off. Furnace controls dead!

He strode over to the bed. The electric blanket, of course, was a mere flimsy fabric. He patted Clare's hunched shoulder. "I'll get another blanket. Where's the flash?"

"On the table," she wheezed, and groped on the far side of the bed. There was a muffled bump, and she lamented weakly, "I had it and it just knocked against something and flipped out of my fingers."

"Don't look for it," he said. "Keep wrapped up. I can find my way in the dark." No use wasting precious minutes, he thought, blundering around looking for the flash, while it, neatly ensconced in some improbable nook, gloated just out of his reach. He started around the foot of the bed toward the bathroom door . . .

Something lashed out of the dark and swathed itself around his ankles. He stumbled disastrously, his out-

stretched hand plunging through air where wall should
have been. His temple and cheek-bone jarred dazingly
against a door frame. He saved himself from falling, but
felt as if he had been battle-axed.

Clare's voice came hoarse and scared: "What happened?
Are you hurt?"

He kept his tone cheerful, if shaky: "Just tripped over the
bedspread turned back on the floor here. I'll throw it over
you till I get the blanket."

Easier said than done. The topologists' puzzle of the
inner tube that can't be turned insideout through a hole in
the side, though infinitely elastic, seemed elementary compared with flattening that eight-by-six rectangle of fluffy
chenille. In the end, he gave up trying to do a perfect job,
and bundled it over the shivering girl any old way, so he
could be free to get that blanket.

The bathroom was utterly black; he could see only the dial
of his wristwatch moving. With a sudden giddy feeling that
the solid fixtures had shifted, he picked his way from sink to
tub and along to the linen-closet over the tub's end. His
exploring fingers felt painted wood and brass knob, cold and
hostile. He opened the door. Folded sheets and shaggy
towels seemed somehow a little friendlier. Sanity began to
steal back as he carefully disengaged a blanket, giving it no
opportunity to emulate the unruliness of the bedspread. As it
came into his arms, a compact, well-folded mass, he let out a
breath he had not known he was holding . . .

Something hit the bottom of the bathtub with an ear-
stunning smash – a big bottle of some kind that had bided
its time up there.

Oh, well – that particular mess could wait till morning,
safely localized inside the tub. He edged back toward the
door, calling, "Okay, honey, just a bottle. Be right with
you." And he felt something hard under his foot, and then a
sharp sting.

His rational brain began parroting, ". . . The first impression is of contact, carried by fast, Group A fibers,
followed by one of pain, carried by slow, Group C fibers.
Pain is of two types: first pain, bright, stinging, well
localized . . ."

But a deeper level of his mind cut in with, "How did that hunk of glass know exactly where I was going to put my foot?"

He got the blanket around Clare, angrily unconcerned that he was soaking the good carpet with gore. Nothing mattered except beating off this peril to Clare, whose teeth were now chattering in the darkness. Now . . . hot water bottles . . .

Eureka! The gas stove would heat the place, and give a little light too . . . why hadn't he thought of that at first? Why, for that matter, hadn't he thought of using the blankets off his couchbed? They surely did exploit your stupidity!

The hot water bottles were in the kitchen. He began to explore his way through the living room.

The darkness was clammy. Windows were dim presences, hardly revealing their own positions. A radiator, when he touched it, was cold as drowned bones. For an endless moment he was groping through a subterranean passage, the weight of ancient rocks pressing down in a sentient and malignant desire to blot out his tiny flicker of life. This was a Thing with which one could have no compromise, because its very being was the sucking down of human aspiration and dream. Its only communication was hate and recognition that he was a special focus of danger, because he knew It for what It was and might rally resistance to It. It was attacking him through Clare; he stood alone between her and faceless Chaos. The bright, somewhat shoddy little apartment had melted like a fragile surface to show an abyss of death.

What would that Presence be like if It once organized and gained the upper hand?

He must not pause, or It *would* gain the upper hand . . .

His touch found the stove where it should be. It had no pilot burner, and he had to locate the match holder. With grim deliberation he struck a match. The instant, blinding flare was no friendly light. He angled it till it burned steadily, then turned on the gas. The gust of air that always precedes the flow from a long-disused burner blew out the match. With the same measured restraint, he got another. But tension and vexation made him strike it a little too petulantly. As the head plumed into flame, it snapped off and vaulted into a far corner.

For a terrifying instant, he thought it had gone into the trash basket full of waxed wrappings and other tinder . . . he dove after it, and struck his bruised cheek sickeningly against a table-corner . . . the match-head died impotently.

He found himself exulting aloud: "Failed, you little bastard!"

On the third try, he got the burner lit, and its eldritch, blue glare made it easier to light the others and get on a kettleful of water. He looked at the flame and admitted he was afraid to bundle Clare out here where it would soon be warm. If he didn't break his neck, or hers, he would probably pitch the two of them into the stove.

While the water was heating, he impulsively went to inspect the fire escape. The window showed nothing but reflections of the burners and his own shadowy image. He raised the sash, and looked out . . .

No wonder the power was off! The street lamps still shone, far below; but they revealed sleet falling like molten drops in Inferno; the trees were deep-sea corals and the windowpane was opaque as a sheet of paraffin.

Queer nausea and faintness swamped him . . . He gripped the sill, and his fingers slipped on the sheath of ice. For a moment he thought he had lost balance and was toppling in the grip of gravity, *Their* master-force, over the low sill . . . Even as he recovered, he could imagine his own nightmare howl as he plunged past scared neighbors' windows to silence on the icy concrete.

He grunted, stepped back, closed the window. He still felt giddy . . .

Then he saw the dark smears on the floor. It took an exploring finger to explain them. He grunted again, a sour sound. Who wouldn't feel giddy if they'd been bleeding like a stuck pig! It took twice as long as it should have to put on a pressure bandage with a napkin.

The water was too hot, now. He hung the bottles on a hook

over the sink while he poured the scalding fluid into them. As he balanced the clumsy kettle, he slipped just a little on a smear of blood and swung the spout where his wrist might have been. But that was a waning threat, he realized – a mere parting shot by a repulsed enemy. The knives, glassware, electrical gadgets, bulks of furniture, all glinted in the blue light, demons and imps ready to frustrate and harass; but the deeper Power had withdrawn – temporarily.

He got the bottles snuggled beside Clare, who murmured gratification.

At that juncture, the lights went on . . .

Next morning, the paper said: EIGHTEEN DIE IN FREAK STORM. There were accounts of linemen slipping to death, highway crashes, frozen tramps, fractured skulls.

Just a skirmish, thought Carl. Imagine that situation spread over the whole country – millions of situations like mine last night, year after year . . .

Driving back to the Institute, he tried to keep his mind on the streets, so that last night could fall into perspective. Soon it began to . . . soon he was smiling a little. But, said his semi-conscious, one thing was sure: Whatever the final verdict on the Major's theory – even if he's wrong – he's wrong with a damn good case!

Carl flung himself into his duties till Matt Loftus came around, about mid-afternoon, flourishing a crisp, folded document. "This is it, son!" said Matt. "We lose the Major, and the Major regains his right to life, liberty and the rebuttal of the inanimate. Want to join the Liberation Committee?"

The Major listened to Matt's announcement with his usual courtesy, but with such reserve that that normally self-assured medico ended rather lamely: "Maybe we should have told you this was coming along, sir. But I figured it as a sort of Christmas surprise. Anyway, we just need your signature . . ."

The Major scanned the paper and then laid it on his work-bench, smiling a little sadly. He said, "I appreciate your efforts, Doctor, and even more I appreciate your motives. But you don't quite understand."

"I – what? What don't I understand?"

The Major seated himself and caressed his mustache for a long moment. Then: "Outside I'd be a target for a concerted attack. They *know* I'm the greatest menace to Them on Earth, and They'd even risk unmasking Themselves – knowing most people would simply gawk at the most fantastic series of accidents and never draw an inference. I wouldn't last a month. Here, I'm safe, with everything under control."

Matt's face was a study: "But . . . what about alerting other people? Don't you have a duty to preach your theory and so on?"

Carl glanced sharply at his friend. That *was* humoring a patient!

"Why, Doctor," said the Major. "I have the best possible audience right here, funny as it sounds. You of the *staff* are the people best equipped to appreciate my theory – scientists, but not convention-bound theorists. You're not only medical men, used to dealing with things as they are: you're psychiatrists, whose job is distinguishing between the rational and the irrational. You can analyze vital phenomena better than an engineer such as myself. And you're the people most likely to be listened to in turn, and best able to defend yourselves from the inevitable attacks by the enemy."

His mild but steady gray eyes considered the young men, and the corners of his mustache quirked: "What better converts could I have than you two?"

Carl turned and stared at Matt, eyes questioning.

Matt set his jaw: "Yes, I'm going to – to follow it up. To see where it goes. And I wouldn't say so till I was sure of at least one competent associate . . . you *are* with me, aren't you?"

"Yes," said Carl, with sudden complete conviction.

The Major leaned back triumphantly. "You see! Of course, this place does put a certain stigma on my ideas. But with the safety factor, and now with grade-A channels, why should I leave? Do you think I'm crazy?"

The Very Pulse
of The Machine

Michael Swanwick

*Michael Swanwick (b. 1950) has been selling science
fiction since 1980, including such complex high-tech
novels as* Vacuum Flowers *(1987),* Griffin's Egg
(1991) and the award-winning Stations of the Tide
(1991). You'll find the best of his early short fiction in
Gravity's Angels *(1991) and the best of his recent work
in* Tales of Old Earth *(2000) including the following
award-winning story.*

C *lick.*
　The radio came on.

"Hell."

Martha kept her eyes forward, concentrated on walking.
Jupiter to one shoulder, Daedalus's plume to the other.
Nothing to it. Just trudge, drag, trudge, drag. Piece of
cake.

"Oh."

She chinned the radio off.

Click.

"Hell. Oh. Kiv. El. Sen."

"Shut up, shut up, shut up!" Martha gave the rope an
angry jerk, making the sledge carrying Burton's body jump
and bounce on the sulfur hardpan. "You're dead, Burton,
I've checked, there's a hole in your faceplate big enough to
stick a fist through, and I really don't want to crack up. I'm

in kind of a tight spot here and I can't afford it, okay? So be nice and just shut the fuck up."

"Not. Bur. Ton."

"Do it anyway."

She chinned the radio off again.

Jupiter loomed low on the western horizon, big and bright and beautiful and, after two weeks on Io, easy to ignore. To her left, Daedalus was spewing sulfur and sulfur dioxide in a fan two hundred kilometers high. The plume caught the chill light from an unseen sun and her visor rendered it a pale and lovely blue. Most spectacular view in the universe, and she was in no mood to enjoy it.

Click.

Before the voice could speak again, Martha said, "I am not going crazy, you're just the voice of my subconscious, I don't have the time to waste trying to figure out what unresolved psychological conflicts gave rise to all this, and I am *not* going to listen to anything you have to say."

Silence.

The moonrover had flipped over at least five times before crashing sideways against a boulder the size of the Sydney Opera House. Martha Kivelsen, timid groundling that she was, was strapped into her seat so tightly that when the universe stopped tumbling, she'd had a hard time unlatching the restraints. Juliet Burton, tall and athletic, so sure of her own luck and agility that she hadn't bothered, had been thrown into a strut.

The vent-blizzard of sulfur dioxide snow was blinding, though. It was only when Martha had finally crawled out from under its raging whiteness that she was able to look at the suited body she'd dragged free of the wreckage.

She immediately turned away.

Whatever knob or flange had punched the hole in Burton's helmet had been equally ruthless with her head.

Where a fraction of the vent-blizzard – "lateral plumes" the planetary geologists called them – had been deflected by the boulder, a bank of sulfur dioxide snow had built up. Automatically, without thinking, Martha scooped up double-handfuls and packed them into the helmet. Really, it was a nonsensical thing to do; in a vacuum, the body wasn't about to rot. On the other hand, it hid that face.

Then Martha did some serious thinking.

For all the fury of the blizzard, there was no turbulence. Because there was no atmosphere to have turbulence *in*. The sulfur dioxide gushed out straight from the sudden crack that had opened in the rock, falling to the surface miles away in strict obedience to the laws of ballistics. Most of what struck the boulder they'd crashed against would simply stick to it, and the rest would be bounced down to the ground at its feet. So that – this was how she'd gotten out in the first place – it was possible to crawl *under* the near-horizontal spray and back to the ruins of the moon-rover. If she went slowly, the helmet light and her sense of feel ought to be sufficient for a little judicious salvage.

Martha got down on her hands and knees. And as she did, just as quickly as the blizzard had begun – it stopped.

She stood, feeling strangely foolish.

Still, she couldn't rely on the blizzard staying quiescent. Better hurry, she admonished herself. It might be an intermittent.

Quickly, almost fearfully, picking through the rich litter of wreckage, Martha discovered that the mother tank they used to replenish their airpacks had ruptured. Terrific. That left her own pack, which was one-third empty, two fully charged backup packs, and Burton's, also one-third empty. It was a ghoulish thing to strip Burton's suit of her airpack, but it had to be done. Sorry, Julie. That gave her enough oxygen to last, let's see, almost forty hours.

Then she took a curved section of what had been the moonrover's hull and a coil of nylon rope, and with two pieces of scrap for makeshift hammer and punch, fashioned a sledge for Burton's body.

She'd be damned if she was going to leave it behind.

Click.

"This is. Better."

"Says you."

Ahead of her stretched the hard, cold sulfur plain. Smooth as glass. Brittle as frozen toffee. Cold as hell.

She called up a visor-map and checked her progress. Only forty-five miles of mixed terrain to cross and she'd reach the lander. Then she'd be home free. No sweat, she thought. Io was in tidal lock with Jupiter. So the Father of Planets would stay glued to one fixed spot in the sky. That was as good as a navigation beacon. Just keep Jupiter to your right shoulder, and Daedalus to your left. You'll come out fine.

"Sulfur is. Triboelectric."

"Don't hold it in. What are you really trying to say?"

"And now I see. With eye serene. The very. Pulse. Of the machine." A pause. "Wordsworth."

Which, except for the halting delivery, was so much like Burton, with her classical education and love of classical poets like Spenser and Ginsberg and Plath, that for a second Martha was taken aback. Burton was a terrible poetry bore, but her enthusiasm had been genuine, and now Martha was sorry for every time she'd met those quotations with rolled eyes or a flip remark. But there'd be time enough for grieving later. Right now she had to concentrate on the task at hand.

The colors of the plain were dim and brownish. With a few quick chintaps, she cranked up their intensity. Her vision filled with yellows, oranges, reds – intense wax crayon colors. Martha decided she liked them best that way.

For all its Crayola vividness, this was the most desolate landscape in the universe. She was on her own here, small and weak in a harsh and unforgiving world. Burton was dead. There was nobody else on all of Io. Nobody to rely on but herself. Nobody to blame if she fucked up. Out of nowhere, she was filled with an elation as cold and bleak as the distant mountains. It was shameful how happy she felt.

After a minute, she said, "Know any songs?"

Oh the bear went over the mountain. The bear went over the mountain. The bear went over the mountain. To see what he could see.

"Wake. Up. Wake. Up."

To see what he could –

"Wake. Up. Wake. Up. Wake."

"Hah? What?"

"Crystal sulfur is orthorhombic."

She was in a field of sulfur flowers. They stretched as far as the eye could see, crystalline formations the size of her hand. Like the poppies of Flanders field. Or the ones in *The Wizard of Oz*. Behind her was a trail of broken flowers, some crushed by her feet or under the weight of the sledge, others simply exploded by exposure to her suit's waste heat. It was far from being a straight path. She had been walking on autópilot, and stumbled and turned and wandered upon striking the crystals.

Martha remembered how excited she and Burton had been when they first saw the fields of crystals. They had piled out of the moonrover with laughter and bounding leaps, and Burton had seized her by the waist and waltzed her around in a dance of jubilation. This was the big one, they'd thought, their chance at the history books. And even when they'd radioed Hols back in the orbiter and were somewhat condescendingly informed that there was no chance of this being a new life-form, but only sulfide formations such as could be found in any mineralogy text . . . even that had not killed their joy. It was still their first big discovery. They'd looked forward to many more.

Now, though, all she could think of was the fact that such crystal fields occurred in regions associated with sulfur geysers, lateral plumes, and volcanic hot spots.

Something funny was happening to the far edge of the field, though. She cranked up her helmet to extreme magnification and watched as the trail slowly erased itself. New flowers were rising up in place of those she had smashed, small but perfect and whole. And growing. She could not imagine by what process this could be happening. Electrodeposition? Molecular sulfur being drawn up from the soil in some kind of pseudocapillary action? Were the flowers somehow plucking sulfur ions from Io's almost nonexistent atmosphere?

Yesterday, the questions would have excited her. Now, her capacity for wonder was nonexistent. Moreover, her instruments were back in the moonrover. Save for the suit's limited electronics, she had nothing to take measurements with. She had only herself, the sledge, the spare airpacks, and the corpse.

"Damn, damn, damn," she muttered. On the one hand, this was a dangerous place to stay in. On the other, she'd been awake almost twenty hours now and she was dead on her feet. Exhausted. So very, very tired.

"O sleep! It is a gentle thing. Beloved from pole to pole. Coleridge."

Which, God knows, was tempting. But the numbers were clear: no sleep. With several deft chin-taps, Martha overrode her suit's safeties and accessed its medical kit. At her command, it sent a hit of methamphetamine rushing down the drug/vitamin catheter.

There was a sudden explosion of clarity in her skull and her heart began pounding like a jackhammer. Yeah. That did it. She was full of energy now. Deep breath. Long stride. Let's go.

No rest for the wicked. She had things to do. She left the flowers rapidly behind. Good-bye, Oz.

Fade out. Fade in. Hours had glided by. She was walking through a shadowy sculpture garden. Volcanic pillars (these were their second great discovery; they had no exact parallel on Earth) were scattered across the pyroclastic plain like so many isolated Lipschitz statues. They were all rounded and heaped, very much in the style of rapidly cooled magma. Martha remembered that Burton was dead, and cried quietly to herself for a few minutes.

Weeping, she passed through the eerie stone forms. The speed made them shift and move in her vision. As if they were dancing. They looked like women to her, tragic figures out of *The Bacchae* or, no, wait, *The Trojan Women* was the play she was thinking of. Desolate. Filled with anguish. Lonely as Lot's wife.

There was a light scattering of sulfur dioxide snow on the ground here. It sublimed at the touch of her boots, turning to white mist and scattering wildly, the steam disappearing with each stride and then being renewed with the next footfall. Which only made the experience all that much creepier.

Click.

"Io has a metallic core predominantly of iron and iron

sulfide, overlain by a mantle of partially molten rock and crust."

"Are you still here?"

"Am trying. To communicate."

"Shut up."

She topped the ridge. The plains ahead were smooth and undulating. They reminded her of the Moon, in the transitional region between Mare Serenitatis and the foothills of the Caucasus Mountains, where she had undergone her surface training. Only without the impact craters. No impact craters on Io. Least cratered solid body in the solar system. All that volcanic activity deposited a new surface one meter thick every millennium or so. The whole damned moon was being constantly repaved.

Her mind was rambling. She checked her gauges, and muttered, "Let's get this show on the road."

There was no reply.

Dawn would come – when? Let's work this out. Io's "year," the time it took to revolve about Jupiter, was roughly forty-two hours fifteen minutes. She'd been walking seven hours. During which Io would've moved roughly sixty degrees through its orbit. So it would be dawn soon. That would make Daedalus's plume less obvious, but with her helmet graphics that wouldn't be a worry. Martha swiveled her neck, making sure that Daedalus and Jupiter were where they ought to be, and kept on walking.

Trudge, trudge, trudge. Try not to throw the map up on the visor every five minutes. Hold off as long as you can, just one more hour, okay, that's good, and another two miles. Not too shabby.

The sun was getting high. It would be noon in another hour and a half. Which meant – well, it really didn't mean much of anything.

Rock up ahead. Probably a silicate. It was a solitary six meters high brought here by who knew what forces and waiting who knew how many thousands of years just for her to come along and need a place to rest. She found a flat spot where she could lean against it, and, breathing heavily, sat down to rest. And think. And check the airpack. Four hours

until she had to change it again. Bringing her down to two
airpacks. She had slightly under twenty-four hours now.
Thirty-five miles to go. That was less than two miles an
hour. A snap. Might run a little tight on oxygen there
toward the end, though. She'd have to take care she didn't
fall asleep.

Oh, how her body ached.

It ached almost as much as it had in the '48 Olympics,
when she'd taken the bronze in the women's marathon. Or
that time in the internationals in Kenya when she'd come
up from behind to tie for second. Story of her life. Always
in third place, fighting for second. Always flight crew and
sometimes, maybe, landing crew, but never the commander. Never class president. Never king of the hill. Just once
– once – she wanted to be Neil Armstrong.

Click.

"The marble index of a mind forever. Voyaging through
strange seas of thought, alone. Wordsworth."

"What?"

"Jupiter's magnetosphere is the largest thing in the solar
system. If the human eye could see it, it would appear two
and a half times wider in the sky than the sun does."

"I knew that," she said, irrationally annoyed.

"Quotation is. Easy. Speech is. Not."

"Don't speak, then."

"Trying. To communicate!"

She shrugged. "So go ahead – communicate."

Silence. Then, "What does. This. Sound like?"

"What does what sound like?"

"Io is a sulfur-rich, iron-cored moon in a circular orbit
around Jupiter. What does this. Sound like? Tidal forces
from Jupiter and Ganymede pull and squeeze Io sufficiently to melt Tartarus, its sub-surface sulfur ocean.
Tartarus vents its excess energy with sulfur and sulfur
dioxide volcanoes. What does. This sound like? Io's metallic core generates a magnetic field that punches a hole in
Jupiter's magnetosphere, and also creates a high-energy ion
flux tube connecting its own poles with the north and south
poles of Jupiter. What. Does this sound like? Io sweeps up
and absorbs all the electrons in the million-volt range. Its

volcanoes pump out sulfur dioxide; its magnetic field breaks down a percentage of that into sulfur and oxygen ions; and these ions are pumped into the hole punched in the magnetosphere, creating a rotating field commonly called the Io torus. What does this sound like? Torus. Flux tube. Magnetosphere. Volcanoes. Sulfur ions. Molten ocean. Tidal heating. Circular orbit. What does this sound like?"

Against her will, Martha had found herself first listening, then intrigued, and finally involved. It was like a riddle or a word-puzzle. There was a right answer to the question. Burton or Hols would have gotten it immediately. Martha had to think it through.

There was the faint hum of the radio's carrier beam. A patient, waiting noise.

At last, she cautiously said, "It sounds like a machine."

"Yes. Yes. Yes. Machine. Yes. Am machine. Am machine. Am machine. Yes. Yes. Machine. Yes."

"Wait. You're saying that Io is a machine? That you're a machine? That you're *Io*?"

"Sulfur is triboelectric. Sledge picks up charges. Burton's brain is intact. Language is data. Radio is medium. Am machine."

"I don't believe you."

Trudge, drag, trudge drag. The world doesn't stop for strangeness. Just because she'd gone loopy enough to think that Io was alive and a machine and talking to her, didn't mean that Martha could stop walking. She had promises to keep, and miles to go before she slept. And speaking of sleep, it was time for another fast refresher – just a quarter-hit – of speed.

Wow. Let's go!

As she walked, she continued to carry on a dialogue with her hallucination or delusion or whatever it was. It was too boring otherwise.

Boring, and a tiny bit terrifying.

So she asked, "If you're a machine, then what is your function? Why were you made?"

"To know you. To love you. And to serve you."

Martha blinked. Then, remembering Burton's long re-
miniscences on her Catholic girlhood, she laughed. That
was a paraphrase of the answer to the first question in the
old Baltimore Catechism: *Why did God make man?* "If I
keep on listening to you, I'm going to come down with
delusions of grandeur."

"You are. Creator. Of machine."

"Not me."

She walked on without saying anything for a time. Then,
because the silence was beginning to get to her again,
"When was it I supposedly created you?"

"So many a million of ages have gone. To the making of
man. Alfred, Lord Tennyson."

"That wasn't me, then. I'm only twenty-seven. You're
obviously thinking of somebody else."

"It was. Mobile. Intelligent. Organic, Life. You are.
Mobile. Intelligent. Organic. Life."

Something moved in the distance. Martha looked up,
astounded. A horse. Pallid and ghostly white, it galloped
soundlessly across the plains, tail and mane flying.

She squeezed her eyes tight and shook her head. When
she opened her eyes again, the horse was gone. A hallucination. Like the voice of Burton/Io. She'd been thinking of
ordering up another refresher of the meth, but now it
seemed best to put it off as long as possible.

This was sad, though. Inflating Burton's memories until
they were as large as Io. Freud would have a few things to
say about *that*. He'd say she was magnifying her friend to a
godlike status in order to justify the fact that she'd never
been able to compete one-on-one with Burton and win.
He'd say she couldn't deal with the fact that some people
were simply better at things than she was.

Trudge, drag, trudge, drag.

So, okay, yes, she had an ego problem. She was an
overambitious, self-centered bitch. So what? It had gotten
her this far, where a more reasonable attitude would have
left her back in the slums of greater Levittown. Making do
with an eight-by-ten room with bathroom rights and a job
as a dental assistant. Kelp and talapia every night, and
rabbit on Sunday. The hell with that. She was alive and

Burton wasn't – by any rational standard that made her the winner.

"Are you. Listening?"

"Not really, no."

She topped yet another rise. And stopped dead. Down below was a dark expanse of molten sulfur. It stretched, wide and black, across the streaked orange plains. A lake. Her helmet readouts ran a thermal topography from the negative 230°F at her feet to 65°F at the edge of the lava flow. Nice and balmy. The molten sulfur itself, of course, existed at higher ambient temperatures.

It lay dead in her way.

They'd named it Lake Styx.

Martha spent half an hour muttering over her topo maps, trying to figure out how she'd gone so far astray. Not that it wasn't obvious. All that stumbling around. Little errors that she'd made, adding up. A tendency to favor one leg over the other. It had been an iffy thing from the beginning, trying to navigate by dead reckoning.

Finally, though, it was obvious. Here she was. On the shores of Lake Styx. Not all that far off course after all. Three miles, maybe, tops.

Despair filled her.

They'd named the lake during their first loop through the Galilean system, what the engineers had called the "mapping run". It was one of the largest features they'd seen that wasn't already on the maps from satellite probes or Earth-based reconnaissance. Hols had thought it might be a new phenomenon – a lake that had achieved its current size within the past ten years or so. Burton had thought it would be fun to check it out. And Martha hadn't cared, so long as she wasn't left behind. So they'd added the lake to their itinerary.

She had been so transparently eager to be in on the first landing, so afraid that she'd be left behind, that when she suggested they match fingers, odd man out, for who stayed, both Burton and Hols had laughed. "I'll play mother," Hols had said magnanimously, "for the first landing. Burton for Ganymede and then you for Europa. Fair enough?" And ruffled her hair.

She'd been so relieved, and so grateful, and so humiliated too. It was ironic. Now it looked like Hols – who would *never* have gotten so far off course as to go down the wrong side of the Styx – wasn't going to get to touch rock at all. Not this expedition.

"Stupid, stupid, stupid," Martha muttered, though she didn't know if she were condemning Hols or Burton or herself. Lake Styx was horse-shoe-shaped and twelve miles long. And she was standing right at the inner toe of the horseshoe.

There was no way she could retrace her steps back around the lake and still get to the lander before her air ran out. The lake was dense enough that she could almost *swim* across it, if it weren't for the viscosity of the sulfur, which would coat her heat radiators and burn out her suit in no time flat. And the heat of the liquid. And whatever internal flows and undertows it might have. As it was, the experience would be like drowning in molasses. Slow and sticky.

She sat down and began to cry.

After a time she began to build up her nerve to grope for the snap-coupling to her airpack. There was a safety for it, but among those familiar with the rig it was an open secret that if you held the safety down with your thumb and yanked suddenly on the coupling, the whole thing would come undone, emptying the suit in less than a second. The gesture was so distinctive that hot young astronauts-in-training would mime it when one of their number said something particularly stupid. It was called the suicide flick.

There were worse ways of dying.

"Will build. Bridge. Have enough. Fine control of. Physical processes. To build. Bridge."

"Yeah, right, very nice, you do that," Martha said absently. If you can't be polite to your own hallucinations . . . She didn't bother finishing the thought. Little crawly things were creeping about on the surface of her skin. Best to ignore them.

"Wait. Here. Rest. Now."

She said nothing but only sat, not resting. Building up

her courage. Thinking about everything and nothing. Clutching her knees and rocking back and forth.

Eventually, without meaning to, she fell asleep.

"Wake. Up. Wake. Up. Wake. Up."

"Uhh?"

Martha struggled up into awareness. Something was happening before her, out on the lake. Physical processes were at work. Things were moving.

As she watched, the white crust at the edge of the dark lake bulged outward, shooting out crystals, extending. Lacy as a snowflake. Pale as frost. Reaching across the molten blackness. Until there was a narrow white bridge stretching all the way to the far shore.

"You must. Wait," Io said. "Ten minutes and. You can. Walk across. It. With ease."

"Son of a bitch!" Martha murmured. "I'm sane."

In wondering silence, she crossed the bridge that Io had enchanted across the dark lake. Once or twice the surface felt a little mushy underfoot, but it always held.

It was an exalting experience. Like passing over from Death into Life.

At the far side of the Styx, the pyroclastic plains rose gently toward a distant horizon. She stared up yet another long, crystal-flower-covered slope. Two in one day. What were the odds against that?

She struggled upward, flowers exploding as they were touched by her boots. At the top of the rise, the flowers gave way to sulfur hardpan again. Looking back, she could see the path she had crunched through the flowers begin to erase itself. For a long moment she stood still, venting heat. Crystals shattered soundlessly about her in a slowly expanding circle.

She was itching something awful now. Time to freshen up. Six quick taps brought up a message on her visor: *Warning: Continued use of this drug at current levels can result in paranoia, psychosis, hallucinations, misperceptions, and hypomania, as well as impaired judgment.*

Fuck that noise. Martha dealt herself another hit.

It took a few seconds. Then – whoops. She was feeling light and full of energy again. Best check the airpack reading. Man, that didn't look good. She had to giggle.

Which was downright scary.

Nothing could have sobered her up faster than that high little druggie laugh. It terrified her. Her life depended on her ability to maintain. She had to keep taking meth to keep going, but she also had to keep going under the drug. She couldn't let it start calling the shots. Focus. Time to switch over to the last airpack. Burton's airpack. "I've got eight hours of oxygen left. I've got twelve miles yet to go. It can be done," she said grimly. "I'm going to do it now."

If only her skin weren't itching. If only her head weren't crawling. If only her brain weren't busily expanding in all directions.

Trudge, drag, trudge, drag. All through the night. The trouble with repetitive labor was that it gave you time to think. Time to think when you were speeding also meant time to think about the quality of your own thought.

You didn't dream in real-time, she'd been told. You get it all in one flash, just as you're about to wake up, and in that instant extrapolate a complex dream all in one whole. It feels as if you've been dreaming for hours. But you've only had one split second of intense nonreality.

Maybe that's what's happening here.

She had a job to do. She had to keep a clear head. It was important that she get back to the lander. People had to *know*. They weren't alone anymore. Damnit, she'd just made the biggest discovery since fire!

Either that, or she was so crazy she was hallucinating that Io was a gigantic alien machine. So crazy she'd lost herself within the convolutions of her own brain.

Which was another terrifying thing she wished she hadn't thought of. She'd been a loner as a child. Never made friends easily. Never had or been a best friend to anybody. Had spent half her girlhood buried in books. Solipsism terrified her – she'd lived right on the edge of it for too long. So it was vitally important that she determine whether the voice of Io had an objective, external reality. Or not.

Well, how could she test it?

Sulfur was triboelectric, Io had said. Implying that it was in some way an electrical phenomenon. If so, then it ought to be physically demonstrable.

Martha directed her helmet to show her the electrical charges within the sulfur plains. Crank it up to the max.

The land before her flickered once, then lit up in fairyland colors. Light! Pale oceans of light overlaying light, shifting between pastels, from faded rose to boreal blue, multilayered, labyrinthine, and all pulsing gently within the heart of the sulfur rock. It looked like thought made visual. It looked like something straight out of DisneyVirtual, and not one of the nature channels either – definitely DV-3.

"Damn," she muttered. Right under her nose. She'd had no idea.

Glowing lines veined the warping wings of subterranean electromagnetic forces. Almost like circuit wires. They crisscrossed the plains in all directions, combining and then converging – not upon her, but in a nexus at the sled. Burton's corpse was lit up like neon. Her head, packed in sulfur dioxide snow, strobed and stuttered with light so rapidly that it shone like the sun.

Sulfur was triboelectric. Which meant that it built up a charge when rubbed.

She'd been dragging Burton's sledge over the sulfur surface of Io for how many hours? You could build up a hell of a charge that way.

So, okay. There was a physical mechanism for what she was seeing. Assuming that Io really *was* a machine, a triboelectric alien device the size of Earth's moon, built eons ago for who knows what purpose by who knows what godlike monstrosities, then, yes, it might be able to communicate with her. A lot could be done with electricity.

Lesser, smaller, and dimmer "circuitry" reached for Martha as well. She looked down at her feet. When she lifted one from the surface, the contact was broken, and the lines of force collapsed. Other lines were born when she put her foot down again. Whatever slight contact might be made was being constantly broken. Whereas Burton's sledge was in constant contact with the sulfur surface of

Io. That hole in Burton's skull would be a highway straight into her brain. And she'd packed it in solid SO_2 as well. Conductive *and* supercooled. She'd made things easy for Io.

She shifted back to augmented real-color. The DV-3 SFX faded away.

Accepting as a tentative hypothesis that the voice was a real rather than a psychological phenomenon. That Io was able to communicate with her. That it was a machine. That it had been built . . .

Who, then, had built it?

Click.

"Io? Are you listening?"

"Calm on the listening ear of night. Come Heaven's melodious strains. Edmund Hamilton Sears."

"Yeah, wonderful, great. Listen, there's something I'd kind a like to know – who built you?"

"You. Did."

Slyly, Martha said, "So I'm your creator, right?"

"Yes."

"What do I look like when I'm at home?"

"Whatever. You wish. To."

"Do I breathe oxygen? Methane? Do I have antennae? Tentacles? Wings? How many legs do I have? How many eyes? How many heads?"

"If. You wish. As many as. You wish."

"How many of me are there?"

"One." A pause. "Now."

"I was here before, right? People like me. Mobile intelligent life forms. And I left. How long have I been gone?"

Silence. "How long –" she began again.

"Long time. Lonely. So very. Long time."

Trudge, drag. Trudge, drag. Trudge, drag. How many centuries had she been walking? Felt like a lot. It was night again. Her arms felt like they were going to fall out of their sockets.

Really, she ought to leave Burton behind. She'd never said anything to make Martha think she cared one way or the other where her body wound up. Probably would've thought a burial on Io was pretty damn nifty. But Martha wasn't doing this for her. She was doing it for herself. To prove that she wasn't entirely selfish. That she did too have feelings for others. That she was motivated by more than just the desire for fame and glory.

Which, of course, was a sign of selfishness in itself. The desire to be known as selfless. It was hopeless. You could nail yourself to a fucking cross, and it would still be proof of your innate selfishness.

"You still there, Io?"

Click.

"Am. Listening."

"Tell me about this fine control of yours. How much do you have? Can you bring me to the lander faster than I'm going now? Can you bring the lander to me? Can you return me to the orbiter? Can you provide me with more oxygen?"

"Dead egg, I lie. Whole. On a whole world I cannot touch. Plath."

"You're not much use, then, are you?"

There was no answer. Not that she had expected one. Or needed it, either. She checked the topos and found herself another eighth-mile closer to the lander. She could even see it now under her helmet photomultipliers, a dim glint upon the horizon. Wonderful things, photomultipliers. The sun here provided about as much light as a full moon did back on Earth. Jupiter by itself provided even less. Yet crank up the magnification, and she could see the airlock awaiting the grateful touch of her gloved hand.

Trudge, drag, trudge. Martha ran and reran and rereran the math in her head. She had only three miles to go, and enough oxygen for as many hours. The lander had its own air supply. She was going to make it.

Maybe she wasn't the total loser she'd always thought she was. Maybe there was hope for her, after all.

Click.

"Brace. Yourself."

"What for?"

The ground rose up beneath her and knocked her off her feet.

★　★　★

When the shaking stopped, Martha clambered unsteadily to her feet again. The land before her was all a jumble, as if a careless deity had lifted the entire plain up a foot and then dropped it. The silvery glint of the lander on the horizon was gone. When she pushed her helmet's magnification to the max, she could see a metal leg rising crookedly from the rubbled ground.

Martha knew the shear strength of every bolt and failure point of every welding seam in the lander. She knew exactly how fragile it was. That was one device that was never going to fly again.

She stood motionless. Unblinking. Unseeing. Feeling nothing. Nothing at all.

Eventually she pulled herself together enough to think. Maybe it was time to admit it: She never *had* believed she was going to make it. Not really. Not Martha Kivelsen. All her life she'd been a loser. Sometimes – like when she qualified for the expedition – she lost at a higher level than usual. But she never got whatever it was she really wanted.

Why was that, she wondered? When had she ever desired anything bad? When you get right down to it, all she'd ever wanted was to kick God in the butt and get his attention. To be a big noise. To be the biggest fucking noise in the universe. Was that so unreasonable?

Now she was going to wind up as a footnote in the annals of humanity's expansion into space. A sad little cautionary tale for mommy astronauts to tell their baby astronauts on cold winter nights. Maybe Burton could've gotten back to the lander. Or Hols. But not *her*. It just wasn't in the cards.

Click.

"Io is the most volcanically active body in the solar system."

"You fucking bastard! Why didn't you warn me?"

"Did. Not. Know."

Now her emotions returned to her in full force. She wanted to run and scream and break things. Only there wasn't anything in sight that hadn't already been broken. "You shithead!" she cried. "You idiot machine! What use are you? What goddamn use at all?"

"Can give you. Eternal life. Communion of the soul. Unlimited processing power. Can give Burton. Same."

"Hah?"

"After the first death. There is no other. Dylan Thomas."

"What do you mean by that?"

Silence.

"Damn you, you fucking machine! What are you trying to *say*?"

Then the devil took Jesus up into the holy city and set him on the highest point of the temple, and said to him, "If thou be the Son of God, cast thyself down: for it is written he shall give his angels charge concerning thee: and in their hands they shall bear thee up."

Burton wasn't the only one who could quote scripture. You didn't have to be Catholic, like her. Presbyterians could do it too.

Martha wasn't sure what you'd call this feature. A volcanic phenomenon of some sort. It wasn't very big. Maybe twenty meters across, not much higher. Call it a crater, and let be. She stood shivering at its lip. There was a black pool of molten sulfur at its bottom, just as she'd been told. Supposedly its roots reached all the way down to Tartarus.

Her head ached so badly.

Io claimed – had *said* – that if she threw herself in, it would be able to absorb her, duplicate her neural patterning, and so restore her to life. A transformed sort of life, but life nonetheless. "Throw Burton in," it had said. "Throw yourself in. Physical configuration will be. Destroyed. Neural configuration will be. Preserved. Maybe."

"Maybe?"

"Burton had limited. Biological training. Understanding of neural functions may be. Imperfect."

"Wonderful."

"Or. Maybe not."

"Gotcha."

Heat radiated up from the bottom of the crater. Even protected and shielded as she was by her suit's HVAC systems, she felt the difference between front and back. It was like standing in front of a fire on a very cold night.

They had talked, or maybe negotiated was a better word for it, for a long time. Finally Martha had said, "You savvy Morse code? You savvy orthodox spelling?"

"Whatever Burton. Understood. Is. Understood."

"Yes or no, damnit!"

"Savvy."

"Good. Then maybe we can make a deal."

She stared up into the night. The orbiter was out there somewhere, and she was sorry she couldn't talk directly to Hols, say good-bye and thanks for everything. But Io had said no. What she planned would raise volcanoes and level mountains. The devastation would dwarf that of the earthquake caused by the bridge across Lake Styx.

It couldn't guarantee two separate communications.

The ion flux tube arched from somewhere over the horizon in a great looping jump to the north pole of Jupiter. Augmented by her visor, it was as bright as the sword of God.

As she watched, it began to sputter and jump, millions of watts of power dancing staccato in a message they'd be picking up on the surface of Earth. It would swamp every radio and drown out every broadcast in the Solar System.

THIS IS MARTHA KIVELSEN, SPEAKING FROM THE SURFACE OF IO ON BEHALF OF MYSELF, JULIET BURTON, DECEASED, AND JACOB HOLS, OF THE FIRST GALILEAN SATELLITES EXPLORATORY MISSION. WE HAVE MADE AN IMPORTANT DISCOVERY . . .

Every electrical device in the System would *dance* to its song!

Burton went first. Martha gave the sledge a shove, and out it flew, into empty space. It dwindled, hit, kicked up a bit of a splash. Then, with a disappointing lack of pyrotechnics, the corpse slowly sank into the black glop.

It didn't look very encouraging at all.

Still . . .

"Okay," she said. "A deal's a deal." She dug in her toes and spread her arms. Took a deep breath. Maybe I am going to survive after all, she thought. It could be Burton was already halfway-merged into the oceanic mind of Io, and awaiting her to join in an alchemical marriage of personalities. Maybe I'm going to live forever. Who knows? Anything is possible.

Maybe.

There was a second and more likely possibility. All this could well be nothing more than a hallucination. Nothing but the sound of her brain short-circuiting and squirting bad chemicals in all directions. Madness. One last grandiose dream before dying. Martha had no way of judging.

Whatever the truth might be, though, there were no alternatives, and only one way to find out.

She jumped.

Briefly, she flew.

High Eight

Keith Roberts

*Occasionally a writer comes along who demands attention
and keeps all the plates spinning on sticks at once. J.G.
Ballard was one such. So were Michael Moorcock and
Roger Zelazny and Ursula K. LeGuin. And so was
Keith Roberts, but in a much quieter, almost apologetic
way. Roberts (1935–2000) sold his first stories in 1964
and was soon appearing in* Science Fantasy, New
Worlds *and* New Writing in SF, *under his own name
and various pseudonyms. His first major work, and the
one for which he will doubtless always be remembered,
was* Pavane *(1968), a wonderful evocation of an alternate Catholic England that arose with the success of the
Spanish Armada and the assassination of Elizabeth I.
He produced many more novels and stories over the years
but grew increasingly disgruntled with publishers and
withdrew from the scene. Roberts had a longing for the
quiet life. Much of his work expresses a caution towards
technology and progress as in the following, which was
first published under a pen name and has only once before
been reprinted, and that thirty years ago.*

For Rick Cameron, the trouble started one bright
morning in Stan Mainwaring's office.

Stan was Outside Works Controller to Saskeega Power,
Rick was line maintenance boss for the company. They
were great buddies; they'd been through school together,
clocked nearly fifteen years together at Saskeega. Rick was

sitting on his boss's desk skinning through a copy of the company magazine when the phone blew. Stan picked up the handset. He said, "What? Yeah, you'd better put him through . . ." The phone squawked a long time. Stan's face changed; his fingers gripped the handset rhythmically, an unconscious reflex. Then, "Yeah, I'll do that. Yeah, straight away." He put the instrument down and sat for a moment staring at it, hands spread on the desk top. Rick glanced resignedly at the ceiling.

They'd been using one of the penstocks as a laboratory to check corrosion characteristics on some new metal dressings, they were due to open her up that morning, have a look at what had been happening. Rick had gone over to Main Block to collect Stan, they'd been going to drive up together. Now he had a strong presentiment they wouldn't be making the trip. He said, "What's the matter, Stan? Trouble?"

The other looked at him sombrely. "Had a suicide in the night. Old guy wrapped himself round a set of bus bars. They only just found him, Billy says it isn't too nice. Sheriff's on the way over, I got to go up and see."

"Where was it, Stan, where'd it happen?"

The other man shrugged. "Of all the crazy places. High Eight."

Half a dozen lines went out from Saskeega; Rick's job was to service and maintain them over a radius of some twenty-five miles from the plant. The shortest run on the sector was the Indian Valley line. That went due west up into the mountains, through Black Horse Pass and down into Indian Valley the other side of the hump. It was the trickiest to service but far and away the most important; it fed the Sand Creek Pool where Sand Creek Atomic Research got their juice. And Sand Creek was about the most important thing in the country. . . . There was something else; the two installations inside the mountain, and the stepdown transformers that fed them. Rick had heard the rumours, he'd heard his boys mutter that they were parts of the Doomsday Brain, that they were bringing the current that ran the Doomsday Brain. He hadn't let himself think too much about it and he certainly hadn't worried. He wasn't the man to worry. His job was to service the lines.

The first transformer was at the bottom of the hill, the second one way up on the Black Horse at the head of the pass. Number two on the line, number eight on the sector; she sat up there in the clouds and that was the name they'd given her, among themselves. High Eight . . .

Rick went along with his boss. Privately, he thought it was his baby as much as Stan's. They drove through Freshet, the little township that had sprung up to house the staff of Saskeega and their families. Passing Rick's place, his wife gave the car a wave. He shook his head slightly. It was just as well she didn't know where they were headed and why, Judy was funny about the lines. They got through town and the road started to climb with the towers striding alongside. Standing room on the mountain was strictly limited, the line followed the road most of the way. When they got high enough Rick could see Saskeega below and miles off, the penstocks running down to it, the white threads of the outfalls.

He turned round to Stan. "How in Hell did he manage to get hold of those bars? He must have been crazy . . ." He wasn't feeling too great himself; once when he was in the army he'd seen a guy take a thousand cycles, hadn't been a thing left but his shoes. And supertension was worse; you couldn't fool with a hundred thousand volts, it played too rough. The bus bars were the big terminals where the contacts were made between the transformers and the cables, they were fenced with guard rails. Drop a spanner over those rails and there it stopped till a Routine Outage. Slide under to get it and the voltage waiting there would come crackling out to meet you, shake you by the hand. Rick ran his fingers through his cropped hair. He said again, "The old guy must've been crazy as a coot to crawl inside . . ."

Stan didn't answer, just put his foot down harder. They passed number seven; a few miles on and they could see High Eight perched over a cliff, its white walls shining in the sun. When they reached it Stan swung off the road and stopped. They got out. There were a couple of cars parked, one of the station service trucks and the Sheriff's estate wagon. They walked towards the building and Sheriff

Stanton came out the door. One of his deputies backed out after him, taking a bulb out of a flash camera. Stanton nodded to the Saskeega men, wagged his thumb at High Eight. He said, "Better take a look, fellers, your steak-frier's sure done him proud."

They went in.

It could have been worse. The body was lying curled up just inside the door, a little old man, grey-haired, clothes ragged. Just an old hobo. The flash had blown him clear instead of taking him in and cooking him, his hands were charred but that was all. He'd smashed the back of his skull on the guard-rail. Not that that mattered, he'd been dead when he hit it. A yard or so away was a tin box. The lid had come off, there were old papers scattered, a couple of photographs. And there were the bus bars shining in the half dark, the transformers singing all round.

An ambulance had been called, they loaded him in as soon as it arrived. Stanton picked up the junk that was spread about, thumbed through it. He shrugged. "No names. Guess if we could trace next of kin they wouldn't want to know. Maybe he's better off, poor old guy. You boys known a thing like this before?"

Rick shook his head slowly. Suicides happened, they just happened all the time, but there weren't many people that chose the lines. It wasn't a nice way to go . . .

The door lock was smashed where the old man had broken in. Stan fingered it; he said slowly, "Maybe he was just lookin' for shelter and a place to sleep awhile. He sure as Hell found that." They told one of the maintenance men to get up there with a new lock, that was about all they could do. Rick drove back down with Stan, tried to put the whole thing out of his mind. He managed it till he got home that night. He saw Judy's face and could tell she knew. He asked her how she'd found out. She said she saw the trouble wagon in town, asked one of the boys. Rick swore under his breath about guys who just had to shoot off their big mouths. It wasn't the sort of thing it did Judy any good to know, not feeling the way she did about the lines. Rick blamed himself partly for that. He'd taken her up to High Eight one day, and it had scared the Hell out of her. The big housings singing like cats, the static over their tops making blue crackles in the dark. She'd lived with the fear for years, but she'd got no better.

He could see the thing was on her back again. She said, "Why'd he do it, Rick, you find out why he did it? Maybe, you know, did he leave a note or something, say why . . . ?"

He said, "No note, honey, nothing. Just wasn't a reason, I guess. Poor old guy was crazy, is all." He stood squarely, facing her and frowning, worrying about something outside his experience and wondering how to quieten her.

She shook her head violently. She said, "I know why he did it, Rick, I can see why, can't you?" She gulped. Then, "Was he . . . much burned?"

"Look, Judy . . ."

She said. "It was the lines. It's always the lines. Like the rails in a . . . station, in a subway, they pull, Rick, you never felt them pull? You stood there with the train coming and the noise and felt the rails pull harder and harder . . ."

"Honey, please . . ."

She ignored him. "It's that way with the lines, Rick. They drew him. Can't you see him up there, that poor old man, lonely, nobody to go to, nobody around? That's when they pull most, when there's nobody around. He was hungry and cold and the night was coming and there were the lights on the wall inside High Eight, like sort of red and amber eyes watching and saying come on, it's OK, come on . . . and the singing all round, and the shining things behind the rail pulling and pulling . . ."

He grabbed her shoulders and shook her. "Judy, for God's sake . . ."

She wrenched away from him, ran into the kitchen. She snapped switches. She said, "Electricity, Rick. It scares me. Look at it all round, Just think, if it was waiting. If it all wanted to pull . . ."

His temper snapped. He yelled at her, "For Christ's sake, *shut up* . . ." He said, "I was the one had to pick him up, get him in the bloodwagon. I didn't like it, honey, I don't *like* that sort of thing. You think I'm a sort of ghoul likes going round picking people off the lines? You want it, you asked to know, yeah, his hands were burned. They were burned black, you could see the bones . . . Now are you happy, I been trying to forget it most of the day . . ."

She screwed her eyes up, hand across her mouth as if she was in pain. A long wait; then, "Rick I'm . . . I'm sorry, honey, I don't know what gets me going like that. It's a thing I got, about the lines . . . I'm sorry . . ."

He sighed, feeling the old trembling he always felt when he rowed with her. "OK, so we both got it out of our systems. Now what say we forget it all. These things happen, honey, isn't any cause to go wild . . ."

"Rick, couldn't we go off? You know, you get some other job, we could go some place miles from Saskeega where we didn't have to see the lines . . ."

They'd been through that fifty, a hundred times before. Rick would have done most things for her even if she wanted them for crazy reasons but he couldn't take another job, the lines were all he knew. Or so he told himself. But there was something else, something he didn't talk about with Judy because she wouldn't understand. The lines did get you, after a time. Oh, not in the crazy way she said, but there was something about them, the towers and the lines soaring off across the country taking power to run peoples' lives, run the world. There was something in that. He used to talk about it odd times with Stan; he never really knew how to get it into words but Stan knew what he meant.

That night Rick kept having a recurring dream. It seemed the phone was ringing and he kept answering it and finding there was another body in High Eight. The fifth or sixth time it happened he sat up in bed, thinking blearily that the crazy talk Judy had given him had somehow gotten on his mind. He looked round. The room was dark, he could see his wristwatch dial on the side table. He picked the watch up. It read just after three. He yawned and rubbed his eyes, then the noise that had woken him started again.

The phone *was* ringing.

He got up and answered it. He listened to what it had to say, then he put the handset down and wondered if he was going to wake up again. But it was no good, this was for real. He went back to the bedroom and started to dress. His hands worked mechanically, almost of their own volition. There was another body in High Eight, the lines were out, he had to get up there quick as he could.

Judy put the light on, and Rick turned round. She was shivering. "Rick, what is it, what goes on? Was it the phone . . . ?"

He said, "Look honey, I gotta go out. They got some trouble, I'll try and not be too long . . ."

She got hold of his arm. "It's another one. In that God-awful place . . ."

"Honey, it isn't, isn't anything like that. They got some trouble down at the plant. Icing on the insulators." He said the first thing that came into his head. It didn't do any good, he could see the look in her eyes, he could tell she knew.

Rick got the car out and drove for the pass. Soon as he left the shelter of town he started to feel the wind pulling and twitching at the steering. There was always a wind on the Black Horse, it blew like a bitch up there night and day. Something came into his mind. He remembered the wind in the poem, the wind that blew in the wasteland where nobody ever came. There was nothing on the mountain either except High Eight.

He didn't care for that idea too much. Essentially, Rick was a rational guy; but the morning had been bad, and with the wind yelling that way and everything black as Hell it was a whole lot worse. He tried to think about something else, started a sort of mental argument with Judy.

"Look honey, there's nothing wrong with electricity. You use it right, it's fine. You fool about and you get in trouble, most things are like that. Look, the lines are good. They light your home, cook your meals, run your television, help you have fun. They keep you warm, they keep you happy. We couldn't do without the lines . . ."

Somehow he knew what she'd answer. It was almost like she was there with him in the car. She said, "The lines are waiting, Rick. Every place, all the time. Just waiting. And one day . . ."

He took a bend. The headlights shone silver off the foot of one of the towers. He wondered suddenly if the thing was a gag, somebody had decided to have a little fun sending him chasing up there in the middle of the night. Didn't seem likely, but there was a chance. That meant he'd get to High Eight, wouldn't be a soul around. Just the wind booming off the cliff and the coloured eyes up there in the housings singing in the dark . . . He tried to see up towards the pass, but as far as he could tell it was all black. He was suddenly sure the thing was a gag. He felt like turning the car and going straight back, but he knew he couldn't do that.

Rick got a cigarette out of his windcheater pocket and fumbled it alight. He was angry with himself; he was acting and thinking like a kid fresh from High School. What he was going to do was ride on up and check the place; and if there was nobody around he was going to phone back to Saskeega and somebody was going to get taken apart. That was all there was to it.

There were folk there. There was a patrol car, he saw the roof-flasher from a couple of miles down the road. Somebody was waving a lamp. He stopped the car and got out. The wind was evil; it felt like a solid, animate thing. He leaned into the gusts, tacked across to High Eight.

It was quieter inside, the wind was muted and the housings were silent because the lines were out. A couple of the night maintenance staff from Saskeega were there, and two cops. They were standing in a group looking at the bus bars. One of the engineers was saying "Gee, *look* at that! Gee, *look* at that!" He was talking softly, like somebody at a pretty firework display. "Gee, look at *that* . . . !"

The Thing squatted with its back turned to Rick, showing him the top of its bald head. Its hands were on the bus bars, but he wasn't holding the contacts any more. Its arms were burned off at the wrists. The stumps sticking out from the body were dried and twisted. The man must have dived in head first, got hold of the bars one in each hand. God alone knew how . . . Then they'd got hold of him and the arcing hadn't stopped till his arms were burned apart. All round for yards across the concrete floor were the black scars where the sparks had drummed and hissed.

The wind howled outside. The man said, "Gee, *look* at that . . . !"

Rick turned round on him, managed to talk somehow. "Turn if off, will you? Just turn it off . . ."

The engineer looked at him and shook his head. "Gee, Rick," he said. "Just look at *that* . . . !"

The overseer walked the length of the building to the phone. He rang through to Saskeega, got the duty engineer in West Power Block. He said harshly, "Donnell, what in Hell you playing at down there?"

There was a lot of static on the line. It was hissing and crackling like it was trying to talk as well, a gibberish of embryonic words. Rick could hardly hear his own voice. He said, "*What in Hell you playing at?*" Suddenly he couldn't stop himself yelling. He felt he wanted to take somebody and pound their face in because of what had happened. But there was no one to blame . . .

Donnell sounded half crazy. "Rick, I don't know what happened, I don't know how in Hell it happened. Trips shoulda pulled the line, they stayed in. Trips didn't work, I don't know what in Hell happened . . ."

Cameron swore. "What are you using for eyes down there, what about your line volts? What you doing down there, what you using for eyes . . . ?"

A great guffaw of static. Then, "I pulled the line soon as the volts. jumped, Rick, I don't know what in Hell happened . . ."

"Soon as Hell you did. Guy's hands fried off up here, Donnell, while you were sitting waiting for your meters to kick. You took his hands off his body, God damn it, you took 'em right off his body . . ."

"Rick, I don't know how in Hell –"

The overseer slammed the phone down and got out. The whole place smelled like somebody had been cooking meat with no salt, and he knew within two minutes he was going to be sick as a dog.

They had to wait while photographs were taken. You always had to have pictures of a thing like that, Rick reflected bitterly, just in case you ever managed to forget it. Then they started clearing the lines. Rick would have called Stan but it would have done no good; he'd gone off to a big convention the afternoon before, he wasn't expected back for a couple of days.

Power was restored about six in the morning, and Rick Cameron drove back down to Saskeega and into a hornets' nest; the feeder had been out most of the night, they'd had to pull juice from half across the country to keep Sand Creek alive. He called Stan long-distance from his office. He still felt pretty shaken up. He had to try three hotels before he reached his boss, when he came on the line he already knew what had happened. Stan flew back the same morning, he was in Saskeega in about six hours. They went down together to see Sheriff Stanton.

They'd taken all the precautions they could; the lock on the door had been fixed, but the second victim hadn't got in that way. There were a couple of windows in the transformer house, they were fairly small and they had heavy bars across, but it looked like the suicide had pulled the bars out with his bare hands and the glass and frame as well. There was no sign of anything he could have used as a lever and there was blood on the sill and on the floor inside, a trail of it to the bus bars. It looked as if he'd torn his hands to pieces smashing the window. Stanton said maybe more would be known after the autopsy, but it looked plain enough; the guy had been crazy, like the hobo. He shook his head. He said he'd known the dead man, he was a farmer from down in Indian Valley. He said, "Beats me how a little guy like that could have busted that window apart. He must have been deranged, crazy as Hell . . . but that don't help us none, what you boys goin' to do about this?"

The Saskeega men looked at each other a little blankly. Then Stan said, "Don't seem to be much we can do, Andy. Like you said, suicides happen. If a guy goes crazy we can't read his mind. We didn't kill those folk."

Stanton grunted. "Your juice did. Look fellers, I seen things like this before. Take my word. Not on the lines, that's something new, but I'm telling you if there's a suicide, say a drowning, and the word goes round, you've got a dozen more. Seems the idea gets in peoples' minds, triggers half the potential nut cases in the county. Now I've seen this and I don't want no more bodies coming down off that mountain, what're you going to do?"

Rick said carefully, "You think maybe the old guy heard about the hobo?"

"Don't see how. Lived on his own, got a little place way out of town, hardly ever saw any folks. I'll check on it, but I don't see how in Hell he could have known."

Stan said, "Well, we can't write it off as just bad luck. What say we put a guard on that place a few nights, Rick, till things quiet down?"

Rick thought of the blackness up there, the wind talking in the wires all the night through. The warning lights that Judy reckoned said come on . . . He said, "Two men, Stan, and better arm 'em. Makes 'em feel better."

Stan looked at the overseer sharply, but nothing more was said. He brought the thing up again that night though, while Rick was driving him home. "Two lots of double time just to watch one bloody little transformer stage, see no more crazy bastards turn themselves into rare steak . . . The old man's going to nail my ears to the wall for this, Rick. They want a guard, I say put on a guard, fine, put a guard on the place. But why the Hell two?"

Rick narrowed his eyes and squinted at a bend. "You like to do it, Stan, you do it on your own?"

He said, "I'd do it if I had to, and you damn well know it, what'n Hell you getting at?" He sounded surly. Rick glanced at him quickly. That wasn't like Stan . . .

They posted the guards and that took care of things at High Eight for a time. But High Eight wasn't the real worry. What Rick wanted to know, what Stan wanted to know, what it seemed everybody in Saskeega wanted to know was why those trips hadn't worked. On all high-tension lines there is gear designed to kill the circuit in an emergency, if, for instance, a tower blows down or gets struck by lightning. If the lines stayed in they'd burn up everything, fry anybody within yards as well. That's what the trips are for, in the event of a major short they pull the plug after three or four seconds at the outside. But the suicide had been on the bars a lot longer than that and the lines didn't cut at all till Donnell shut down by hand.

That was another mystery, of course. How could Donnell and the whole night staff have missed seeing things were wrong? Donnell swore he took action as soon as the voltage went crazy and he was a good engineer, Stan knew that. "But the Hell, Rick," he said worriedly. "He didn't pull those lines till there was nearly nothing left of the guy, he didn't pull till the voltage had steadied again. He could have had the whole feeder burn out under his nose. Under all their noses . . ."

The Controller questioned everybody, but he could get no leads. There just didn't seem to be a reason for any of it. The trip gear was checked a dozen times, there wasn't a thing out of place. That line just had to pull. And yet it didn't.

They had to leave things like that. Nobody liked it, but there wasn't anything to be done. The guards were kept on High Eight a couple of weeks, but nothing else happened. Rick put another set of bars on the window, had the door double-locked and hoped the line had settled down for good. But it had not. The day after the guards were removed Saskeega lost three men.

Two of them were killed in a chopper that crashed into the cliff right below High Eight. Nobody could explain it; a farmer who saw it happen said the machine just turned and flew straight at the rock. The Company ran half a dozen helicopters, they were good for patrolling lines in awkward country. Stan grounded the rest as soon as he heard; that didn't make Rick's job any easier. He tried to make the best of it. He was sanguine enough to realize there was nothing else his boss could have done.

The other death was on the Indian Valley feeder as well. The man's name was Halloran, Rick had known him very well. He was half Irish, hadn't seemed to have a nerve in his body. He was boss of one of the maintenance gangs, he'd been with Saskeega for years.

He took a truck out that day, nobody saw him go. Nobody missed him either. About five in the afternoon a patrol came through from Indian Valley on a routine job, saw something they never would have believed. One of the men told Rick later, they drove down and stopped and got out of the car and stood staring, and they still could hardly believe. Parked beside one of the towers was the trouble wagon; and up above it, way up in the sky, Jim Halloran was crouched over an insulator stack, blue fire in his hands and the pain of the Pit in his eyes . . .

Rick began to lose staff. They sloped off in ones and twos, found other jobs where they wouldn't have to keep looking over their shoulders wondering who was going next. Halloran's death hit them harder than anything else that had happened. Old farmers can go crazy, bums can get tired of life, but Halloran was a guy they'd worked with, got drunk with. He wouldn't have killed himself, that was what they muttered. Something dragged him up to that tower, he didn't take his own life, and whatever the something was, if it could kill a guy like Halloran it could do anything.

Rick knew the rumours were going round, but there wasn't a thing he could do. He'd got his hands full as it was; there was a lot of routine work on the lines, repair jobs were always coming up; kids out for kicks shooting up the insulators, all sorts of things like that. The choppers were still being taken apart to find out what made them fly into rock walls, he'd had to split the remnants of half a dozen gangs and make up new bosses, and there was trouble there. Always friction when a thing like that has to be done. He was working most hours God gave, his wife was headed for a nervous breakdown on account of all the trouble, he'd just about had enough. Then he heard about Stallion Jim.

It seemed one of the gangers was a halfbred Indian. Whatever the truth of his tale, he reckoned years back his people had owned most of Saskeega County. He said that Indian Valley had been their chief hunting ground, which explained its name, and that the Black Horse was sacred land, the home of the tribal gods. Stallion Jim was the boss spirit or totem, and there was a legend that one day he would return and drive the white-eyes back into the east. There would be portents when that happened, thunder and lightning on the peak, and people would be killed by fire from the sky. It all fitted in very nicely, and it was just about what was needed to start a general rout.

Rick decided this was one thing he could knock over the

head. He had the Indian – Joey, they called him – in his office, and had the mother, father and grand-daddy of all rows. He told him one more word out of him about phantom horses or curses or fire from above and there'd be more fire than he knew what to do with right down on earth, and he'd personally kick him to the other side of Saskeega. Joey didn't answer much; but even while his boss was bawling him out his eyes were flicking to the window of the office. The lines were visible from that window, threading away towards the hills, and the Black Horse was lowering in the distance . . .

The Indian saved Rick his trouble. He lit out the same day, they never saw him again.

But the damage had been done. Saskeega lost more men than ever till Rick was practically working with skeleton crews. He didn't have a day off for a month; then he got sick and tired. He told Judy to pack a lunch, they'd be getting out for a time. He'd seen as much of the Company as he wanted, if the whole shebang fell apart while he was away it was just too Goddam bad.

They drove round the long way to Indian Valley. It had always been one of Judy's favourite spots. It was a hot day, Rick pulled the car off the road under a group of trees. They sat and talked and ate the meal; then he leaned back and smoked a cigarette, and looked through the leaves to where he could see the Black Horse framed in the distance. The top of the mountain seemed to move as he stared at it, crawling forward against the clouds and not getting anywhere. Rick started to doze; he was feeling at peace with the world.

There was the most fearsome noise he'd ever heard. It wasn't like thunder, wasn't like anything he could think of. It filled the air, it was deep and hollow at the same time, a series of concussions that hit him like punches under the heart. There was nothing to see, just the mountain and the sailing clouds. He sat with the cigarette in his fingers and his mouth open. The row lasted maybe ten seconds, maybe twenty. When it finished Judy started to whimper. She said, "Stallion Jim . . ." She ducked, like the sight of the mountain was burning her. It was the first time Rick knew she'd heard the story.

He shoved her in the car and started up. He had no idea what he was going to do, he just knew he was going to get away from that place but fast. The noise had shaken him up badly, more badly than he was prepared to admit either then or later. He heard himself saying over and over, "Was a storm, honey, it was thunder, that's all . . ." But he didn't even believe that himself. The din hadn't sounded like any thunder he'd ever heard. It had sounded just like it should; like the beat of huge, horrid hooves round the mountain . . .

They got home, the phone was raising Hell. Would Rick Cameron go up to the Black Horse right away, Station Seven had exploded.

He didn't waste time explaining that transformer stages don't explode, he just put Judy back in the motor and drove down to Stan's place. Jeff was at home; he thanked God for that at least. She looked pretty white herself; Rick said things were under control, could she look after Judy while he went up the hill. He felt better after that; he knew his wife would be OK. He drove for the Black Horse.

He didn't make good time. Traffic was stalled on the mountain, somebody said a tower was down across the road. Rick would have got through faster with a trouble wagon, but he'd only got his private car and no identification. In the end he gave up arguing. He drove through on the wrong lane and the Hell with everybody. He got up to Number Seven, the tower wasn't down, but she was leaning out across the road like she'd come any minute. The sky was full of cables. Rick left the car and walked.

It looked like half Saskeega had got there in front of him. Stan was there and Sheriff Stanton, they said old man Perkins had been up but he'd cleared off again. That suited Rick fine. He went and had a look at what was left of the stage. There wasn't much; a few bits of metal scattered around, some lumps of concrete, pieces of the insulator stacks. Where the transformers had stood was a hole. A crater. It was twelve, maybe fifteen feet deep and thirty feet across. It had an obscene look about it, it was black inside like the earth had been burned, and it threw rays and arms out across the road like a filthy star. Rick walked to the edge of it with Stan, stood looking down. He didn't know what to think. He said quietly. "How do you read this, mister?"

His boss shook his head. "Only one answer. Somebody blew it. We been sabotaged but good . . ."

The linesman stared at him, grinning without humour. "No. Oh, no . . . somebody blew it? You mean, they blew this thing up? You just see that hole, Stan, you know what it'd take to dig that out? You worked out what size charge you'd put in to make a hole like that?"

Stan looked angry. "So they didn't know what they were doing. They used a big charge."

Rick nodded. "Yeah, they did. They used a big charge. And that row I heard was the charge going off. Yeah."

He walked round the lip of the crater. Stan followed up. He said, "So it blew on its own. How's that, Rick, it just sort of blew up. Just like so."

Rick could feel the sweat starting out on his face. It was like he was going crazy. He said, "Transformer stages do not explode. I am a working stiff, I am not too bright in the head, I just know this, transformer stages do not spontaneously . . . explode."

He'd never had a row with Stan. He didn't have one then, but it got mighty close, When things had calmed down a bit, the overseer said, "OK, Rick, OK So we take first things first. What do we do?"

Rick was still glaring at the hole. He said, "Block that road, Stan, east at Saskeega, west at the end of Indian Valley."

"It's done."

"Relieving tackle on that downhill tower. Then get the traffic all through, get it clear. We can guy her then so she won't fall, if she does we'll have the line laying down right back to Saskeega. When we've secured her we go back down the hill and face the music. By then they'll be playing a real pretty tune . . ."

They got busy. Supporting the tower was a ticklish job, it was nearly night before they'd finished, and a storm was blowing up over the Black Horse. A queer fancy came into Rick's mind, wedged itself there somehow so it wouldn't be driven away. The next tower downhill was the one Jim

Halloran had died on. He kept thinking he'd look up and see him still up there, riding the wires like a big, ragged crow as the stalk was winched upright. When everything was tied off, the vehicles convoyed back down. Rick couldn't stop from looking in his mirror and seeing the red hood just behind and feeling glad he wasn't the last in line. He was still pretty badly shaken up, he just felt like that. Glad he wasn't the last in line . . .

If he thought he'd had trouble over the suicides he soon found out that had been nothing. There was trouble and trouble and trouble. Saskeega was important, whatever happened there was important. Saskeega fed Sand Creek, and Sand Creek was part of the National Effort and that was very important. Nobody thought too much about sleep until the stage was rebuilt and the lines were in again. Stan and Rick were grilled by the FBI, they asked did they think the feeder had been sabotaged, they said the Hell yes, there didn't seem to be anything else they could say. Yes, somebody blew that stage, somebody that wanted Sand Creek shut down. And that was all that was needed. The state troopers were turned out, and after that Rick complained bitterly he needed a counter-signed pass to get from his house across to his own garage and back.

A patrol crossed the Black Horse the night the stage blew, to check that the tower was OK and the tackles holding. The driver said later it was queer up there, the wind gusting so strong the tail of the car got nearly snatched off the road a couple of times. Nothing impossible in that; as Stan said, anything could happen on that mountain in a blow and most times it did. The other linesman acted strangely, wouldn't talk on the hill, just sat making bug-eyes up at the wires in the dark. He killed himself the same night, ran his car in the garage. That made six . . .

Rick found out something about himself. He was scared of the Black Horse.

It was crazy, he knew that, he told himself it was crazy, but he couldn't shake it off. The Black Horse was a hill. A lump of dirt stuck there in the way so they'd had to put the lines across it, give it a wire necklace. Rick told himself the lines were just lines, they carried supertension up from Saskeega to Indian Valley, across to Sand Creek. Just power lines, that was all. But some part of him insisted there was something else.

He'd get up nights, go to the windows and watch the green lightning-flicker over the mountain, listen to the war-drums of the thunder. That was the line where people died. That was where they took hold of bus bars, scalded themselves into mummies. That was where they climbed towers, reached out and got a good firm grip on Death. That was where transformers exploded, and blew half the mountain out doing it. That was the line to High Eight.

He'd never felt like that, never had a thing in his mind that was crazy but that he couldn't drive away. He tried to tell himself there was a Reason, there was always a Reason for everything, but that didn't help because then he'd try and imagine what the Reason looked like. He'd see it stalking up there on its own two legs, he'd see it walking empty roads under the lightning flashes and glaring down at Saskeega, scurrying home to a little white building, nesting down before the dawn caught up with it. That was how he got to feel about High Eight.

They built the new stage. They costed it and ordered the parts and put them together, and tested and checked and corrected until it was all fine. Then they started the feeder again and Rick hoped he'd get some peace.

He did, for a couple of months. He got Judy to go away to her folks, she came back looking brown and well. They started going down to Stan's place again, had a lot of fun. And the Indian Valley line stayed like it should, it was just a string of well-behaved towers humping away across a hill. Everything was OK.

Then Rick got a call that started it all again. This time for keeps.

He was over in his office one afternoon. It was a nice day, the sun was shining and he was sitting up there with his feet on the desk and a cup of coffee in his hand. Then the phone rang. He picked it up. "Yeah, line maintenance, Cameron here . . ."

A voice gabbled in his ear. "That you, Rick? For Chrissake come up here, Rick, come up for Chrissake, we got a tower m-mm."

Cameron frowned. "What? Say again?" It sounded like the phone had said, "We got a tower melting."

It had.

Rick didn't know what to make of one of his boys gone crazy, raving on the line like that. He said, "Er . . . Look, Johnny, you on your own? Who you got with you, pal, who's with you?"

"Rick, for Chrissake . . ."

"Take it easy, Johnny, you got Grabowski with you? You get him on the line, will you? and, Johnny, take it easy . . ."

The phone swore. It said, "Damn it to Hell an' gone, Rick, I ain't shook my bolts, I'm at High Eight and the place is goin' crazy again and there's people all over, will you damn well come . . . ?" The line went dead.

The fear had a galvanic effect, it bounced Rick out of his chair and out of the office. He jeeped across to Main Block and burst in on Stan. He said breathlessly, "High Eight again, Stan, something wrong with a tower. Can you come?" The Controller didn't waste time answering, just grabbed his hat and ran after him.

There was an accident truck outside, they jumped in and Stan set the siren blaring. He drove for the gates scattering people right and left. Rick yelled at him. "There'll be Hell for this, the old man'll give us Hell, using a siren without a main alarm . . ."

He shouted back. "If it's a phoney we give out we got a short on the button. If it's the real thing, best we keep it to ourselves. What the Hell they say's the matter?"

"Say we got a tower melting."

"*What?*"

Rick bawled, "*Melting* . . ." Stan didn't ask anything else, just put his foot down and kept it there. They bounced through the gate and screeched onto the main road.

There was plenty wrong.

They passed Number Seven, everything still looked OK. The truck swung round the last bend but one and there was High Eight, above and tiny in the distance. Rick said "Jesus Christ . . ." He couldn't help it.

Strain towers are extra-heavy stalks put in to take the pull where the cables change direction. Last one before Indian Valley was just below High Eight, and like the linesman had said it was melting. There wasn't any doubt it was melting. Metal was dropping off the arms, running like solder under a torch, splashing down onto the rock in gobs a foot across. While Rick stared the whole thing sagged, shoved a spar towards the mountain like a man thrusting his knee out, bracing himself for a big yawn. Beyond the tower was a trouble wagon, and a little figure in Saskeega blue was running like Hell down the mountain. In front of him were the people.

The road was full. There were a couple of hundred of them, maybe more. They were formed in a ragged column, moving up the middle of the carriageway towards High Eight. All sorts of people. There was a garageman still in his soiled whites, a girl in a blowy dress. . . . And in front of them the tower was bending into crazy shapes and over their heads the wires were waltzing from side to side.

Rick slammed the siren in again and the truck came down behind them howling and bellowing. Stan was leaning out of the cab yelling at the top of his voice. "Get out from under the wires . . . Get back, get off the road, *get out from under the wires . . .*"

For all the notice they took the wagon might not have been there. Stan left it nearly too late to stop. At the last instant he trod on the anchors and wrenched the wheel round and the truck screeched and broadsided onto the rough. It dragged a plume of dust behind it forty, fifty yards, then it smashed its pan across a rock and the ride was over. Rick banged his head on the screen, fell back and heard the cables part. Something slapped on the road behind the truck's tail, the Saskeega men curled up instinctively away from the cab sides, there was the rush and whimper of the arcing then the cutoffs killed the line. Stan got out; Rick followed him cautiously, feeling himself to see he was still in one piece. The Sand Creek feeder was out again . . .

Boris Grabowski reached the truck. His face was as near white as it could get and his eyes looked as if they were bolting out of his head. He said, "Boss, I'm going bloody-crazy."

Rick said heavily, "You and me both, Boris, you and me both." He looked up towards the strain tower. She was mostly all gone; there was a stump about six or eight feet tall, and the struts of that were twisted and blackened. What was left of the head had been dragged ninety, a hundred feet downhill, and all the road was a jumble of wires. The people were standing about in the middle of the mess. The cables had come down right among them, but they were still all on their feet, God alone knew how. The Saskeega men tried to talk to them, but it was no use. They started pushing them clear of the cables. It was hard work. The strangers stared straight ahead, walked when they were being shoved, stopped still as soon as they were left alone. "What we need," said Rick furiously, "is a bloody sheep-dog."

He sent Boris down to phone for roadblocks and ambulances and lifting gear to clear the carriageway. Then he walked on up to High Eight with Stan. They got another shock. The people they'd seen had been only the second wave, the first crowd of zombies had got there before the lines parted. There were red smears on the door where they'd torn the locks apart. They were the folk Johnny had tried to tell about on the phone.

Rick went inside. Johnny was very dead. It looked like he'd tried to hold the folk back from the bus bars. He hadn't had a chance, they'd picked him up bodily and shoved him onto the contacts . . . Six had managed to die, a dozen more were hanging round the gear looking stupid, fumbling at the bars like something ought to have happened but hadn't. Rick hauled one of them up and shoved him away. He came right back and the overseer shoved him off again. He came back again and Rick hit him, he couldn't stop himself. He didn't feel it. He rolled across the floor, got up slobbering blood and started feeling for the contacts again. Rick let him be. It was like giving a kid a toy to keep it quiet . . .

The only one of the victims that showed any sign of being human was a girl. She sat just outside the door and she was crying. Stan put his jacket round her shoulders. He said, "God knows what's with the others, but this looks like plain shock." He started talking to her. He found out her name was Allison Foster, she'd lived with her aunt a few miles out of Freshet. She said they'd heard the music. That was all. They'd heard the music. They'd got the car out and driven up, following whatever was calling them. They'd had a blowout on the trail, had to walk the rest of the way. She told Stan, the music had stopped now. It had gone away. Then she started in crying again.

The Controller looked up and shook his head, and they heard the sirens going way off towards Saskeega . . .

The mountain was cordoned. The road was closed to traffic from Freshet right to Indian Valley. It seemed every research lab in the country had a team up there scraping about. They even sent some people over from Cape Kennedy. What the spaceboys wanted with bits of the busted stalk, Rick couldn't figure. Stan said sardonically that maybe they thought the Company had little green men.

Just about everything got analysed, the tower struts, the insulators, the rock face, bits of the cables. If there were ever any reports Stan and Rick didn't get to see them. They were no wiser than they had been the day the thing happened. All they knew was one bright morning that tower melted. It couldn't have happened, but it did.

They re-rigged the feeder. A piece was blasted out of the rock, the new cables were brought inside the line of the old so the eggheads could keep their playground. Power was restored two days after the accident. The troops stayed put; Black Horse Pass was stiff with guards.

Within a week the people who'd been saved were all dead, and that started a national scare on its own. There was talk of putting the whole of Saskeega County under quarantine. That would have been done, but nobody could find out why the victims died. Wasn't anything physical, they just seemed to fade away. Nobody could do a thing. Rick heard the day the power went back on they had to strap them down to stop them walking to the Black Horse and doing the same thing all over. The girl Stan had talked to didn't seem too bad, they didn't watch her like they watched the others. They let her ram her fingers in a light socket. Somehow she kept them there till her heart stopped . . .

Rick moved over to Stan's place for a time because he didn't like the idea of Judy being on her own any more. When she was with Jeff she wasn't too bad. About ten days after the trouble he got back from Saskeega one evening and Stan asked him to go down to the workshop. He'd got something he wanted to show him.

He'd got a nice little place rigged up at the bottom of the lot, a shed with a couple of lathes and a milling machine. The thing he wanted to talk about was standing in the middle of the floor. Rick stared at it. "What'n Hell is it, Stan?"

He said, "Take a look. Guess at its operation."

Rick looked. The device was about four feet tall, a square box set on thin, dural legs. Most of the housing was taken up with circuitry. Rick was no electronics man but he knew an oscillator pack when he saw one. There was a metal cone speaker mounted above it on a horizontal baffle, and on top of that a thing that looked like the element of an electric fire. Over that again was a fine wire-mesh frame.

Cameron shrugged. "Lower part's obvious. Rest looks like it'd be good for warming the house. What's it supposed to do?"

Stan said, "It's a bugtrap."

Rick was fogged. "What does it trap?"

"It's set for 'skeeters at the moment. Give me a hand with it, I'll show you." They lifted the machine outside and Stan plugged in a wander lead from the shop distributor board. He pointed at a line of potentiometers on the chassis. He said, "You get a sort of list comes with it, you set these things up for your homing frequencies. Composite note."

Rick had read something about that somewhere; how the females of certain insects emit a note to attract the males, or the other way round. He wasn't too sure about that, but the principle was obvious. He said, "You mean the pack generates the call frequency, the 'skeeters fly in . . ."

"And land on the hotplate over the sound source. Quick and easy. And it works, it works fine." Stan switched the thing on. There was no audible sound; the side panels just got a sort of velvety feel, that was all. The elements started to glow orange-red; within seconds something dropped down onto the gauze, wriggled and vanished. Then another and another. Soon a stream of insects were flying down to incinerate themselves. Stan switched off. He said, "That's enough for a demonstration. I don't even care for killing 'skeeters at the moment, I'm beginning to know what they feel like."

It took a few moments for the implication to sink in. When it did, Rick felt like he'd been kicked in the gut. He said, "Stan, if you're suggesting what I think . . . It's crazy. And it's too bloody horrible for words . . ."

Stan shrugged. "I didn't suggest a thing. I showed you an insect trap, you made your own comparisons." He picked up a gauze frame. "I left the thing running last night. This was the result." Rick took it from him. It was like he'd expected. The thing was coated with insects, black drifts and skeins of them. He chucked it down and Stan walked away.

Rick followed him. Somehow, although a thing that had been in his mind for a long time had been verbalized, he still felt he had to argue. He felt mad at Stan for saying something he was so scared might be true. He said, "Stan, if you expect me to go along with a crazy thing like that –"

The other man swung round on him. "Christ, Rick, can't you play this quiet . . . ?" He said, "Look, I don't believe." He spread his hands. "I can't believe. But I've followed this thing through and there's only one answer satisfies my logic. I can't *believe* that answer. But I also know, I *know*, Rick, that what you saw that machine do, is a model of what's going on at High Eight. This I swear before God and His angels." He ducked back into the workshop.

Rick stepped after him helplessly. Stan opened a cupboard. There was a bottle of Scotch and a couple of glasses. He got the whisky down and poured a couple of slugs. Rick picked his drink up, and the glass chattered suddenly against his teeth. He set it down and looked at it. "Now I know I'm going crazy."

Stan rubbed his face. "Rick, listen and hear me. I may not have the chance to repeat what I'm going to say. You can't explain the Black Horse, I can't, none of us can. So we'll take the things that have happened as pointers and see

what they can show us. If we see something outside our
technology, that's a pity. Because, like the guy said, once
you've eliminated the impossible whatever remains, however improbable, is the truth."

He took a swig of whisky. He said, "We'll eliminate
sabotage. If you wanted to wreck our lines, OK, but how
would you melt a tower? And we'll eliminate the chance
that we're all asleep and dreaming this, I cut my face
shaving this morning, I bled . . . We'll also discount the
idea that we've suffered a series of unconnected mishaps
because a probability of that order is strictly in the mon-
keys-play-Beethoven class. We'll take the facts as interre-
lated events and work from there.

"An old hobo died. Then there was the farmer. Then the
boys in the chopper, they flew nearly straight at High Eight.
And Halloran up on the wires. Then the people we saw the
day the tower melted. Now, I know and you know, Jim
Halloran wouldn't have killed himself. It's like the guys
said, he was pulled up there. The zombies didn't kill
themselves *consciously* either; you know that, you were with
me, you helped drag 'em off the lines. They weren't conscious of a damn thing. I don't believe any of the deaths
have been suicides, except maybe the old tramp. People
have been drawn to the lines, in particular to High Eight,
and there hasn't been a damn thing they could do about it.
To me that suggests a force, a Will if you want to think of it
like that. Something stronger than humans, something that
can cut across the basic instinct to survive, make you go up
there and . . . char yourself into a union with it. And the
figures say something else. First it was one, then two, then
three, then a hundred. The Will is getting stronger. So I
maintain it's a process of *feeding* . . ."

Rick said hoarsely, "For the sake of God . . ."

Stan kept on talking, overrode him. "It's very strong now
because it took the ones that died in hospital. It's strong and
it's mean. It's made mistakes in the past. Bad ones. But it
won't make any more. What happened to Station Seven we
shall never know. Or the tower. I'd say that last time it got
over-keen. It was hauling in its biggest batch to date, it got
careless, allowed too big a concentration of itself in one

place. Because it *can* concentrate and disperse. It can adjust our voltage to what it needs. This I've proved."

Rick said, "But our juice –"

Stan stopped him savagely. "It isn't our juice. He . . . it . . . uses the current somehow as a carrier. It can work the voltage the way it wants. For instance, it can keep surges away from the trip gear when it doesn't want the hotplate turned off. They read on the dials, they read every place, but the lines don't pull out."

"That's crazy –"

"Rick, you don't know about this because it was done behind your back. For that, I'm sorry. I put recording voltmeters on that line. One on the output at Saskeega, one in High Eight, one at Station Seven, half a dozen more in between. They were set up one night and taken down again before dawn. I got the rolls here." He turned on a shaded lamp and opened a drawer. He handed Rick the graphs. The overseer stared at them. It seemed to him in that moment the shadows in the workshop started to darken and crowd. Theories were great, but they were still just playing with words, this was something you could touch. Rick was a working stiff, he believed in something he could touch.

The line up to the Black Horse was full of knots and snarls. The graphs showed it. There were pulses in the voltage, peaks and zeroings. There were rhythms where something had raced all night up the wires and back between Saskeega and High Eight. Something impossible, something malevolent, something terribly strong. Allison had talked about music. This was the notation of the tune she'd heard . . .

Stan said quietly, "I ran the same test in Indian Valley. Beyond High Eight the voltage doesn't move. The lines are clean."

Rick could only whisper. "What in Hell is it? You know what in Hell it is, Stan?"

He shrugged. "How can I answer that? How can anybody? Maybe it's the old man, the hobo. Maybe he somehow got caught in the lines. And he's lonely, wants some company . . . Maybe it's something that blew in with the cosmic rays, maybe we generated it ourselves from cobalt and hydrogen, maybe there was a second Creation down there in the windings, deep in the darkness and warmth, and this is the new Adam. Demon or spirit, Stallion Jim or AntiChrist himself, I don't know. But I know why it uses our lines, why it's sitting up there in High Eight."

"Why?"

He said, "Use your head, Rick. We're the biggest feeder into the Sand Creek Pool. And there's the gear on the hill, the Doomsday units. Whatever we think, whatever happens, those lines are going to stay intact. The thing could flow off, it's got a whole country to travel in, hunt in. It must have moved when it blew the stage, it must have got out when the tower went. But it comes back each time to where it knows its safe."

Cameron was just beginning to see possibilities. He had to lick his lips to make his voice come. "Stan," he said. "what's going to be the end of this . . ."

The Controller was standing in the half dark outside the circle of lamplight. Rick saw him shrug. He said, "This is still supposition. But the way I see it, there need be no end. Look at the lines, Rick, think about them. Think about them the way Judy does. Think how they go out from the power companies to the substations, how they split into street mains, how the street mains split into the risers. Think about how they wind themselves through towns and villages, into shops and movie houses and theatres, factories, farms, hospitals . . . A forest, that's what the lines are. A million trees on the same trunk. And if those lines go bad, and it's starting here at High Eight . . . they could touch us all. There'd be no getting away.

"Nobody would realize when it really started to pull. Maybe it would take the scientists, the politicians, anybody who could understand it, know what it was trying to do. Maybe we'd start a few wars, help it on with the job. One thing's certain; until the very last of us went, Saskeega would still be manned, those lines to Sand Creek would be alive. And after that, when there was nobody left . . . Who knows? Perhaps Saskeega would still be manned . . .

"If I wasn't an engineer, if I wasn't works controller for

Saskeega and if I *believed* this, I'd get out. I'd go live in Tibet. That way I might manage to die apart from it. But I'm not a free agent. I have to say this is rubbish, this is all fools' talk. I have to get on with the job."

He lit a cigarette. The sudden flare of light was startling. Rick saw his face for a second. He looked worried nearly to death. The overseer said suddenly, "We can kill it, Stan. Cut the lines at Saskeega and beyond High Eight, quarantine it, starve it to death . . ."

Stan laughed. He said bitterly, "Kill it? Can you see that happening, can you see me running to old man Perkins, to the Government? What would I say, cut the lines over the Black Horse, cut 'em each end because the Devil's in the wires and we got to starve him out? Can you see me doing that? And can you imagine them listening? I told you it was smart. It's damn smart. There's no way out."

Rick said, "Take it in your own hands. You know what's happening, you've sold me on it . . . I'm with you, my boys'd do it . . ."

Stan was quiet for a moment. Then he said, "I'll forget you said that, Rick. But I'll give you this warning. I forbid you as your superior to do anything that would prejudice the running of Saskeega Power. I'm still Works Controller, and, by God, if that's my job I'm going to see it keeps on getting done. You clear on that, Rick?"

Cameron shook his head. It was like he couldn't think straight any more. "You can't just let it build, Stan. It's too bloody awful to think about. If this thing gets started . . ."

Mainwaring shook his head. "Rick, I'm in a vice. I'm caught in the same trap as everybody else. It's the sort of trap only the human race could have invented for itself. It could have sprung any time. It's chosen now. We're hooked on our own technology.

"Those lines have got to stay in. We *need* 'em. We're dead without them. Could be we're dead with them as well, that's just too bad. But we can't turn the clock back. We can't scrap electricity just because it's turned mean.

"I've told you what I *know* is true. But I didn't tell you I believed it. This is one of those times when knowing and believing are two different things. I can't let myself believe this because of what I am at Saskeega. I can't believe it on a personal basis either because it represents the descent to what I've been taught to regard as unreason. I can't take a fall like that."

He walked across the shed and turned on another light. Then another. Then he started one of the lathes. He said, "I stand or fall on what I've told you. I'm about to prove it one way or the other."

Suddenly, Rick was scared. "Stan, what the Hell . . ."

He turned on the other lathe, the drilling machine. He looked round but there was nothing else left to start up. The whole place was humming and clacking, light streaming out across the lawn in the dusk. And far-off was the Black Horse, a shadow in the night. The mountain looked ten miles tall. Stan said, "This filth can come down the wires. It got to the people in hospital. It got to the girl Allison. It made her do something I still shudder to think about. So it could be with us now. In the lamps, the lathes.

"I say the Thing, whatever it is, is logical. So far it's moved in steps that can and have been explained. Being logical, it knows I'm the only guy understands it and can order its death. I've absolved you from responsibility and also for the moment from risk by giving you the orders I did. So if it wants to stay alive it's got to take me. And it's got to move fast." He put his hand on the housing of one of the lathes and looked at the mountain. He said, "I'm challenging you, you bastard. And whichever way you move you're through. Because if I go off the book people will finally know you're real, and they'll know how to carve your heart out . . ."

Nothing happened. The mountain hung in the sky like a cloud and the lathes turned softly and the belts went click-click-click over the pulleys and that was all. They waited; then Stan shut down the gear and Rick followed him back to the house.

They heard a late night newscast. The news was weird. Throughout the States ten thousand people had been reported missing from their homes within the last twenty-four hours. The FBI were conducting nation-wide enquiries. An airliner had crashed in the Rockies, nearly five hundred miles off course. A cowboy, riding a boundary miles from anywhere, had seen a strange thing. He swore he'd met an army of ragged, empty-faced folk who swarmed past without speaking, pushed on to God knew where. There was a lot more stuff like that.

Stan hunted out some maps and did a little plotting. The course of the aircraft, the sightings of wandering people . . . he wound up with a set of lines. They all pointed to one place.

Rick felt he couldn't believe his eyes. But he had to believe. He said, "Stan, by God, it's moving. It's started to move . . ." Stan just sat and shook his head. He didn't answer.

They talked the girls into going east. They couldn't say what they were afraid was happening, they just told them, over and over, there was something badly wrong. They had a hard job convincing them, but they gave in finally. Stan left it that Judy would drive out in the morning, he'd follow on as soon as he could. Then they tried to get some rest. Rick was up at dawn. It was pretty early, but Stan had beaten him to it. The garage was empty, he'd already gone to Saskeega.

Rick drove up to his own place. Everything was quiet. He changed, hunted out an old cutthroat razor and had a shave. He didn't fancy using his Remington. Then he went and stood outside where he could see the valley, the mountain beyond, the lines moving up there like cobwebs miles away. He kept thinking he ought to be packing, they all ought to be getting out. But it was still too crazy. It was like throwing away job and future and home and all the folk you knew because one night you'd had a bad dream. It was all so peaceful. The air smelled good, there just couldn't be a Thing in the wires that was fixing to kill everybody on earth . . .

He drove down to Saskeega. There were troops on the road, everything was confused. Nobody knew for sure what was happening. He saw tanks, and there were guns pointed about. Nowhere to aim them. He heard somebody ask if they'd started another war.

Saskeega was empty. Deserted. It was crazy. Rick could

hear the noise of the turbines, the roaring the place always made. The power was going out, but the station was running itself.

A siren was howling someplace, but even the siren sounded sort of lonely. Like there was nobody to shout to and it knew it. Rick went into Main Block, got to the old man's office. The door was swinging open, his chair was overturned, there were papers scattered about the floor. Like he'd jumped up suddenly and run out like a mad thing. There was no help there. Rick drove across to West Power.

The sun was well up now, it was going to be a hot day. He got out of the car, ran across the macadam. His footsteps were the only thing there was. He got to the control room, Donnell was there on his own. Rick asked where the Hell were the shift staff, why hadn't he yelled for help. He was sweating, looked half crazy. He'd tried, phones wouldn't answer, he couldn't leave the place on its own. Voltage had been jumping over the Black Horse, the trips hadn't pulled the line. Mr Mainwaring had been in, Mr Mainwaring had driven up to High Eight. He'd said he would call from the pass. He hadn't called yet . . .

Rick looked at the dials on the main panel, they were reading steady. The building was pulsing. Wasn't what you could call a noise, it was the feeling of a dozen turbines threshing power into the lines, driving it up and away over the Black Horse. Donnell couldn't keep still. The wires were bad, they'd gone bad again, something was far wrong. He'd buy his lot if he let the line burn out, he'd buy his lot if he pulled the plug without an authority. Would Rick authorize him, would he clear him to close the line?

Cameron swore at him. It was Donnell's baby, not his. The engineer looked like he was going to burst out crying. He started patting panels and controls like he couldn't believe anything was real any more. The phone rang.

Rick grabbed it. But it wasn't Stan, it was Judy. Somehow the call had got through, they couldn't have all been dead in the exchange . . . Judy on the line, wanted to know were things OK? She was packing, they were getting on the road, were things OK?

Donnell was yanking Rick's arm. Muttering something

about music. He knocked him off and he started to yell. "The music, Rick, it started again, was the music last time, I saw those dials move, we all did, couldn't do a thing, just had to hear the music. Christ, Rick, the music . . ." He was down on his knees, groping about. Donnell was through.

Rick stood feeling the power through the soles of his shoes and there was Judy on the line and he didn't know what to do, couldn't think any more. The voltage was going to waltz again and he couldn't think. He said, "Look, Judy, get this and get it good. Things aren't OK, there's something crazy happening. Just get out, Judy, make it fast. . . ." Then it hit him. She was packing, meant she was calling from home. They shouldn't have gone back up there, he wanted them away and clear. He yelled at her. "Judy, *get out of that house . . .*!"

"What –."

He gagged, but it had to be said. "Judy, the lines. Like you said, there's something wrong with the lines. Judy, don't go near any lines. Don't try and cook, don't use any lights, don't take any more calls. Just get out. Tell Jeff that's from Stan and me. Tell her we'll come soon as we can, tell her I'll bring Stan along, I'll bring him if I have to carry him. But *get out*! You got that, Judy, you got that OK?"

"Ye-es . . ."

"Well, be a good girl, finish that packing and get out. Shoo, scat . . . I'll see you soon as I can . . ."

He put the handset down, ran to the line phone. Donnell was yelling. "I heard it last time, Rick, couldn't tell you, couldn't lose my job, you'd have said I was crazy, couldn't say what I heard . . ."

He said, "For Chrissake, *get out of the way* . . ." He got past him, got to the phone. He rang High Eight. Nobody there. The static on the line was horrible, it was wailing and gibbering at the same time, it was like hearing a mad army. He'd never heard static like that before. He yelled, "Anybody there? Come on, come on somebody, are you there . . . ?"

He thought he heard a handset being picked up. "Stan, that you? You up at High Eight?"

Something like a groan. It sounded like a groan. And a word, all threaded through and underlaid with static. Sounded like, "Can't . . ." Then there was nothing.

Cameron banged the receiver rest. He yelled, "Stan? Stan, you there? West Power to High Eight, *are you there* . . . ?"

High Eight answered. They both saw it, saw every dial on the board kick its stops as the voltage jumped up there on the mountain . . .

Rick made a noise like a horse neighing. He jumped at the board and pulled the line, killed it stone dead. Then he ran for the car.

There was a shortcut onto the mountain, missing Freshet. A rough road, barely more than a track. He took the car on that and held her flat out, squealing her into bends, breaking off into the rough, smashing her chrome chops on boulders. He was trying to break her up like he was busting up inside. When he got to High Eight the lines were live again. Somebody had authorized Donnell to put them back in. Or they'd put themselves back in. It didn't make any difference to Rick. Didn't make any difference to the folk who had got there before him either.

All through the night they'd been coming, the poor folk, the first of the ragged armies . . . They were piled round the bars, the transformers were singing there shoulder deep. And there were black skeins round the walls like the bugs in the trap, and overhead in the wires like a crop of filthy fruit. There'd been a cordon of troopers round the hill. It was hard to tell, but it looked like the guards were mostly underneath.

Rick started to laugh. A thin noise, wild and high. Laughing at the people, at High Eight, at what he'd seen there, at what he'd promised Jeff. He'd said he'd bring Stan. If he had to carry him. But he couldn't carry him. He couldn't move him, he'd have broken, he was too brittle . . .

He went back down the mountain. He never knew how he reached the bottom. He had to run the last half mile. He'd busted the car, she was seized solid.

There was a big line store about a mile from Number

Seven, they'd set it up when they did all the work on the hill. Rick was lucky; when he reached it one of the Company trucks was standing outside. There was nobody around. He broke the door open, loaded what he wanted in the back of the wagon. When she wouldn't take any more he started up and went for Freshet like a bat from Hell. He couldn't think any more. He just wanted to see Judy had got away, he wanted her clear.

He drove into trouble. A roadblock. It hadn't been there when he'd come down. There were poles across the road, he could see the army moving about behind. He stopped the truck and a soldier came over. He had a carbine in his hands and looked like he'd been told he could use it. Rick yelled at him he was Saskeega maintenance, he'd got an urgent job. He shoved his pass under his nose and the man fetched his sergeant.

Cameron felt he was going crazy. What he'd got wouldn't keep and he knew it. The sergeant came across. He was scared. He had a big, pasty face and the fear was in his face, he smelled of fright. He wagged his thumb at the truck. "Down, bud . . ."

Just along the road Hell started breaking loose, shots and screams. A column of people was coming along. Soldiers firing over their heads, trying to turn them. It wasn't making any difference, they were walking like they didn't hear.

Rick jabbed the throttle and let the clutch go. He heard the smack as the shoulder of the truck shoved the sergeant's face out of the way then he was through the block, bouncing and skidding on the timbers and poles and scattering men every which way. Something rattled behind him; blue sky opened up over the windshield, then he was clear. They never came after him. It looked as if they had their hands too full.

Rick got to his place, Jeff's car was still in the drive. He rammed the truck in alongside and got out. Something made him look across to the garage. The port was up, his wife's old Pontiac was gone. He tried to tell himself, it's OK, they took the Pontiac instead, it's OK, but it wasn't any good. He felt fear. It was like a hand round his heart squeezing it until it could get no smaller, no colder. He walked slowly into the house. He called, "Judy . . . ?"

Nothing. No answer. Water running somewhere and another noise. He followed it. Came from the lounge. He walked in. There was a hairdryer lying buzzing on the carpet, a cord up to the wallplug.

Jeff was in the kitchen, of all the crazy places. Sitting over the sink with her head down. Cameron lifted her. Blood was all down the side of the sink, spattered, red and pink, a pink fan spreading to the plug. Her face was gouged, hair to chin. Like she'd been clawed by a mountain cat. She'd gone to the sink to try to stop the blood but she couldn't, she was hurt too bad. He let go of her, wasn't anything he could do. He stood there and knew he couldn't go crazy, not just for a while.

He knew what had happened, he could see it so clearly. Judy did what she said, she kept off all electric things, but she forgot the drier. She bathed and changed and then she started the drier and let High Eight talk, held the motor right up by her face so she could hear it clear. He should have remembered, he should have told her about the drier . . .

Jeff tried to stop her. When she heard . . . whatever it was you heard, she went out and got the Pontiac and Jeff tried to hold her and she beat and beat and tore her face apart . . . But it wasn't Judy that had done that, it wasn't his Judy, it was a Thing that already belonged to High Eight . . . And that was where she went, she left Jeff on the ground and drove up the road, and God can you hear me, *she drove to High Eight . . .*

He should have done what she said. He should have taken her away, she was always so scared of the lines, she knew one day she'd have to go to the lines.

It had taken Stan and it had taken Judy, it had taken everything he had. It had to take him. It knew he hated it, it knew he could kill it. It was up there sulking, deep in the windings, it was full and lazy, but it knew it had to move because he was coming to kill.

Rick tried to hold his mind on what he had to do. On his back he had a box of caps, the truck outside was loaded with blasting sticks. Linked charges on the tower heads each side of High Eight, blow the lines and pin it. Then flatten High Eight, burst its foul blue heart . . . But he wasn't going to make it. He had the caps ready, he was checking them, but he knew he wasn't going to make it. He didn't want to make it because he'd have to go inside, he'd have to pick Judy off the wires . . .

It hit him, on the dot.

High Eight calling . . .

He reeled, hand to his head. It was like all the sound there ever was. Like music but not like music. Like the wind in trees. Like voices. Like Mom and Pop. Lovely and lovely and ugghh . . .

Ugghh . . .

Like Judy . . .

It didn't take him all at once. It tried, but it couldn't. It had to rack up and down, and slide, move and slide, look for him, pinpoint . . .

He was moving again, draggingly. The caps in his hand, blasting sticks in the truck, and the wind in the trees soughing, Judy calling and not to let go of the caps don't ever forget . . . and up ahead on the hill, movement. A shifting and crawling. A motion that was no motion. Molecules that were not molecules forming and dissolving, bubbling, frothing . . .

And for the first time, *fear* . . .

Shards

Brian W. Aldiss

Brian Aldiss (b. 1925) has been one of Britain's leading sf writers since the 1950s and has also long established himself as one of the field's critics and historians with his study The Trillion-Year Spree *(1986) and other works. He won his first sf award with the series of stories which made up* Hothouse *(1962) set on a far-future Earth and has won many awards since including ones for his story "The Saliva Tree" (*F&SF, *September 1965) and the first of his Helliconia trilogy* Helliconia Spring *(1982). What has always struck me about Aldiss's work is that he does not follow trends. He pursues his own thoughts and ideas whether he's in step or out. He managed to champion the New-Wave movement of the sixties with such profound works as* Report on Probability A *(1968) – which remained unpublished for six years – without wholly being associated with it. He has weaved in and out of the mainstream with a number of books and has done more than any other British sf writer, to bring sf to the attention of the literary establishment. The following story is an example of Aldiss's experimentalism. You won't have a clue what this story is about until you finish it, and then you'll never forget it.*

I

The way of telling the time down here in Mudland was very ingenious. Double A had a row of sticks stuck in the mud in the blackness before his eyes. With his great spongy hands that sometimes would have nothing to do with him, he gripped the sticks one by one, counting as he went, sometimes in numbers, sometimes in such abstractions as lyre birds, rusty screws, pokers, or seaweed.

He would go on grimly, hand over fist against time, until the beastly old comfort of degradation fogged over his brain and he would forget what he was trying to do. The long liverish gouts of mental indigestion that were his thought processes would take over from his counting. And when later he came to think back to the moment when the take-over occurred, he would know that that had been the moment when it had been the present. Then he could guess how far ahead or behind of the present he was, and could give this factor a suitable name – though lately he had decided that all factors could be classified under the generic term Standard, and he named the present time Standard O'Clock.

Standard O'Clock he pictured as a big Irish guardsman with moustaches sweeping round the roseate blankness of his face. Every so often, say on pay day or on passing out parade, the Lance-Standard would chime, with pretty little cuckoos popping out of all orifices. As an additional touch of humour, Double A would make O'Clock's pendulum wag.

By this genial ruse, he was slowly abolishing time, turning himself into the first professor of a benighted quantum. As yet the experiments were not entirely successful, for ever and anon his groping would communicate itself to his hands, and back they'd come to him, slithering through the mud, tame as you please. Sometimes he bit them; they tasted unpleasant; nor did they respond.

"You are intellect," he thought they said. "But we are the tools of intellect. Treat us well."

II

Another experiment concerned the darkness.

Even sprawling in the mud with his legs amputated unfortunately represented a compromise. Double A had to admit there was nothing final in his degradation, since he had begun to – no, nobody would force him to use the term "enjoy the mud", but on the other hand nobody could stop him using the term "ambivelling the finny claws (clause?)" with the understanding that in certain contexts it might be interpreted as synonymous with "enjoying the mud".

Anyhow, heretofore, and nutmeggaphonically, it remained to be continued that everywhere was compromise. The darkness compromised with itself and with him. The darkness was sweet and warm and wet.

When Double A realised that the darkness was not utter, that the abstraction utterness was beyond it, he became furious, drumming imaginary heels in the mud, urinating into it with some force and splendour, and calling loudly for dark glasses.

The dark glasses were a failure, for they became covered in mud, so that he could not see through them to observe whether or not the darkness increased. So They came and fitted him with a pair of ebony contact lenses, and with this splendid condescension on their part, Double A hoped he had at last reached a point of non-compromise.

Not so! He had eyelids that pressed on the lenses, drawing merry patterns on the night side of his eyeballs. Pattern and darkness cannot exist together, so again he was defeated by myopic little Lord Compromise, knee-high to a pin and stale as rats' whiskers, but still Big Reeking Lord of Creation. Well, he was not defeated yet. He had filled Application No. Six Oh Five Bark Oomph Eight Eight Tate Potato Ten in sticks and sandbars and the old presumption factor for the privilege of Person Double A, sir, late of the Standard O'Clock Regiment, sir, to undergo total partial and complete Amputation of Two Vermicularform Appendages in the possession of the aforesaid Double A and known henceforth as his Eyelids.

Meanwhile until the application was accepted and the scalpels served, he tried his cruel experiments on the darkness.

He shouted, whispered, spoke, gave voice, uttered, named names, broke wind, cracked jokes, split infinitives, passed particles, and in short and in toto interminably talked, orated, chattered, chatted, and generally performed vocal circumbendibusses against the darkness.

Soon he had it cowering in a corner. It was less well equipped orally than Double A, and he let it know with a "Three wise manias came from the Yeast, causing ferment, and bringing with them gifts of gold and Frankenstein and murder" and other such decompositions of a literary-re-ligio-medico-philisophico-nature.

So the powers of darkness had no powers against the powers of screech.

"Loot there be light!" boomed Double A: and there was blight. Through the thundering murk, packed tight with syllables, he could see the dim mudbound form of Gasm.

"Let there be night!" doomed Double A. But he was too late, had lost his chance, had carried his experiment beyond the pale. For in the pallor and the squalor, Gasm remained revolting *there*, whether invisible or visible. And his bare-ness in the thereness made a whereness tight as harness.

III

So began the true history of Mudland. It was now possible to have not only experiments, which belong to the old intellect arpeggio, but character conflict, which pings right out of the middle register of the jolly old emotion chasuble. Amoebas, editors, and lovers are elements in that vast orchestra of classifiable objects to whom or for whom character conflict is ambrosia.

Double A went carefully into the business of having a C.C. with Gasm. To begin with, of course, he did not know whether he himself had a C.: or, of course squared, since we are thinking scientifically, whether Gasm had a C. Without the first C., could there be the second? Could one have a C.-less C.?

Alas for scientific enquiry. During the o'clock sticks that passed while Double A was beating his way patiently through this thicket of thorny questions, jealousy crept up on him unawares.

Despite the shouting and the ebony contact lenses, with which the twin polarities of his counter-negotiations with the pseudo-dark were almost kept at near-maximum in the fairly brave semi-struggle against compromise, Gasm remained ingloriously visible, lolling in the muck no more than a measurable distance away.

Gasm's amputations were identical with Double A's: to wit, the surgical removal under local anesthetic and two aspirin of that assemblage of ganglions, flesh, blood, bone, toenail, hair, and kneecap referred to hereafter as Legs. In this, no cause for jealousy existed. Indeed, They had been scrupulously democratic: one vote, one head; one head, two legs; two heads, four legs. Their surgeons were paragons of the old equality regimen. No cause for Double A's jealousy.

But. It was within his power to *imagine* that Gasm's amputations were other than they were. He could quite easily (and with practice he could perfectly easily) visualise Gasms as having had not two legs but one leg and one arm removed. And that amputation was more interesting than Double A's own amputation, or the fact that he had fins.

So the serpent came even to the muddy paradise of Mudland, writhing between the two bellowing bodies. C.C. became reality.

IV

Double A abandoned all the other experiments to concentrate on beating and catechising Gasm. Gradually Mudland lost its identity and was transformed into Beating and Catechising, or B & C. The new regimen was tiring for Double A, physically and especially mentally, since during the entire procedure he was compelled to ask himself why he should be doing what he was, rather than resting contentedly in the mud.

The catechism was stylised, ranging over several topics and octaves as Double A yelled the questions and Gasm screamed the answers.

"What is your name?"

"My name is Gasm."

"Name some of the other names you might have been called instead."

"I might have been called Plus or Shob or Fred or Droo or Penny-feather or Harm."

"And by what strange inheritance does it come about that you house your consciousness among the interstices of lungs, aorta, blood, corpuscles, follicles, sacroiliac, ribs and prebendary skull?"

"Because I would walk erect if I could walk erect among the glorious company of the Higher Vertebrates, who have grown from mere swamps, dinosaurs and dodos. Those that came before were dirty brates or shirty brates; but we are the vertebrates."

"What comes after us?"

"After us the deluge."

"How big is the deluge?"

"Deluge."

"How deep is the deluge?"

"Ai, deluge."

"How deluge is the deluge."

"Deluge, deluger, delugest."

"Conjugate and decline."

"I decline to conjugate."

"Who was that dinosaur I dinna saw you with last night?"

"That was no knight. That was my dinner."

"And what comes after the vertebrates?"

"Nothing comes after the vertebrates because we are the highest form of civilization."

"Name the signs whereby the height of our civilization may be determined."

"The heights whereby the determination of our sign may be civilized are seven in number. The subjugation of the body. The resurrection of the skyscraper. The perpetuation of the species. The annihilation of the species. The glorification of the nates. The somnivolence of the conscience. The omniverousness of sex. The conclusion of the Hundred Year War. The condensation of milk. The conversation of muts. The confiscation of monks –"

"Stop, stop! Name next the basic concept upon which this civilization is based."

"The interests of producer and consumer are identical."

"What is the justification of war?"

"War is its own justification."

"What is the desire to feed on justice?"

"A manifestation of opsomania."

"Let us sing a sesquipedalian love-song in octogenerian voices."

At this point they humped themselves up in the mud and sang the following tuneless ditty:

"No constant factor in beauty is discernable.
Although the road that evolution treads is not
    eturnable,
It has some curious twists in it, as every shape and size
And shade of female breast attestifies.
Pointed, conical, flat or sharp or bonical,
Pendulous or cumulus, pearshaped, oval, tumulus,
Each one displays its beauty or depravity
In syncline, incline, outcropping or cavity.
Yet from Peru to Timbuctu
The bosom's lines are only signs
Of all the pectoral muscles' tussles
With a fairly constant factor, namely gravity."

They fell back into the mud, each lambasting his
    mate's nates.

V

Of course for a time it was difficult to be certain of everything or anything. The uncertainties became almost infinite, but among the most noteworthy of the number were the uncertainty as to whether the catechisings actually took place in any wider arena of reality than Double A's mind; the uncertainty as to whether the beatings took place in any wider arena of reality than Double A's mind; the uncertainty as to whether, if the beatings actually took place, they took place with sticks.

For it became increasingly obvious that neither Double A nor Gasm had hands with which to wield sticks. Yet on the other appendage, evidence existed tending to show that some sort of punishment had been undergone. Gasm no longer resembled a human. He had grown positively torpedo shaped. He possessed fins.

The idea of fins, Double A found to his surprise, was not a surprise to him. Fins had been uppermost in his mind for some while. Fins, indeed, induced in him a whole watery way of thinking; he was flooded with new surmises, while some of the old ones proved themselves a wash-out. The idea, for example, that he had ever worn dark glasses or ebony contact lenses . . . Absurd!

He groped for an explanation. Yes, he had suffered hallucinations. Yes, the whole progression of thought was unravelling and clarifying itself now. He had suffered from hallucinations. Something had been wrong in his mind. His optic centres had been off-centre. With something like clarity, he became able to map the area of disturbance.

It occurred to him that he might some time investigate this cell or tank in which he and Gasm were. Doors and windows had it none. Perhaps like him it had undergone some vast sea change.

Emitting a long liquid sigh, Double A ascended slowly off the floor. As he rose, he glanced upwards. Two drowned men floated on the ceiling, gazing down at him.

VI

Double A floated back to his former patch of mud only to find his hands gone. Nothing could have compensated him for the loss except the growth of a long strong tail.

His long strong tail induced him to make another experiment; no more nor less than the attempt to foster the illusion that the tail was real by pretending there was a portion of his brain capable of activating the tail. More easily done than thought. With no more than an imaginary flick of the imaginary appendage, he was sailing above Gasm on a controlled course, ducking under but on the whole successfully ignoring the two drownees.

From then on he called himself Doublay and had no more truck with time or hands or ghosts of hands and time.

Though the mud was good, being above it was better, especially when Gasm could follow. They grew new talents – or did they find them?

Now the questions were no sooner asked than forgotten, for by a mutual miracle of understanding, Doublay and Gasm began to believe themselves to be fish.

And then they began to dream about hunting down the alien invaders.

VII

The main item in the laboratory was the great tank. It was sixty feet square and twenty feet high; it was half full of sea water. A metal catwalk with rails round it ran along the top edge of the tank; the balcony was reached by a metal stair. Both stair and catwalk were covered with deep rubber, and the men that walked there wore rubber shoes, to ensure maximum quiet.

The whole place was dimly lit.

Two men, whose names were Roberts and Collison, stood on the catwalk, looking through infra-red goggles down into the tank. Though they spoke almost in whispers, their voices nevertheless held a note of triumph.

"This time I think we have succeeded, Dr Collison," the younger man was saying. "In the last forty-eight hours, both specimens have shown less lethargy and more awareness of their form and purpose."

Collison nodded.

"Their recovery has been remarkably fast, all things considered. The surgical techniques have been so many and so varied . . . Though I played a major part in the operations myself, I am still overcome by wonder to think that it has been possible to transfer at least half of a human brain into such a vastly different metabolic environment."

He gazed down at the two shadowy forms swimming round the tank.

Compassion moving him, he said, "Who knows what terrible traumas those two brave souls have had to undergo? What fantasies of amputation, of life, birth and death, of not knowing what species they were."

Sensing his mood, Roberts said briskly, "They're over it now. It's obvious they can communicate. The underwater mikes pick up their language. They've adjusted well. Now they're raring to go."

"Maybe, maybe. I still wonder if we had the right –"

Roberts gestured impatiently, guessing Collison spoke only to be reassured. He knew how proud the old man secretly was, and answered him in the perfunctory way he might have answered one of the newspaper men who would be round later.

"The security of the world demanded this drastic experiment. The alien ship 'landed' a year ago in the North Atlantic, off Bermuda. Our submarines have investigated its remains on the ocean bed. They have found proof that the ship landed where it did *under control*, and was only destroyed when the aliens left it.

"The aliens were fish people, aquatics. The ocean is their element, and undoubtedly they have been responsible for the floods extending along the American and European seaboards and inundating the West Indies. Undoubtedly the popular press is right to claim we are being defeated in an alien invasion."

"My dear Roberts, I don't doubt they're right, but –"

"There can be no buts, Dr Collison. We've failed to make any contact with the aliens. They have eluded the most careful submarine probes. Nor is there any 'but' about their hostile intent. It seems more than likely that they have killed off all the eel family in some unimaginable slaughter under the Sargasso Sea. Before they upset our entire oceanic ecology, we must find them and gain the information about them without which they cannot be fought. Here are our spies, here in this tank. They have post-hypnotic training. In a couple more days, when they are fit, they can be released into the sea to go and get that information and return with it to us. There are no buts; only imperatives in this equation."

Slowly the two men descended the metal stairway, the giant tank on their left glistening with condensation.

"Yes, it's as you say," Collison agreed wearily. "I would so much like to know, though, the insane sensations passing through those shards of human brain embedded in fish bodies."

"Ethics don't enter into it," Roberts said firmly.

In the tank, in the twilight, the two giant tunnies swam restlessly back and forth, readying themselves for their mission.

Except My Life³

John Morressy

The previous story was a fairly early example of genetic engineering. It was some years before the word "clone" entered the vernacular and the whole subject of cloning continues to be hotly debated. Assuming the inevitable John Morressy (b. 1930) – who is probably better known for his fantasy stories about the magician Kedrigern, though he has been writing sf for thirty years – considers a future where clones are everywhere.

Since the agency opened for business, I've worked out a mutually satisfactory division of labor among myself. I[3] manage the office, I[1,2] do the legwork, and I[4] take care of the deep thinking. So far, the system works.

It's not entirely the result of good organization. Cracking a couple of spectacular cases has helped a lot. Word got around that if you're having trouble with a clone or with the entertainment business – and especially with both combined – the Lucky Clover Detective Agency, Joe Kilborn sole owner and proprietor, is the place to go for help.

So I[3] wasn't surprised when Serena Siddons appeared in the office, pointed a finger at my[3] chest, and said, "I want you, Kilborn."

"A lot of people do, ma'am," I[3] said, rising. "It's been busy around here lately."

"I need you more than they do, and I can pay."

I[3] gave her a businesslike smile and waved her to a chair. When she had seated herself, she tossed back her great mane of silver hair and fixed her emerald eyes on me[3], then took a slow look around the office. I[3] said, "You have me at a disadvantage, ma'am. I don't believe I know –"

"Don't play dumb, laddie. Everybody in this city knows me."

She was absolutely right, but I[3] make it a practice to be unimpressed by clients, even when I[3]'m impressed. Most of the people who walk into the office have enough ego to fill Central Park. Even so, this particular client would have impressed Napoleon.

"Would you by any chance be Serena Siddons?"

She flashed a smile as frosty as a January moonrise. "At a rough estimate, laddie, there are twenty thousand people in this city who *would* be Serena Siddons, if they could. I *am*."

I[3] had never seen her in person before. Serena Siddons was a legend, and she worked at keeping the legend alive and public. But she worked at it in very different circles from the ones I[1,2,3] moved in. She had been in the theater – "on Broadway" is what people called it then, and sometimes, just to confuse things, "off-Broadway" or even "off-off-Broadway" – back in the days of the old Times Square, when year after year, thirty or forty theaters regularly offered live drama and musicals. When live drama in this country went the way of black-and-white films and two-dimensional television, she organized an international touring company. After twenty-five years of touring, she took two years off to write her autobiography, then became a screenwriter and eventually director and producer of her own vehicles. Why she was here I[3] couldn't imagine, but it was a pretty safe bet that theater had something to do with it.

"I'm pleased to meet you," I[3] said. "What is it you'd like me to do?"

"I have an investment, Kilborn. I want it protected."

"What's the investment, ma'am?"

"You've heard of Three For The Show, I assume?"

"An acting group, isn't he?"

"The three finest actors I've ever seen, Kilborn. The best in the business today by far. Maybe the best ever."

"A clone, isn't he, ma'am?"

"Yes. Surely that doesn't bother you, Kilborn," she said, narrowing those chilly green eyes.

"Not a bit, ma'am. I'm just looking for the facts."

"I'll give you all the facts you want. You've heard of Count Proteus, too, I suppose?"

I[3] had to think for a minute. "He's an impressionist, isn't he?"

"You're a master of understatement, Kilborn. Count Proteus doesn't do impressions, he becomes other people. He can be man, woman, child. He can be tall or short, fat or thin, anything he wants. He's the best."

"If you say so, ma'am. But what do they have to do with you and me?"

For the first time, she looked as though she approved of what was going on. "You keep to the point, Kilborn. That's good. And here's the connection. I've signed Three For The Show and Count Proteus to do *Hamlet* live, on stage, before an audience." She gave me a cold smile. "You've heard of *Hamlet*, I take it?"

"It's a play, isn't it, ma'am?"

"It's *the* play, Kilborn. There hasn't been a live *Hamlet* in this city since I played Ophelia thirty-six years ago, and we're going to put on the performance that will stand as definitive for as long as there are two people to act and one to applaud. I'm talking theater history, Kilborn."

"Yes, ma'am. And what's my part in it?"

"I'm also talking about a two billion dollar property which will be worth ten billion before we're through. Maybe twenty. Maybe fifty. I want you to keep an eye on Proteus and Three until every frame is in the can."

"Then you'll be filming it for the hollies?"

"You bet I'll be filming it. And until I do, every cent is at risk."

"If all you want is a bodyguard, then maybe –" I[3] started to say, but broke off when I[3] saw me[4] walk in. At sight of the client, I[4] stopped in my[4] tracks and stood for a moment astonished; then I[4] whipped off my[4] hat, stepped before her chair, and made a low sweeping bow.

"Madame Siddons, you do this humble office a great honor," I[4] said in my[4] most solemn voice. The cool glance of those green eyes warmed just a bit as I[4] went on, "Should anything be causing you concern, Madame, I hope you will allow me to assist you, the most illustrious figure of the modern theater, with all the resources at my command."

I[4] was good at this kind of thing, and I[3] was glad to see me[4]. It goes back to what I[3] was saying about division of labor. This kind of client was my[4] meat, not mine[3]. I[1,2] wouldn't know how to deal with her at all.

"I spoke to Lieutenant Gutierrez this morning. She asked about the Gunderson papers," I[4] said to me[3].

I[3] clapped a hand to my[3] brow and exclaimed, "I completely forgot about the Gunderson business! I've got to bring up that whole file and check every entry by . . . I'll never make it."

"If Madame has no objection to dealing with me, I'll be glad to fill in," I[4] said, turning to Siddons with an expectant smile.

She shot one frigid glance at me[3] and then looked up at me[4] warmly. "No objection at all, laddie," she said. "It's not a question of bodyguards. I know where I can get bodyguards. I want *you*, Kilborn."

I[4] studied her for a moment, then took a seat facing her. Placing my[4] fingertips together, I[4] gazed up into the corner of the ceiling. "Aside from the obvious facts that you have come on a matter relating to the theater, involving a clone, and with a large amount at risk, I can deduce nothing," I[4] said, ". . . except for your initial reluctance to deal with me and your haste in coming here once you had decided, despite concern over the health of your white cat."

Even I[3] was impressed with that, and regretted that I[3] had to leave the office before I[3] could see the expression on her face. Not that there was anything wrong. "Gunderson" was a convenient code I used among myself to make sure clients were best handled. Right now, it meant that I[3] had to make a show of rushing out, and be content to eavesdrop.

Once I[3] was gone, I[4] said, "Now, if you'd begin –"

"Just a minute, laddie," Siddons broke in. "Don't think you can get away with spying on me. Who put you up to it?"

"Spying, Madame?"

"That's what I said, damn it, *spying*! Who is it, Kilborn –

my maid? The cook? Has somebody bought off my whole staff?"

"I require no spies," I[4] said with dignity. "I observe, and I deduce."

"That I have a white cat? And she's sick?" She laughed and made as if to rise.

"There are tufts of cat hair at the hem of your skirt, Madame. The skirt was brushed, but in haste. You were hurrying out even as your maid was brushing," I[4] said. She settled back into the chair. I[4] went on, "The presence of white hairs on a black skirt suggests that concern for the cat overcame your habitual attention to grooming. The quantity of hair attests to the animal's ill health."

She was silent for a time. She reached down to pick a few white hairs from her skirt; then she demanded, "What about the rest? How did you know those other things?"

"You have seen my methods. It should be obvious."

"Well, it's not, and I didn't come here to play detective. You just walked in – how do you know why I'm here?"

"First, since your life has been spent in the world of theater, and this agency's most celebrated cases have dealt with the theater, it is unlikely that you would wish to engage me on some other matter. Secondly, the Lucky Clover Detective Agency is owned and operated by a clone and is known for dealing successfully with clone-related cases. Thirdly, my fees are the highest in the city. I am not engaged for trivial matters."

"Now that you explain it, it makes sense. It's really very simple."

"It always is, Madame – once I've explained."

"Don't be touchy, Kilborn. I had to know if there was a leak. This project is absolutely secret, and I want it to stay secret until I'm ready to open the publicity campaign."

She gave me[4] a recap of the information she had given me[3] before I[4] arrived. I[4] was impressed. The theater has always been one of my[4] chief interests, and this production of *Hamlet* was sure to be as significant a theatrical event as Serena Siddons was touting it to be.

"Naturally, I'm pleased that you thought of this agency," I[4] said, "but I still don't understand why ordinary bodyguards won't do. You could hire a platoon of good ones for what you'll have to pay me."

"I don't want ordinary bodyguards, Kilborn. If it was up to me, I wouldn't be here. But I've got backers who put a lot of money into this, and they want to see some protection. And if I have to hire protection, I want the best."

"Very sensible," I^4 said.

"Besides, you're a clone. You think like a clone. There's going to be a lot of pressure on Three and Proteus over the next few months. This is their first live production, and the first *Hamlet* in this city since I was a girl. I don't want anybody making them jumpy. Clones trust clones."

I^4 let that ridiculous bit of folklore pass without comment. "Proteus isn't a clone," I^4 pointed out.

"He's more like a clone than any other solo I've ever met," Siddons said. "You're a four-clone, Kilborn. My boys are a three-clone. Count Proteus has been a thousand people at one time or another."

"But only one at a time. It's not the same."

"Maybe not the same as being a true clone, but it's a lot closer to clone experience than to typical solo experience. You'd get along with him, Kilborn. Others wouldn't. And it's important to me and to the whole project that Proteus and Three be kept as calm and relaxed and happy as possible until we open."

I^4 certainly could not argue her last point. Show people are a temperamental lot under the best of circumstances. In these times, with live performance fighting to make a comeback and The Great Mulroney scandal still fresh in the public's mind, being a clone and an actor was a stressful condition. I^4 could see where the Lucky Clover Detective Agency would be helpful. And this was probably the only chance I^4'd ever get to see a live *Hamlet*.

Two days later I assembled one by one at Serena Siddons's apartment to meet Three For The Show. She was taking no chances. At her insistence, I came disguised as a reporter, accountant, outercom repairman, and analyst, while Three showed up as a hairdresser, fencing instructor, and dietician.

When we had all arrived, Siddons swept in to make the introductions and offer drinks. In the interests of secrecy, her staff had been given the day off, so we fixed our own. I[4] stuck to mineral water, but I[1,2,3] homed in on the twenty-four-year-old scotch. Three had a double vodka martini, a bourbon sour, and something blue with fruit in it.

The martini Three broke the ice clone-style by asking me[1], "Was your original a detective?"

"Until shortly after he got his legs blown off," I[1] said.

"How dreadful!"

"His very words." I[1] took a good swallow of the scotch and savored it with half-closed eyes and an expressionless face.

Turning to me[2], Three[1] asked, "Was it an accident?"

"Sort of. Somebody accidentally planted a bomb in his roller, and it went off."

I[1,2] am sometimes off-putting in social situations. I[4] could sense Three's uneasiness, so I[4] moved in and said, "Joe Kilborn survived and brought in the people who planted the bomb. After that, he retired from the force and became a private investigator and student of criminology. He wrote the standard work on the evolution of electronic jurisprudence."

Three[3] said, "He wrote detective stories, too, didn't he?"

"Yes, in the last years of his career," I[4] said.

"What was your original, a bartender or a decorator?" I[2] asked, pointing to the gaudy drink in Three[3]'s hand.

"I'm cloned from Sir Herbert Three," Three[3] announced.

"The finest actor of his day," Three[1] added proudly.

"One of the finest of all time. It's a pity we have so few examples of his work. Some scenes from his *Henry V*, a single speech from *Cyrano de Bergerac* . . ." I[4] fell silent, shaking my[4] head ruefully.

"When the last theater in London closed its doors, he swore he'd never act again," said Three[1].

"But I've got a hollie of his *Cyrano*, if you'd care to see it. And his entire *Richard III*," Three[3] said.

I[4] was delighted. Sir Herbert Three's acting was legendary, but his reluctance to have his performances recorded in any way meant that there was little to go upon but the legend. I[1,2] refilled my[1,2] glass and rejoined Three and me[4]. Meanwhile, I[3] spoke to our hostess apart from the others.

"How's everyone getting on?" she asked.

"We'll be all right, ma'am. It just takes a while to loosen up."

"Why? You're all clones. Isn't that the important thing?"

"He's a three-clone and I'm a four-clone. Three-clones have a reputation for never agreeing. Always two against one. Four-clones learn to agree. There's no tie-breaking vote."

"Three gets along together very well. I've never seen any serious disagreement."

"Well, then, things should be just fine, ma'am," I[3] said.

By this time, I[4] had gotten Three on the subject of his *Hamlet*. He was bursting to talk about the project, sometimes all at once, and his enthusiasm was even making me[1,2] ease up on the wisecracks and pay attention.

"For the first time, Hamlet's divided nature will be made physically manifest to the audience. I'll be playing Hamlet, Laertes, and Fortinbras," said Three[3].

"And, of course, Claudius," Three[1] added.

"And others, too. And I'll be switching back and forth constantly," said Three[2].

"So the facet of Hamlet's personality in each of these characters will at last be plainly visible," Three[1] concluded.

"That will be tricky, won't it?" I[4] asked. "As I recall, Hamlet, Laertes, Claudius, and Fortinbras all appear or stage in the very last scene, along with other major characters."

"That's right. A couple of other scenes presented problems, too, but we've worked them out. We'll have to make quick changes, but we're used to that. And we'll have other actors to help out in the tricky spots."

"We'll need them for Horatio, and Rosencrantz and Guildenstern, and all those courtiers and ambassadors and soldiers," said Three[1]. "Serena's found some first-rate actors. Solos, of course, but they're very good."

"Proteus is a solo," said our hostess, who had joined us. "Have you forgotten?"

"Ah, but Proteus is one of a kind," said Three[2].

"My point exactly. So glad you agree," said Siddons icily.

"He solves a lot of problems," Three[2] went on. "He'll be Ophelia –"

"Ophelia?!" I[4] blurted, astonished.

"Proteus is very versatile," Three[3] assured me. "He'll take one of the major roles when all four have to be on the stage at once."

"And he'll play important minor characters, too, like Osric. And he'll be Fortinbras, in the last scene," said Three[2].

The sheer complexity of it impressed me[1,2], even though I[2]'m not fond of theater and I[1] haven't read a book for years. "How do you plan to do this without falling all over yourselves?" I[2] asked.

"I'm directing, laddie. And when I direct, people don't fall all over themselves," said our hostess.

"I thought you were the producer," I[4] said.

"I am. I'm playing Gertrude, too. I think I can bring something to the part."

I[4] nodded, and so did I[2], even though Siddons's words meant nothing to me[2]. I[1] looked at the others and grinned. "At least there's one role this guy Proteus won't get to play," I[1] said.

"Where is Proteus? Is he coming?" I[4] asked.

"He can't make it, Kilborn. You're going to meet him at his place," she said. "In fact, you just left."

Proteus had a townhouse at the end of a cul-de-sac overlooking the river. It was evening when my[3] roller pulled up at the door. A light rain had begun to fall. I[3] paid the driver and took a look at the building.

It was a classic of its kind, clean white limestone with every detail carefully preserved – or restored by experts. But I[3] wasn't interested in the architecture. I[3] was going to be watching out for Count Proteus for the next few months, and I[3] wanted to know whether his house was going to make the job harder or easier.

The house had the standard urban security systems, but

it was no fortress. That was reassuring. Watching over someone who thinks he's invulnerable and immortal is hard, but being around someone who jumps out of his skin at every sound and sudden movement is worse. This place suggested an occupant who was more interested in protecting his privacy than his skin. I[3] liked that.

Count Proteus was expecting me.[3] The outer gate clicked open as soon as I[3] gave my[3] name and code, and I[3] waited only a few seconds before the massive front door swung wide and a tall, deadpan butler greeted me[3] with a mournful, "Good evening, Mr Kilborn. The master will be with you shortly. Please come this way."

I[3] followed him down a darkened hall lined with photographs and into a dimly lit library. A fire was burning in the fireplace. It was a real fire, with real logs. My[3] estimate of Proteus went up. Only the very rich could afford to burn wood these days, and only the very classy would have a fire burning in an empty room for the comfort of a private eye.

The butler took my[3] coat and hat and assured me[3] that the master would join me[3] in a few minutes. That was just fine. It gave me[3] time to look around.

I[3] was studying the bookshelf near the window when a round little woman dressed all in black, with graying hair pulled back in a knot, entered the room and in a soft, motherly voice asked, "Would you like a cup of tea while you're waiting, Mr Kilborn? It will warm you up after that nasty drizzle."

"No, thank you, ma'am," I[3] said. "But I'd appreciate it if you'd answer a few questions."

"Oh, dear me, there isn't any trouble, is there?" she asked, wringing her hands and glancing anxiously around the room.

"No trouble at all, ma'am. I'm going to be working very closely with Count Proteus for the next few months, and I'd like to learn all I can about him and the household. You can be a great help."

She shrank back. "You're not a reporter, are you?"

"No, ma'am. I'm a private detective."

"Oh, I see. Middleton didn't say you were a detective,

Mr Kilborn, so I assumed . . . oh, dear, I am sorry," she said, resuming her hand-wringing.

"No need to apologize, ma'am. Is Middleton the butler?"

"That's right, Mr Kilborn. He's been with the master for nearly six years now. I'm Mrs Etherege. Georgina Etherege. The housekeeper."

"And Mr Etherege?"

"He died in 2034," she said, lowering her gaze.

"I'm sorry to hear that, ma'am. Is there anyone else in the household besides you and Middleton and Count Proteus?"

"Well, there's Otway, the cook. And the girl who helps out in the kitchen, poor thing."

"Why do you call her 'poor thing,' ma'am?"

"Ida's not in full possession of her senses, Mr Kilborn. She has delusions. She thinks she's the Gish sisters."

"That's too bad, ma'am," I[3] said, assuming from her solemn tone that it in fact was. I[4] would have known who the Gish sisters were, but I[3] didn't have a clue. Maybe I[4] should cover Proteus instead of me[3], I[3] thought. But then, without me[4] around, I[1,2] would probably make Three uneasy. This was something to talk over back at the office.

"Oh, it's not so bad. After all, there were only the two, Lillian and Dorothy. Sometimes Ida's one, sometimes the other. It doesn't affect her work at all," said Mrs Etherege.

"She's never both at the same time, then?"

"Oh, dear, no. And most of the time she's just our poor Ida."

I[3] nodded and tried to look sympathetic. It was necessary to remember that solos had problems, too, and most of the time a solo had no one around to listen and understand. If solos started talking to themselves, people thought they were crazy.

"Would you like to speak with them?" Mrs Etherege asked. "I mean with Otway or Ida," she added quickly.

"Maybe before I go, ma'am. I want to be ready to talk with Count Proteus as soon as he can see me."

"Of course you do. Oh, and there's one other person. I expect you'll be meeting her this evening."

"Who's that, ma'am?"

"Millwood, the master's business manager. She attends to all his professional affairs. She's not available right now, but you should be able to see her before you leave," said Mrs Etherege, backing toward the door. "Are you sure you don't want tea?"

"I'm sure, ma'am."

She slipped noiselessly out of the room, leaving me[3] alone once again. It was too dark now to read the titles, so I[3] pulled a chair up before the fireplace and stretched my[3] feet out to the warmth. A real wood fire was a rare treat. It seemed only sensible to enjoy it while I[3] could.

A few minutes passed, and then I[3] was aware of someone in the room. In the shadows by the door stood a figure all in black. Count Proteus had entered the library as silently as his housekeeper had left.

I[3] started up, but he gestured for me[3] to stay seated. In a hushed, cultured monotone, he said, "Please don't rise, Mr Kilborn. I like my guests to be comfortable."

"You surprised me, Count."

"It is my profession to surprise . . . to astound . . . to astonish. Tell me, Mr Kilborn, what do you think of my household?"

"I've only met the butler and the housekeeper. They looked all right to me."

"I'm glad to hear that, Mr Kilborn." The Count didn't move from the shadows by the door. Even if he had, the rest of the room was so gloomy by now that it would have made no difference. He showed no interest in turning up the lights.

I[3] remembered then some of the things I[3]'d read about Count Proteus. He was a very private person. In fact, he was almost pathological about his privacy. When he was not working, he was invisible. He avoided photographers, granted no interviews, permitted no one near him. I[3] was probably the first outsider to enter his house, and I[3] certainly wasn't getting a good look. It was hard to say whether this was all real, and I[3] really didn't care whether it was or not. What I[3] wondered was whether it was going to make my[3] work easier or harder.

Proteus laughed softly and said, "So you found nothing unusual about Mrs Etherege and Middleton."

"No, I didn't."

"Well, I'll have to tell that to the master, Mr Kilborn. And are you sure you don't want a nice cup of tea?" It was Mrs Etherege's voice, no question about it, and Proteus seemed to have gotten smaller and rounder as he stood there wringing his hands. Then, abruptly, he seemed to grow and swell, and I³ heard Middleton's plummy voice say, "It is most gratifying, sir, to know that you do not find us suspicious characters."

"That's pretty impressive, Count," I³ said, trying not to show how impressive it really was. It was so impressive that it made me³ suspicious of everything I³'d seen.

"It is my profession," Proteus said in his normal voice – in the voice he'd first used, anyway – "And I am good at it. Are you as good at yours?"

"I've done pretty well so far. You've heard of the Great Mulroney case, I suppose."

"I have indeed. A tragic affair."

"It could have been worse. I prevented a murder."

"I was referring to the tragic waste of talent, Mr Kilborn. The Great Mulroney was a gifted clone, but he squandered his gifts on pratfalls and pie-throwing. I am saddened by the thought of what he might have achieved."

"He almost achieved the murder of his manager."

Again Proteus laughed that soft private laugh. "We speak at cross-purposes, Mr Kilborn. But no matter. Serena has explained the reason for your presence. I feel no need for protection, but I have no wish to be difficult. You are welcome so long as you do not interfere with my work or make any attempt to violate my privacy. Is that understood?"

"Understood."

"Millwood will acquaint you with my schedule and the household routine, and provide any necessary information. Good evening, Mr Kilborn."

He turned to leave. I³ said, "Just a minute, Count. I have a question."

"I have no time for it, Mr Kilborn. Question my staff, if you like."

"It's about your staff. Is there really a Middleton and a

Mrs Etherege, or are you playing games with me? Is there really a Millwood?"

He stopped at the door, deep in the shadows, and said, "Millwood is real. As for the others . . . you claim to be a good detective. Find out for yourself."

He was gone before I^3 could respond. I^3 stood by the chair, trying to get things straight. It wasn't easy. Proteus's impersonation of Middleton and Etherege had been so flawless that I^3 couldn't be sure that the butler and house-keeper hadn't been Proteus in disguise. But why would he do that? To test me^3? If so, I^3 had flunked. It might be some private joke, his own way of staying in practice, or keeping the world at arm's length. Whatever his reasons, Count Proteus was going to be a tough client. I^4 had the brains to handle him, but I^3 felt that he could make me^3 look foolish with very little effort. I^3 decided that the smart thing to do was to wash my^3 hands of Proteus after tonight, and turn him over to me^4. Proteus would never know the difference. Solos never do.

Then she entered the room, and any thought of changing assignments vanished at the sight of her. She was tall and slender, with a beautiful figure and the carriage of a queen. Her perfume was delicate; it made me^3 think of spring and flowers and soft rain. Her honey-blonde hair was worn long and loose; her eyes were pale blue, her features perfect in an oval face. I^3 looked at her in the glow of the fire, and knew that I^3 would do anything this woman asked. I^3 had fallen in love with her on the spot, and though I^3 had no previous experience in permanent undying love, I^3 knew that this was it. Fortunately, I^3've learned to keep my^3 feelings from showing, so when I^3 introduced my^3self, my^3 voice was steady.

Her voice was a match for her appearance. It was soft and husky, a voice perfectly suited to firelight and a cozy room. "Morgana Millwood, Mr Kilborn. I'm pleased to meet you," she said, holding out her hand. "Let's sit by the fire. Is this light sufficient?"

"It's perfect, ma'am," I^3 said. She wore a dark blue dress of soft clinging material. The firelight struck highlights from it, and I^3 had the crazy image of a goddess come down to earth wrapped in the night sky, stars and all. I[3] had never thought like that before in my[3] life, but the sight of Morgana Millwood was turning me[3] into a poet.

"Call me Morgana, please. And may I call you Joe?"

"I'd be happy if you did."

Neither of us had moved. We stood looking into one another's eyes without speaking, then we both spoke at once, in a rush, and then we laughed, embarrassed. She laid her hand on mine[3] and said, "Joe, I'm sorry. I don't know what's come over me."

I[3] don't know how to be subtle. I[3] took her hand in both of mine[3] and said, "If it's the same thing that came over me, don't be sorry."

"Joe, do you feel . . . ?"

"I do, Morgana. I never did before, but I do now."

Then she was in my[3] arms. I[3] can't describe how I[3] felt. If you've been there you know, and if you haven't you don't, and no words will help you. After a time she took my[3] face in her hands and looked up at me[3], and then she laughed, a little shy laugh, so happy and innocent it made me[3] fall for her all over again.

"Joe, what's happening to us? We're not a couple of kids. We're supposed to be talking about business," she said.

"Let's talk business later."

"Business now, Joe. Then we'll have time for other things."

We sat before the fire, drawing the chairs close, and she filled me[3] in on the household routine and Proteus's daily schedule. It was hard to keep my[3] mind on business, but long habit carried me[3] through when inclination made me[3] want to consign to hell Count Proteus and Three for the Show and Serena Siddons and everything and everybody else but Morgana Millwood.

Proteus ran his life like an elaborate timepiece. Everything was scheduled, and the schedule was sacred. He spent most of the day in his fourth-floor retreat, a combination of theater, gymnasium, studio, and rehearsal hall that was permanently off limits to the rest of the human race. Even Morgana had never set foot in it. He breakfasted every morning at nine-fifteen, then vanished upstairs. Mrs Ether-

ege brought his lunch up at one-fifteen and placed it on a
table outside the door. She picked up the tray, sometimes
untouched, at two o'clock sharp. Proteus left his sanctum at
four-thirty, when he withdrew to rest before going to
theater or studio, or wherever he was playing. He was
always home in time for a light supper at midnight, after
which he vanished once again, presumably to sleep. This
was his routine, day after day. Everything revolved around
this schedule and a few inflexible rules: no visitors, no
prying, no contact with the media.

I[3] would have thought that working for such a clock-
bound fanatic had to rank low on anyone's list of favorite
occupations, but Morgana insisted otherwise, and claimed
that Middleton, Mrs Etherege, and the rest of the staff
agreed with her. If you could mind your own business and
be punctual in the things that mattered to him, Proteus
asked little else and paid generously for your service. And,
she added, there was a kind of excitement in being so close
to such a great and mysterious man.

"So Middleton and Mrs Etherege are real," I[3] said. "For
a time, I wondered. Proteus is so good I couldn't tell him
from the real thing. But why did he do it? He doesn't have
to impress me."

She shrugged. "Maybe he just felt playful."

"Maybe. He couldn't fool me if he tried to impersonate
you, though. Has he ever tried?"

"I wouldn't know. That's another of his rules: none of us
is ever to see him perform. He doesn't even allow us near
the theater."

"You mean you've never seen him act?"

"None of us on the staff have. He's adamant on that
point."

"What about tapes? There must be tapes, and hollies."

"Very few, and he'd destroy those if he could. He doesn't
allow his work to be recorded. He believes that performance
should be seen live or not at all."

"You work for a very strange guy, Morgana."

"Not so strange, Joe. He came up the hard way. Now that
live theater is coming back, Count Proteus is in demand
everywhere, and he can name his own terms."

"What about this *Hamlet* deal? There'll be tapes and hollies of that. Does he know?"

"Of course. He's willing to compromise, just this once, for the chance to act in *Hamlet*. It will be the great achievement of his career. But there won't be any recording of any kind until he's satisfied with the performance. That's in the contract."

"I still think he's strange."

She looked at me[3] earnestly and leaned forward to take my[3] hands in a firm grip. Her perfume caressed me[3] like a gentle spring breeze. "Think of what his life has been like, Joe. He's impersonated all the giants of the stage in their great roles. He's been Barrymore and Olivier and Gielgud as Hamlet, Walter Hampden and José Ferrer as Cyrano, Jason Robards as Hickey, Laurette Taylor as Amanda Wingfield – he's always been playing the part of someone playing the part of someone else, always wearing one more mask than everyone else on stage. His idea of reality is bound to be different from yours and mine. Try to understand, Joe. He needs your understanding."

None of those names meant much to me[3], but it was plain that they meant a lot to her, and I[3] got the general idea. Proteus had made it to the top, but like all successful people he had changed along the way, and the changes hurt. A clone can have a thousand faces, but they'll all be the same. It provides a certain security. For a solo, every face is different. No wonder there are so many crazy solos.

"I'll try to understand him, sweetheart. For your sake. You think a lot of Count Proteus, don't you?"

"He's done a lot for me, Joe. I'll always be grateful to him."

"Is that as far as it goes?"

"I never loved Proteus as a woman loves a man, if that's what you mean. Until today, I've never loved anyone. I still can't believe what's happened. The minute I saw you . . ." She looked at me[3], wide-eyed, and shook her head helplessly.

"Believe it. It happened to me, too," I[3] said.

Morgana and I[3] decided to keep things quiet, at least for a while. It's unprofessional for someone in my[3] business to fall for a client, and she didn't want to do anything that might upset Proteus.

As things turned out, it was not difficult to keep our relationship secret. The next few weeks were busy, and I[3] got together with me[1,2,4] only two or three times a week for a quick exchange of information. Morgana was free when Proteus was in his fourth-floor hideaway, but we couldn't leave the house. Once he started rehearsing with Three, I[3] had to stick with him and she couldn't come along, thanks to his crazy rules. Rehearsals went on well into the night, and sometimes into the morning, and when Proteus and I[3] returned to the townhouse, I[3] still wouldn't see Morgana for an hour or more. It was part of Proteus's routine to dictate all his observations on the rehearsal to her, so she could organize them for study and have them printed out by breakfast time. The crazy hours were knocking Morgana out, but she didn't complain. She knew that Proteus was a perfectionist. She had her job, and she did it.

Seeing Proteus on stage gave me[3] a different view of him. Sure, he was strange, but he knew his business. When he came on as Ophelia – she's maybe sixteen years old, innocent and sweet – Proteus was little and frail. He was your kid sister, the girl next door, the beautiful princess from all the fairy tales you've ever heard. And not long after that, he was a bald, squat, pot-bellied old gravedigger with a boozer's rasp in his voice and a wheezing cough. At the end of the play he was Fortinbras, a tough professional soldier, and he looked about six-foot-six with shoulders that wouldn't go through a doorway head-on.

He played other parts, too. They all did, and after a while I[3] lost track and stopped trying to tell one from the other. But Proteus was the marvel on that stage. Nobody could stretch and shrink and bloat up and trim down like that night after night, I[3] kept telling my[3]self. But Proteus did it, and seemed to do it just a little bit better every time. It made me[3] feel spooky when we rode home in his private roller after rehearsals. I[3] was always afraid he'd start changing right before my[3] eyes.

Not that I[3] could have seen it even if he had. Proteus could have turned into an octopus and I[3] wouldn't have known, the way he kept the roller darkened, and had his hat pulled down and his collar up. It bothered him to have anyone in the roller at all, even though I[3] was seated up front and could only catch a glimpse of him by twisting around until my[3] neck ached. Every time I[3] did, he'd shrink into himself a little more. Proteus loved secrecy as much as he loved perfection.

Just how much he loved his secrecy had become clear right away, when I[4] ran the routine check on everyone involved in this project. Serena Siddons's printout could have papered every wall in the office, with enough left over for the hall. Three's was almost as extensive. The printout for Count Proteus ran to two sheets. Most of it was white space.

I[4] was furious. "Look at this! Date of birth: blank. Place of birth: blank. I can't even get a continent!"

"I told you he likes his privacy," I[3] reminded me[4], and I[1,2] got a laugh out of my[4] reaction.

I[4] was not amused. This was a challenge to my[4] skill, and I[4] was ready now to sit at the terminal until doomsday in order to access Proteus's background.

"What's the problem?" I[2] asked. "That kind of privacy costs. If Proteus spent the money, let him enjoy it."

"He's just building up his image as a mystery man. It's strictly business," I[3] added.

I[4] was adamant. "Nobody is that secretive unless he has something to hide."

I[1,3] exchanged a patient smile and I[3] said, "So maybe he's Wally Zunkfuddle from North Pinhole, Montana. People change their names when they go on stage, don't they?"

"Especially if the name is Wally Zunkfuddle," I[1] said.

I[4] still wasn't happy, but there was no point arguing, and no reason to do a deep background search. After that, there was never enough time for one, or for anything else.

Rehearsals went along smoothly, and soon opening night was a week away. It couldn't come soon enough for me[3]. Even though there hadn't been a hint of trouble, these clients were taking up a lot of time. I[1,2,4] was down to four hours sleep a night. Between Proteus and Morgana, I[3] wasn't even getting that.

Morgana was having it tough, too. Proteus turned up the pressure as opening night drew near, and she was run off her feet. That last week we spent our time together – never more than ten minutes at a stretch – sitting in his library, hand in hand, her head on my[3] shoulder, both of us too tired to do anything but talk. In very short sentences.

I[3] still hadn't told me[1,2,4] about Morgana. I[3] had the feeling that I[4] suspected that I[3] had something on my[3] mind, but I[1,2] didn't seem to notice a thing. And even I[4] probably didn't suspect that a woman was involved. I[3] wondered what I[1,2,4]'d say when I[3] announced that I[3] meant to get married. Clones and solos marrying isn't all that unusual, but it had never come up before among me.

The night before *Hamlet* was to open, I[3] asked Morgana to marry me[3], and she accepted. We were both half knocked out with exhaustion, but I[3]'ll never forget taking her in my[3] arms, just holding her close, breathing in the soft fragrance of her perfume, being happier than I[3]'d ever been before. She let a lot of painful things come out then, in that rush of happiness, things she'd never told anyone else. I[3] had always figured that life was easy for a smart, beautiful woman. Morgana taught me[3] otherwise.

She'd been a foundling, an abandoned kid brought up in a series of homes, some good, some bad. The last one was the worst, so bad she ran away and was on her own at fifteen. She was a beauty even then, and that had caused her more problems than it solved. Her looks got her into show business, and after a few tough years she landed a job assisting a small-time impressionist who was just starting his career, doing the scroungy club circuit that was all the work he could get in those days. But in time, both he and the opportunities for live entertainers improved considerably, and he took to calling himself Count Proteus. She'd stayed with him as he went to the top.

"He'll miss you if you leave him after all these years," I[3] said.

"I don't think he will, Joe. He might even retire after this *Hamlet*. He can afford it now."

"I can't picture a guy like him retiring."

"He will. And when he does, he may just disappear completely."

"If anybody can do it, Proteus can. But why would he?"

"He's tired, Joe. He's worn out."

"He's not the only one."

We both yawned, and that set us laughing, very softly and wearily, hardly making a sound. She said, "Only one more night, Joe."

"You'll still be knocking yourself out for Proteus."

"Once the show's opened, we'll have a lot more time together. I have a feeling that Proteus will agree to the hollies early on. It won't be a long run, and once it closes, we'll be free to marry whenever we like."

"I'll get the license tomorrow – just in case the show is a flop," I[3] said.

But when tomorrow came, I[3] didn't even have time to get my[3] breakfast. Serena Siddons called Proteus's house a dozen times that day, checking on his health. I[3] saw Morgana exactly twice, for a total of about forty seconds. The rest of the time she was working with Proteus. The whole house was charged up. Middleton ran up and down stairs like a teenager, Mrs Etherege scurried from room to room wringing her hands, and Ida scrubbed everything in the kitchen twice: once as Dorothy, once as Lillian. And the theater was even worse.

When the play finally started, I[3] was ready to drop. I[3] took the seat reserved for me[3] in the third row, while I[1,2] stayed in the wings and I[4] took a seat in the stage manager's booth. I[3] expected to doze off, job or no job, as soon as the lights went down. But no one slept through that performance. It was magnificent.

Three was as good as everyone expected him to be, but I[3] had a special interest in Proteus. Whenever he was on stage, I[3] fixed on him, and he was onstage almost constantly. This night he did something he'd never done in rehearsal. He played Ophelia as Morgana. It was unmistakable. He had her voice and every gesture down pat. It was strange to sit there seeing and hearing painful things happen to the woman I[3] loved and all the time knowing that she was safe across town, waiting for me[3]. When the account of Ophelia's drowning was given, I[3] choked up, and an awful feeling of doom came over me[3] at the thought of ever losing Morgana.

I[3] didn't like Proteus for doing that, but I[3] couldn't deny his brilliance as an actor. Minutes after doing Ophelia's mad scene he was a gravel-voiced gravedigger, with bulging red nose and swaying belly. And in the last scene of the play, with all the main characters dead by trickery and treachery, he strode on as Fortinbras. That's a small part, but he stretched it to something big. Here's a guy who's fought and never won the prize, been held back and kept down and made to wait, and now it all drops into his lap. The way Proteus played him, Fortinbras was a giant – proud, confident, self-assured, a man whose faith in himself had never wavered and now was justified before the world.

When the lights went down, there was a moment of absolute silence, and then an outburst of applause that went on and on. It got louder, and still the lights did not come on. I[3] slipped from my[3] seat and went backstage to see what was wrong. This was not part of the play.

The first person I[3] saw was Serena, leaning on my[4] arm. Under the heavy makeup she looked weary and shrunken. I[3] had the same feeling of doom I[3] had felt at Ophelia's death.

She grabbed at my[3] sleeve. "He's dead. All of him. Murdered," she said in a shaky voice.

"Who?"

"Three. All three."

"What happened?" I[3] asked me[4].

"The sword. It was razor-sharp, and something was smeared on the tip," I[4] said.

"So whoever did it stuck to the script."

"No. The wine wasn't poisoned, or Serena would be dead, too. Someone wanted to kill Three and no one else. He was playing Hamlet, Laertes, and Claudius, and they're the only ones touched by the sword," I[4] explained.

"What will we do?" Serena moaned.

"Leave that to me. But first I want you to give the best performance of your life . . . if you can," I[4] said.

Serena covered her face with her hands for a moment, then looked up and nodded. "I can."

I[4] laid my[4] hands on her shoulders. "Go out there and tell them that there won't be any curtain calls tonight. Give any reason you like, Serena, or none at all, but get them out of the theater quietly, without panic."

"But how? What can I say?" she asked, wavering.

"Improvise. You can do it," I[4] said.

She took a deep breath, then straightened and looked me[3,4] in the eye. "I'll do it," she said. She turned, and walked out cool and poised as a queen.

As soon as she was gone, I[4] said, "I've called Homicide, and I'm staying with the bodies and the murder weapon. I've given word that no one backstage is to leave."

"Is it wise to let the audience go?"

"There's no way of keeping them here. Anyway, this wasn't done by anyone in the audience. No one came backstage once the play started."

"The sword could have been poisoned before," I[3] pointed out.

"No. I checked them all at intermission, and they were clean."

"But they were blunted, weren't they?"

"There was a transparent sheath covering the last fifteen inches of the blade. Someone stripped it off just before the fencing match," I[4] said.

"Any ideas?"

I[4] shrugged. "It could have been anyone. Anyone but Three."

That feeling of doom came over me[3] again. I[3] grabbed my[4] arm and said, "How can I be sure that all three Three are Three? One of them could be Count Proteus."

"Three played Hamlet, Laertes, and Claudius in that scene, and they're the ones who died. Proteus played Fortinbras."

"What if they decided to switch roles at the last minute? They changed roles a few times during the play. They could have done it in the last scene, too."

"But why would they?"

"Who knows why actors do anything?"

"It's a possibility," I^4 conceded. "And it's easy to check. All I have to do is find Fortinbras and –"

A guard came running up, stopped in front of me^{3,4}, and panted, "Mr Kilborn, sir, I'm sorry. I didn't know. I let him go."

"Who?"

"Mr Three, sir. He was in a hurry, and I didn't know anything had happened. He just rushed right by."

"Are you sure it was Three?" I^3 asked.

"Yes, sir. No doubt about it."

So I^3 was right. For some reason, Proteus had switched roles with one of Three for that scene, and now he was dead. But why had he done it on opening night? Why did he do it at all? Was his death the outcome of a careful plot that had been a long time in matching, or a case of mistaken identity? No matter how things appeared, no one could be sure of anything until all the people who might be involved were physically present and clearly visible. So far, the chief suspects were actors and stagehands – people who spent their lives making audiences believe that fantasy was reality.

"It could still have been Proteus, you know," I^4 said. "He could have fooled the guard into thinking he was Three."

"We won't know for sure until we get the makeup off the bodies," I^3 said.

While $I^{3,4}$ was pondering the guard's news, a second guard rushed up. He was carrying a bundle, which he thrust into my^4 arms.

"I found this behind the steps, Mr Kilborn. It's a costume," he said.

"Fortinbras's costume," I^4 said.

"This may be the proof that they did switch roles. Let's see it."

I^4 tossed me^3 the costume. It looked heavy, but it wasn't. Most of it was the lightweight padding that built the person wearing it up to heroic size. As I^3 examined it more closely, I^3 caught a faint whiff of a familiar fragrance. I^3 dropped the costume as if it were on fire, and took an unsteady step backwards. As I^3 did so, a great roar of applause and cheering swept over me^{3,4} from the front of the house, drowning the cries and questions. When it subsided, I[3] was aware of my[4] hand on my[3] shoulder, and Serena looking at me[3] as if I[3] were a ghost.

"What's wrong?" I[4] asked.

"I have to go. Give me an hour, then meet me at Proteus's house," I[3] said.

I[3] let my[3]self in at the servants' entrance and went directly to the fourth floor. Morgana was there, at a desk, sorting through papers. A small suitcase was on the floor beside the desk. She gave a start when she saw me[3].

"Joe! I didn't expect you so early."

"I left before it was over. I've had enough *Hamlet* to last a long time."

"Then . . . you didn't see the end?"

I[3] laughed. "I know how it ends, don't I? But what are you doing here? I thought this place was off limits."

"Proteus told me to come here, Joe. He said there was a surprise for me – for us."

"Us?"

"I told him everything, Joe. He was happy. I've never seen him so happy."

"I've never seen him happy at all. He seemed pretty keyed-up to me, especially these past few days."

"Did you notice it, too?"

"Couldn't help it. He was as jumpy as a man getting ready to commit a murder."

She winced. "Don't say things like that, Joe."

"Sorry. What's this surprise he had?"

"Oh, Joe, it's incredible! Count Proteus is the kindest, most generous man I ever knew. Look at this."

She held out a letter. I[3] read it over quickly and gave a single low whistle. The letter gave Morgana Millwood a half interest in Proteus's share of *Hamlet*.

"We can be together for the rest of our lives, Joe, just the two of us, anywhere we want to be. We can go away tonight, right now, and never tell a soul," she said, coming into my[3] arms, putting her soft mouth to mine[3], nestling close. I[3] breathed in the sweetness of her perfume, and wanted to keep this moment forever. But I[3] knew it couldn't last.

"Joe, let's go now. Right now," she whispered.

I[3] took her hand and led her to a chair. "Sit down, Morgana. I want to tell you something."

"Later, Joe. Let's go now, right away."

"I lied to you. I stayed to the end of *Hamlet*."

"Oh? What's so important about that, Joe? I thought you had a big confession to make."

"I made mine. Now it's your turn. Sit down." She sat and looked up at me[3], frowning slightly, looking genuinely puzzled. "I want you to tell me the truth about that small-time impressionist. It's the one thing I can't figure out."

"Joe, what do you mean? What are you trying to say?"

"Did he die, or did you kill him, too?"

She whispered my[3] name once, very softly, then she turned away and stared blankly into the darkness of the far corner of the room. I[3] pulled up a chair and sat facing her.

"Let me see if I have it right. You were a kid with the face of an angel and a body that every man you met was hungry for – every one but this guy. He was different. Sure, he saw that you were beautiful, but he saw something else that the others didn't. He spotted that one-in-a-million gift, and he helped you to bring it out."

"I didn't kill him, Joe. Not in the way you mean. I'll always be grateful to him."

"What happened?"

"He made me his assistant, and started teaching me everything he knew. He had all the theory, but not much talent. I was a natural – like a chameleon. In three months, I was the act and he was the assistant. People didn't even bother to talk to him any more, except to ask for me. He tried to keep up a front, but one night in San Francisco he took a walk across the bridge and never got to the other side."

"And that's when Count Proteus was born."

"No. That came later. I knew I had the talent, but I still had a lot to learn if I was going to be the best, and I meant to be the best. I had some money by then, so I found the best teachers and worked hard with them. I traveled around Europe and the East, and when I was ready, I came back here as Count Proteus. When people asked questions, I just smiled and referred them to my assistant, Millwood, who told them nothing. The more mysterious I was, the better they liked it."

"Why Count Proteus? Why not Countess?"

She smiled and shrugged. "Just one more mask, Joe. I felt safer behind it."

"When did you find out where all that talent came from? You must have wondered."

"Genius, Joe. Not talent, sheer genius," she said. "Yes, I wondered. I nearly went crazy wondering. I spent a fortune trying to find out who my real parents were, and I learned nothing." She took my[3] hand in hers. "The other private investigators aren't in your league."

"I try harder. So when did you find out?"

"Not until I signed with Serena and met Three for the first time. It hit me like a bolt of lightning, Joe. You know how it is. We can sense these things."

"Three didn't sense it."

"I was Count Proteus at the time. Safe behind my impenetrable mask." Her expression hardened and she drew her hands back. "Besides, Three couldn't even begin to imagine the truth. He had my original's full freight of misogyny."

"Sir Herbert Three was no woman-hater, Morgana. He was married four times and had dozens of mistresses. He couldn't keep away from women."

Morgana looked at me[3] clinically for a time; then she shook her head and laughed a faint, humorless laugh. "I know the stories better than you do, Joe. Sir Herbert Three believed in loving and leaving, breaking hearts, treating women like disposable cups you use once and then crumple and throw away. He had his wives and he had his affairs, but no woman was good enough to bear his child. He left orders to be cloned. He wanted four male heirs, four perfect little images of himself uncontaminated by a woman's touch." She sat back. She smiled, then she laughed, and it was a laugh of sheer delight. "But something went wrong. A chromosome decided it wasn't going to go along with the process of making four little Sir Herberts. And then there were three. And me – the dirty little secret that had to be hidden away."

"You didn't have to kill him, Morgana," I[3] said.

"I didn't want to, Joe, I swear I didn't. I kept waiting for one of him to show a single glimmer of recognition. We were closer than sister and brother, closer than twins – but all that Three ever saw was Count Proteus. He was cold, Joe, cold as ice! I thought of all those years I was alone, and frightened . . . the things I did to stay alive . . . while Three was together, never feeling that awful loneliness. I wanted to kill him, one by one." She rose and stood with her fists clenched, ramrod stiff from head to foot. "I thought about it every day. I planned it to the last detail. But I never really meant to do it, Joe. Tonight I gave him one last chance. I dropped the mask. I played Ophelia as myself. I was sure he'd see who I really was. All I wanted was one word, one look of recognition . . . and when it didn't come, I told myself that Three didn't deserve to live. It was no problem. I was Osric, remember? I handed out the foils. 'A hit, a very palpable hit,'" she cried in Osric's foppish voice, then turned to me[3]. "That's the whole story, Joe. Now you know. You've solved this case. And now let's go far away where no one will ever find us. Come on, Joe. Don't you want me?"

I[3] looked from her hair to her feet and up to her eyes again. "I do, Morgana. I want you more than I've ever wanted anything in the world. But the law wants you, too."

"Joe," she said softly, in a voice that was barely a whisper. "Joe, don't let it end like this. Please, Joe."

She reached out to me[3]. Just as our hands were about to touch, the door burst open. Lieutenant Chupka of Homicide and I[1,2,4] had arrived, right on time.

"Here's your murderer, Chupka," I[3] said. "Morgana Millwood, also known as Count Proteus. Her real name's Herbert Three[4]."

"All right, Kilborn," Chupka said. He nodded, and two policewomen took Millwood by the arms and led her out. She didn't look at me[3].

"Go easy," I[3] said. "She had a pretty good reason for killing him."

"They always do, don't they?" Chupka pushed his hat back and surveyed the room. The little suitcase caught his eye. "Looks like she was getting ready to skip. Alone?"

"I don't know. You'll have to ask her," I[3] said.

"That was fast work, Kilborn. How did you figure this one out?"

I[1] said, "It was easy."

"Easy?"

I[2] shrugged. "She killed Three and she's going over for it."

Chupka nodded. "Yeah. A fine-looking woman, too. It's a shame."

I[4] looked after her thoughtfully and murmured, "A lovely woman, with a face that a man might die for."

"Three did," Chupka growled. Turning to me[3], he added, "But you got her, Kilborn. Nice work. You must feel pretty good."

I[3] turned away without answering and went to the window. I[3] didn't feel good. I[3] felt a way I[3]'d never felt before, a way I[3] thought only a solo could feel.

I[3] felt lonely.

Into Your Tent I'll Creep

Eric Frank Russell

Britain has produced some of the world's greatest science fiction writers. One has only to mention the names Arthur C. Clarke, John Wyndham, J.G. Ballard and, of course, H.G. Wells, to achieve instant recognition. Whereas Clarke, Wyndham, Ballard and a few others went on to establish a world-wide reputation, as accepted by the mainstream and literary establishment as by the sf world, there were others who remained mighty in their own world but unknown beyond. Such a one was Eric Frank Russell (1905–78). Russell began selling science fiction, mostly in America, from 1937 onwards and scored a big hit with his novel Sinister Barrier, *published in the magazine* Unknown *in 1939. Russell established a special rapport with the editor of* Unknown *and of the leading science-fiction magazine* Astounding *(still published today as* Analog*), John W. Campbell, Jr. Russell was Campbell's favourite sf writer and most of his best work appeared in* Astounding *during the forties and fifties. But Russell found it increasingly difficult to sell his work elsewhere and by the sixties had tired of the hassle. He thus faded from the sf scene. If you hunt around you should find his collections* Deep Space *(1954) or* Far Stars *(1961) or the later compendium* The Best of Eric Frank Russell *(1978). Russell won a Hugo-award for a clever British satire of bureaucracy in space, "Allamagoosa" (1955), and though not typical of his work, it was typical of his habit to be light-hearted about intrinsically far-reaching matters. The following story is another such example.*

M orfad sat in the midship cabin and gloomed at the wall. He was worried and couldn't conceal the fact. The present situation had the frustrating qualities of a gigantic rat-trap. One could escape it only with the combined help of all the other rats.

But the others weren't likely to lift a finger either on his or their own behalf. He felt sure of that. How can you persuade people to try to escape a jam when you can't convince them that they're in it, right up to the neck?

A rat runs around a trap only because he is grimly aware of its existence. So long as he remains blissfully ignorant of it, he does nothing. On this very world a horde of intelligent aliens had done nothing about it through the whole of their history. Fifty skeptical Altairans weren't likely to step in where three thousand million Terrans had failed.

He was still sitting there when Haraka came in and informed, "We leave at sunset."

Morfad said nothing.

"I'll be sorry to go," added Haraka. He was the ship's captain, a big, burly sample of Altairan life. Rubbing flexible fingers together, he went on, "We've been lucky to discover this planet, exceedingly lucky. We've become blood brothers of a life-form fully up to our own standard of intelligence, space-traversing like ourselves, friendly and cooperative."

Morfad said nothing.

"Their reception of us has been most cordial," Haraka continued enthusiastically. "Our people will be greatly heartened when they hear our report. A great future lies before us, no doubt of that. A Terran-Altairan combine will be invincible. Between us we can explore and exploit the entire galaxy."

Morfad said nothing.

Cooling down, Haraka frowned at him. "What's the matter with you, Misery?"

"I am not overjoyed."

"I can see that much. Your face resembles a very sour *shamsid* on an aged and withered bush. And at a time of triumph, too! Are you ill?"

"No." Turning slowly, Morfad looked him straight in the eyes. "Do you believe in psionic faculties?"

Haraka reacted as if caught on one foot. "Well, I don't know. I am a captain, a trained engineer-navigator, and as such I cannot pretend to be an expert upon extraordinary abilities. You ask me something I am not qualified to answer. How about you? Do you believe in them?"

"I do – *now*."

"Now? Why now?"

"The belief has been thrust upon me." Morfad hesitated, went on with a touch of desperation. "I have discovered that I am telepathic."

Surveying him with slight incredulity, Haraka said, "You've discovered it? You mean it has come upon you recently?"

"Yes."

"Since when?"

"Since we arrived on Terra."

"I don't understand this at all," confessed Haraka, baffled. "Do you assert that some peculiarity in Terra's conditions has suddenly enabled you to read my thoughts?"

"No, I cannot read your thoughts."

"But you've just said that you have become telepathic."

"So I have. I can hear thoughts as clearly as if the words were being shouted aloud. But not your thoughts nor those of any member of our crew."

Haraka leaned forward, his features intent. "Ah, you have been hearing *Terran* thoughts, eh? And what you've heard has got you bothered? Morfad, I am your captain, your commander. It is your bounden duty to tell me of anything suspicious about these Terrans." He waited a bit, urged impatiently, "Come on, speak up!"

"I know no more about these humanoids than you do," said Morfad. "I have every reason to believe them genuinely friendly but I don't know what they think."

"But by the stars, man, you –"

"We are talking at cross-purposes," Morfad interrupted. "Whether I do or do not overhear Terran thoughts depends upon what one means by Terrans."

"Look," said Haraka, "whose thoughts *do* you hear?"

Steeling himself, Morfad said flatly, "Those of Terran dogs."

"Dogs?" Haraka lay back and stared at him. "*Dogs?* Are you serious?"

"I have never been more so. I can hear dogs and no others. Don't ask me why because I don't know. It is a freak of circumstance."

"And you have listened to their minds ever since we jumped to Earth?"

"Yes."

"What sort of things have you heard?"

"I have had pearls of alien wisdom cast before me," declared Morfad, "and the longer I look at them the more they scare hell out of me."

"Get busy frightening me with a few examples," invited Haraka, suppressing a smile.

"Quote: the supreme test of intelligence is the ability to live as one pleases without working," recited Morfad. "Quote: the art of retribution is that of concealing it beyond all suspicion. Quote: the sharpest, most subtle, most effective weapon in the cosmos is flattery."

"Huh?"

"Quote: if a thing can think it likes to think that it is God – treat it as God and it becomes your willing slave."

"Oh, no!" denied Haraka.

"Oh, *yes!*" insisted Morfad. He waved a hand toward the nearest port. "Out there are three thousand million petty gods. They are eagerly panted after, fawned upon, gazed upon with worshiping eyes. Gods are very gracious toward those who love them." He made a spitting sound that lent emphasis to what followed. "The lovers know it – and love comes cheap."

Haraka said, uneasily, "I think you're crazy."

"Quote: to rule successfully the ruled must be unconscious of it." Again the spitting sound. "Is that crazy? I don't think so. It makes sense. It works. It's working out there right now."

"But –"

"Take a look at this." He tossed a small object into Haraka's lap. "Recognize it?"

"Yes, it's what they call a cracker."

"Correct. To make it some Terrans plowed fields in all kinds of weather, rain, wind and sunshine, sowed wheat, reaped it with the aid of machinery other Terrans had sweated to build. They transported the wheat, stored it, milled it, enriched the flour by various processes, baked it, packaged it, shipped it all over the world. When humanoid Terrans want crackers they've got to put in man-hours to get them."

"So –"

"When a dog wants one he sits up, waves his forepaws and admires his god. That's all. Just that."

"But, darn it, man, dogs are relatively stupid."

"So it seems," said Morfad, dryly.

"They can't really *do* anything effective."

"That depends upon what one regards as effective."

"They haven't got hands."

"And don't need them – having brains."

"Now see here," declaimed Haraka, openly irritated, "we Altairans invented and constructed ships capable of roaming the spaces between the stars. The Terrans have done the same. Terran dogs have not done it and won't do it in the next million years. When one dog has the brains and ability to get to another planet I'll eat my cap."

"You can do that right now," Morfad suggested. "We have two dogs on board."

Haraka let go a grunt of disdain. "The Terrans have given us those as a memento."

"Sure they gave them to us – at whose behest?"

"It was wholly a spontaneous gesture."

"Was it?"

"Are you suggesting that dogs put the idea into their heads?" Haraka demanded.

"I know they did," retorted Morfad, looking grim. "And we've not been given two males or two females. Oh no, sir, not on your life. One male and one female. The givers said we could breed them. Thus in due course our own worlds can become illuminated with the undying love of man's best friend."

"Nuts!" said Haraka.

Morfad gave back, "You're obsessed with the old, out-of-date idea that conquest must be preceded by aggression. Can't you understand that a wholly alien species just naturally uses wholly alien methods? Dogs employ their own tactics, not ours. It isn't within their nature or abilities to take us over with the aid of ships, guns and a great hullabaloo. It *is* within their nature and abilities to creep in upon us, their eyes shining with hero-worship. If we don't watch out, we'll be mastered by a horde of loving creepers."

"I can invent a word for your mental condition," said Haraka. "You're suffering from caniphobia."

"With good reasons."

"Imaginary ones."

"Yesterday I looked into a dogs' beauty shop. Who was doing the bathing, scenting, powdering, primping? Other dogs? Hah! Humanoid females were busy dolling 'em up. Was *that* imaginary?"

"You can call it a Terran eccentricity. It means nothing whatever. Besides, we've quite a few funny habits of our own."

"You're dead right there," Morfad agreed. "And I know one of yours. So does the entire crew."

Haraka narrowed his eyes. "You might as well name it. I am not afraid to see myself as others see me."

"All right. You've asked for it. You think a lot of Kashim. He always has your ear. You will listen to him when you'll listen to nobody else. Everything he says makes sound sense – to you."

"So you're jealous of Kashim, eh?"

"Not in the least," assured Morfad, making a disparaging gesture. "I merely despise him for the same reason that everyone else holds him in contempt. He is a professional toady. He spends most of his time fawning upon you, flattering you, pandering to your ego. He is a natural-born creeper who gives you the Terradog treatment. You like it. You bask in it. It affects you like an irresistible drug. It works – and don't tell me that it doesn't because all of us know that it *does*."

"I am not a fool. I have Kashim sized up. He does not influence me to the extent you believe."

"Three thousand million Terrans have four hundred million dogs sized up and are equally convinced that no dog has a say in anything worth a hoot."

"I don't believe it."

"Of course you don't. I had little hope that you would. Morfad is telling you these things and Morfad is either crazy or a liar. But if Kashim were to tell you while prostrate at the foot of your throne you would swallow his story hook, line and sinker. Kashim has a Terradog mind and uses Terradog logic, see?"

"My disbelief has better basis than that."

"For instance?" Morfad invited.

"Some Terrans are telepathic. Therefore if this myth of subtle mastery by dogs were a fact, they'd know of it. Not a dog would be left alive on this world." Haraka paused, finished pointedly, "They don't know of it."

"Terran telepaths hear the minds of their own kind but not those of dogs. I hear the minds of dogs but not those of any other kind. As I said before, I don't know why this should be. I know only that it *is*."

"It seems nonsensical to me."

"It would. I suppose you can't be blamed for taking that viewpoint. My position is difficult; I'm like the only one with ears in a world that is stone-deaf."

Haraka thought it over, said after a while, "Suppose I were to accept everything you've said at face value – what do you think I should do about it?"

"Refuse to take the dogs," responded Morfad, promptly.

"That's more easily said than done. Good relations with the Terrans are vitally important. How can I reject a warm-hearted gift without offending the givers?"

"All right, don't reject it. Modify it instead. Ask for two male or two female dogs. Make it plausible by quoting an Altairan law against the importation of alien animals that are capable of natural increase."

"I can't do that. It's far too late. We've already accepted the animals and expressed our gratitude for them. Besides, their ability to breed is essential part of the gift, the basic intention of the givers. They've presented us with a new species, an entire race of dogs."

"You said it!" confirmed Morfad.

"For the same reason we can't very well prevent them from breeding when we get back home," Haraka pointed. "From now on we and the Terrans are going to do a lot of visiting. Immediately they discover that our dogs have failed to multiply they'll become generous and sentimental and dump another dozen on us. Or maybe a hundred. We'll then be worse off than we were before."

"All right, all right." Morfad shrugged with weary resignation. "If you're going to concoct a major objection to every possible solution we may as well surrender without a fight. Let's abandon ourselves to becoming yet another dog-dominated species. Requote: to rule successfully the ruled must be unconscious of it." He gave Haraka the sour eye. "If I had my way, I'd wait until we were far out in free space and then give those two dogs the hearty heave-ho out the hatch."

Haraka grinned in the manner of one about to nail down a cockeyed tale once and for all. "And if you did that it would be proof positive beyond all argument that you're afflicted with a delusion."

Emitting a deep sigh, Morfad asked, "Why would it?"

"You'd be slinging out two prime members of the master race. Some domination, eh?" Haraka grinned again. "Listen, Morfad, according to your own story you know something never before known or suspected and you're the only one who does know it. That should make you a mighty menace to the entire species of dogs. They wouldn't let you live long enough to thwart them or even to go round advertising the truth. You'd soon be deader than a low-strata fossil." He walked to the door, held it open while he made his parting shot. "You look healthy enough to me."

Morfad shouted at the closing door, "Doesn't follow that because I can hear their thoughts they must necessarily hear mine. I doubt that they can because it's just a freakish –"

The door clicked shut. He scowled at it, walked twenty times up and down the cabin, finally resumed his chair and sat in silence while he beat his brains around in search of a satisfactory solution.

"The sharpest, most subtle, most effective weapon in the cosmos is flattery."

Yes, he was seeking a means of coping with fourfooted warriors incredibly skilled in the use of Creation's sharpest weapon. Professional fawners, creepers, worshipers, man-lovers, ego-boosters, trained to near-perfection through countless generations in an art against which there seemed no decisive defense.

How to beat off the coming attack, contain it, counter it?

"Yes, God!"

"Certainly, God!"

"Anything you say, God!"

How to protect oneself against this insidious technique, how to quarantine it or –

By the stars! that was it – *quarantine* them! On Pladamine, the useless world, the planet nobody wanted. They could breed there to their limits and meanwhile dominate the herbs and bugs. And a soothing reply would be ready for any nosy Terran tourist.

"The dogs? Oh, sure, we've still got them, lots of them. They're doing fine. Got a nice world of their very own. Place called Pladamine. If you wish to go see them, it can be arranged."

A wonderful idea. It would solve the problem while creating no hard feelings among the Terrans. It would prove useful in the future and to the end of time. Once planted on Pladamine no dog could ever escape by its own efforts. Any tourists from Terra who brought dogs along could be persuaded to leave them in the canine heaven specially created by Altair. There the dogs would find themselves unable to boss anything higher than other dogs, and, if they didn't like it, they could lump it.

No use putting the scheme to Haraka, who was obviously prejudiced. He'd save it for the authorities back home. Even if they found it hard to credit his story, they'd still take the necessary action on the principle that it is better to be sure than sorry. Yes, they'd play safe and give Pladamine to the dogs.

Standing on a cabin seat, he gazed out and down through the port. A great mob of Terrans, far below, waited to witness the coming takeoff and cheer them on their way. He noticed beyond the back of the crowd a small, absurdly groomed dog dragging a Terran female at the end of a thin, light chain. Poor girl, he thought. The dog leads, she follows yet believes *she* is taking *it* some place.

Finding his color-camera, he checked its controls, walked along the corridor and into the open air lock. It would be nice to have a picture of the big send-off audience. Reaching the rim of the lock he tripped headlong over something four-legged and stubby-tailed that suddenly intruded itself between his feet. He dived outward, the camera still in his grip, and went down fast through the whistling wind while shrill feminine screams came from among the watching crowd.

Haraka said, "The funeral has delayed us two days. We'll have to make up the time as best we can." He brooded a moment, added, "I am very sorry about Morfad. He had a brilliant mind but it was breaking up toward the end. Oh well, it's a comfort that the expedition has suffered only one fatality."

"It could have been worse, sir," responded Kashim. "It could have been you. Praise the heavens that it was not."

"Yes, it could have been me." Haraka regarded him curiously. "And would it have grieved you, Kashim?"

"Very much indeed, sir. I don't think anyone aboard would feel the loss more deeply. My respect and admiration are such that –"

He ceased as something padded softly into the cabin, laid its head in Haraka's lap, gazed soulfully up at the captain. Kashim frowned with annoyance.

"Good boy!" approved Haraka, scratching the newcomer's ears.

"My respect and admiration," repeated Kashim in louder tones, "are such that –"

"Good boy!" said Haraka again. He gently pulled one ear, then the other, observed with pleasure the vibrating tail.

"As I was saying, sir, my respect –"

"Good boy!" Deaf to all else, Haraka slid a hand down from the ears and massaged under the jaw.

Kashim favored Good Boy with a glare of inutterable hatred. The dog rolled a brown eye sideways and looked at him without expression. From that moment Kashim's fate was sealed.

A Death in the House

Clifford D. Simak

Although his best work was produced in the 1950s and early 1960s, and his later work became perhaps a little too repetitive of old themes, I would still rank Simak (1904–88) amongst my top ten favourite sf writers. And that's because he was a voice on his own. No one else produced science fiction like Simak. Although he could write high-tech stuff if he chose, most of the time he chose not to. What interested Simak were everyday folks with their everyday robots and everyday dogs (sentient or otherwise) and everyday aliens. The typical Simak story involves a loner in a rural setting, quite often a farmer in the American mid-west, to whom something unusual happens. Simak reworked that theme over and over again but always with remarkable freshness, often with humour, sometimes with profound poignancy, as in the following. He could achieve this at novel length – check out his masterpiece, the award-winning Way Station *(1963). He could do it at novella length – the award-winning "The Big Front Yard"* Astounding, *November 1958). He could do it with the short story – the award-winning "Grotto of the Dancing Deer" (*Analog, *April 1980). Oh, and he could do it with the story series – yep, another award-winner;* City *(1952). The Science Fiction Writers of America voted Simak a Grand Master in 1976, and I doubt there'll ever be another like him.*

O ld Mose Abrams was out hunting cows when he found the alien. He didn't know it was an alien, but it was alive and it was in a lot of trouble and Old Mose, despite everything the neighbors said about him, was not the kind of man who could bear to leave a sick thing out there in the woods.

It was a horrid-looking thing, green and shiny, with some purple spots on it, and it was repulsive even twenty feet away. And it stank.

It had crawled, or tried to crawl, into a clump of hazel brush, but hadn't made it. The head part was in the brush and the rest lay out there naked in the open. Every now and then the parts that seemed to be arms and hands clawed feebly at the ground, trying to force itself deeper in the brush, but it was too weak; it never moved an inch.

It was groaning, too, but not too loud – just the kind of keening sound a lonesome wind might make around a wide, deep eave. But there was more in it than just the sound of winter wind; there was a frightened, desperate note that made the hair stand up on Old Mose's nape.

Old Mose stood there for quite a spell, making up his mind what he ought to do about it, and a while longer after that working up his courage, although most folks offhand would have said that he had plenty. But this was the sort of situation that took more than just ordinary screwed-up courage. It took a lot of foolhardiness.

But this was a wild, hurt thing and he couldn't leave it there, so he walked up to it and knelt down, and it was pretty hard to look at, though there was a sort of fascination in its repulsiveness that was hard to figure out – as if it were so horrible that it dragged one to it. And it stank in a way that no one had ever smelled before.

Mose, however, was not finicky. In the neighborhood, he was not well known for fastidity. Ever since his wife had died almost ten years before, he had lived alone on his untidy farm and the housekeeping that he did was the scandal of all the neighbor women. Once a year, if he got around to it, he sort of shoveled out the house, but the rest of the year he just let things accumulate.

So he wasn't as upset as some might have been with the

way the creature smelled. But the sight of it upset him, and it took him quite a while before he could bring himself to touch it, and when he finally did, he was considerably surprised. He had been prepared for it to be either cold or slimy, or maybe even both. But it was neither. It was warm and hard and it had a clean feel to it, and he was reminded of the way a green corn stalk would feel.

He slid his hand beneath the hurt thing and pulled it gently from the clump of hazel brush and turned it over so he could see its face. It hadn't any face. It had an enlargement at the top of it, like a flower on top of a stalk, although its body wasn't any stalk, and there was a fringe around this enlargement that wiggled like a can of worms, and it was then that Mose almost turned around and ran.

But he stuck it out.

He squatted there, staring at the no-face with the fringe of worms, and he got cold all over and his stomach doubled up on him and he was stiff with fright – and the fright got worse when it seemed to him that the keening of the thing was coming from the worms.

Mose was a stubborn man. One had to be stubborn to run a runty farm like his. Stubborn and insensitive in a lot of ways. But not insensitive, of course, to a thing in pain.

Finally he was able to pick it up and hold it in his arms and there was nothing to it, for it didn't weigh much. Less than a half-grown shoat, he figured.

He went up the woods path with it, heading back for home, and it seemed to him the smell of it was less. He was hardly scared at all and he was warm again and not cold all over.

For the thing was quieter now and keening just a little. And although he could not be sure of it, there were times when it seemed as if the thing were snuggling up to him, the way a scared and hungry baby will snuggle to any grown person that comes and picks it up.

Old Mose reached the buildings and he stood out in the yard a minute, wondering whether he should take it to the barn or house. The barn, of course, was the natural place for it, for it wasn't human – it wasn't even as close to human as a dog or cat or sick lamb would be.

He didn't hesitate too long, however. He took it into the house and laid it on what he called a bed, next to the kitchen stove. He got it straightened out all neat and orderly and pulled a dirty blanket over it, and then went to the stove and stirred up the fire until there was some flame.

Then he pulled up a chair beside the bed and had a good, hard, wondering look at this thing he had brought home. It had quieted down a lot and seemed more comfortable than it had out in the woods. He tucked the blanket snug around it with a tenderness that surprised himself. He wondered what he had that it might eat, and even if he knew, how he'd manage feeding it, for it seemed to have no mouth.

"But you don't need to worry none," he told it. "Now that I got you under a roof, you'll be all right. I don't know too much about it, but I'll take care of you the best I can."

By now it was getting on toward evening, and he looked out the window and saw that the cows he had been hunting had come home by themselves.

"I got to go get the milking done and the other chores," he told the thing lying on the bed, "but it won't take me long. I'll be right back."

Old Mose loaded up the stove so the kitchen would stay warm and he tucked the thing in once again, then got his milk pails and went down to the barn.

He fed the sheep and pigs and horses and he milked the cows. He hunted eggs and shut the chicken house. He pumped a tank of water.

Then he went back to the house.

It was dark now and he lit the oil lamp on the table, for he was against electricity. He'd refused to sign up when REA had run out the line and a lot of the neighbors had gotten sore at him for being uncooperative. Not that he cared, of course.

He had a look at the thing upon the bed. It didn't seem to be any better, or any worse, for that matter. If it had been a sick lamb or an ailing calf, he could have known right off how it was getting on, but this thing was different. There was no way to tell.

He fixed himself some supper and ate it and wished he knew how to feed the thing. And he wished, too, that he knew how to help it. He'd got it under shelter and he had it warm, but was that right or wrong for something like this? He had no idea.

He wondered if he should try to get some help, then felt squeamish about asking help when he couldn't say exactly what had to be helped. But then he wondered how he would feel himself if he were in a far, strange country, all played out and sick, and no one to get him any help because they didn't know exactly what he was.

That made up his mind for him and he walked over to the phone. But should he call a doctor or a veterinarian? He decided to call the doctor because the thing was in the house. If it had been in the barn, he would have called the veterinarian.

He was on a rural line and the hearing wasn't good and he was halfway deaf, so he didn't use the phone too often. He had told himself at times it was nothing but another aggravation and there had been a dozen times he had threatened to have it taken out. But now he was glad he hadn't.

The operator got old Doctor Benson and they couldn't hear one another too well, but Mose finally made the doctor understand who was calling and that he needed him and the doctor said he'd come.

With some relief, Mose hung up the phone and was just standing there, not doing anything, when he was struck by the thought that there might be others of these things down there in the woods. He had no idea what they were or what they might be doing or where they might be going, but it was pretty evident that the one upon the bed was some sort of stranger from a very distant place. It stood to reason that there might be more than one of them, for far traveling was a lonely business and anyone – or anything – would like to have some company along.

He got the lantern down off the peg and lit it and went stumping out the door. The night was as black as a stack of cats and the lantern light was feeble, but that made not a bit of difference, for Mose knew this farm of his like the back of his hand.

He went down the path into the woods. It was a spooky place, but it took more than woods at night to spook Old Mose. At the place where he had found the thing, he looked around, pushing through the brush and holding the lantern high so he could see a bigger area, but he didn't find another one of them.

He did find something else, though — a sort of outsize birdcage made of metal lattice work that had wrapped itself around an eight-inch hickory tree. He tried to pull it loose, but it was jammed so tight that he couldn't budge it.

He sighted back the way it must have come. He could see where it had plowed its way through the upper branches of the trees, and out beyond were stars, shining bleakly with the look of far away.

Mose had no doubt that the thing lying on his bed beside the kitchen stove had come in this birdcage contraption. He marveled some at that, but he didn't fret himself too much, for the whole thing was so unearthly that he knew he had little chance of pondering it out.

He walked back to the house and he scarcely had the lantern blown out and hung back on its peg than he heard a car drive up.

The doctor, when he came up to the door, became a little grumpy at seeing Old Mose standing there.

"You don't look sick to me," the doctor said. "Not sick enough to drag me clear out here at night."

"I ain't sick," said Mose.

"Well, then," said the doctor, more grumpily than ever, "what did you mean by phoning me?"

"I got someone who is sick," said Mose. "I hope you can help him. I would have tried myself, but I don't know how to go about it."

The doctor came inside and Mose shut the door behind him.

"You got something rotten in here?" asked the doctor.

"No, it's just the way he smells. It was pretty bad at first, but I'm getting used to it by now."

The doctor saw the thing lying on the bed and went over

to it. Old Mose heard him sort of gasp and could see him standing there, very stiff and straight. Then he bent down and had a good look at the critter on the bed.

When he straightened up and turned around to Mose, the only thing that kept him from being downright angry was that he was so flabbergasted.

"Mose," he yelled, "what *is* this?"

"I don't know," said Mose. "I found it in the woods and it was hurt and wailing and I couldn't leave it there."

"You think it's sick?"

"I know it is," said Mose. "It needs help awful bad. I'm afraid it's dying."

The doctor turned back to the bed again and pulled the blanket down, then went and got the lamp so that he could see. He looked the critter up and down, and he prodded it with a skittish finger, and he made the kind of mysterious clucking sound that only doctors make.

Then he pulled the blanket back over it again and took the lamp back to the table.

"Mose," he said, "I can't do a thing for it."

"But you're a doctor!"

"A human doctor, Mose. I don't know what this thing is, but it isn't human. I couldn't even guess what is wrong with it, if anything. And I wouldn't know what could be safely done for it even if I could diagnose its illness. I'm not even sure it's an animal. There are a lot of things about it that argue it's a plant."

Then the doctor asked Mose straight out how he came to find it and Mose told him exactly how it happened. But he didn't tell him anything about the birdcage, for when he thought about it, it sounded so fantastic that he couldn't bring himself to tell it. Just finding the critter and having it here was bad enough, without throwing in the birdcage.

"I tell you what," the doctor said. "You got something here that's outside all human knowledge. I doubt there's ever been a thing like this seen on Earth before. I have no idea what it is and I wouldn't try to guess. If I were you, I'd get in touch with the university up at Madison. There might be someone there who could get it figured out. Even if they couldn't they'd be interested. They'd want to study it."

Mose went to the cupboard and got the cigar box almost full of silver dollars and paid the doctor. The doctor put the dollars in his pocket, joshing Mose about his eccentricity.

But Mose was stubborn about his silver dollars. "Paper money don't seem legal, somehow," he declared. "I like the feel of silver and the way it clinks. It's got authority."

The doctor left and he didn't seem as upset as Mose had been afraid he might be. As soon as he was gone, Mose pulled up a chair and sat down beside the bed.

It wasn't right, he thought, that the thing should be so sick and no one to help – no one who knew any way to help it.

He sat in the chair and listened to the ticking of the clock, loud in the kitchen silence, and the crackling of the wood burning in the stove.

Looking at the thing lying on the bed, he had an almost fierce hope that it could get well again and stay with him. Now that its birdcage was all banged up, maybe there'd be nothing it could do but stay. And he hoped it would, for already the house felt less lonely.

Sitting in the chair between the stove and bed, Mose realized how lonely it had been. It had not been quite so bad until Towser died. He had tried to bring himself to get another dog, but he never had been able to. For there was no dog that would take the place of Towser and it had seemed unfaithful to even try. He could have gotten a cat, of course, but that would remind him too much of Molly; she had been very fond of cats, and until the time she died, there had always been two or three of them underfoot around the place.

But now he was alone. Alone with his farm and his stubbornness and his silver dollars. The doctor thought, like all the rest of them, that the only silver Mose had was in the cigar box in the cupboard. There wasn't one of them who knew about the old iron kettle piled plumb full of them, hidden underneath the floor boards of the living room. He chuckled at the thought of how he had them fooled. He'd give a lot to see his neighbors' faces if they could only know. But he was not the one to tell them. If they were to find it out, they'd have to find it out themselves.

He nodded in the chair and finally he slept, sitting upright, with his chin resting on his chest and his crossed arms wrapped around himself as if to keep him warm.

When he woke, in the dark before the dawn, with the lamp flickering on the table and the fire in the stove burned low, the alien had died.

There was no doubt of death. The thing was cold and rigid and the husk that was its body was rough and drying out – as a corn stalk in the field dries out, whipping in the wind once the growing had been ended.

Mose pulled the blanket up to cover it, and although this was early to do the chores, he went out by lantern light and got them done.

After breakfast, he heated water and washed his face and shaved, and it was the first time in years he'd shaved any day but Sunday. Then he put on his one good suit and slicked down his hair and got the old jalopy out of the machine shed and drove into town.

He hunted up Eb Dennison, the town clerk, who also was the secretary of the cemetery association.

"Eb," he said, "I want to buy a lot."

"But you've got a lot," protested Eb.

"That plot," said Mose, "is a family plot. There's just room for me and Molly."

"Well, then," asked Eb, "why another one? You have no other members of the family."

"I found someone in the woods," said Mose. "I took him home and he died last night. I plan to bury him."

"If you found a dead man in the woods," Eb warned him, "you better notify the coroner and sheriff."

"In time I may," said Mose, not intending to. "Now how about that plot?"

Washing his hands of the affair entirely, Eb sold him the plot.

Having bought his plot, Mose went to the undertaking establishment run by Albert Jones.

"Al," he said, "there's been a death out at the house. A stranger I found out in the woods. He doesn't seem to have anyone and I aim to take care of it."

"You got a death certificate?" asked Al, who subscribed to none of the niceties affected by most funeral parlor operators.

"Well, no, I haven't."

"Was there a doctor in attendance?"

"Doc Benson came out last night."

"He should have made you out one. I'll give him a ring."

He phoned Doctor Benson and talked with him a while and got red around the gills. He finally slammed down the phone and turned on Mose.

"I don't know what you're trying to pull off," he fumed, "but Doc tells me this thing of yours isn't even human. I don't take care of dogs or cats or –"

"This ain't no dog or cat."

"I don't care what it is. It's got to be human for me to handle it. And don't go trying to bury it in the cemetery, because it's against the law."

Considerably discouraged, Mose left the undertaking parlor and trudged slowly up the hill toward the town's one and only church.

He found the minister in his study working on a sermon. Mose sat down in a chair and fumbled his battered hat around and around in his work-scarred hands.

"Parson," he said, "I'll tell you the story from first to last," and he did. He added, "I don't know what it is. I guess no one else does, either. But it's dead and in need of decent burial and that's the least that I can do. I can't bury it in the cemetery, so I suppose I'll have to find a place for it on the farm. I wonder if you could bring yourself to come out and say a word or two."

The minister gave the matter some deep consideration.

"I'm sorry, Mose," he said at last. "I don't believe I can. I am not sure at all the church would approve of it."

"This thing may not be human," said Old Mose, "but it is one of God's critters."

The minister thought some more, and did some wondering out loud, but made up his mind finally that he couldn't do it.

So Mose went down the street to where his car was waiting and drove home, thinking about what heels some humans are.

Back at the farm again, he got a pick and shovel and went into the garden, and there, in one corner of it, he dug a grave. He went out to the machine shed to hunt up some boards to make the thing a casket, but it turned out that he had used the last of the lumber to patch up the hog pen.

Mose went to the house and dug around in a chest in one of the back rooms which had not been used for years, hunting for a sheet to use as a winding shroud, since there would be no casket. He couldn't find a sheet, but he did unearth an old white linen table cloth. He figured that would do, so he took it to the kitchen.

He pulled back the blanket and looked at the critter lying there in death and a sort of lump came into his throat at the thought of it – how it had died so lonely and so far from home without a creature of its own to spend its final hours with. And naked, too, without a stitch of clothing and with no possession, with not a thing to leave behind as a re-membrance of itself.

He spread the table cloth out on the floor beside the bed and lifted the thing and laid it on the table cloth. As he laid it down, he saw the pocket in it – if it was a pocket – a sort of slitted flap in the center of what could be its chest. He ran his hand across the pocket area. There was a lump inside it. He crouched for a long moment beside the body, wondering what to do.

Finally he reached his fingers into the flap and took out the thing that bulged. It was a ball, a little bigger than a tennis ball, made of cloudy glass – or, at least, it looked like glass. He squatted there, staring at it, then took it to the window for a better look.

There was nothing strange at all about the ball. It was just a cloudy ball of glass and it had a rough, dead feel about it, just as the body had.

He shook his head and took it back and put it where he'd

found it and wrapped the body securely in the cloth. He carried it to the garden and put it in the grave. Standing solemnly at the head of the grave, he said a few short words aid then shoveled in the dirt.

He had meant to make a mound above the grave and he had intended to put up a cross, but at the last he didn't do either one of these. There would be snoopers. The word would get around and they'd be coming out and hunting for the spot where he had buried this thing he had found out in the woods. So there must be no mound to mark the place and no cross as well. Perhaps it was for the best, he told himself, for what could he have carved or written on the cross?

By this time it was well past noon and he was getting hungry, but he didn't stop to eat, because there were other things to do. He went out into the pasture and caught up Bess and hitched her to the stoneboat and went down into the woods.

He hitched her to the birdcage that was wrapped around the tree and she pulled it loose as pretty as you please. Then he loaded it on the stoneboat and hauled it up the hill and stowed it in the back of the machine shed, in the far corner by the forge.

After that, he hitched Bess to the garden plow and gave the garden a cultivating that it didn't need so it would be fresh dirt all over and no one could locate where he'd dug the grave.

He was just finishing the plowing when Sheriff Doyle drove up and got out of the car. The sheriff was a soft-spoken man, but he was no dawdler. He got right to the point.

"I hear," he said, "you found something in the woods."

"That I did," said Mose.

"I hear it died on you."

"Sheriff, you heard right."

"I'd like to see it, Mose."

"Can't. I buried it. And I ain't telling where."

"Mose," the sheriff said, "I don't want to make you trouble, but you did an illegal thing. You can't go finding people in the woods and just bury them when they up and die on you."

"You talk to Doc Benson?"

The sheriff nodded. "He said it wasn't any kind of thing he'd ever seen before. He said it wasn't human."

"Well, then," said Mose, "I guess that lets you out. If it wasn't human, there could be no crime against a person. And if it wasn't owned, there ain't any crime against property. There's been no one around to claim they owned the thing, is there?"

The sheriff rubbed his chin. "No, there hasn't. Maybe you're right. Where did you study law?"

"I never studied law. I never studied nothing. I just use common sense."

"Doc said something about the folks up at the university might want a look at it."

"I tell you, Sheriff," said Mose. "This thing came here from somewhere and it died. I don't know where it came from and I don't know what it was and I don't hanker none to know. To me it was just a living thing that needed help real bad. It was alive and it had its dignity and in death it commanded some respect. When the rest of you refused it decent burial, I did the best I could. And that is all there is to it."

"All right, Mose," the sheriff said, "if that's how you want it."

He turned around and stalked back to the car. Mose stood beside old Bess hitched to her plow and watched him drive away. He drove fast and reckless as if he might be angry.

Mose put the plow away and turned the horse back to the pasture and by now it was time to do chores again.

He got the chores all finished and made himself some supper and after supper sat beside the stove, listening to the ticking of the clock, loud in the silent house, and the crackle of the fire.

All night long the house was lonely.

The next afternoon, as he was plowing corn, a reporter came and walked up the row with him and talked with him when he came to the end of the row. Mose didn't like this reporter much. He was too flip and he asked some funny questions, so Mose clammed up and didn't tell him much.

★   ★   ★

A few days later, a man showed up from the university and showed him the story the reporter had gone back and written. The story made fun of Mose.

"I'm sorry," the professor said. "These newspapermen are unaccountable. I wouldn't worry too much about anything they write."

"I don't," Mose told him.

The man from the university asked a lot of questions and made quite a point about how important it was that he should see the body.

But Mose only shook his head. "It's at peace," he said. "I aim to leave it that way."

The man went away disgusted, but still quite dignified.

For several days there were people driving by and dropping in, the idly curious, and there were some neighbors Mose hadn't seen for months. But he gave them all short shrift and in a little while they left him alone and he went on with his farming and the house stayed lonely.

He thought again that maybe he should get a dog, but he thought of Towser and he couldn't do it.

One day, working in the garden, he found the plant that grew out of the grave. It was a funny-looking plant and his first impulse was to root it out.

But he didn't do it, for the plant intrigued him. It was a kind he'd never seen before and he decided he would let it grow, for a while at least, to see what kind it was. It was a bulky, fleshy plant, with heavy, dark-green, curling leaves, and it reminded him in some ways of the skunk cabbage that burgeoned in the woods come spring.

There was another visitor, the queerest of the lot. He was a dark and intense man who said he was the president of a flying saucer club. He wanted to know if Mose had talked with the thing he'd found out in the woods and seemed terribly disappointed when Mose told him he hadn't. He wanted to know if Mose had found a vehicle the creature might have traveled in and Mose lied to him about it. He was afraid, the wild way the man was acting, that he might demand to search the place, and if he had, he'd likely have found the birdcage hidden in the machine shed back in the corner by the forge. But the man got to lecturing Mose about withholding vital information.

Finally Mose had taken all he could of it, so he stepped into the house and picked up the shotgun from behind the door. The president of the flying saucer club said good-by rather hastily and got out of there.

Farm life went on as usual, with the corn laid by and the haying started and out in the garden the strange plant kept on growing and now was taking shape. Old Mose couldn't believe his eyes when he saw the sort of shape it took and he spent long evening hours just standing in the garden, watching it and wondering if his loneliness were playing tricks on him.

The morning came when he found the plant standing at the door and waiting for him. He should have been surprised, of course, but he really wasn't, for he had lived with it, watching it of eventide, and although he had not dared admit it even to himself, he had known what it was.

For here was the creature he'd found in the woods, no longer sick and keening, no longer close to death, but full of life and youth.

It was not the same entirely, though. He stood and looked at it and could see the differences – the little differences that might have been those between youth and age, or between a father and a son, or again the differences expressed in an evolutionary pattern.

"Good morning," said Mose, not feeling strange at all to be talking to the thing. "It's good to have you back."

The thing standing in the yard did not answer him. But that was not important; he had not expected that it would. The one important point was that he had something he could talk to.

"I'm going out to do the chores," said Mose. "You want to tag along?"

It tagged along with him and it watched him as he did the chores and he talked to it, which was a vast improvement over talking to himself.

At breakfast, he laid an extra plate for it and pulled up an extra chair, but it turned out the critter was not equipped to use a chair, for it wasn't hinged to sit.

Nor did it eat. That bothered Mose at first, for he was hospitable, but he told himself that a big, strong, strapping youngster like this one knew enough to take care of itself, and he probably didn't need to worry too much about how it got along.

After breakfast, he went out to the garden, with the critter accompanying him, and sure enough, the plant was gone. There was a collapsed husk lying on the ground, the outer covering that had been the cradle of the creature at his side.

Then he went to the machine shed and the creature saw the bird-cage and rushed over to it and looked it over minutely. Then it turned around to Mose and made a sort of pleading gesture.

Mose went over to it and laid his hands on one of the twisted bars and the critter stood beside him and laid its hands on, too, and they pulled together. It was no use. They could move the metal some, but not enough to pull it back in shape again.

They stood and looked at one another, although looking may not be the word, for the critter had no eyes to look with. It made some funny motions with its hands, but Mose couldn't understand. Then it lay down on the floor and showed him how the birdcage ribs were fastened to the base.

It took a while for Mose to understand how the fastening worked and he never did know exactly why it did. There wasn't, actually, any reason that it should work that way.

First you applied some pressure, just the right amount at the exact and correct angle, and the bar would move a little. Then you applied some more pressure, again the exact amount and at the proper angle, and the bar would move some more. You did this three times and the bar came loose, although there was, God knows, no reason why it should.

Mose started a fire in the forge and shoveled in some coal and worked the bellows while the critter watched. But when he picked up the bar to put it in the fire, the critter got between him and the forge and wouldn't let him near. Mose realized then he couldn't – or wasn't supposed to – heat the bar to straighten it and he never questioned the entire rightness of it. For, he told himself, this thing must surely know the proper way to do it.

So he took the bar over to the anvil and started hammering it back into shape again, cold, without the use of fire, while the critter tried to show him the shape that it should be. It took quite a while, but finally it was straightened out to the critter's satisfaction.

Mose figured they'd have themselves a time getting the bar back in place again, but it slipped on as slick as could be.

Then they took off another bar and this one went faster, now that Mose had the hang of it.

But it was hard and grueling labor. They worked all day and only straightened out five bars.

It took four solid days to get the bars on the birdcage hammered into shape and all the time the hay was waiting to be cut.

But it was all right with Mose. He had someone to talk to and the house had lost its loneliness.

When they got the bars back in place, the critter slipped into the cage and starting fooling with a dingus on the roof of it that looked like a complicated basket. Mose, watching, figured that the basket was some sort of control.

The critter was discouraged. It walked around the shed looking for something and seemed unable to find it. It came back to Mose and made its despairing, pleading gesture. Mose showed it iron and steel; he dug into a carton where he kept bolts and clamps and bushings and scraps of metal and other odds and ends, finding brass and copper and even some aluminum, but it wasn't any of these.

And Mose was glad – a bit ashamed for feeling glad, but glad all the same.

For it had been clear to him that when the birdcage was all ready, the critter would be leaving him. It had been impossible for Mose to stand in the way of the repair of the cage, or to refuse to help. But now that it apparently couldn't be, he found himself well pleased.

Now the critter would have to stay with him and he'd

have someone to talk to and the house would not be lonely. It would be welcome, he told himself, to have folks again. The critter was almost as good a companion as Towser.

Next morning, while Mose was fixing breakfast, he reached up in the cupboard to get the box of oatmeal and his hand struck the cigar box and it came crashing to the floor. It fell over on its side and the lid came open and the dollars went free-wheeling all around the kitchen.

Out of the corner of his eye, Mose saw the critter leaping quickly in pursuit of one of them. It snatched it up and turned to Mose, with the coin held between its fingers, and a sort of thrumming noise was coming out of the nest of worms on top of it.

It bent and scooped up more of them and cuddled them and danced a sort of jig, and Mose knew, with a sinking heart, that it had been silver the critter had been hunting.

So Mose got down on his hands and knees and helped the critter gather up all the dollars. They put them back into the cigar box and Mose picked up the box and gave it to the critter.

The critter took it and hefted it and had a disappointed look. Taking the box over to the table, it took the dollars out and stacked them in neat piles and Mose could see it was very disappointed.

Perhaps, after all, Mose thought, it had not been silver the thing had been hunting for. Maybe it had made a mistake in thinking that the silver was some other kind of metal.

Mose got down the oatmeal and poured it into some water and put it on the stove. When it was cooked and the coffee was ready, he carried his breakfast to the table and sat down to eat.

The critter still was standing across the table from him, stacking and restacking the piles of silver dollars. And now it showed him, with a hand held above the stacks, that it needed more of them. This many stacks, it showed him, and each stack so high.

Mose sat stricken, with a spoon full of oatmeal halfway to his mouth. He thought of all those other dollars, the iron kettle packed with them, underneath the floor boards in the living room. And he couldn't do it; they were the only thing he had – except the critter now. And he could not give them up so the critter could go and leave him too.

He ate his bowl of oatmeal without tasting it and drank two cups of coffee. And all the time the critter stood there and showed him how much more it needed.

"I can't do it for you," Old Mose said. "I've done all you can expect of any living being. I found you in the woods and I gave you warmth and shelter. I tried to help you, and when I couldn't, at least I gave you a place to die in. I buried you and protected you from all those other people and I did not pull you up when you started growing once again. Surely you can't expect me to keep on giving endlessly."

But it was no good. The critter could not hear him and he did not convince himself.

He got up from the table and walked into the living room with the critter trailing him. He loosened the floor boards and took out the kettle, and the critter, when it saw what was in the kettle, put its arms around itself and hugged in happiness.

They lugged the money out to the machine shed and Mose built a fire in the forge and put the kettle in the fire and started melting down that hard-saved money.

There were times he thought he couldn't finish the job, but he did.

The critter got the basket out of the birdcage and put it down beside the forge and dipped out the molten silver with an iron ladle and poured it here and there into the basket, shaping it in place with careful hammer taps.

It took a long time, for it was exacting work, but finally it was done and the silver almost gone. The critter lugged the basket back into the birdcage and fastened it in place.

It was almost evening now and Mose had to go and do the chores. He half expected the thing might haul out the birdcage and be gone when he came back to the house. And he tried to be sore at it for its selfishness – it had taken from him and had not tried to pay him back – it had not, so far as he could tell, even tried to thank him. But he made a poor job of being sore at it.

It was waiting for him when he came from the barn carrying two pails full of milk. It followed him inside the house and stood around and he tried to talk to it. But he didn't have the heart to do much talking. He could not forget that it would be leaving, and the pleasure of its present company was lost in his terror of the loneliness to come.

For now he didn't even have his money to help ward off the loneliness.

As he lay in bed that night, strange thoughts came creeping in upon him – the thought of an even greater loneliness than he had ever known upon this runty farm, the terrible, devastating loneliness of the empty wastes that lay between the stars, a driven loneliness while one hunted for a place or person that remained a misty thought one could not define, but which it was most important one should find.

It was a strange thing for him to be thinking, and quite suddenly he knew it was no thought of his, but of this other that was in the room with him.

He tried to raise himself, he fought to raise himself, but he couldn't do it. He held his head up a moment, then fell back upon the pillow and went sound asleep.

Next morning, after Mose had eaten breakfast, the two of them went to the machine shed and dragged the birdcage out. It stood there, a weird alien thing, in the chill brightness of the dawn.

The critter walked up to it and started to slide between two of the bars, but when it was halfway through, it stepped out again and moved over to confront Old Mose.

"Good-bye, friend," said Mose. "I'll miss you."

There was a strange stinging in his eyes.

The other held out its hand in farewell, and Mose took it and there was something in the hand he grasped, something round and smooth that was transferred from its hand to his.

The thing took its hand away and stepped quickly to the birdcage and slid between the bars. The hands reached for the basket and there was a sudden flicker and the birdcage was no longer there.

Mose stood lonely in the barnyard, looking at the place where there was no birdcage and remembering what he had felt or thought – or been told? – the night before as he lay in bed.

Already the critter would be there, out between the stars, in that black and utter loneliness, hunting for a place or thing or person that no human mind could grasp.

Slowly Mose turned around to go back to the house, to get the pails and go down to the barn to get the milking done.

He remembered the object in his hand and lifted his still-clenched fist in front of him. He opened his fingers and the little crystal ball lay there in his palm – and it was exactly like the one he'd found in the slitted flap in the body he had buried in the garden. Except that one had been dead and cloudy and this one had the living glow of a distant-burning fire.

Looking at it, he had the strange feeling of a happiness and comfort such as he had seldom known before, as if there were many people with him and all of them were friends.

He closed his hand upon it and the happiness stayed on – and it was all wrong, for there was not a single reason that he should be happy. The critter finally had left him and his money was all gone and he had no friends, but still he kept on feeling good.

He put the ball into his pocket and stepped spryly for the house to get the milking pails. He pursed up his whiskered lips and began to whistle and it had been a long, long time since he had even thought to whistle.

Maybe he was happy, he told himself, because the critter had not left without stopping to take his hand and try to say good-bye.

And a gift, no matter how worthless it might be, how cheap a trinket, still had a basic value in simple sentiment. It had been many years since anyone had bothered to give him a gift.

It was dark and lonely and unending in the depths of space with no Companion. It might be long before another was obtainable.

It perhaps was a foolish thing to do, but the old creature had been such a kind savage, so fumbling and so pitiful and eager to help. And one who travels far and fast must likewise travel light. There had been nothing else to give.

Refugium

Stephen Baxter

I opened this anthology with a brand new story and I'm closing it with one. Stephen Baxter (b. 1957) is one of Britain's major writers of science fiction. His first stories appeared in Interzone *from 1987, introducing his Xeelee sequence, but he first rose to international attention with* The Time Ships *(1995), his sequel to Wells's* The Time Machine. *He has since produced several highly acclaimed sf novels such as* Voyage *(1996) and* Titan *(1997), as well as collaborating with Arthur C. Clarke on* The Light of Other Days *(2000). He has recently started his Manifold series. This is planned as a multiverse epic exploring Fermi's Paradox: are we alone? It centres around astronaut Reid Malenfant and his family. The first book was* Time: Manifold One *(1999). The following story is the latest in the series.*

C elso and I were ejected from the *Sally Brind*. Frank Paulis had brought us to the Oort Cloud, that misty belt far from the sun where huge comets glide like deep-sea fish.

Before us, an alien craft sparkled in the starlight.

On the inside of my suit helmet a tiny softscreen popped into life and filled up with a picture of Paulis. He was wizened, somewhere over eighty years old, but his eyes glittered, sharp.

Even now, I begged. "Paulis. Don't make me do this."

Paulis was in a bathrobe; behind him steam billowed. He

was in his spa at the heart of the *Brind* – a luxury from which Celso and I had been excluded for the long hundred days it had taken to haul us all the way out here. "Your grandfather would be ashamed of you, Michael Malenfant. You forfeited choice when you let yourself be put up for sale in a debtors' auction."

"I just had a streak of bad luck."

"A streak spanning fifteen years hustling pool and a mountain of bad debts?"

Celso studied me with brown eyes full of pity. "Do not whine, my friend."

"Paulis, I don't care who the hell my grandfather was. You can see I'm no astronaut. I'm forty years old, for Christ's sake. And I'm not the brightest guy in the world –"

"True, but unimportant. The whole point of this experiment is to send humans where we haven't sent humans before. Exactly who probably doesn't matter. Look at the Bubble, Malenfant."

The alien ship was a ten-foot balloon plastered with rubies. Celso was already inspecting its interior in an intelligent sort of way.

Paulis said, "Remember your briefings. You can see it's a hollow sphere. There's an open hatchway. We know that if you close the hatch the device will accelerate away. We have evidence that its effective final speed is many times the speed of light. In fact, many millions of times."

"Impossible," said Celso.

Paulis smiled. "Evidently, not everyone agrees. What a marvellous adventure! I only wish I could come with you."

"Like hell you do, you dried-up old bastard."

He took a gloating sip from a frosted glass. "Malenfant, you are here because of faults in your personality."

"I'm here because of people like you."

Celso took my arm.

"In about two minutes," Paulis said cheerfully, "the pilot of the *Sally Brind* is going to come out of the airlock and shoot you both in the temple. Unless you're in that Bubble with the hatch closed."

Celso pushed me towards the glittering ball.

I said, "I won't forget you, Paulis. I'll be thinking of you every damn minute –"

But he only grinned.

My name is Reid Malenfant.

You know me, Michael. And you know I was always an incorrigible space cadet. I campaigned for, among other things, private mining expeditions to the asteroids. I hope you know my pal, Frank J. Paulis, who went out there and did what I only talked about.

But I don't want to talk about that. Not here, not in this letter. I want to be more personal. I want you to understand why your grandpappy gave over his life to a single, consuming project.

For me, it started with a simple question: What use are the stars?

Paulis had installed basic life-support gear in the Bubble. Celso already had his suit off and was busy collapsing our portable airlock.

Through the net-like walls of the Bubble I looked back at the *Sally Brind*. I could see at one extreme the fat cone shape of Paulis's Earth return capsule, and at the other end the angular, spidery form of the strut sections that held the nuke reactor and its shielding.

Beside our glittering toy-ship the *Brind* looked crude, as if knocked together by stone axes.

I had grown to hate the damn *Brind*. In the months since we left lunar orbit, she had become a prison to me. Now, as I looked back at her, drifting in this purposeless immensity, she looked like home.

When I took off my suit I found I'd suffered some oedema, swelling caused by the accumulation of fluid under my skin – in the webs of my fingers, in places where the zippers had run, and a few other places where the suit hadn't fitted as well as it should. The kind of stuff the astronauts never tell you about. But there was no pain, no loss of muscle or joint function that I could detect.

"Report," Paulis's voice, loud in our ears, ordered.

"The only instrument is a display, like a softscreen," said

Celso. He inspected it calmly. It showed a network of threads against a background of starlike dots.

"Your interpretation?"

"This may be an image of our destination. And if these are cosmic strings," Celso said dryly, "we are going further than I had imagined."

I wondered what the hell he was talking about. I looked more closely at the starlike dots. They were little spirals.

Galaxies?

Celso continued to poke around. "The life support equipment is functioning nominally."

"I've given you enough for about two months," said Paulis. "If you're not back by then, you probably won't be coming back at all."

Celso nodded.

"Time's up," Paulis said. "Shut the hatch, Malenfant."

I shot back, "You'll pay for this, Paulis."

"I don't think I'll be losing much sleep, frankly." Then, with steel: "Shut the hatch, Malenfant. I want to see you do it."

Celso touched my shoulder. "Do not be concerned, my friend." With a lot of dignity he pressed a wall-mounted push-button.

The hatch melted into the hull, closing us in.

The Bubble quivered. I clung to the soft wall.

Paulis's voice cut out. The sun disappeared. Electric-blue light pulsed in the sky. There was no sensation of movement.

But suddenly – impossibly – there was a planet outside, a fat steel-grey ball. A world of water. *Earth?*

It looked like Earth. But, despite my sudden, reluctant stab of hope, I knew immediately it was not Earth.

Celso's face was working as he gazed out of the Bubble, his softscreen jammed against the hull, gathering images. "A big world, larger than Earth – but what difference does that make? Higher surface gravity. More internal heat trapped. A thicker crust, but hotter, more flexible; lots of volcanoes. And the crust couldn't support mountains in that powerful gravity . . . Deep oceans, no mountains tall enough to peak out of the water – life clustering around deep-ocean thermal vents –"

"I don't understand," I said.

"We are already far from home."

I said tightly, "I can see that."

He looked at me steadily, and rested his hands on my shoulders. "Michael, *we have already been projected to the system of another star*. I think —"

There was a faint surge. I saw something like streetlamps flying past. And then a dim pool of light soaked across space below us.

Celso grunted. "Ah. I think we have accelerated."

With a click, the hull turned transparent as glass.

The streetlamps had been stars.

And the puddle of light was a swirl, a bulging yellow-white core wrapped around by streaky spiral-shaped arms.

It was the Galaxy. It fell away from us.

That was how far I had already come, how fast I was moving.

I assumed a foetal position and stayed that way for a long time.

As a kid I used to lie out on the lawn, soaking up dew and looking at the stars, trying to feel the Earth turning under me. It felt wonderful to be alive — hell, to be ten years old, anyhow. Michael, if you're ten years old when you get to read this, try it sometime. Even if you're a hundred, try it anyhow.

But even then I knew that the Earth was just a ball of rock, on the fringe of a nondescript galaxy. And I just couldn't believe that there was nobody out there looking back at me down here. Was it really possible that this was the only place where life had taken hold — that only here were there minds and eyes capable of looking out and wondering?

Because if so, what use are the stars? All those suns and worlds, spinning through the void, the grand complexity of creation unwinding all the way out of the Big Bang itself . . .

Even then I saw space as a high frontier, a sky to be mined, a resource for humanity. Still do. But is that all it is? Could the sky really be nothing more than an empty stage for mankind to strut and squabble?

And what if we blow ourselves up? Will the universe just

*evolve on, like a huge piece of clockwork slowly running down,
utterly devoid of life and mind? What would be the use of that?*

*Much later, I learned that this kind of "argument from
utility" goes back all the way to the Romans – Lucretius, in
fact, in the first century AD. Alien minds must exist, because
otherwise the stars would be purposeless. Right?*

Sure. But if so, where are they?

*I bet this bothers you too, Michael. Wouldn't be a Mal-
enfant otherwise!*

Celso spoke to me soothingly. Eventually I uncurled.

The sky was embroidered with knots and threads. A fat
grey cloud drifted past.

After a moment, with the help of Celso, I got it into
perspective. The embroidery was made up of galaxies. The
cloud was a supercluster of galaxies.

We were moving fast enough to make a supercluster shift
against the general background.

"We must be travelling through some sort of hyper-
space," Celso lectured. "We hop from point to point. Or
perhaps this is some variant of teleportation. Even the
images we see must be an illusion, manufactured for our
comfort."

"I don't want to know."

"But you should have been prepared for all this," said
Celso kindly. "You saw the image – the distant galaxies, the
cosmic strings."

"Celso –" I resisted the temptation to wrap my arms
around my head. "Please. You aren't helping me."

He looked at me steadily. Supercluster light bathed
his aquiline profile; he was the sort you'd pick as an
ambassador for the human race. I hate people like that.
"If the builders of this vessel are transporting us across
such distances, there is nothing to fear. With such
powers they can surely preserve our lives with negligible
effort."

"Or sit on our skulls with less."

"There is nothing to fear save your own human failings."

I sucked weak coffee from a nippled flask. "You're
starting to sound like Paulis."

He laughed. "I am sorry." He turned back to the drifting supercluster, calm, fascinated.

Just think about it, Michael. Life on Earth got started just about as soon as it could – as soon as the rocks cooled and the oceans gathered. Furthermore, life spread over Earth as fast and as far as it could. And already we're starting to spread to other worlds. Surely this can't be a unique trait of Earth life.

So how come nobody has come spreading all over us?

Of course the universe is a big place. But even crawling along with dinky ships that only reach a fraction of lightspeed – ships we could easily start building now – we could colonise the Galaxy in a few tens of millions of years. 100 million, tops.

100 million years: it seems an immense time – after all, 100 million years ago dinosaurs ruled the Earth. But the Galaxy is 100 times older still. There has been time for Galactic colonisation to have happened many times since the birth of the stars.

Remember, all it takes is for one race somewhere to have evolved the will and the means to colonize; and once the process has started it's hard to see what could stop it.

But, as a kid on that lawn, I didn't see them.

Advanced civilizations ought to be very noticeable. Even we blare out on radio frequencies. Why, with our giant radio telescopes we could detect a civilization no more advanced than ours anywhere in the Galaxy. But we don't.

We seem to be surrounded by emptiness and silence. There's something wrong.

This is called the Fermi Paradox.

The journey was long. And what made it worse was that we didn't know *how* long it would be, or what we would find at the end of it – let alone if we would ever come back again.

The two of us were crammed inside that glittering little Bubble the whole time.

Celso had the patience of a rock. Trying not to think about how afraid I was, I poked sticks into his cage. I ought to have driven him crazy.

"You have a few 'human failings' too," I said. "Or you wouldn't have ended up like me, on sale in a debtors' auction."

He inclined his noble head. "What you say is true. Although I did go there voluntarily."

I choked on my coffee.

"My wife is called Maria. We both work in the algae tanks beneath New San Francisco."

I grimaced. "You've got my sympathy."

"We remain poor people, despite our efforts to educate ourselves. You may know that life is not easy for non-Caucasians in modern California. . . ." His parents had moved there from the east when Celso was very young. "My parents loved California – or at least, the dream of California – a place of hope and tolerance and plenty, the society of the future, the Golden State." He smiled. "But my parents died disappointed. And the California dream had been dead for decades . . ."

It all started, he said, with the Proposition 13 vote in 1978. It was a tax revolt, when citizens began to turn their backs on public spending. More ballot initiatives followed, to cut taxes, limit budgets, restrict school spending discretion, bring in tougher sentencing laws, end affirmative action, ban immigrants from using public services.

"For fifty years California has been run by a government of ballot initiative. And it is not hard to see who the initiatives are favouring. The whites became a minority in 2005; the rest of the population is Latino, black, Asian and other groups. The ballot initiatives are weapons of resistance by the declining proportion of white voters. With predictable results."

I could sympathise. As a kid growing up with two radicals for parents – in turn very influenced by my grandfather, the famous Reid Malenfant himself – I soaked up a lot of utopianism. My parents always thought that the future would be better than the present, that people would somehow get smarter and more generous, overcome their limitations, learn to live in harmony and generosity. Save the planet and live in peace. All that stuff.

It didn't work out that way. Where California led, it seems to me, the rest of the human race has followed, into a pit of selfishness, short-sightedness, bigotry, hatred, greed – while the planet fills up with our shit.

"But," Celso said, "your grandfather tried."

"Tried and failed. Reid Malenfant dreamed of saving the Earth by mining the sky. Bullshit. The wealth returned from the asteroid mines has made the rich richer – people like Paulis – and did nothing for the Earth but create millions of economic refugees."

And as for my grandfather, who everybody seems to think I ought to be living up to: his is a voice from the past, speaking of vanished dreams.

Celso said, "Is there really no hope for us? Can we really not transcend our nature, save ourselves?"

"My friend, all you can do is look after yourself."

Celso nodded. "Yes. My wife and I could see no way to buy a decent life for our son Fernando but for one of us to be sold through an auction."

"You did that knowing the risk of coming up against a bastard like Paulis – of ending up on a chute to hell like this?"

"I did it knowing that Paulis's money would buy my Fernando a place in the sun – literally. And Maria would have done the same. We drew lots."

"Ah." I nodded knowingly. "And you lost."

He looked puzzled. "No. I won."

I couldn't meet his eyes. I really do hate people like that.

He said gently, "Tell me why *you* are here. The truth, now."

"Paulis bought me."

"The laws covering debtor auctions are strict. He could not have sent you on such a hazardous assignment without your consent."

"He bought me. But not with money."

"Then what?"

I sighed. "With my grandfather. Paulis knew him. He had a letter, written before Reid Malenfant died, a letter for me . . ."

A paradox arises when two seemingly plausible lines of thought meet in a contradiction. Throughout history, paradoxes have been a fertile seeding grounds for new ways of looking at the world. I'm sure Fermi is telling us something very profound about the nature of the universe we live in.

But, Michael, neither of the two basic resolutions of the Paradox offer much illumination – or comfort.

Maybe, simply, we really are alone.

We may be the first. Perhaps we're the last. If so, it took so long for the Solar System to evolve intelligence it seems unlikely there will be others, ever. If we fail, then the failure is for all time. If we die, mind and consciousness and soul die with us: hope and dreams and love, everything that makes us human. There will be nobody even to mourn us . . .

Celso nodded gravely as he read.

I snorted. "Imagine growing up with a dead hero for a grandfather. And his one communication to me is a lecture about the damn Fermi Paradox. Look, Reid Malenfant was a loser. He let people manipulate him his whole life. People like Frank Paulis, who used him as a front for his predatory off-world capitalism."

"That is very cynical. After all this project, the first human exploration of the Bubbles, was funded privately – by Paulis. He must share some of the same, ah, curiosity as your grandfather."

"My grandfather had a head full of shit."

Celso regarded me. "I hope we will learn enough to have satisfied Reid Malenfant's curiosity – and that it does not cost us our lives." And he went back to work.

Humans fired off their first starships in the middle of the twentieth century. They were the US space probes called Pioneer and Voyager, four of them, launched in the 1970s to visit the outer planets. Their primary mission completed, they sailed helplessly on into interstellar space. They worked for decades, sending back data about the conditions they found. But they haven't gone too far yet, all things considered; it will take the fastest of them tens of thousands of years to reach any nearby star.

The first genuine star probe was the European-Japanese *D'Urville:* a miniaturised robot the size of a hockey puck, accelerated to high velocity. It returned images of the Alpha Centauri system within a decade.

The *D'Urville* found a system crowded with asteroids

and rocky worlds. None of the worlds was inhabited . . . but one of them had been inhabited.

From orbit, *D'Urville* saw neat buildings and cities and mines and what looked like farms, all laid out in a persistent hexagonal pattern.

But everything had been abandoned. The buildings were subsiding back into the yellow-grey of the native vegetation, though their outlines were clearly visible. *Farms and cities*: they must have been something like us. We must have missed them by no more than millennia. It was heartbreaking.

So what happened? There was no sign of war, or cosmic impact, or volcanic explosion, or eco-collapse, or any of the other ways we could think of to trash a world. It was as if everybody had just up and gone, leaving a *Marie Celeste* planet.

But there were several Bubbles neatly orbiting the empty world, shining brightly, beacons blaring throughout the spectrum.

Since then more probes to other stars, followers of the *D'Urville*, have found many lifeless planets – and a few more abandoned worlds. Some of them appeared to have been inhabited until quite recently, like Alpha A-IV, some deserted for much longer. But always abandoned.

And everywhere we found Bubbles, their all-frequency beacons bleeping invitingly, clustering around those empty worlds like bees around a flower.

After a time one enterprising microprobe was sent *inside* a Bubble.

The hatch closed. The Bubble shot away at high speed, and was never heard from again.

It was shortly after that that Bubbles were found in the Oort cloud of our own Solar System. Hatches open. Apparently waiting for us.

Paulis had set out the pitch for me. "Where do these Bubbles come from? Where do they go? And why do they never return? My company, Bootstrap, thinks there may be a lot of profit in the answers. Our probes haven't returned. Perhaps you will."

Or perhaps not.

It doesn't take a Cornelius Taine to figure out that the Bubbles must have something to do with the fact that my grandfather's night sky was silent.

. . . Or maybe we aren't alone, but we just can't see them. Why not?

Maybe the answer is benevolent. Maybe we're in some kind of quarantine – or a zoo.

Maybe it's just that we all destroy ourselves in nuclear wars or eco collapse.

Or maybe there is something that kills off every civilization like ours before we get too far. Killer robots sliding silently between the stars, which for their own antique purposes kill off fledgling cultures.

Or something else we can't even imagine.

Michael, every outcome I can think of scares me.

Celso called me over excitedly. "My friend, we have travelled for days and must have spanned half the universe. But I believe our journey is nearly over." He pointed. "Over there is a quasar. Which is a very bright, very distant object. And over there –" He moved his arm almost imperceptibly. "I can see the same quasar."

"Well, golly gee."

He smiled. "Such a double image is a characteristic of a cosmic string. The light bends around the string. You see?"

"I still don't know what a cosmic string is."

"A fault in space. A relic of the Big Bang, the birth of the universe itself . . . Do you know much cosmology, Michael?"

"Not as such, no." It isn't a big topic of conversation in your average poker school.

"Imagine the universe, just a few years old. It is mere light years across, a soup of energy. Rapidly it cools. Our familiar laws of physics take hold. The universe settles into great lumps of ordered space, like – like the freezing surface of a pond.

"But there are flaws in this sober universe, like the gaps between ice floes. Do you understand? Just as liquid water persists in those gaps, so there are great channels through which there still flows energy from the universe's earliest hours. Souvenirs of a reckless youth."

"And these channels are what you call cosmic strings?"

"The strings are no wider than ten hydrogen atoms. They are very dark, very dense – many tons to an inch." He cracked an imaginary whip. "The endless strings lash through space at almost the speed of light, throwing off loops like echoes. The loops lose energy and decay. But not before they form the kernels around which galaxies crystallize."

"Really? And what about this primordial energy?"

"Great electric currents surge along the strings. Which are, of course, superconductors."

It sounded kind of dangerous. I felt my stomach loosen – the reaction of a plains primate, utterly inappropriate, lost as I was in this intergalactic wilderness.

But now there was something new. I looked where Celso was pointing – and made out a small bar of light. It moved like a beetle across the background.

"What's that? A bead sliding on the string?"

He grabbed a softscreen, seeking a magnified image. His jaw dropped. "My friend," he said softly, "I believe you are exactly right."

It was one of a series of such beads, I saw now. The whole damn string seemed to be threaded like a cheap necklace.

But now the perspective changed. That nearest bar swelled to a cylinder. To a wand that pointed towards us. To a tunnel whose mouth roared out of infinity and swallowed us.

We sailed along the tunnel's axis, following a fine thread beaded with toy stars – a thread that had to be the cosmic string. The stars splashed coloured tubes on the tunnel walls; they hurtled by like posters in a subway to hell.

I clung to the Bubble walls. Even Celso blanched.

"Of course," he yelled – and stopped himself. There was no noise, just the feeling there ought to have been. "Of course, we have still less reason to fear than before. Our speed must be vastly less than when we were in free space. And I believe we're still slowing down."

I risked a look.

We were dipping away from the axis. Those tremendous bands of light flattened out and became landscapes that streamed beneath us.

We slowed enough to make out detail.

One model sun was a ruddy giant. By its light, fungi the size of continents lapped vast mountain ranges.

The next sun was a shrunken dwarf; oceans of hydrogen or helium slithered over the tunnel walls. I saw something like an enormous whale. It must have had superconducting fluid for blood.

So it went, sun after sun, landscape after landscape. A subway filled with worlds.

Celso's dark eyes shone with wonder. "This tunnel must be a million miles across. So much room . . ."

We dipped lower still. Atmosphere whistled. The latest sunlight looked warm and familiar, and the walls were coated with a jumble of blue and green.

The huge curved floor flattened out into a landscape, exploded into trees and grass and rivers; suddenly we landed, as simple as that.

Gravity came back with a thump. We fell into the base of our Bubble.

Without hesitation Celso pulled on his suit, set up our inflatable airlock, and kicked the hatch open.

I glimpsed grassy hills, and a band of night, and a white dwarf star.

I buried my face in the wall of the Bubble.

Celso came to me that evening.

(Evening? The toy sun slid along its wire and dimmed as it went. In the night, I could see Earthlike landscape smeared out over the other side of the sky.)

"I want you to know I understand," Celso said gently. "You must come to terms with this situation. You must do it yourself. I will wait for you."

I shut my eyes tighter.

The next morning, I heard whistling.

I uncurled. I pulled on my suit, and climbed out of the Bubble.

Celso was squatting by a stream, fishing with a piece of string and a bit of wire. He'd taken his suit off. In fact, he'd stripped down to his undershorts. He broke off his whistling as I approached.

I cracked my helmet. The air smelt funny to me, but then I'm a city boy. There was no smog, no people. I could smell Celso's fish, though.

I splashed my face in the stream. The water felt pure enough to have come out of a tap. I said: "I'd like an explanation, I think."

Celso competently hauled out another fish. (At least it looked like a fish.) "Simple," he said. "The line is a thread from an undergarment. The hook is scavenged from a ration pack. For bait I am using particles of food concentrate. Later we can dig for worms and –"

"Forget the fishing."

"We can eat the fish, just as we can breathe the air." He smiled. "It is of no species I have ever seen. But it has the same biochemical basis as the fish of Earth's oceans and rivers. Isn't that marvellous? *They* knew we were coming – they brought us here, right across the universe – they stocked the streams with fish –"

"We didn't come all this way to bloody fish. What's going on here, Celso?"

He wrapped the line around his wrist and stood up. Then, unexpectedly, he grabbed me by the shoulders and grinned in my face. "You are a hero, my friend Michael Malenfant."

"A hero? All I did was get out of bed."

"But, for you, that step across the threshold of the Bubble was a great and terrible journey indeed." He shook me gently. "*I understand*. We must all do what we can, yes? Come now. We will find wood for a fire, I will build a spit, and we will eat a fine meal." He loped barefoot across the grass as if he'd been born to it.

Grumbling, I followed.

Celso gutted the fish with a bit of metal. I couldn't have done that to save my life. The fish tasted wonderful.

That night we sat by the dying fire. There were no stars,

of course, just bands of light on the horizons like twin dawns.

Celso said at length, "This place, this segment alone, could swallow more than ten thousand Earths. So much room . . . And we flew over dozens of other inside-out worlds. I imagine there's a home for every life form in the universe – perhaps, in fact, a refuge for all logically possible life forms . . ."

I looked up to the cylinder's invisible axis. "I suppose you're going to tell me the whole thing's built around a cosmic string. And the power for all the dinky suns comes from the huge currents left over from the Big Bang."

"I would guess so. And power for the gravity fields we stand in – although there may be a simpler mechanism. Perhaps the tube is spinning, providing gravity by centripetal forces."

"But you'd have to spin the tube at different rates. You know, some of the inhabitants will be from tiny moons, some will be from gas giants . . ."

"That's true." He clapped me on the shoulder. "We'll make a scientist of you yet."

"Not if I can help it." I hunched up, nostalgic for smog and ignorance. "But what's the point of all this?"

"The point – I think – is that species become extinct. *Even humans* . . . I did not always work in the algae farms. Once I had higher ambitions." He smiled. "I would have been an anthropologist, I think. Actually my speciality would have been palaeoanthropology. Extinct homs."

"Homs?"

"Sorry: field slang. Hominids. The lineage of human descent. I did some work, as a student, in the field in the desert heartlands of Kenya. At Olduvai I was privileged to make a key find. It was just a sharp-edged fragment of bone about the size of my thumb, the colour of lava pebbles.

"But it was a bit of skull.

"Homs don't leave many fossils, Michael. You very rarely find ribs, for example. Until humans began to bury each other, a hundred thousand years ago, ribs were the first parts of a corpse to be crunched to splinters by the carnivores. It took me months before I learned to pick out the relics, tiny specks against the soil . . .

"Well. Believe me, we were very excited. We marked out the site. We broke up the dirt. We began to sieve, looking to separate bits of bone from the grains of soil and stone. After weeks of work you could fit the whole find into a cigarette packet. But that counts as a phenomenal find, in this field.

"What we had found was a trace of a woman. She was *Homo Erectus*. Her kind arose perhaps two million years ago, and became extinct a quarter-million years ago. They had the bodies of modern humans, but smaller brains. But they were highly successful. They migrated out of Africa and covered the Old World."

I said dryly, "Fascinating, Celso. And the significance –"

"*They are gone*, Michael. This is what my field experiences taught me. Here was another type of human – *extinct*. All that is left is shards of bone from which we have to infer everything– the ancient homs' appearance, gait, behaviour, social structure, language, culture, tool-making ability – everything we know, or we think we know about them. *Extinction*. It is a brutal, uncompromising termination, disconnecting the past from the future.

"And for an intelligent species this over-death is an unbearable prospect. Everything that might make a life valuable after death – memory, achievement – is wiped away. *There is nobody even left to grieve*. Do you see?"

He was genuinely agitated; I envied his intensity of emotion. "But what has this to do with the builders?"

He lay on his back and stared at the empty sky. "I think the builders are planning ahead. I think this is a *refugium*, as the ecologists would say. A place to sit out the cold times to come, the long Ice Age of the universe – a safeguard against extinction." He sighed. "I think your grandfather understood about extinction, Michael."

I stared at the fire, my mind drifting. He was thinking of the destiny of mankind. I was just thinking about myself. But then, I hadn't asked to be here. "Maybe this is okay for you. Sun, trees, fishing, mysterious aliens. But I'm a city boy."

"I am sorry for you, my friend. But I, too, am far from my family."

It was a long night, and not a whole lot of laughs.

A new sun slid down the wire. The dew misted away.

I rubbed my eyes; my back was stiff as hell from sleeping unnaturally without a mattress on the ground.

There were two alien Bubbles. They bobbled in the breeze, side by side.

One was ours. Its door gaped; I recognised our kit inside it. Within the second Bubble I thought I could make out two human forms.

I shook Celso awake. "We've got company."

We stood before the new vessel. Its hatch opened.

There was a woman; a small boy clung to her. They were a terrified mess. When they recognised Celso –

Look, I have some decency. I took a walk along the stream.

After an hour I rejoined the family. They were having a nice fish breakfast, talking animatedly.

Celso grinned. "My friend Michael Malenfant. Please meet my wife, Maria, and Fernando, my son."

Maria still wore the grimy coverall of an algae tank worker. She said: "The Bubble came and scooped me up from work; and Fernando from his school."

I gaped. "The Bubbles have come to Earth?"

They had, it seemed: great gossamer fleets of them, sailing in from the Oort Cloud, an armada perhaps triggered by our foolhardy jaunt.

"They make the sky shine," said the boy, beaming.

"Of course it is logical," said Celso. "The aliens would want to reconstruct stable family units."

"I wonder how they knew who to bring."

Celso smiled. "I would guess they studied us – or rather the Bubble did – during the journey. Whoever was most in our thoughts would be selected. The puzzles of the human heart must be transparent to the builders of such a monumental construct as this."

"We were scared," said Fernando proudly, chewing the flesh off a fishy spine.

"I'll bet." I imagined the scenes in those nightmarish farms as a Bubble came sweeping over the algae beds . . . "So now what? Do you think you'll stay here?"

Celso took a deep breath. "Oh, yes."

"Better than the algae farms, huh."

"It is more than that. This will be a fine land in which to build a home, and for Fernando to grow. Other people will be brought here soon. We will farm, build cities." He took my arm. "But you look troubled, my friend. I must not forget you in my happiness. Was no one in your heart during our journey?"

In my hop-skip-and-jump life I'd never made the time to get close enough to anyone to miss them.

He put his hand on my arm. "Stay with us." His son smiled at me.

Once again I found myself unable to meet Celso's kind eyes.

Michael, much of my life has been shaped by thinking about the Fermi Paradox. But one thing I never considered was the subtext.

Alone or not alone – why do we care so much?

I think I know now. It's because we are lonely. On Earth there is nobody closer to us than the chimps; we see nobody like us in the sky.

But then, each of us is alone. I have been alone since your grandmother, Emma, died. And now I'm dying too, Michael; what could be lonelier than that?

That's why we care about Fermi. That's why I care.

Michael, I'm looking at you, here in this damn hospital room with me; you're just born, just a baby, and you won't remember me. But I'm glad I got to meet you. I hope you will learn more than I have. That you will be wiser. That you will be happier. That you won't be alone.

I said, "I guess we know the truth about Fermi now. As soon as intelligence emerges on some deadbeat world like Earth, along come the Bubbles to take everybody away. Leaving all the lights on but nobody home. That's all there is to it."

"But what a vast enterprise," Celso said. "Remember, a key difficulty with the Fermi Paradox has always been consistency. If there is a mechanism that removes intelligent life from the stars and planets, it must do so unfailingly and everywhere: it must be all but omniscient and omnipotent."

"So the universe must be full of those damn Bubbles."

"Yes." He smiled. "Or perhaps there is only one . . ."

"But *why?* Why go to all this trouble, to build this – this vast theme park?"

He grinned. "Extinction, Michael. This is a dangerous universe for fragile beings such as ourselves. Left to our own devices, it doesn't look as if we are smart enough to get through many more centuries, does it? Maybe the Bubbles have come just in time. And remember that life can be readily destroyed – by impact events, volcanism and other instability – by chance events like nearby supernovae or the collision of neutron stars – by more dramatic occurrences like the collision of galaxies – and in the end, of course, all stars will die, all free energy sources dwindle . . . We are stalked by extinction, Michael; we are all refugees.

"But one energy source will not fade away: the energy trapped in the cosmic strings. So I think they built this place, and they sent out their trawler-like vessels. The refugium is a defiance of extinction – a mechanism to ensure that life and mind may survive into the unimaginable future –"

I sniffed, looking up at a fake sun. "But isn't that a retreat? This great sink of life isn't our world. To come here is an end to striving, to ambition, to the autonomy of the species." I thought of the Bubbles clustering around Earth, like antibodies around a source of infection. I thought of human cities, New York and London and Beijing, emptied and overgrown like the dismal ruins of Alpha Centauri A-IV.

But Celso said, "Not really. They were just thinking of their children. Rather like me, I guess. And there are adventures to be had here. We will design flying machines and go exploring. There may be no limit to the journeys we, or our children, will make, up and down this great corridor, a corridor that encircles the universe, no limit to the intelligences we might meet. And here, sheltered in this refugium, the human species could last *forever* . . . think of that." He studied me. "As for you, I didn't know you were so restless, Michael. Heroism, now wanderlust. You have travelled across half the cosmos, and at the end of your journey you found yourself. Maybe your grandfather's genes really are working within you."

The boy spoke around a mouthful of fish. "If you are lonely, sir, why don't you go home?"

I smiled. "Easier said than done."

"No, really. You know the screen in the Bubble – the one that showed our destination?"

"The cosmic string picture . . . what about it?"

"Well, in your Bubble it's changed."

Celso stared at the boy, then ran to the Bubble. "He's right," he breathed.

The screen showed a picture of the Earth – continents, grey-blue oceans – unmistakeable and lovely.

I kissed that damn kid.

Celso nodded. "They know you wish to leave." He shrugged. "The choice of the species is surely clear; *this*, not that beautiful, fragile blue bauble, is mankind's destiny. But individuals are free . . ."

There was a distant shiver of motion. A third Bubble sailed across the plain. I hardly noticed it.

Without hesitation I jumped into the open hatchway of our Bubble. "Listen," I said to Celso, "are you sure you don't want to come? It's going to be a tough life here."

He rejoined his family. "Not for us. Goodbye, my friend. Oh – here." He handed me his softscreen. "With the information I have gathered in this you will become a rich man."

The new vessel drifted to rest.

I couldn't have cared less. I banged the button to shut the hatch. My Bubble lifted.

Through the net walls I could see the new arrival tumble out onto the raw earth. I recognised him. The person who'd made sure he'd been on my mind throughout the whole journey.

Frank J. Paulis was wearing his bathrobe. He wailed.

Celso caught my eye and winked. Paulis would be doing a lot of worm digging before he was allowed back to his spa and Bootstrap and his sprawling empire. I wished I'd been there when that damn Bubble had shown up to scoop him away.

But maybe Paulis had got what he wanted, at that. *The answer* – in this universe, anyhow. My grandfather would have been pleased for him, I thought.

The landscape fell away, and I flew past toy stars.